# THE NEW WOMAN

# CATHOLIC WOMEN WRITERS

# THE NEW WOMAN

Carmen Laforet

TRANSLATED FROM SPANISH BY CLAIRE WADIE
WITH AN INTRODUCTION BY
CARAGH WELLS

The Catholic University of America Press
WASHINGTON, D.C.

First published in 1955 by
Ediciones Destino, Barcelona
Support for the translation of this book
was provided by Acción Cultural Española,
AC/E. Additional support for this translation
was provided by the Maynooth Scholastic Trust.

Cataloging-in-Publication Data available
from the Library of Congress
ISBN 978-0-8132-3980-4
ISBN 978-0-8132-3981-1

# CONTENTS

The Catholic Literary Revival was concentrated primarily in Britain, France, and America. Spanning the hundred years between the late nineteenth century and the late twentieth century, the movement saw an unprecedented quantity of writing by and about Catholics emerging after a protracted absence of Catholic faith and culture from the public sphere. In Britain the catalysts for this flourishing of poetry, prose fiction, and nonfiction were the beginning of the Oxford Movement, John Henry Newman's conversion to Rome, and the re-establishment of the Catholic hierarchy after three hundred years of persecution. In France, amid continuing anti-clericalism following the revolution, Catholic literature flourished alongside new religious orders and lay spiritual communities. And in America, European immigrants arriving in the nineteenth century were entering a society marked by a long history of anti-Catholicism. They utilized literature to explore a dimension of human thought and experience that was still largely absent from the American imagination.

The Catholic Literary Revival is exemplified by the work of Hilaire Belloc, Robert Hugh Benson, Georges Bernanos,

Léon Bloy, G. K. Chesterton, Graham Greene, Gerard Manley Hopkins, Jacques Maritain, Thomas Merton, Charles Péguy, Walker Percy, J. R. R. Tolkien, and Evelyn Waugh. The works of all of these writers have been consistently in print, in modern editions, throughout the last century and up to the present day. The Revival's most numerous members, however, were women, and although some of these women remain well known—Muriel Spark, Antonia White, Kate O'Brien, Flannery O'Connor, Dorothy Day—many have been almost entirely forgotten. These include Mary Beckett, Kathleen Coyle, Enid Dinnis, Anna Hanson Dorsey, Alice Thomas Ellis, Eleanor Farjeon, Rumer Godden, Caroline Gordon, Clotilde Graves, Caryll Houselander, Sheila Kaye-Smith, Jane Lane, Marie Belloc Lowndes, Alice Meynell, Kathleen Raine, Pearl Mary Teresa Richards, Edith Sitwell, Gladys Bronwyn Stern, Josephine Ward, and Maisie Ward.

There are various reasons why each of these writers fell out of print. Broadly, we can point to changes in the commercial publishing world after World War II as well as changes within the Church itself and in the English-speaking universities that redefined the literary canon in the last decades of the twentieth century. Yet it remains puzzling that a body of writing so creative, so attuned to its historical moment, and so unique in its perspective on the human condition should have fallen into obscurity for so long.

This series brings together the English-language prose work of Catholic women from the nineteenth and twentieth centuries, work that retains its literary excellence and its accessibility to a broad range of readers. Although the series includes some short stories and nonfiction, it concentrates primarily on the novel. The novel was modernity's chief literary innovation. It grew out of several prose traditions, especially the spiritual autobiography, and yet it has been called both a Protestant and a secular form. The novel usually concentrates on the personal lives of a small cast of characters drawn from a range of social demographics; its demand for psychological realism and the nuances of lives lived in the material world mean its vision is usually more earthly than spiritual. The novel is able to contain and explore religious concerns, especially the roles of providence and personal conscience, and many great novels depict elements of religious experience. Yet these novels nonetheless tend to remain worldly, secular or materialist in structure and vision. This is no surprise, for the novel is ultimately resistant to "the pressures put upon it by many writers to transcend the limits" of the secular world.[1]

However, many of the writers in this series used the novel as an opportunity to rethink the form and its capacity to express a uniquely Catholic perspective. In doing so, they not only developed and advanced the form itself but also brought an ancient faith to bear on life in the modern world. There is a certain paradox here: Catholic writers effectively helped to push the novel into newer, and therefore more "modern," forms even though they did so in pursuit of a truth that sometimes required a rejection or questioning of modernity's broader cultural movements.

The novel has often been characterized, especially in its early-eighteenth-century form, as primarily concerned with

---

1. George Levine, *Realism, Ethics and Secularism: Essays on Victorian Literature and Science* (Cambridge University Press, 2011), 210. See also Deirdre Shauna Lynch, "Gothic Fiction and 'Belief in Every Kind of Prodigy,'" in *The Routledge Companion to Literature and Religion*, ed. Mark Knight (Routledge, 2016), 252.

female experience and the domestic sphere. Although prominent counter-examples to this thesis exist, such as in the work of Fielding and Dickens, the genre nonetheless frequently explores the internal lives of female characters and their negotiation of personal relationships within the more limited geographical settings of a single house, village, or city. But the novel is also a genre well suited to the exploration of social and political change. Unlike drama or epic, it can provide a voice for those who do not possess great social power, who must navigate moral challenges, often on their own and in direct conflict with the culture around them, and who, in doing so, offer criticisms of the society in which they find themselves. In this respect, the novel offered a perfect vehicle for exploring the challenges faced by a Catholic in modern society.

The historical period in which the Catholic Literary Revival emerged witnessed a complex renegotiation of almost all European social institutions, from the aristocracy and the family to party politics and the role of the state. There were Catholic writers among the many voices calling for change as well as among the many questioning its validity. Many of the novels in this series are concerned with distinguishing between stale social conventions that confine, suppress, or limit human capacities and timeless spiritual traditions that are morally and doctrinally true and authentic. Indeed, Catholic writers of the period drew on their faith to interrogate their society while also exploring how modern Catholics could live faithfully in a rapidly changing world.

The nineteenth and twentieth centuries were religiously tumultuous; they were often defined, even at the time, as an age of both faith and doubt. Writers and artists of every stripe examined the role of institutional religion in public life and the personal consequences of lives lived with faith or without it. The period has been described as the beginning of a modern secular society, but it also witnessed powerful resistance to secularization; writers from Austen to Eliot, Wilde to Waugh identified religious belief as newly urgent and necessary. A nonreligious or strictly materialist worldview was for many an increasingly dangerous proposition. In 1935, T. S. Eliot criticized writers who failed to resist the drift toward secularism: "the whole of modern literature is corrupted by what I call Secularism.... [I]t is simply unaware of, simply cannot understand the meaning of, the primacy of the supernatural over the natural life ... something which I assume to be our primary concern."[2] Indeed, the period saw many conversions to Catholicism, notably among writers and artists, all of whom helped to shape in new and dynamic ways the "Catholic imagination."

This term can be broadly defined as a vision of the world in which the drama of salvation is played out in the mundane experiences of the everyday, in which the visible and created things of the world, the development of individual character and community identity, and the adventure of human relationships—all these are phenomena through which readers can touch spiritual realities. The Catholic imagination is that state of awareness through which the seemingly abstract doctrines of Church teaching are played out in a person's day-to-day experiences and moral actions, to the point that some of the smallest human endeavors become nothing less than matters of life and death. From a technical point of view, the novel was uniquely

2. T. S. Eliot, "Religion and Literature," in *Selected Prose*, ed. Frank Kermode (Harcourt Brace Jovanovich, 1975), 104–5.

suited to exploring these varied levels of human experience. Its innovations in voice and point of view, in narrative time and the role of description and world-making in constructing human interiority, predispose it to the dramatization of both earthly and cosmic dimensions and moral or spiritual battles both social and personal.

The neglected female representatives of the Catholic literary revival cast a distinct and important light on the Catholic imagination. Typically writing from within more introspective, domestic and romantic contexts, they often root Catholic experience in the everyday, revealing its relevance in and to the lives of ordinary men and women. This less socio-political touch may be one reason for their fall from the public eye, but it is also what makes them so uniquely relevant to contemporary life. As politico-cultural and religious institutions continue to drift into separate spheres of public influence, Christians today often struggle to grasp how faith should or does inform their day-to-day lives. Through fiction, the authors in this series provide a bridge over the divide between religious belief and everyday experience.

If the women writers involved in the Catholic literary revival often wrote from a more domestic or interpersonal angle, they were by no means unaware or uncritical of the social, cultural, political, and ecclesial developments of their time. Indeed, their more marginal role in Anglo-American society often allowed them to adopt a uniquely perceptive outsider's view. For many of the women in this series it was precisely their Catholic faith that empowered them to adopt a prominent voice. Inspired by the rich intellectual tradition of the Church and the prominent female saints throughout history, these writers made important contributions to Catholic thought on human dignity and the sacramental potential of the ordinary.

A large number of writers in this series were converts from Anglicanism or from no religion at all. Their imaginations were therefore shaped by a radical change in perspective. Becoming Catholic meant accepting a place outside of the British and American establishment, but it also meant they could often see their society with clear eyes for the first time. Many of the writers in this series also experienced personal suffering to an inordinate degree. Catholic teaching on the salvific nature of suffering provided them with means by which to understand the role that their loss played in the small drama of their own life as much as the bigger cosmic drama in which we are all players. Caryll Houselander, for example, understood personal suffering to be a means by which Christians could "give birth to Christ" in the lives of others. Like many writers, she understood that the novel is itself a vehicle for understanding suffering. Houselander turned to the novel after decades of writing spiritual prose. She did so because she no longer wanted to "preach" to her fellows; she wanted instead to "take sinners by the hand" and walk in their lives for a time. The wounds experienced by our writers, when combined with the existential awakening of a conversion to faith, shaped their particular view of human experience and divine truth. Faced with the emotional and spiritual reality of deep suffering, convert novelists often saw in Catholicism what they saw in the novel itself: a space able to contain all the mysteries of human experience.

Benedict XVI said that "the only really effective apologia for Christianity comes down to two arguments, namely, the *saints* the Church has produced and the *art* which has grown in her womb."[3] We should not, therefore, underestimate the importance of artists for defending the credibility of the Christian faith. This pertains also to the Catholic women writers of this series. Few of these writers will go on to be canonized; indeed some of them may not have been particularly saintly, but through their interventions in literary tradition, these women powerfully reshaped the literary and religious landscape.

For the Catholic reader, the writing in this series provides a fictional exploration of the moral and spiritual adventure offered by Catholic life. It also offers a way of holding together themes that have become increasingly partisan in the Church today. Most of the women in this series were writing at a time when the Church was grappling to define its relationship to an increasingly secular world. They were innovators who raised questions that would eventually be posed at the Second Vatican Council, but they were also loyal to many of the traditions and doctrines that disappeared after the Council. Their vision incorporates both a rigorous personal morality and a concern for social justice; an awareness of God's grandeur and an appreciation of his presence in the ordinary; and the importance of both piety and charitable works.

For the non-Catholic reader, the writing in this series offers a crucial but overlooked vision of modernity. It provides insight into a unique form of female experience but also a unique means of understanding how the Catholic faith is played out in the everyday. For those interested in the history of the novel, these writers demonstrate some of the ways in which the genre is able to explore and express the highest and most timeless spiritual

3. Joseph Cardinal Ratzinger (with Vittorio Messori), *The Ratzinger Report: An Exclusive Interview on the State of the Church*, trans. Salvator Attanasio and Graham Harrison (Ignatius Press, 1985), 129.

realities, often through the application of the most avant-garde novelistic techniques.

*Bonnie Lander Johnson and Julia Meszaros*

## FURTHER READING

Tom Woodman. *Faithful Fictions*. The Catholic University of America Press, 2022.

James Emmett Ryan. *Faithful Passages*. University of Wisconsin Press, 2013.

## PREVIOUS BOOKS IN THE SERIES

Caryll Houselander. *The Dry Wood*, 2022.
Sheila Kaye-Smith. *The End of the House of Alard*, 2022.
Josephine Ward. *One Poor Scruple*, 2023.
Enid Dinnis. *The Complete Short Stories, Volume 1*, 2024.
Mary Beckett. *Give Them Stones*, 2025.

*The New Woman* is the first title in the Catholic Women Writers series from outside the English-speaking world. Carmen Laforet was one of Spain's greatest modern literary talents: her work has been translated into multiple languages, but *La mujer nueva* has never before been translated into English. Like so many novels in this series, *The New Woman* explores forms of personal and domestic suffering known to its author: in Laforet's case, the early loss of her mother. By the time Laforet wrote this novel, she was well known for creating heroines whose suffering made them hard and selfish: only in *The New Woman*, the novel that followed Laforet's own conversion experience, do we find a heroine who discovers the redemptive capacity of suffering and the mysterious connection between heartbreak and growing in love.

*The New Woman* tells the story of Paulina, a young woman in search of personal freedom in a broken world. Paulina's marriage and motherhood are a genuine burden and yet also become a catalyst for her being made "new." As Caragh Wells' introduction highlights, the social context in which Paulina's domestic unhappiness occurs is itself one of brokenness: it involves a fascist regime and a Church that, having allowed itself to be instrumentalised politically, has become spiritually hollow. Not unlike another volume in this series, Mary Beckett's *Give Them Stones*, Laforet's *The New Woman* confronts the socio-political realities of its time and place from the perspective of a woman's domestic life and relationships. In doing so, it unearths the ways in which the life of the spirit and that of the political subject are interconnected. The corruption of Church and state contributes to the spiritual and emotional desert in which Paulina finds herself. Yet when she leaves this desert behind, it is not through a social or political rebellion but through the experience of participating in a power that transcends social reality and which makes possible an interior liberation that, in turn, transforms her exterior circumstances.

As it traces the protagonist's inner journey, Laforet's novel disrupts conventional readings of conflict—between the individual and society, between male and female, between freedom and obligation—by considering them in reference to the life of the spirit. Paulina's search is not defined solely by the social possibilities emerging at the cusp of second-wave Feminism, or by the political defiance that characterised resistance movements during the decades of Revolution, but by a hunger for truth and meaning. The novel is an emancipation story, but not the kind we might expect from a mid-twentieth-century author.

Caragh Wells' introduction reveals the degree to which Paulina's story can be and has been interpreted through different modes of spiritual experience. To the Catholic reader, *The New Woman* will most likely appear to be a straightforward conversion narrative—one that probes the psychological dynamics of a religious conversion with unusual subtlety and sensitivity. But Paulina's story functions in a variety of ways: scholars have accounted for her transformation through a number of modern intellectual paradigms. The novel's depiction of a woman yearning for change, and the arrival of an inspired knowledge with which to bring about that change, will speak to every reader.

*Bonnie Lander Johnson and Julia Meszaros*

## BY CARAGH WELLS

## The Author

Carmen Laforet (1921–2004) was born in Barcelona but spent her early and teenage years on the Canary Island of Gran Canaria where she was encouraged by her father Eduardo to live an active life, close to nature and the sea.[1] Her mother Teodora supported her studies and instigated her love of literature, reading to Laforet and her siblings after lunch and encouraging them to read from the same book to enhance their education. When Carmen was thirteen Teodora died, and her father remarried quickly, which resulted in a form of compounded trauma for the young Carmen as her stepmother ordered all her mother's belongings to be removed from the family home and did not allow her name to be mentioned again. In 1939 Laforet travelled to Barcelona to study at the Central University and her observations of postwar life and its impact on society are

---

1. Water is a recurring trope in Laforet's fiction, symbolising merger and the search for experiences that promote oneness as a means of psychological relief.

partly reflected in her first novel *Nada* which won the Premio Nadal in 1944.

Laforet's first novel and the voluminous number of critical studies it has generated since its publication overshadows her other novels and wider literary production, although more recently scholars have sought to adjust the view that *Nada* remains her most important work.[2] Alongside having five children, Laforet published five novels, short stories, travelogues, children´s fiction, and articles for *Destino* and other cultural magazines.[3] More recently, her letters to fellow Spanish writers Ramón J. Sender and Elena Fortún have been published.[4] Laforet's literary oeuvre reveals a writer whose concerns were simultaneously situated in the contemporary context of the Franco regime as well as being intricate studies in human psychology. Laforet's fiction is therefore very much of her time, yet also timeless, making her writing enduringly modern. This perhaps explains the sustained interest in her fiction and her ongoing popularity as a writer both within Spain and internationally. Although *Nada* has been translated into multiple languages since its publication, Laforet's other novels have not received the same level of interest from translators, primarily due to the prominence of her first novel within academic literary scholarship. This translation of *La mujer nueva* enables readers to gain a deeper insight into Laforet's fiction beyond the scope of her

2. *Carmen Laforet: Después de Nada, mucho. Nuevas perspectivas al conmemorar el centenario de su nacimiento (1921–2021)*, ed. Mark P. Del Mastro and Caragh Wells (Albatros, 2022).

3. Her articles published in *Destino* are collected in *Carmen Laforet: Puntos de vista de una mujer* (Destino, 2021).

4. *Carmen Laforet/Ramón J. Sender: Puedo contar contigo. Correspondencia* (Destino, 2004); *Carmen Laforet & Elena Fortún: De corazón y alma (1947-1952)* (Fundación Banco Santander, 2017).

famous first novel. It would now be an opportune moment to open up Laforet's writing to an even wider audience through a translation of all her fictional work in order to appreciate the complexity and depth of one of Spain's most significant postwar writers.[5]

Although Laforet's novelistic production defies any clear categorisation or genre, she has been described as a psychological realist which provides the closest definition of her work.[6] Her five novels represent detailed insights into each protagonist's psyche and the impact that their environments and the people who surround them have on their psychological development, or lack thereof. What unifies all the protagonists is the absence of either one or both parents; each novel may be read as a repeated search to fill the void of the missing maternal or paternal figure through various means, either through friendship, religion, nature, reason, or, in her final posthumous novel, *Al volver la equina* (2004), psychoanalysis. Thus, the theme of flight or *fuga* forms the axis of each novel, following a pattern of moving away from one situation and towards another and, often, not finding a true locus of stability for any length of time, but using whatever means becomes available to generate a sense of connection with another human or, in the case of *La mujer nueva*, religious object, albeit temporary. Each novel

5. Prior to Laforet's death in 2004, she began to distance herself from writing in her later years, falling into a state of contemplative silence, as if locked into a private world of peaceful interiority. This is described in Laforet's daughter's memoir of her mother's life: Cristina Cerezales Laforet, *Música blanca* (Destino, 2009).

6. Graciela Illanes Adaro was the first literary critic to describe Laforet as a psychological realist. See Illanes Adaro, *Graciela: La novelística de Carmen Laforet* (Editorial Gredos, 1971). In his study guide to Nada, Barry Jordan was one of the first critics to apply psychoanalytical theory to Laforet's writing. See Barry Jordan, *Laforet: Nada* (Grant and Cutler in association with Tamesis Books, 1993).

is therefore built upon a similar trajectory based on the pursuit of relief from psychological suffering, revealing the unhealed wound that marked Laforet's own life through the loss of her mother, replicated through the trajectories of her protagonists' existential journeys within each novel.

*La mujer nueva*, Laforet's third novel, which won the Premio Menorca in 1955 and the Premio Nacional de la Literatura in 1956, at first appears to sit incongruously alongside her other four longer works of narrative fiction due to its subject matter and the choice of an older, female protagonist who is married and has a child. *Nada* focuses on the experiences of Andrea, a young university student, across one year of her life with her extended family in Barcelona. *La isla y los demonios* (1952) similarly explores the experiences of a young woman Marta Camino and her encounters with her family when they flee from the Spanish Civil War to the Canary Islands. In Laforet's fourth novel, *La insolación* (1963), the story focuses on a teenage boy Martín Soto and his relationship with fellow teenagers during three summers in Alicante. In her final novel, published posthumously in 2004 but completed around 1976, Martín's story is continued as a young adult. And although the backdrop to all of these novels connects readers to the society and culture of the Franco regime and the Catholic Church as an integral part of Spanish society, it is only in *La mujer nueva* that religion is foregrounded as a central theme. Central to the novel is Paulina's struggle to formulate and understand her relationship with Catholicism and to find an authentic, living relationship with God that provides meaning within her life. The choice of an older protagonist is therefore significant as readers gain an insight into the complex struggle of an adult woman, wife and mother living under the authoritarian and misogynistic ideology of the Francoist dictatorship. Paulina's search for spiritual freedom is therefore arguably both personal and political as she navigates how to live beyond the realm of any ideology and, perhaps, as will be discussed below, any prescribed religion, to find a truer sense of Self and greater maturation.

## The Novel

Although Laforet repeatedly refuted any biographical connection between her fiction and her life, it proves difficult to disentangle the interconnections between the personal and existential struggles that her protagonists experience and her own life circumstances, particularly in the case of *La mujer nueva*.[7] Paulina's search for a deeper meaning beyond her identity as wife and mother is directly reflected in Laforet's own engagement with Catholicism between 1951 and 1958. In 1951, while walking in Madrid, Laforet had a profound mystical experience and subsequently converted to Catholicism, and this experience forms the basis for the second part of the novel during the detailed narrative description of Paulina waking up on the train to Madrid. As was the case for most Spaniards of her generation, Laforet had been brought up as a Catholic, but she had not practiced her religion strictly. However, in addition to Laforet's religious experience in 1951, the influence of one person would shape her life and relationship with Catholicism

7. See Caragh Wells, *The Novels of Carmen Laforet: An Aesthetics of Relief* (Legenda, 2019) and Federico Bonaddio, "'The Unsuspected Truth': Silence and Trauma in Carmen Laforet's *Nada*," in *Memory and Trauma in the Postwar Spanish Novel: Revisiting the Past*, ed. Sarah Leggott and Ross Woods (Bucknell University Press, 2014).

for the next seven years—Lilí Álvarez.

Lilí Álvarez (1905–98), was a prominent sportswoman, writer, and feminist thinker of sorts who was active in the religious environment of postwar Spain.[8] She sought to combine a modern understanding of women's role in society with Catholicism, so that "a new woman" could emerge from within the Church and act as a wider force for regeneration. She advocated for the Church playing a greater role in secular society, rather than remaining detached from the realities of women´s lives in Spain and stigmatising them as a corrupting influence within the Church. *La mujer nueva* is dedicated to Lilí with the following words: "A Lilí Álvarez, con agradecimiento, con mi grand carino, como madrina mía de confirmación."[9] This dedication illustrates the profound nature of their friendship and Lilí's influence on Laforet during this period of her life; she is believed to be the person on whom the character of Blanca in the novel is based.

Although Lilí has been described by some cultural historians as a feminist thinker since she wrote widely on the need for women's increased participation in sport in Spain, her feminism stopped short of, for example, the work of Betty Friedan's *The Feminine Mystique*, for which she wrote the introduction to the Spanish translation in 1965.[10] She instead tried to unfold her progressive ideas within the framework of Catholicism, perhaps signalling the very real constraints that women faced

8. See Conrad Vilanou i Torrano, Raquel de la Arada, and Guillem Turró i Ortega, "Lilí Álvarez, tenista e intelectual: Entre el Eterno femenino y la mujer eterna," *Ars Brevis* (2013): 216–50. Catherine G. Bellver, "Lilí Alvarez: Star Athlete, Writer, and Feminist 'a su Manera.'" *Letras Hispanas* 7, No. 1 (2010): 17–26.

9. "For Lilí Álvarez, godmother at my confirmation, with my gratitude and great affection."

10. Betty Friedan, *La mística de la feminidad.* Prólogo de Lilí Álvarez, condesa de la Valdene (Sagitario, 1965).

while trying to implement change within a dictatorial society. Although we may read such efforts as a type of toned down feminism, adopting a position that was less revolutionary than some second wave feminism ideas, and endeavouring to adapt them to their current circumstances, was perhaps the only way for women such as Lilí and Carmen to make their voices heard within Spain at the time.

The imprint of Lilí's influence can be felt in the novel's critique of a hypocritical and debased form of Catholicism which was distorted to uphold the ideology of the Franco regime and was a far cry from the spiritual essence of Santa Teresa de Jesús and Juan de la Cruz, two of the most famous sixteenth-century Spanish mystics. For example, in chapter six of the novel, Paulina is slapped across the face by her father for laughing in church when the priest speaks about women and their corrupting influence on society, illustrating Laforet´s critique of forms of misogyny within the Church under the Franco dictatorship. Similarly, the representation of Paulina's father as a man of upright character and a devout Catholic is sharply undermined by the narrator's exposure of his philandering and relationship with the household maid. Her mother, who seeks solace from confession, must suffer in silence, highlighting the base misogyny and double standards in operation within Spain at the time. Given the level of criticism directed at clericalism in *La mujer nueva*, it is hard to understand how the novel was published within the strict climate of censorship at the time, although the ending may have been a mitigating factor as the institution of marriage "por la iglesia" is upheld.

The question then to consider is whether *La mujer nueva* is in fact a Catholic novel at all, as it was interpreted at the time of its publication, or whether it signals to the type of muted feminism reflected in Lilí Álvarez's 1964 study *Feminismo y espiritualidad*.[11] Indeed Rolón-Barada suggests in his introduction to *La mujer nueva* that "Laforet ofrece a sus lectores una contribución personal al movimiento feminista de la literatura de posguerra."[12] There are undoubtedly clear feminist tones in the novel, irrespective of its wider religious themes. For example, the opening scene represents Paulina leaving her husband and son to travel to Madrid and live on her own for a period due to a depressive episode linked to emotional estrangement from her husband and suffering a miscarriage. Her backstory also reveals how she lived as a single mother in Madrid for several years working as a teacher to support her son while Eulogio was in exile after the Spanish Civil War. Paulina is consistently represented as a "chica rara," a woman who existed outside the dominant norms of the "buena esposa" espoused by the Sección Femenina of the far-right Falange Española.[13] She refuses to wear make-up, smokes, has an affair with her husband's second cousin Antonio, and discusses her feelings of sexual desire, a topic Álvarez also explored in her writing in which she suggested that men and women had equal sexual needs.

The thematic dynamics within the novel therefore appear to move in opposite directions—towards a modern, feminist role for women and, due to the ending, towards a more traditional representation of wife and mother. As her biographers note,

11. Lilí Alvarez, *Feminismo y espiritualidad* (Taurus, 1964).

12. "Laforet provides readers with her own unique feminist contribution to postwar Spanish literature." Carmen Laforet, *La mujer nueva*, edición y prólogo de Israel Rolón-Barada (Destino, 2003), 13.

13. The term "chica rara" is derived from an essay by Carmen Martín Gaite based on Andrea, the protagonist of *Nada*. Carmen Martín Gaite, *Desde la ventana: enfoque femenino de la literatura española* (Espasa Calpe, 1993).

"Podría decirse que su novela es tanto regresiva como progresiva."[14] It therefore proves hard to fit *La mujer nueva* under the label of either a feminist or a Catholic novel. Instead, Laforet delineates a type of spirituality that has more in common with mysticism and a deeply personal relationship with God, rather than one prescribed by dogma or the clerical and masculinist culture of the time. It is interesting to observe that Laforet's relationship with Lilí Álvarez and her role as spiritual mentor to the author drew to an end towards 1959, as did Laforet´s intense engagement with Catholicism. Although Laforet never renounced her religion, she sought her own spiritual path, and in her later years she read the work of Gary Snyder, a Zen-Buddhist poet and ecologist, and began sketching Chinese Hanzi on pieces of paper, even though she was not trained in the language.

The realms of the spiritual and transcendental as well as other forms of religion appeared to draw Laforet's interest as she grew older. It is also important to note that representations of states of oneness and transcendence recur across all her novels, beginning with *Nada*. Thus, Paulina's conversion on the train to Madrid could be read as a deeper exploration of states of consciousness and transcendental experiences that were already present in her previous two novels and would be developed further in the first two novels of her trilogy *Tres pasos fuera del tiempo*.[15] These states of merger align with Abraham Maslow's "peak experiences" during which the protagonists temporarily

14. "One could say the novel is as much about forward thinking as it about tradition." Ana Caballé and Israel Rolón-Barada, *Carmen Laforet: una mujer en fuga* (RBA Libros, 2010), 259.

15. The manuscript of the final novel of the trilogy *Jacque mate* was never published and remains lost. *La insolación* and *Al volver la equina* form the first two novels of the trilogy.

lose their egoic selves and enter a blissful condition akin to William James's accounts of "pure experience."[16] For example, a state of transcendence is achieved by Andrea in *Nada* while listening to her uncle Román play the violin and also when she stands in front of Barcelona's neo-Gothic cathedral in the old city one evening. Another example can be found in *La isla y los domonios* when Marta enters the sea naked, under a full moon, and feels profound happiness. The pursuit of relief from suffering through transcendence thus forms an undercurrent that runs through each of Laforet's novels, and the question to consider with reference to *La mujer nueva* is whether Paulina's conversion on the train to Madrid is another iteration of this search for inner peace or is somehow distinct from other accounts of transcendence within Laforet's literary oeuvre.

The entire "segunda parte" of *La mujer nueva*, which only contains two chapters, is dedicated to Paulina's religious conversion and her first encounters with Father Pedro González who has been recommended by Blanca as a spiritual guide. The distinctive lyricism and reliance on language drawn from the mystical writings of Santa Teresa de Jesús and Juan de la Cruz separate this description of transcendence from other representations in Laforet's fiction.[17] While disagreeing with Laforet's choice of ending for the novel, the well-known Hispanist Gerald Brenan praised Laforet's prose style in the "segunda parte" in the highest terms: "Dudo que haya en castellano

16. Abraham Maslow, *The Farthest Reaches of Human Nature* (Viking Press, 1971). *Pure Experience: The Response to William James*, ed. E. I. Taylor and R. H. Wozniak (Thoemmes Press, 1996).

17. For a detailed discussion of the influence of the Spanish mystics on the writing of this novel see Samuel O'Donoghue, "Carmen Laforet and the Spanish Mystics: Spiritual Renewal and Social Critique in *La mujer nueva*" in Del Mastro and Wells, 217–44.

unas páginas más maravillosamente poéticas que éstas. Ésta es la cosa major del libro."[18] Waking up on the train to Madrid, Paulina becomes absorbed in the changing landscape outside her window and begins to feel a sense of merger with the natural world, but it is important to note that Laforet does not initially draw on mystical vocabulary to describe the protagonist's feelings. Paulina's gaze merges with the landscape of the Spanish planes, delighting in their colours and the contrasting morning light. As she observes small dwellings on the horizon, Paulina is propelled into a state whereby she begins to feel a loss of self and projects herself into the environment passing in front of her eyes. Gradually, this experience of absorption in nature evolves into a sense of universal love towards her fellow human beings as her soul fills up with a sense of beauty and she gently notices with curiosity what is happening to her. Again, the narrative initially focuses on nature and not God as the source of the first stage of transcendence.

As the chapter develops, the use of capital letters signals the increasingly religious and mystical nature of Paulina's experience of love which she comes to realise is God's grace entering her: "El Amor es Dios—supo Paulina—; Dios, esa inmensa hoguera de felicidad."[19] The word "arrebato" recurs many times to convey the sense of ecstasy that Paulina is experiencing in this mystical state; similarly, 'gozo' is repeated to signify the joyous sense of blissful union with God's love and the experience of entering into a state of Grace. As the train finally comes to the

18. "I doubt whether there are any pages in the Castilian language more wonderfully poetical than these. They're the best thing about the book." Caballé and Rolón-Barada, 262.

19. "Love is God," Paulina realised, "God, that immense blazing hearth of happiness." Carmen Laforet, *La mujer nueva*, 139.

end of its journey, Paulina arrives in Madrid "recién nacida"—a woman reborn—filled with God's Grace and ready to embark on her journey towards religious fulfilment. William James, in his detailed analysis of mystical states, avers that these types of experiences have "an unusually close relation to the transmarginal or subliminal region," in other words the unconscious.[20]

Paulina's conversion therefore remains open to interpretation as it could be understood less as a mystical, religious experience and more of an encounter with the deepest realms of her unconscious mind. However, since Laforet was in the middle of a period of religious fervour and under the spiritual guidance of Lilí Álvarez, it is understandable why the conversion sequence is framed within the language of Spanish mysticism and not psychoanalysis even though key figures from this field—Freud and Adler—are mentioned in *La mujer nueva*.[21] It therefore proves difficult to say definitively whether Paulina's experience on the train is religious or psychological, or perhaps both, as James suggested was integral to such transcendental moments. It is important to mention that Laforet's immersion in religious thought, as well as her friendship with Lilí Álvarez, was coming to an end by 1958, no doubt due to the author's fierce love of freedom and resistance to any constraints on her liberty. Given Laforet's later statements on her feelings about her third novel, discussed below, it is difficult to formulate a definitive interpretation of Paulina's religious epiphany in the

20. William James, *The Varieties of Religious Experience: A Study in Human Nature* (Penguin, 1985), 483.

21. Laforetian scholar and close friend of Laforet Roberta Johnson states that "by the time Laforet wrote this novel, she had been reading the great psychologists of the first half of the 20th century," in "Carmen Laforet's *La mujer nueva*: a feminist response to Gabriel Miró's Nuestro Padre San Daniel and El Obispo leproso?," in Del Mastro and Wells, 245.

"segunda parte." Nonetheless, the autobiographical alignment between the author's personal experience of conversion and those of her protagonist in *La mujer nueva* appear indisputable. Similarly, Paulina´s name also signals to St Paul whose mystical conversion requires no explanation and serves as a key influence on the novel.

The final section of the novel might be considered diffuse and fragmented, yet it sets out to convey Paulina's ongoing struggle to integrate her experience of entering into God's grace into her life alongside her ongoing personal struggles involving her feelings towards her husband and her lover Antonio. The sub-story of Julián and his plot to rob jewels from a woman in the neighbourhood is perhaps inserted too bluntly into Paulina's spiritual journey in the third part of the novel, but the story serves as a critique of the emerging materialism in Spain in the 1950s as the economy began to recover after the postwar austerity of the 1940s.[22]

We must now turn to the ending of *La mujer nueva* and examine the complex nature of Paulina's choice to return to her husband and son, end her affair with Antonio, and agree to her husband's request to marry "por la Iglesia," as their existing civil marriage during the Civil War was deemed invalid under the dictatorship. O'Donoghue suggests that "the end of *La mujer nueva* is the only logical conclusion for a novel so steeped in the worldview of the Spanish mystics."[23] Conversely, Brenan felt dissatisfied with the ending and interpreted Paulina´s actions as a form of defeat.[24] A feminist reading of Paulina's decision

22. Some of Laforet´s articles published in *Destino* suggest her disapproval towards the direction Spain was heading in the mid to late 1950s.

23. O´Donoghue, 242.

24. Cerezales Laforet, 227.

would concur that her actions smack of capitulation to the gender roles of Franco's Spain, while a more conservative, religious interpretation might suggest that she is simply fulfilling her previous commitments as a wife and mother.

Laforet herself later appeared to regret the ending of the novel and echoed Brenan's observations that Paulina's return to her husband was unsatisfactory. She suggested that she accommodated Paulina´s actions within her own knowledge and direct experiences of religious devotion at the time of writing the novel, but she remained dissatisfied with the outcome: "en lo más íntimo de mi ser no lo sentía, quería convencerme de ello haciéndoselo vivir a Paulina."[25] The meaning of Paulina's actions however carry within them a typical Laforetian ambiguity which transcends any definitive interpretations.[26] Critics have missed the opportunity to explore the fact that the protagonist returns to her husband with an awareness of her capacity to embrace solitude, which will now be bearable due to feeling supported by God's love; thus her homecoming may be construed as a return to her Self and her capacity to be and feel alone, which she was unable to bear at the beginning of the novel due to her estrangement from her husband and subsequent depression as a result of her miscarriage. With this knowledge that she will be able to tolerate solitude, she begins to feel "una gran confianza," as she is not only returning to her husband with "esa paz de Cristo" but also an awareness of her capacity to be alone.[27] According to D. W. Winnicott,

25. "In the depths of my being, I didn't feel it, but I wanted to convince myself by making Paulina feel it." Cerezales Laforet, 227; 77–78.

26. Laforet was an adept short story writer and utilized the technique of ambiguous endings, one of the key features of the genre, in many of her stories.

27. Carmen Laforet, *La mujer nueva,* 335.

an individual's ability to bear their own company represents an important stage of maturation and psychological development, which Paulina may have missed due to her adverse early life circumstances within her family.[28] In this regard, perhaps Paulina truly becomes a new woman due to growth of Self as much as spiritual renewal.

## FURTHER READING

Caballe, Ana, and Israel Rolón-Barada. *Carmen Laforet: Una mujer en fuga.* RBA Libros, 2010.

Cerezales Laforet, Cristina. *Música blanca.* Destino, 2009.

Cerezales Laforet, Agustín. *Carmen Laforet: Vista por sí misma.* Destino, 2021.

Del Mastro, Mark P., and Caragh Wells. *Después de nada mucho: nuevas perspectivas al conmemorar el centenario de su nacimiento (1921–2021).* Albatros, 2022.

Illanes Adaro, Graciela. *La novelística de Carmen Laforet.* Editorial Gredos, 1971.

Johnson, Roberta. *Carmen Laforet.* Boston, 1981.

Laforet, Carmen. *La mujer nueva.* Edición y prólogo de Israel Rolón-Barada. Destino, 2003.

Laforet, Carmen. *Puntos de vista de una mujer.* Edición de Ana Cabello y Blanca Ripoll. Destino, 2021.

Wells, Caragh. *The Novels of Carmen Laforet. An Aesthetics of Relief.* Legenda, 2019.

28. D. W. Winnicott, *The Maturational Processes and the Facilitating Environment; Studies in the Theory of Emotional Development* (Hogarth, 1965).

# THE NEW WOMAN

Carmen Laforet

*For Lilí Álvarez, godmother at my confirmation,*
*with my gratitude and great affection*

AUTHOR'S NOTE

The characters in this novel, along with several villages, a river and a valley have been invented and situated in the province of León. The intention was not in any way to create a "novel of manners." The author, who has only a visitor's knowledge of this marvellous region with all its contrasts, felt that it would provide a suitable geographical location for her invented valley and a convenient setting for her story. The region has been chosen for no reason other than this.

*For neither circumcision counts for anything,
nor uncircumcision, but a new creation.*

*Paul's Letter to the Galatians*

# PART ONE

# I

The sky lay heavy behind them. Voracious green, striped flies buzzed, hovering above the large cow pats that lay scattered over the road and, through the gravel and the dust, a desire for moisture, a longing for the coming storm, wound its way upwards.

Paulina was not thinking about where she placed her feet as she hurried down the slope. She was conscious only of the beating of her heart; that too was heavy. Her husband, Eulogio, caught her arm to steady her whenever her flimsy shoes buckled between the stones, or she lost her footing.

"The train doesn't leave till seven," he reminded her.

Below them, on the other side of the river, the little station was bathed in an unusual glow that summer afternoon. Shafts of sunlight were streaming out from between the crusts of ever-swelling, jostling clouds. The river glimmered darkly. On its bank, by the tracks, loomed huge mounds of coal. The mines were a few miles away from the village and the ore would be brought in by lorry before being transferred to the coal trains… Coal heaps aside, nothing about Villa de Robre betrayed the presence of the mines. Verdant meadows, large herds of cattle, hillsides abundant with oak and chestnut trees, and beyond, the immense crags in a semi-circle around the widening in the valley where the village nestled. For now, these crags were invisible, hidden by the bilious clouds that were slowly bearing down on all of it.

As Paulina and Eulogio crossed the new bridge to the station, the first rumbles of thunder echoed in the distance. Paulina felt the sound of the coming storm vibrate through her body. She looked upwards, her eyes wide, serious. Her gaze followed the course of the river. Very close, a mile or so from the station, on a hill, and beside what was known as the old bridge (the ancient bridge built from Roman stone, the one carriages weren't allowed to cross) she could see the battlements of the castle, their dark lines sharp against the dark clouds. The river, reflecting them.

Eulogio's bright blue eyes followed Paulina's gaze.

"I don't understand why you won't go to Ponferrada in Antonio's car. I'm sure if we telephone from the station…"

Paulina turned her head without answering. She was a slender woman, with intensely black hair and eyes. Her husband, still a young man, broad-shouldered, solidly built, was carrying the suitcase. Eulogio was fair-haired, with blue eyes, like most of his family, the Nives, wealthy cattle farmers in the Robre valley. He wore a thick hand-woven jacket, made for the country. His white shirt, no tie, was undone at the collar. He had a self-assured air, a look that was clean yet seemingly effortless. His expression was stubborn. When he caught Paulina's arm to stop her falling, she could feel the strength of his hand through the light fabric of her summer dress, a gabardine dress the colour of straw… At her neck, Paulina wore a green silk scarf that didn't do her any favours. Her small slender face seemed to pick up reflections, also green, from the neckerchief.

Eulogio was carrying his wife's coat and the case, while she held nothing save her white handbag. It was surprising how little she had to bring… The decision to leave had been made in little more than an hour. And she was going… Nobody had tried to stop her. Mariana, Eulogio's mother, had simply raised her eyebrows. Then her eyes had sought out her son's. The two held each other's gaze for a few moments… Mariana thought that Paulina was not of completely sound mind. Eulogio's opinion was that he couldn't prevent Paulina from doing anything she wanted to do. Neither morally nor legally. Paulina hadn't expected him to so casually pick up the suitcase and the white wool coat and accompany her. During the short stretch of time that had ensued between the announcement of her departure and its obstacle-free realisation, Paulina had felt a strange sensation: like someone who had prepared themselves for a titanic effort to push over a wall, only to discover the wall to be no more than an optical illusion.

"I'm going to call Antonio," Eulogio had said as they left the manor house, "it'll be best if he takes us to Ponferrada in his car. That way I can go with you until you get on the express train… I'm sure he'd be happy to have an excuse to dine out."

"No."

The *no* had been so abrupt that Eulogio had stopped there.

"I don't want to say goodbye to anyone. I don't feel like talking to anyone… I won't go with Antonio."

As they crossed the bridge over the Robre, the couple had looked across to the castle. That was where Antonio lived now.

He was Eulogio's cousin and was married to the daughter of the owners of the ancient castle, the Count and Countess of Vados de Robre.

The village, viewed from the station that afternoon, had the look of an engraving. Grey and black. It was a terraced village, its houses mostly stone-built, and with slate roofs. The houses appeared stuck on, two dimensional, against the backdrop of a forest of chestnut trees and the dark sky. Plumes of smoke rose from some of the chimneys. They emerged sluggishly, weary from the heat and the oppressive sky.

Eulogio approached the booth to buy the tickets. Paulina remained motionless, gazing out to the village. It seemed unfamiliar, a shadowy image, almost dreamlike.

"I've got you a seat in first class; it's only two hours but you'll be more comfortable."

Casually, he took some large notes out of his wallet. At the same time, he carried on talking slowly, deliberately.

"Take this. I'll come in October; if you run short before then, you'll let me know, won't you? When I come, we'll sort everything out properly. I feel it'll give you time to think, two months… Me too… I'm sure, though, that I'll decide to stay here. This is what I've been searching for, for years, without realising. You'll think it all through. I don't want to force you… You know I don't want to force you… But don't forget about Miguel; well, you'll see… In any case, I'll bring Miguel with me in October. He'll have to board, or… We'll see."

Paulina sensed that what Eulogio was saying was of the utmost importance, despite its vagueness. Yes, maybe it was important… It related to the life of the two of them and to the future of their son. She was listening, her dark eyes wide, like

two large, black ink stains. But she couldn't speak. She couldn't
even think about what she was hearing.

She was still holding the tickets in her hand, undecided as
to whether to put them in her handbag. Her face looked slightly
rigid. Eulogio insisted:

"If you need anything else, I mean it, call me, drop me a
line… Good… And if you change your mind, you know…"

Eulogio's attitude was caring, protective. As if he were
talking to a child or an invalid.

Paulina knew it would be very hard to speak. If she spoke,
her eyes would fill with tears and she didn't want to make a
scene. She waited a few moments and then put her money
away slowly. When she judged that the little narrow-gauge
train was about to leave, she uttered an abrupt "thank you,"
her voice hoarse.

Eulogio, who had already stowed his wife's case on the
train, held her shoulders and kissed her quickly and simply.
Afterwards he watched her disappear inside the train.

The train was tiny, preposterous, with its three classes of
passenger. An old engine, with a large funnel, whistled and
belched balls of white steam into the gloomy, sultry afternoon.
Paulina didn't look out of the window.

Eulogio stood alone, a stiff, rather forlorn figure on the
platform. "Poor Paulina!" he thought, not really knowing quite
why she was so poor… But even he, not usually one to delve
into such things, could see the sadness in her eyes. In the past,
before he had discovered happiness through meaningful work,
when problems, setbacks and ambition had gnawed at his soul,
Eulogio had found that black, sad well in Paulina's eyes both
unsurprising and unattractive. Things were different now. Be-

sides, she had been so seriously unwell…

The train vanished around a curve in the valley. It would continue to follow the entire course of the River Robre along the bed of the steep-sided valley. Then it would veer off towards Ponferrada. This was where Paulina would have to change for the express train from Galicia to Madrid. Just then, it occurred to Eulogio that he had neglected his duty entirely. He should have accompanied her all the way there, made sure she was comfortable… There were things that Eulogio had been taught from a young age about women. Small details his mother had ensured he viewed as sacred. This didn't mean he couldn't be hard as stone, on occasion… Now he felt ashamed of the long, unpleasant arguments he'd had with Paulina only a few months ago… Shame is a strange thing. It buries itself deep inside you and then it bursts out at the most unexpected moments. Eulogio hadn't felt any compassion for Paulina during the long past year, when every one of his wife's gestures had irritated him. And at the time she'd tried to please him, or at least submit meekly to his demands… but now that Paulina had changed so much that she was like a stranger, now that she no longer bothered about him (had they even spoken together alone since she'd been able to get out of bed again after the illness that had nearly killed her?), now that in Eulogio's mother's house she behaved as if she were a guest of honour, spoilt, demanding… It was now that Eulogio had begun to feel a vague sense of remorse, an odd kind of shame, and because of this he didn't dare to judge Paulina, nor to contradict her.

Eulogio crossed the bridge. His blue eyes shone bright and wide in his tanned, healthy face. He was frowning. The air was suffocating, and he wished the storm would break at last.

A fair-haired little boy was leaning over the railings on the bridge, looking down at the water. Some other little rascals were swimming in the river below, naked. Eulogio remembered that Paulina hadn't even waited for Miguel—who had been spending a fortnight in a house they owned in a small village in the forest—to come home so she could say goodbye to him… Lately it seemed that not even her son mattered to her. Yet she had dedicated her life to the boy for ten years.

The thunder claps began to fill the world with warnings, as if at any moment, the mountains would fall. The calm in the village, the stillness of the chimney smoke, the black roofs and the black trees felt eerie. He saw the clear zigzag of a lightning bolt among the clouds, and a terrific noise reverberated throughout the valley, as if the crags had indeed come crashing down… The flash and the peal of thunder made Eulogio happy. It would soon rain.

# II

When he arrived home, the first drops had not yet begun to fall.

Every generation of the Nives, all of them gentlemen-farmers, had sprung from that wide, solidly-built manor house, and now it belonged to him, although like all his assets, his mother held it in usufruct.

Others of Eulogio's relatives had settled in Madrid and in various provincial capitals. Nearly all were wealthy bourgeoisie, much richer than Miguel Nives, Eulogio's father, had been, although their lifestyle was not superior to the one that Mariana had carved out for their own family. Nives Commercial Enterprises, for example, with a capital of many millions, belonged almost entirely to his uncles and cousins… And all this mattered, much more so in Eulogio's family than in most Spanish families at the time, because the Nives had an extremely strong sense of family loyalty. Paulina used to say that the Nives were a sort of freemasonry scattered throughout the nation. Not even the civil war had threatened their unity. All the family members, of various political persuasions, had set aside any differences of opinion to help each other out whenever they could. Eulogio's relatives helped him when he was in America; and when he returned to Spain they had reached out to him too. Eulogio felt more secure in his life once he understood that he was not alone, that he belonged to a clan. A clan of hard-workers, full of determination, and good fortune.

Eulogio's second cousin, Antonio Nives, the one Paulina had refused to go to Ponferrada with, was the most affluent and the least typical of the Nives; son of a successful lawyer from Barcelona, he was wealthy but not on his own merit. He was rich purely by chance. His mother—a young woman originally from the Philippines, possessed of a huge fortune—died giving birth to him, and he'd now inherited this vast fortune. The lawyer, his father, who had put him through a law degree, intending to employ him in his cabinet, despaired when he saw the life of absolute idleness and extravagance that Antonio chose to lead. He had counted on Antonio's marriage being the cure, but since marrying, his son had become even worse…

All the Nives had certain reservations about Antonio. They had been very surprised at the marriage he'd made, because Rita Vados, Antonio's wife, was exactly the class of person that any Señora Nives would have desired for her son, in the same way that Paulina, Eulogio's wife, would have been considered an embarrassment by any of them… And yet, Eulogio, a sensible boy, who always did what his parents expected of him, had chosen Paulina, and it was Antonio, the restless one, the "artist"—and his relatives imbued this word with a certain inflection it rather warranted as Antonio fancied himself a poet and a writer, without any basis—who had selected and then courted the daughter of the Count and Countess of Vados de Robre, the best family in the land, and the only aristocratic one in the village.

All the Nives felt rather attached to the village of Villa de Robre, where there were several summer chalets belonging to various members of the family. They all liked to drop by from time to time, no matter how far away they lived. And because of this Antonio had known Rita Vados since childhood, and had married her... But for all the Nives, the most important house was Eulogio's. Mariana had looked after the house so well, managing to introduce every new convenience without ruining the charm of its solid stone walls. It was a pleasant place to live. The best place in the world.

In a narrow street, a studded gate, half embedded within a wall... Almost the entire street was taken up with an enormous yellow automobile. Antonio's automobile... A few minutes more and Paulina would have had no excuse for her eccentric idea of setting off alone to Ponferrada in the little narrow-gauge train... Nearly every afternoon, after taking his invalid wife out for a drive, Antonio would pull up at the mansion.

The gate was part-open. Eulogio pushed it. He stepped into a patio garden, adorned with large flowerbeds filled with blue and pink-hued hydrangeas. Wisteria and bougainvillea trailed across the walls of the house: the flowers quiet, as if sleeping in the agonising peace of the moment. A wide porch, rather like a room with one wall missing, decorated with antique furniture, seemed to wait on stone steps. The patio was paved with flagstones, grass pushing up between them.

There was no one in the porch, but as soon as Eulogio entered the house he heard voices coming from the room they called "the small sitting room" or "Mariana's room," because it was his mother's refuge. A beautiful, light-filled room with a piano, and an open fire that in winter, despite the efficient heating system, Mariana liked to have burning all the time… A bookshelf with Mariana's favourite books, in attractive editions, and the desk where she would settle her accounts with the tenant farmers; a couch, various armchairs and pretty, brightly coloured curtains.

When Eulogio walked in, the curtains were drawn shut and the fire lit. In the room were Antonio and Rita, his wife: tall, slim, pretty and very young, with the gentle languor of a green reed, though her serious illness deformed her face. It was impossible to say exactly how Rita had changed, but she wasn't the same as she'd been a few months earlier. Something soft and white, sad, indefinable, seemed to be erasing her features.

Antonio's parents-in-law were there too. The Count of Los Vados was a tall, spindly, bespectacled old man, very polite and cheerful, who, so people said, was quite mad, and the Countess, a plump lady who at first glance looked like an elegant housekeeper, was dressed in what appeared to be a cassock or perhaps a black sack. Her grey hair was rolled into a little bun and fastened at the nape of her neck, her face was as happy and rosy as a baby's, and her eyes the same greenish colour as Rita's. She also had the voice of a baby, which formed an odd contrast with its volume. They were having drinks with Mariana.

Eulogio's mother was the same age as the Countess, but her figure was trim and she was tastefully dressed. In fact, she'd been tall and plump in her prime. As she had slimmed down her face had become wrinkled, although she prided herself on her still beautifully smooth forehead. Her eyes were restless, like those of a businessman. She had a fear of missing anything going on around her. Mariana would have been extremely surprised if she'd known that her friend, the Countess of Los Vados, thought her very innocent and lacking in insight…This opinion was not widely shared, however. The villagers considered that Mariana managed her affairs very efficiently, and so attributed her with all kinds of wisdom and guile.

It was hot; even in the large room the air was oppressive.

"We had to close the windows. The thunder claps were frightening Rita," Mariana explained.

Rita, ensconced in an armchair, her exceedingly long and beautiful legs stretched out in front of her, was smiling.

Eulogio on that afternoon felt strangely inclined to compassion. He noted this as he looked at Rita's smile and the slightly trembling hand—very delicate and, since some time ago, withered—in which she held her glass.

They heard more thunder claps. The house, with its thick walls, felt protective.

"Like this, inside a house, it's almost enjoyable listening to the noise…"

"No rain yet, Eulogio?"

"No."

Antonio Nives, who bore no resemblance whatsoever to his family from Villa de Robre, was a young man of twenty-five, tall and very slight, with brown, thoughtful eyes. He was smoking quietly, sitting on one of the arms of his wife's chair. But you could tell from his ears that he was attentive. He seemed to be listening to something other than the sound of the storm. As if he were listening out for footsteps on the stone staircase that swept upwards from the nearby hallway.

"Is Paulina not coming?" he asked finally.

Unexpectedly, Rita blushed.

Mariana looked at Eulogio. Eulogio said with some effort:

"Please accept her apologies, but you know how impulsive she is…" He smiled in an attempt to make his words sound natural, and in doing so made them sound contrived. "She decided she needed to go to Madrid right away, today. I've come from the station; she was catching the seven o'clock train."

There was a slight pause. An almost agonising pause. The Count could be heard singing softly to himself:

*Woman is fickle*
*Like a feather in the wind…*

Rita began to laugh. It was a nervous, silly laugh. Antonio crushed his cigarette into the ashtray. The Countess, who was standing a little apart, in her black dress, turned her bright, wide eyes towards Antonio and her daughter. She couldn't quite see her daughter's face, which was half hidden by the husband's body.

Antonio looked at his watch:

"What time does Paulina's train for Madrid leave from Ponferrada?… I could have taken her."

"I'm not really sure. I think the express train goes through at eleven or twelve. I'd rather you had taken us and we could have had dinner there… But you know what she's like. She gets some crazy notion into her head and…"

The Count asked the question no one had dared to ask: "You haven't had an argument, have you?"

"For heaven's sake, Alfonso, not at all! You know very well that since her illness, she's suffered with her nerves… She has to do things just like that, in the moment, as soon as she thinks of them…"

Mariana's voice resonated. It was a piercing voice. A voice that could be heard from all corners of the house, though she didn't shout.

"Yes, we felt it best to let her do what she wanted. You know what Joaquín advised. Not to upset her. Let her recuperate… In any case, in my opinion she's completely recovered, physically speaking. Some days she's been perfectly cheerful. Almost overly so… To the point of being irritating. We've all seen how she's taken to laughing, running around with the dogs in the orchard, as if she were a little girl, and as we all know, she's not a little girl anymore… She kept wanting to go and hunt for insects in the fields, for her son's collection, holding the boy by the hand! All her toing and froing was making us quite dizzy… And then other days she was unbearable, feeling sorry for herself, self-absorbed… Then, Blanca wound her up into an even more agitated state… It has to be said."

The Countess turned her extraordinary eyes towards her friend. Mariana was in the habit of blaming Blanca for anything inexplicable that happened around them.

"Yes, you, you dear, with your piety and all your nonsense… Well, no one can accuse Paulina of being superstitious, it's one of the few faults she doesn't have; she's not even religious. But Blanca insisted on taking Paulina to visit some of her friends, those funny nuns, the Altozano Foundation ones… Yes, the Carmelites… Well, I don't know why I'm bothering to explain what you all already know. She took her there one day and my silly daughter-in-law found it all fascinating. What I mean is, she was horrified… That's the word. But horror in the sense of an unhealthy fascination. Lately her only topic of conversation has been these women—who are buried alive and eat in the company of a skull—and whether their way of life is humane or inhumane… But she went back to see them again. And then she took it into her head to go to the cemetery… Well… That was fatal… She said it was the best entertainment to be had in the village. Anyway, today she comes out with the idea that this village disturbs her too much, that she's seeing skulls and religious fanatics and nuns all over the place and that she's leaving. What could we do? I think the best thing was what we did do; say goodbye as if everything were normal… and keep the door open in case she arrives in Madrid and decides to come straight back home again."

Eulogio was smiling a little. Paulina hadn't offered any of the explanations his mother had volunteered. She'd simply said she was leaving. And she'd added: "Right now, as soon as I've packed." All that about nuns and skulls and religious fanatics, Mariana had invented.

Antonio stood up. He was looking at Rita.

"Okay, baby, I think it's calming down… Anyway, I'll drive; so there's absolutely nothing to worry about. It's no distance from here to home… A short hop… We do need to go."

Not only was the thunderstorm not calming down, it was positively raging. The closed windows and the curtains drawn across them meant they couldn't see the lightning flashes, but the cracks of thunder were becoming louder and louder.

Mariana stopped still in the middle of the room.

"All right, but don't you want to stay for dinner?… I'd thought… I wanted to tell you I was reading about a case of instability very like my daughter-in-law's, I'm not sure if it was Adler or perhaps Freud himself…"

"No, no…You know Rita has her dinner in bed. It's already enough that we've had a good walk this afternoon. We have to take it slowly… Don't we baby? Don't give me that cute face… You know it's true. You'll thank me for it later…"

Rita was truly tired. She didn't dare protest at the abrupt departure into the storm, the lightning flashes, the ear-splitting crashes of thunder… Of course, in a few minutes she would be home. The walls there were solid and welcoming too.

*Wild thunderstorms…*
*rock the small boat…*
*of Peter's successor…*
*abandoned, adrift…*

The Count sang this song—which none of them knew originated in a faraway school and a faraway nursery—to himself with his usual ironic little smile. It was his way of expressing himself. After singing it he kissed Mariana's hand affectionately. Blanca was smiling, as if to excuse her husband. There was a tremendous roar of thunder. A roar that grew louder and louder, seeming to shake the house, although of course the house remained solid as ever. Far off in the kitchen, a maid screamed.

Blanca glanced at her daughter, who had stood up and was leaning on her husband, holding his arm, her face pale. Then she eyed her son-in-law. With her timid, bright child's voice she asked: "Couldn't we… Antonio?"

Antonio had decided they were leaving. You could see it in his face, in his narrowed eyes, which usually wore a caring, gentle expression, and now resembled two dark slits, their expression unfathomable.

"Thank you very much, Aunt," he said to Mariana, ignoring his mother-in-law; "Now let's see… ah, yes… here's Rita's coat. Put it on, baby."

Sometimes he would enunciate the word baby like a hammer banging down on each syllable. Like he was giving an order. He always called his wife baby.

He barely glanced at Eulogio as they said goodbye. The Count, on the other hand, patted him affectionately on the back, to make up for his son-in-law's curtness.

When they opened the door, the porch was flooded with blue light for a few seconds. Rita leaned against Antonio, burying her face in his shoulder. This frailty was excusable given that she was so sick. The latest tests gave her very little hope, all pointing to a very serious leukemia. Even so, her husband put an arm around her shoulders and dragged her across the patio while lightning flashes followed the rumbling that had so startled her.

A few very large drops of rain began to fall.

The Cadillac's headlights lit up the evening gloom, deepening the surrounding darkness. It was almost night-time.

"I don't know son, that Antonio," Mariana began, "there's something about him… He was so rude to Rita. I don't know how Blanca allows him… Well, no, I do know. Antonio pays all the family expenses… They let him do whatever he wants…"

Eulogio remained in the porch for a moment. He liked to listen to the rain, stubborn and warm, that soon would lash down furiously. He liked the smell of the earth, already rising from the hydrangea beds. He could sense the bougainvillea and the wisteria springing back to life.

When he entered his mother's small sitting room, he saw that Mariana, who wasn't afraid of anything, had thrown the windows wide open. The delicious aromas of earth and rain drifted in and flashes of white illuminated the room. Eulogio sighed contentedly. He poured himself a small amount of cordial with ice and water, and began to sip it slowly.

When his mother sat down opposite him, in another of the armchairs, he sensed that she was about to launch into one of her speeches in that nervy, brisk, terse way of hers; that a cascade of words would come gushing out, full of reason and good sense and urging him to act. He halted the stream with a hand before it could begin.

Mariana was sitting on the edge of the seat, upright, her mouth almost open to speak.

"Mother. I'm going to Las Duras tomorrow... I want to see how Miguelito is getting on."

Las Duras is a miserable hamlet, with no communications, in the large area of forest where León borders Galicia and Asturias. The Nives owned a house there, built on the ruins of an old convent by one of Eulogio's ancestors. This gentleman had acquired it very cheaply at the time of the state confiscation of church property, as well as a large swathe of forest, impossible to exploit because of the lack of roads or tracks. The house was a luxury that had been earned by three generations of hard-working Nives. They used it as an occasional hunting lodge. When Eulogio was young he would enjoy a few days there every summer... Now his son was there, being looked after by the gamekeepers and his friend José Vados.

Mariana sat back again, sinking into the armchair and leaning back.

"That's fine… You all do whatever you must…"

She closed her eyes, as if she were tired. She wasn't. She opened them immediately, listening to the sounds that were coming from the kitchen, through the vegetable garden, through the open windows.

"That stupid woman Justa, the cook, thinks it's funny to scare the girl and…"

Eulogio wasn't listening to his mother, but to the rain that was now falling heavily and it felt to him as though it were washing away the dust, bringing fresh, new life to his soul too. It felt as if it were spurring him on with the strong aroma it was summoning from the earth, as if it were reinvigorating him.

When Mariana, her housekeeping instinct awoken, left the room, Eulogio didn't even notice.

The rain and that smell of the earth brought memories of the many desires he had experienced throughout his thirty-six years.

Eulogio had been brought up to live here in this village. It was expected that he would take over his father's cheese and butter factory and manage the land. He had a degree in industrial engineering. The countryside suited him. He had been brought up, too, to live in great comfort and with all his material needs satisfied, to live the same lifestyle to which his family had become accustomed. And he'd been blessed with much more besides. He had enormous physical strength, which he nurtured. He was fond of the good things in life but since boyhood he'd enjoyed hunting and hiking, plus he was resilient and resourceful… The war took him away from the village and then away from Spain. When his son Miguel was due, at the end of the civil war, he'd been forced to leave Paulina in Barcelona, practically abandon her to her fate… And though his intention had been to return to Spain, the way things had turned out, he'd set off for Central America and a year and a half had gone by before he returned to his own country. He remembered one or two opportunities to become wealthy that had come his way yet, for some reason, he hadn't taken; a kind of strange destiny always derailed his ambitious plans. He could remember the worst of those times, an occasion when he'd contemplated taking advantage of certain arbitrary laws in Mexico to obtain a divorce, so that he could marry a crazy millionairess. If he'd married her, he might have become fabulously rich… As it happened, the millionairess had tired of him before he'd made up his mind. Paulina never knew… Women had not been a very important factor in Eulogio's life. Only his desire to triumph, to do things, to shape his life. And of course, he never forgot he had a son. He was a very virile man, with a deep paternal instinct. Eventually he realised he needed to come back to his home and his son… But even after his return he wrestled with a sense of thwarted ambition for over a year, while he and his family lived in a modest rented furnished flat, waiting for his big chance to take over the reins at Nives Commercial Enterprises where he worked. It was a year of hardship, of bad moods, of a demanding Paulina, who had to learn to get used to his lower wage, and who was unwell… A year during which he ignored his mother's calls, visits and letters… Eventually, when Paulina came to Villa de Robre, practically kidnapped by Mariana, and gave birth to a premature, still-born son, he came back through a sense of duty… And simply by inhaling the smell of the valley, hearing the unique way people spoke, rediscovering Mariana's comfortable armchairs and seeing the brick chimney towering above the factory, he knew it was his destiny. The destiny that had always awaited him. And… he was staying. Just now, this afternoon, he had decided to stay. Mariana had been right since day one. It was logical that when the term of the lease ended on the factory, he should take it on. He had to build what was his. Look after the land and the livestock. And even, who knows, the huge, exhilarating forests of Las Duras could be a greater adventure than any he could have had elsewhere in the world. In the scent of the storm showers, in the swaying branches he sensed something both new and old. There were things that his forebears had begun and that he would continue, and things that he himself could begin, there on his own land, and that his children would continue…

The thought of children made him frown. He didn't know if there would be any other children apart from Miguel.

He pictured the boy's straight, fair hair, his smiling mouth and his straight ten-year-old legs. In any case, Miguel was worth many sons.

Mariana came back in, her movements agitated, her bright eyes worried.

"Really? You're going to smoke now?"

Eulogio had his pipe in his hand and was about to fill it. "I didn't realise."

"It's that we're going to have dinner in a minute, son… Then you must tell me what luggage you'll take to Las Duras."

Eulogio politely put the pipe down. When a gust of wind banged the doors, knocked over two tall glasses lined with straw and blew some sheets of music off the piano stand, he stood to tidy up as much as he could of the mess.

Now Mariana was talking. Talking, talking… Not about Paulina, as he'd feared, but about Miguel and the bad influence that a crackpot like Pepe Vados could have on a ten-year-old boy.

"You need to fetch him back straight away, son. What were you thinking? Pepe has a streak of his father's madness in him. It's true… You only need look at his face… A crazy father and a simple mother; because Blanca is a very decent woman, but simple; who knows how a child of theirs could have turned out… I was surprised that the boy was so clever."

She was talking about Pepe Vados, who now called himself Don José González and was the parish priest of Las Duras and other hamlets in the surrounding area; godforsaken, miserable hamlets that remained cut off for several months of the year and hadn't had a doctor or a priest for years… González was the Vados de Robre family's surname, but people usually called them by their parents' title. And so, the transformation of Pepe Vados—eldest son of the Count and Countess, engineer from Montes, free-thinker, close friend of Eulogio Nives and spoilt, adopted child of Mariana—into a village priest called Don José González, was one of the strangest things to greet Eulogio on his return to Spain.

Pepe had asked him for part of the Las Duras house—the former church that had been used as a granary—so that it could provisionally become a church again. And it now was…

Eulogio's eyes narrowed a little, and changed colour slightly as he listened to his mother. He couldn't find the right words to express what he felt. And anyway, it would have been too hard to condense a truth that even he found confusing... Pepe Vados, alongside the smell of the Leonese earth and the comfortable, familiar atmosphere of his house, had been the most important factor in his decision to stay forever. It was Pepe who, almost without mentioning it, had helped him imagine the boundless opportunities that lay in his forests... Just like when they were boys, Pepe had revealed that beauty to him.

Pepe Vados was Eulogio's youth. His companion through childhood to adolescence, closer than a brother to him, and Eulogio had dreaded seeing him again now that he'd transformed into something no one would have dreamt of in Pepe's case; a priest... Everything he heard about Pepe on his return to Villa de Robre made him uneasy... And when eventually he'd made up his mind to go up to Las Duras, his state of mind had been similar to whenever he decided to see a dentist. Out of necessity. Because it was necessary for him to convince himself, once and for all, that his friend no longer existed... Then something profound had happened, something majorly significant, when, as soon as they embraced he realised that, astonishingly, Pepe Vados was still his friend and his brother, as if the terrible events of the years they hadn't seen each other had never happened, and as if they had both remained unchanged.

Eulogio had made the trip to Las Duras three weeks ago, together with Paulina, Miguel, and Antonio Nives. They had hastily organised the small expedition to take up some provisions and medicines the priest had requested.

Antonio drove them to the last village you could reach by road: Doña Urraca. From there, it was five hours on mules, up into the forest... Eulogio had been reminded of his youth and the hiking trips that began at Doña Urraca. He and Pepe Vados, in shorts, rucksacks on their backs, drenched in clean, golden sweat in the warm, humid, and smouldering half-light of the forest, during the long treks to the summit. As he reminisced, his joints had felt old and rusty… As for Antonio Nives, who was still a young man, what a disaster! He got bitten by all the mosquitoes, he insisted on explaining all the dreadful sensations running through his long legs—feeling broken, beaten, ground down—he was sweating buckets, and he kept moaning about it. Horrified and hysterical, he brushed an insect off his neck; a hard, gold, marvellous insect that Miguel then claimed for his collection… Paulina had been braver; even when she'd had to spend a morning in bed afterwards, when they arrived in Las Duras, she hadn't complained.

Miguel was magnificent. Eulogio had felt proud of him. He never got tired. Eulogio had found it immensely moving to return to this vast, alien landscape, with its colossal, moisture-laden trees. Miguel kept saying it was like being in the jungles of Africa.

It was raining when they arrived. This is a land of rain and fever. It was raining and a warm smell rose from the earth. José Vados, almost unrecognisable, his coarse, grey hair shaved close, approached them with a smile, and deep wrinkles appeared in his tanned skin, around cheerful eyes.

"You look twenty years older than me," Eulogio had told him, "but your body is twenty years younger. You're as fit as ever."

The expedition party had brought José a large chest of medicines sent by Joaquín, another of the Vados family who also lived in the castle and was a doctor. José examined the medicines enthusiastically, and straight away began to read the long explanations typed by the good doctor.

"I would have done better studying for a degree in medicine… It would have served me well now. In winter, there's no way to get anybody up here… these four hamlets are completely cut off."

Everything was very simple, very unimportant. It was only that Pepe Vados's gestures, the determined set of the chin, the clear eyes, were the same, as was the closeness rekindled between the two men the moment they began to walk alongside each other through the wilderness that had shaped them.

Bringing Pepe and Miguelito together filled Eulogio with an unfamiliar, unadulterated pride. How could he ever explain these things?

The week they spent together, Eulogio, Father José, and Miguelito, was extraordinary. They went to the places they used to hike to long ago and told the boy stories of their childhood adventures.

They told him about their first hunting trip when they had tagged along with a group of seasoned hunters.

"Your father and I were young then, you see. Not as young as you… Four or five years older than you are now." José laughed when he saw the amazement in Miguel's face. "Yes, that night we didn't sleep in Las Duras; we were going to hunt chamois; do you know what they are? Wild goats. The hardest creature in the world to hunt… Your father was sure that it was all about physical strength and swore blind that he would bring back two of those little goats slung over his shoulders… Do you remember Eulogio?"

Eulogio remembered how exhausting and how magical that late autumn day had been; they had walked for hours, beyond the forests, up onto the bare ridges of the mountain crest, and then slept on the straw-covered floor of a shepherd's hut. The shepherd was an unkempt old man who had made a lasting impression on Eulogio. He had black teeth and his stinking pipe smoke blotted out the crystalline horizons of the mountains. When he finished smoking, the man would scrape out the bowl of the pipe with his knife. He would carefully press together the saliva-soaked tobacco with a hand that looked as if it had been hewn from dark wood... and later, he would eat it.

Eulogio could picture the bearded man silhouetted in the doorway of the hut, surrounded by stars.

"So, how many chamois did you kill?" asked Miguel.

Eulogio and José laughed. Eulogio said that he couldn't remember. José put it simply:

"None that day."

Four or five little kids from the hamlet—José with the patience of an animal tamer was training them up as future altar boys—followed them wherever they went and listened to these stories alongside Miguel. If anyone spoke to them, they never replied. It must have been a hard few days for Paulina and Antonio. They seemed bored and almost afraid of the natural world around them. They must have been sick of the interminable forests and the dirty, hungry people who seemed to lie in wait.

"I'd never be able to live here. It's dreadful," Paulina said. "All the locals believe in spirits and with all the fog I can understand why... Goodness me, it must be awful here in winter!"

Paulina appeared even more fragile, pale and delicate in those wet, wild woods. It couldn't have been more obvious she was from the city; her white hands, hardly ever without a cigarette, and her impractically fine leather shoes, seemed to scream it out. She was at odds with her surroundings... When

Eulogio came upon her unexpectedly during that time, in the damp patio of the ruined house or curled up, smoking, by the fire, he experienced a bizarre feeling inside. Something that Pepe Vados's embrace had laid bare, something mysteriously connected to his joy at having found his friend… A compassion that was faint but insistent, like a mist. He began to feel sorry for Paulina, perhaps because he himself felt rejuvenated and full of confidence. Whenever he left the house, excitedly, he felt happy that at least Antonio was there to keep Paulina company. Antonio, too, seemed out of place and bored. But Paulina especially would gaze about her, astonished that anyone could put up with the climate and the isolation.

She would look at José as if he were crazy. José would laugh. Over the last few years he had done everything he could to get himself sent to these parts. His dream was to breathe life back into the old, defunct parish. They were already rebuilding the church in Las Duras. In the meantime, Mass was being celebrated in Eulogio's house… This was a standing joke, because it was well known that Eulogio's family were anticlerical. At least, his father, and Mariana, who was known as "the foreigner" because of her Swiss origins, had publically declared themselves enemies of the Church. Eulogio was agnostic… As a courtesy, however, he would listen to José Vados recite Mass in the verdant mornings, in the old barn José himself had whitewashed, and he would find himself moved.

He and Miguelito and two old ladies from Las Duras were the only ones to hear them, apart from the snotty-nosed, scabby-headed kids to whom José would then dish out sweets. He always requested large quantities from Villa de Robre… That stripped-back Mass, the shabby tabernacle, the pine table altar and the solitary crucifix; the tall shaven-headed kid, surely the cleverest in the village, who could read aloud the responses that José had painstakingly written out for him; the birdsong drifting in through the windows and, above all, the strange reverential expression José wore when he officiated, all of this, Eulogio found moving. Paulina and Antonio never wanted to get up in time to attend Mass.

Now Mariana was going on and on about José.

"A boy could turn superstitious under that kind of influence. And he's a very young boy. He needs looking after and you should never, ever have left him…"

"At his age, I'd have liked to stay there too. Anyway, I'm going to get him back tomorrow. I'll stay a few days…"

The door opened and the maid appeared. The maid was a girl from the village who still felt somewhat self-conscious in the cap and gloves that Mariana made her wear to serve the evening meals.

"Dinner is served ladies and gentlemen," she announced in a whisper.

# III

There are times when a man feels tears of rage well up in his eyes. The engine had begun to fail. Just as he was accelerating on the old road, in the warm rain that was now bucketing down, illuminated by flashes of lightning.

He pulled over on the roadside, in the treacherous mire where the road overhung the abyss. Antonio was a good driver, but he didn't have a clue about mechanics, not even the basics. All he knew right now was that he needed to reach Ponferrada at the same time or before the narrow-gauge train Paulina was travelling in, that he would do whatever it took, and that it felt like a sharp stab of pain.

He gripped the steering wheel tighter and tighter until his palms hurt. Physical pain. More bearable than the fury consuming him. He switched off the headlights for a moment, so he could detect any other lights out there in the night. Complete darkness enveloped him. A smell of wild grass, the sound of rushing water, of water bouncing off the car's shiny exterior, of water saturating the earth. Down below in the valley, the lights of the tiny villages were scattered like fireflies along the tracks. He was sure he'd heard, far in the distance, as it carried through the damp air, the unmistakable whistle of the train.

He had left the house as quickly as he possibly could. But one cannot do exactly as one desires. It is not done to leap over the whole family, push aside one's invalid and frightened wife, kick the old Count out of one's way in the hall, spit in the face of one's brother-in-law, Joaquín, as he sits calmly in his armchair reading the paper, nor at Joaquín's wife, Ana María, an insipid being… He wouldn't have done any of these things. Usually he didn't want to either but tonight he almost could have.

Instead, he had simply been rude and extremely disagreeable towards all of them. He'd practically pushed Rita into her bedroom. Then he had begun pacing up and down the hallway, complaining that the storm, and being shut up in the house, was upsetting him.

"Go for a walk around the garden," Joaquín had suggested.

He fancied he heard a hint of irony in Joaquín's voice. But his brother-in-law's dove-like face betrayed nothing, nor did it ever. As for Joaquín's wife, she hadn't even looked up from her knitting. What Antonio didn't know was that the family considered him an ill-tempered and dangerous man, and at such times would try not to irritate him. The Count was an exception, of course. Alfonso lived in his own little world.

*"O clouds of the tempest, by light'ning kiss'd,*
*Your edges shot with the fire of its love…"*

The Count recited the lines in a quavering voice, a mischievous smile on his lips.

The garden was within the crenelated walls of the former parade ground. The huge castle keep had been transformed by the current count into a lovely country house. Before the war, the Count and Countess used to spend their summers there. Now they lived there all year round, to save money, as did their son Joaquín, a mediocre doctor who had never quite made his mark in the city. Rita, when she began to feel unwell, had wanted to come too.

"What use is a walk in the garden to me? You must be joking…"

He stood in the glass-panelled vestibule for a few minutes, watching the lashing rain wreak destruction on the flower beds. The lights from the house revealed the borders filled with rose bushes, now stripped of their petals, eerie and pale in the electric glow. They lit the gentle willow trees, troubled, teary almost and the two magnolia trees that Blanca liked so much. The chapel too—rebuilt by Antonio after the wedding as a gift to the devout family—was illuminated.

"I'm going. I'm very sorry but I'm going. I'll eat out… I need some inspiration for my book."

He threw this out as a challenge, but no one rose to it.

They didn't even smile when they heard the usual excuse of the book. Blanca had gone up to Rita's room, the Count was walking around with his hands on his back. The timid couple, who to top it all were called Joaquín and Ana like the saints, looked at each other. That was it. Antonio was indeed free to set off for the garden, and from there to the garage. It was when he switched on the garage light that Blanca, who was closing the curtains of her daughter's room, saw him from the upper floor.

"Won't you take your mac?" he heard Joaquín shout when he was already out in the rain.

"Have it brought out."

As he drove the car out, a maid appeared sheltering under a large umbrella, with the raincoat under her arm.

Sat at the wheel of his recently acquired American car, which was in perfect condition and ate up the miles, Antonio felt powerful and relieved. He sensed a connection with the machine, with its speed. He could feel its efficient suspension, which guaranteed a level of comfort, a smoothness, even over those infernal potholes. That powerful yet mellow engine was his ally, as at one with him as a good horse. At times he urged it on, encouraged it as if the car could understand him.

And now it was failing him. Not even a gasp. When an animal is spent, you hear a gasp. A gasp means something; a hope, a justification, a life. Nothing. The coldness of a broken engine. While a machine functions, man endows it with the poetry it lacks, even begins to feel blood and friendship flow between the two. When it fails, it becomes a frightening, unfathomable mass of cold, twisted steel and tin.

And, it was possible that no one would come along this road tonight. Antonio would be stranded there, suspended ridiculously above the valley, in the storm, until dawn, and Paulina would have escaped now, at the very moment he'd realised how much everything that had happened between them meant to him. It wasn't simply a casual fling. How could he have thought such a thing?

Yes, he felt a terrible rage when he realised that Paulina was getting away. After years and years during which the woman's unique charm had obsessed him, after forgetting her and then meeting her again, after finally knowing what she was like when she was falling in love, after having been completely certain he was her master in body and spirit, after having even begun to tire of this feeling… after all this, Paulina had packed her bag, without a word, without a definitive ending, without an ultimatum and was disappearing… And he couldn't even catch up with her tonight, to ask for explanations, to demand them, to defeat her…

As he put on the raincoat to get out of the car, he felt hysterical, like a woman, wanting to bite his fists.

Torch in hand, he examined the wheels. Behind the illuminated curtain of water, he could see there was nothing wrong with the tyres.

He began to hurl insults at himself, because he could have avoided this. He vaguely remembered the chauffeur saying that the car was almost out of petrol… What with Rita's fears of the storm he had forgotten to fill the tank… That was it. Fortunately, he always carried a few litres in a jerry can. It would get him to the town. After that…

His impatience caused his hands to tremble. The caps and screws fell to the ground. But eventually he managed to quench the parched engine. He could, finally, take off his mac inside the car and dry his hair, drenched by the downpour, with the dirty old chamois cloth he kept with the petrol can and the jacks. It reeked of grease.

The automobile started again. That purr of the engine was a beautiful sound. A sound that made his lips twitch. The car's clock read half past eight. He had only lost a quarter of an hour but it seemed like a century. He didn't stop to think about whether this woman was worth all this torture… an ancient hunting instinct propelled him to chase after her. He would never have even believed this, a few days earlier, when to tell the truth he'd felt almost a little bored of all that passion. He had amused himself by watching Paulina's reactions while he laid out travel plans that would separate them. He'd spoken very seriously, almost sadly:

"I should convince Rita to go to Switzerland... I should be doing everything I possibly can to cure her... Yet I'm here putting up with all Joaquín's snide comments... Putting up with it all because you're here." Maybe it was callous. That was when Paulina spoke up. The colour had drained from her face.

"You know there's absolutely no hope of a cure. You said yourself the specialists' verdict was exactly that: no hope... Only one of them said it could be years; the rest gave her just months. The cruellest thing would be to take her away from everything she loves."

He'd laughed at Paulina then, very gently tracing the line of her throat with his finger, pausing at the corner of her soft, full lips. Beside her mouth, there were faint lines in her skin, and at the outer edges of her lids too, beside her large slightly drooping eyes. In that moment of course, Paulina had been lying on the ground, looking up at the canopy of the old oak trees, and he had been beside her, propped up on his elbows, looking down at her. It had been a hot day. He'd noticed a film of sweat on Paulina's neck, at the base of her thick black hair...

Even now he could taste her sweet mouth, her moist skin.

Back then it had been Paulina trembling, afraid of losing him. Now, she had found the strength to run away without saying goodbye, without a word... That very morning, she'd squeezed his hand, with an urgency he could sense when she caressed him secretly, in front of people who should have seen them, but who saw nothing.

Rita was jealous, certainly, but wasn't she jealous of everything and everyone? No one had seen anything. This was the curious thing. This tumultuous affair had been going on for almost two months, begun and cemented under the noses of the entire family and no one had noticed. Mariana, perhaps because her own body was cold and passive; Blanca and Alfonso because they were innocents, the rest—Antonio smiled—the rest because either they were idiots or distracted, or for whatever reason. Nobody knew how Paulina looked for him, and waited for him on the outskirts of the village, how he had the power to make her ecstatic or miserable, depending on how he felt, and how he experienced a curious pleasure in making her cry, she, who in the past had always boasted that she never did…

But now she'd gone. She hadn't even threatened to go. Once only had he seen something resembling distress in her eyes. Sometimes she would say she felt overwhelmed, driven almost insane by the pursuit, and the physical passion, which she found degrading.

"I never thought I could sink this low, never."

Antonio had thought all this anguish was simply more lies. He couldn't shake the idea that Paulina must have lived a very independent, exciting life during the years Eulogio had been out of the country.

Most men feel a kind of need to be the judge of the woman they love. Antonio was no exception. Though she swore it wasn't true, he was convinced that she had lovers.

"A woman like her doesn't sleep alone," he thought more than once. "She cheated on me while she lived on her own and she's cheating on the others now."

In his mind, it had been a knowing deceit, carefully planned. Antonio had fallen in love with her when he was a young boy, only just out of short trousers. The classic teenage crush on a woman eight years his senior. A mad passion, bursting with all the sentimental tosh he had lapped up from those idiotic books he used to read in his youth. A mad passion full of romantic gestures, and wicked desires too. Antonio was living in Barcelona and Paulina in Madrid, with her son. The young man made as many trips as he could, simply to see her. Years and years of seeing her on and off brought him out in the angry welts of infatuation.

Paulina was like no one else. This was what kept his love for her alive. Antonio didn't know if she was beautiful or ugly, he didn't notice whether she was looking older—he who attached so much importance to appearances—or if she were well or badly dressed. Her charm was so physical, yet, paradoxically, seemed to transcend her body and features. Antonio had never met a woman who spoke with the same mixture of pride and sweetness, or who held up her head with such a lively, intelligent expression, or whose laugh had such depth but never any harshness, as if joy were bubbling out of her. And he always looked on her as a pure, unblemished creature. That was the funniest thing. She taught maths for a living. She looked after her child... She would smile at his declarations and once she spoke to him about what true love meant for her, with an emotion that was almost contagious.

"Liar!" he muttered out loud, in the darkness of the car. "Liar!

You and I know what true love is. You and I… Plain and simple."

His mouth filled with saliva. He swallowed it.

Now the road was veering away from the track, and from the valley floor where the train meandered. After the descent, the going got easier. He accelerated. He could see the lights of Ponferrada, phantasmal in the softly falling rain, no lightning flashes now. Chimneys were spewing smoke and flames into the night. Several buildings emerged from the shadows, lights blazing, glass walls exposing the cold abandoned entrails of offices… Flames were reflected in the River Sil. Something huge, strange, exciting seemed to be taking shape that night, under the lights of the flood plain. An ancient village, on the route of the Camino de Santiago, discovers rich mineral deposits and grows, spilling out from its old stones, and the foundries transform the night into a fantastical fire-and-smoke beast battling the cotton clouds.

He was at the wrong station. Various rail routes start at Ponferrada. How many stations does it have? Antonio didn't know there were so many.

"No sir; from here the trains go to Laciana."

Finally, he arrived. It was quarter past nine. He'd almost given up. "Even if she's here already, I'll find her. Ponferrada isn't that big. I'll find her."

He peered into a small office in search of a ticket clerk. A stench emanated from sacks full of rotting potatoes that had taken over almost the entire room, leaving barely enough space for an ink-stained table covered in papers, some large spiders' webs on the ceiling and a scrawny attendant wearing a railway uniform cap and spectacles.

"Haven't you looked at the timetable sir? How can the Villa

de Robre train have arrived, if it's coming in at half past nine?"

The railway employee returned to what he was doing. Antonio saw that it was a crossword in a children's newspaper. The man was screwing up his face. The tip of his tongue was sticking out… In front of him a clock was ticking.

Antonio smiled, remembering how anxious he'd felt on the way, remembering the rain drenching his hair, dripping down inside the collar of his raincoat and soaking into his shirt. He felt victorious. Paulina would belong to him forever simply because of this, because he'd got there on time. It was odd. All along he had been convinced that Paulina's train would arrive at nine.

Laughing at his own weakness he went into a urinal. He came out revolted, pale.

"I'm like a squeamish woman, but that made me want to vomit. Disgusting!"

The night smelled good. It was raining. In front of the small station stood two pristine trees bathed in the light from the streetlamps, speckled with rain.

Antonio's raincoat was completely saturated, water dripped from the hem onto his trousers. He was a young, very slender man, and the raincoat, as it moved along under the station canopy, appeared disconnected from its human owner. As though it were hung out to dry, turning slowly in the wind, with dark droplets slowly falling from it.

# IV

The reflection of Paulina's face quivered and changed shape in the carriage window She looked critically at it, this face, with its overly large eyes, its gently outlined cheekbones, its delicate nose. Its full mouth. According to her grandmother, the wickedness was right there. If there were any wickedness in that face, it was hidden in those lips of hers, and in the end, as her grandmother had warned her a thousand times would happen if she didn't keep a tight hold on things, she had lost control…

"If you're not careful, Paulina, that mouth of yours will betray you. You've a good head on your shoulders, you're proud. You're tough. But I never saw a mouth like it on any woman in our family. That comes from your father. But you must remember that I knew my grandmother and she knew hers. There has never been a single scandal in our family… Eh? You're growing up with such freedom. You must be prepared and heed my warning."

Paulina had remembered her grandmother's warning well. She'd felt revulsion on hearing it. She had run to look at herself in the bathroom mirror and had scrubbed at her thick, soft lips. She decided then she would never paint them, and she didn't for years… She shuddered with distaste at the thought of their similarity to those thick, red, sensual lips beneath the moustache, the tobacco smell those lips exhaled: her father's lips… In the mirror that day a sullen face stared back at her, a face that her grandmother wouldn't recognise, an expression she wore almost exclusively during her summers in the village. Her grandmother would shrug when her daughter Isabel wrote, from Villa de Robre, that she was worried that Paulina was miserable and unpleasant. In Madrid, the girl was the complete opposite, affectionate and chatty… Her grandmother didn't know that years earlier Paulina, in the very depths of her being, had rejected her parents.

The grandmother had begun to be concerned about Paulina when the girl reached fifteen. A girl who isn't particularly pretty and yet attracts all the boys in her year like flies, is a frightening thing for a grandmother. The phone didn't stop ringing with boys asking for Paulina. She was never left out of any outing, walk, or meetup that those boys, like prawns according to Grandmother Bel, could dream up. And the girl was having a ball. She flirted like the devil. She was fashionable, cheerful, carefree.

The grandmother also worried about the frostiness between Paulina and other girls.

"Can't you find yourself a nice friend?"

"They think I'll steal their boyfriends, they're jealous."

The grandmother thought about this while she studied her granddaughter's face with its still somewhat exaggerated features.

"It's absurd to talk like that at your age."

"How old were you when you married?"

"Around your age, but…"

Paulina would laugh. She loved her grandmother very much. She spent the winters with her when she was studying in Madrid, in a lower-ground-floor flat on Calle Monte Esquinza, crammed with shabby antique furniture, souvenirs of the grandmother's adventures in various Spanish cities, as a military wife. She was the widow of a colonel, no less… That was how she was, a little old lady like a raisin dusted in white powder. The grandmother was old and honest and strong. Paulina's mother had been the youngest of seven children. The grandmother, who everyone including Paulina used to call Mama Bel, had none of her children left by her side. Two of Paulina's uncles were in America: the rest had died. And Paulina's mother had always lived in the provinces. Paulina's father was a mining engineer.

Mama Bel died alone, during the war. She sold all her furniture and gave a family the use of her flat in exchange for providing her with food. They swore to Paulina that they had done so, but the poor old woman died all the same, during the Hunger Years in wartime Madrid.

She had been the one person in the family who had spoiled Paulina. The one who had worried about her and yet had never been unfair, and despite the infamous mouth, had trusted her… The grandmother had kept hidden from Paulina's father—the violent Don Pedro Goya—Paulina's long engagement with a young Philosophy and Literature graduate.

"When you are about to marry, then we'll tell him. With men like your father, the only thing you can do is lie to them.

That's what we've always done… I believe in you… I know there's good inside you."

Paulina revelled in the phrase "that's what we've always done." In her grandmother's opinion men might be scary but they were also naive, like naughty little boys, and it was up to the women to pass down through the generations the secrets and tricks to keeping them happy… While simultaneously doing exactly as they, themselves, wanted.

"So long as he's well-made, like a girl needs. Eh, my little sweetie?"

The grandmother didn't know, of course, that her granddaughter, in an affectionate way, thought of her as a little girl, too, ignorant of the harsh realities of life, and needing to be protected from ever finding out about them.

Paulina demanded her fiancé put on an elaborate charade in her grandmother's presence, which the old lady appreciated, although she would have preferred, she said, "something better" for her granddaughter.

The girl thought that her grandmother would have died of shock if she'd known about their liberal attitudes towards some of the issues of the day, like free love, for example, which they both believed in. Except that Paulina believed in her own way.

In practice, she behaved as well as her grandmother would have wished… Except that she wasn't afraid of kissing, in the eerie light at dusk, in Madrid's deserted building sites… But she wouldn't go any further, though Victor wanted much more.

"It's not about 'trapping you legally,' like some provincial girl desperate for a husband. It's not about that. But I must be true to myself, Victor. I hate hypocrisy. I've had my fill of it in my own house. I despise uncleanliness in actions. If you want

me to go away with you, I'll go with you to your house tomorrow. But like this, in the daylight, with my bundle of clothes
under my arm… don't laugh, no; I tell you it's true. No legal
tricks, no signed paper… But no pretence either. No deceiving
my grandmother and receiving the allowance from my father
like it doesn't matter… I won't be your lover until you decide
to take on the responsibility."

This language was fashionable. But Victor understood…
No more than kisses. No further than that.

Victor was thinking, wisely, that living together openly could
have as many disadvantages as marriage… If they were to do it,
he would have to think like a bourgeois and get himself a proper
job, because Victor, even though he'd finished his degree, was
at the time living comfortably off a generous helping from the
family pot of stew, and before the war there had been plenty
to feed everyone.

In addition, Victor suffered from a crippling fear, which
he passed off as dislike, of Don Pedro Goya whose great bulk
he'd glimpsed once or twice when the engineer had visited
Madrid. Don Pedro, Mama Bel had repeated innocently and
apparently horrified, making sure she was in earshot of Victor,
was one of those old-fashioned gentlemen who would shoot
a man to avenge the honour of his daughter, without so much
as a second thought.

As the years passed, Paulina sometimes wondered if Mama
Bel's ingenuity only existed in her granddaughter's imagination.
Mama Bel "managed" Victor in her own way, instilling a healthy
fear into him.

Paulina can't help but smile for a moment as, on this stormy
night, with darkness descending swiftly because of the pouring

rain, and her reflection quivering below that of the lightbulb, she remembers those kisses during her first engagement and how innocent they were. The glass reflects empty seats too, with their white covers and a large open newspaper. The newspaper belongs to the owner of the grocery shop, positioned opposite Villa Robre's town hall. The shopkeeper is a thickset man with reddish hair, who has greeted her very formally… No one else. She's alone.

Víctor was ten years older than Paulina. He was slim and sported a little pencil moustache. A poet, he would compose very convoluted verse in the style of Luis de Góngora. Friend to all the literati of the age, he introduced Paulina to them too. He gave his fiancée all the most daring—but well-written—literature he could lay his hands on, with the aim of refining Paulina's slightly dull taste… Víctor was amused by the courage she showed whenever an obstacle stood in her way, by her frustration with the old way of life, which she said was suffocating her, and it amused him too that, incomprehensibly, she'd elected to attend the Faculty of Exact Sciences and was what people called "a bluestocking." Outstanding after outstanding… During the entire month of May, Víctor didn't set eyes on Paulina. She came out of her exams, laden with awards and dark circles round her eyes, and they enjoyed a few short days of walks in the pollen-filled air under the leafy branches of the Parque del Oeste or the Retiro.

Afterwards, Paulina had to take the train from the Estación del Norte to Villa de Robre where she was to spend the summer with her parents.

"I'm counting the years, you know? I'm counting the years until I'm twenty-one… Then I won't go back. Once I'm old enough I'm not going back to that godforsaken village."

She had thought through the practicalities, she explained to him:

"I'll have my degree…"

"Won't you tell me what they're like, your parents?" Víctor would encourage her.

Paulina was thoughtful for a few moments. But she didn't tell him everything.

"My father is one of those gentlemen who are very friendly with the priests, very involved in the church, organising the processions but who at the same time has… lady friends… and… bah, my parents are boring."

She fell silent. It was too embarrassing to tell Víctor that her father swore like a trooper, that he had a devil of a temper, that despite his degree and his being supposedly a gentleman, he was boorish with her mother, who he'd sometimes hit when she complained of his infidelities. For Paulina, this was more shameful than the lady friends… She didn't tell Víctor that the housemaid, a certain Leonela, had been her father's lover since their arrival in Villa de Robre, and that her mother had never been able to dismiss her. There were many things that she couldn't tell Víctor. She didn't tell him, for example, how she suffered at night, aged five, when in her darkened room, she would be woken by her father hurling insults at her mother, who would be crying in the next room. She didn't tell him how she would kneel on her bed, praying to God that her parents would make up and be good and there would be happiness in the house for ever and ever…

Víctor was Paulina's only friend, the all-consuming boyfriend, her only confidant, and yet he didn't fully know her, even at this age when confidences are shared so easily. The young woman would very quickly skate over the topic of her parents and her childhood if it came up.

Víctor—she realised now—had known a cheerful young woman, who could be cheeky, but was slightly pedantic and judgemental, and very cynical, none of which was the real Paulina. When she claimed that she'd seen too much hypocrisy in her house, and too much impurity, not to be genuine and pure herself as a result, her fiancé didn't appreciate how true this was. Nor did he realise how an expression glimpsed on her father's face one day as he looked at a woman, and seared into her memory, had made Paulina often distant and cold with Víctor during their relationship…

"You're a girl who's never known real suffering. That's why you're so cruel."

This rather pretentious phrase of Víctor's rang in her ears now. "But I," Paulina was thinking while the little train drew away from another of the innumerable stations on the route, and she heard it whistle. "But I know suffering like no one else. I've experienced it in all its facets, I've felt the very depths of its writhing pain… And I knew it then. Yes, I did, I knew it then."

"I," thought Paulina, "need sincerity and I can't conceive of life without a great love. I'm one of those who will always suffer. Now I know it will always be so."

The train was pulling into another station. Paulina saw a man in the rain; a tall, thin man approaching the train. She felt paralysed. It was completely absurd. The tall, thin man was running along in the rain, opening an umbrella to meet a woman from the village who was carrying a huge basket and had a child with her. Why on earth would Antonio be here?… The man didn't even look like Antonio.

All the stations on the line blurred into each other in the blackness that was engulfing everything. The night and the rain. The same yellowish bulbs, illuminating the thick threads of rain. The same station master, with his whistle and his flag. The same village women with the same baskets… Then the rows of coal heaps, the lights of the washhouses beside the tracks, smalls patches of reflected light in the darkness that betrayed the presence of the river. And sometimes the murmur of the river swollen by the rain.

Now and then a blast of the rich smell of earth watered by a summer storm. The heady, exhilarating aroma mingled with that of the soot from the train.

Paulina could think of nothing but Antonio now. Every turn of the wheels, every mile the train covered, was taking her away from Antonio. She loved him without expectation, with absolute generosity. She knew that she awoke cruel instincts in him and that he liked nothing better than to see her suffer. But she felt tied to him. Tied. Except that… She hadn't been able to bear it. She hadn't been able to bear the sudden realisation of what had happened to the self-image that she had spent an entire proud and righteous lifetime creating.

"I'm just like my father," she'd thought.

Could she explain this to Antonio? She hadn't had the courage, she'd barely managed to tell him, timidly, that she was suffering. He'd laughed a lot.

"It was you, woman, you came looking for me…" Her temples were throbbing. Her head hurt with the tension. Pain seared through her bones.

She fell back in her seat. She closed her eyes. This was the thing she'd never felt able to admit to anyone she loved: "I'm suffering."... But she'd said it, because she had found him when she was already too tired, already too stripped of all her armour to defend herself with a pride that no longer existed... For Antonio, she had reserved her soul's deepest scream. But he mocked her without even listening.

She was living through unimaginable torment. It was true that sometimes she felt happy. Sometimes, a powerful happiness pierced her, surged through her. She had lived through too many months of apathy, half-dead from tiredness, exhaustion and miserable emptiness, since Eulogio arrived from America, to not appreciate the pain of being alive... But it was too hard.

She opened her eyes and there in the window pane, hovering against a backdrop of dark countryside, and surrounded by a yellowish glow from the lightbulb, was a small face, its pupils darting frantically. The eyes began to slow down as Paulina looked at them. Then she covered her eyes so as not to see them. She curled up in her corner.

There were times when she would have loved to know what she meant to Antonio. She liked to recall those years when she'd looked upon him indulgently, as a little boy who wasn't very bright, but sensitive and in love. A sweet young man, who was quite artistic or certainly a good judge of art. A boy who, in Barcelona, when she most needed the family's protection, had been the one to obtain it, and had then put her in such a false, difficult situation with his clinging infatuation that she had decided to run away to Madrid, taking her young son with her... Antonio's father and stepmother were under the impression that Paulina was "encouraging" the boy's eccentric behaviour... Nothing could be further from the truth, at the time.

What was I like when I met Antonio? The thought struck her suddenly… a fright; I'd never looked so ugly… I'd just come out of prison, I was wearing a faded dress and carrying my child of only a few months… I was so skinny, and not even pale and interesting because I caught so much sun in the prison gallery where I spent the mornings beside the child, sewing. My nose was covered in freckles, my hair was practically shaved… What did the kid see in me?

Antonio wasn't much to look at either. Tall, spotty, the fluff on his upper lip… If she'd been the Paulina from before the civil war, the Paulina Víctor had known, she would have relished teasing the youngster, but at that point in her life when everything had turned bitter and all she had was her youth and the desire to be with Eulogio again, in that moment, that sensitive, tiresome, irritating, lovesick boy had touched her.

She didn't "encourage" him, as the alarmed relatives believed, but neither could she treat him harshly, nor tell on him to his parents, nor ridicule him. She preferred to take her son and reject the hospitality Antonio's parents had shown her, setting off for Madrid, without any money, or any kind of security… That was how Antonio came into her life. Making it difficult even then… Perhaps because of this he always made his presence felt, because of this, he'd eventually imposed his will on her completely.

Later, Antonio and Paulina had argued. He was making increasingly frequent trips to Madrid to see her, and maybe already at that point he held a sinister attraction for Paulina. But during that period, she managed to keep alive her innocent, youthful romanticism. She was convinced that she could only love fully once in her life, and that she loved Eulogio from the depths of her soul. Pride, too, played a part in sustaining her romantic dream. Pride, above all.

Antonio, during a particularly bad patch, even accused her of flirting with him and leading him on. They quarrelled bitterly. They said spiteful things to each other… Paulina smiled as she remembered them. But Antonio held grudges. He thought he'd been deceived… And many things happened before they saw each other again. Antonio married his childhood friend, Rita Vados, and settled in Madrid. They never bumped into each other… Eulogio returned from America and Paulina received him with a mixture of desperate longing and joy. She found it hard to reconcile the self-contained man who stepped off the aeroplane with the muscular youth whose hard lips had pressed against hers as he left… And afterwards…

Afterwards, Paulina experienced a dark time, that she preferred not to think about. A shameful time during which she'd been forced to account for every centime, during which she'd felt as though she were trapped in an absurd school where every preference was criticized, every expression, every innocent phrase. Eulogio wanted a different Paulina, a different woman. And the worst thing was that he didn't simply want this different woman, he was prepared to create her, moulding her, over months. It was a dreadful time. She felt unwell, and would shuffle round the small apartment they'd rented with its ugly furniture, the apartment they still rented, in her slippers. She was sick, she was pregnant again. She was vomiting. She felt she was dying. She didn't have the strength to fight, nor to do anything. Not to leave Eulogio either.

Towards the end of that period Eulogio had become fixated on the idea of them marrying again, this time in a church.

Paulina refused. They had married during the war, in the Red zone, a civil ceremony. She knew that those marriages were considered valid. That was enough… Eulogio's reaction to her refusal was unexpected.

Eulogio began to treat her better, more affectionately. Mariana arrived in Madrid one day, and immediately took charge of the disastrous situation in the house. For the first time, she was kind to her daughter-in-law.

"You must come to Villa de Robre. Eulogio might want nothing to do with the land, but his son should be born in the manor house… Come, you must. Antonio will take us in his automobile. He's going back the day after tomorrow."

And that was when she saw Antonio again. Feeling utterly exhausted, falling apart. Seven months pregnant. Ugly. Old.

Antonio appeared much more confident than before. Very confident. Here was a man who was very sure of himself, very particular in his manners, in his dress… Empty-headed? The excessive attention to appearances would suggest that, yes, he was a superficial man. He treated Paulina with the same attentiveness he would have shown an elderly relative. With a gently mocking smirk. That car journey was the beginning of her suffering… And then, she had felt extreme pangs of jealousy at the sight of Antonio's young, pretty wife! The terminally ill woman sparked an envy in her, like a cancer that wouldn't allow her to breathe or live.

Paulina opened her eyes once more and once more was met with her likeness reflected in the carriage window.

The salesman had fallen asleep, the newspaper open on his knees, his head dropped to his chest… The yellow light, the white covers on the seats, her thick, black, curly hair, her black eyes, all of it was still there, hovering, against the black and rainy night, reflected in the glass of the little train.

She caught a glimpse of the lights of Ponferrada in the distance.

Sadness weighed on her heart again. No. She didn't believe in Antonio's affection for her. It tasted like her own, bitter. She had no faith in the boy. He craved her with a kind of physical torment. He liked to make her cry... But could she bear this self-imposed separation from him, the separation that would be determined by however much time Rita had left?

Eventually she began to cry. Two solitary tears... They fell between the excessively long lashes that she had lowered to hold them in. She bit a finger. When she opened her eyes again, the salesman was still sleeping.

"I can't cry here. I mustn't cry here." She quickly wiped her eyes with a handkerchief. Her throat was throbbing with pain, as if she had been hung by it. Even her ears were hurting.

"Tomorrow, when I write to him."

She frowned as she realised that if she even began to draft the letter in her head she would cry again.

She didn't know what to do, it seemed that any action would trigger a painful reaction. If she opened her bag she'd find photographs of Antonio, of her son Miguel, of Eulogio... She didn't feel strong enough. She didn't want to think... It was like being entangled in barbed wire. It was like being in hell.

# V

She was struggling to get her bag down. Eulogio had lifted the small suitcase effortlessly in one hand, but to Paulina it felt extremely heavy as she tried to drag it off the luggage rack.

Her wrists were slender, which was a nuisance. It was practically impossible to carry any weight in her hands. Despite this, she didn't see herself as weak. She had stamina… Even on that long expedition to Las Duras, she'd shown resilience, at least, more than Antonio had… But that had nothing to do with her hands.

In any case, she managed to lift the case down from the rack eventually and then checked her reflection in the train carriage window, unconsciously smoothing her hair, and putting on her coat. It occurred to her that she should have brought a mackintosh.

The shopkeeper from the village square had left the carriage some time ago, perhaps fearful he might have to help her. She headed towards the exit. From the door, she could see how hard the rain was falling; she paused a moment to watch it… Her face was illuminated by the station lamps, like the rain. Serious.

It was only when she stepped down onto the platform that she saw Antonio. When he took the suitcase from her hands.

Antonio had been observing her, as she fastened her coat inside the carriage, and when just now she'd stood for a few seconds on the platform, under the light that made her face look triangular and sad.

"Come," said Antonio. "Come."

He pulled her out of the station towards the yellow car. Once they were inside it felt like home; that familiar tick of the clock or of the engine running. Antonio took Paulina's hands and began to kiss them.

They couldn't say a word to each other. But neither could they remain there, among the old, benign streets, on the edges of town, between one yellowish street lamp and the next, opposite a billiard Hall, its feeble spotlight sadder even than the yellow glow from the streetlights.

"You've got time, right? We'll head towards the main road… Any main road. Into the countryside. Then we'll find somewhere to have dinner."

"Yes, my love."

There it was. That one word brought warmth with it. It took away the bitterness and the struggle that had humiliated her. It left the soul as smooth as oil.

He touched her cheekbones in the dark but Paulina wasn't crying. She smiled at his gesture, and kissed his hand, gently.

"Do you know where I'm going to take you, Paulina? You've never been? I'm going to take you to the region's wine-making village, Cascabelos. Isn't it a funny name?"

Paulina said yes. She was happy, as if they were setting off to live forever in that village with its funny jingle-bells name. As if nothing stood in their way, and she and Antonio were to spend the rest of their lives together.

It is a curious thing that meetings with the people we love are always surprising. These people, those whom we truly love, are never the same when we're face to face with them as they are when we think about them. This was in Paulina's mind, and in Antonio's too, as he was filled with an unexpected, raw tenderness… For Paulina, Antonio, a few minutes earlier, had meant unbearable pain. Now he meant happiness. He was happiness…

"It reeks of petrol in here!" She wrinkled her nose. "What happened?"

Antonio laughed.

"I'll tell you later… And then your nose will be close to my hair and you'll understand."

The car began to cross Ponferrada, with its urban sprawl, its shop windows, its life spilling out of the ancient network of streets, and over the old height of the buildings, that was no longer enough.

As they emerged into the countryside, Antonio let out a deep sigh.

"Pass me a cigarette, Paulina. They're in my jacket."

Paulina took the cigarettes from his pocket.

"I'm happy. I'd forgotten they existed. But I've missed them." She handed Antonio a lit cigarette. She took another and let its heat comfort her. Along with the warmth and the smoke a sense of feeling safe with Antonio, that she had never felt before, began to grow in her.

"Now explain this madness, Paula."

"I can't keep on deceiving your wife…"

There was a silence.

Antonio was pulling up slowly at the side of the road. It was barely raining now. There was even a star visible, up there towards the north.

"I love your romantic notions. And why only my wife, may I ask?"

"Yes, you may. I'll tell you…"

It was very difficult. Then Antonio took her hand. It was easier.

"Firstly," Paulina's began in a faltering voice, "because Rita loves you, while the love between Eulogio and me died a long time ago. Yes, it's dead, dead and buried now… But apart from that—that's only part of the reason, a small part. What matters is that your wife is sick, she's dying and you can't abandon her and I can't go on like this; I don't know how to keep lying like this, day after day, seeing her and smiling at her… I can't do it. I wasn't born for this. Being with Mariana and Eulogio all day long, but thinking of you… I've hardly ever, practically never had you in any other way than thinking about you. But it never goes away and it's dark… and you know it."

Eventually, Paulina began to weep. For the first time, Antonio was moved by her tears.

"I was going to write tomorrow to tell you everything, Antonio. I didn't feel brave enough to tell you face to face like this… But I didn't honestly believe either, you see, that my leaving would matter so much to you that you would come racing into the night after me…"

"You're the most important thing in the world to me," said Antonio.

As he spoke these words, he realised that somewhere deep inside himself, to his astonishment, they were true.

Paulina tossed her cigarette out of the window. Maybe she enjoyed weeping. She did it with remarkable naturalness, as if a tragedy had befallen her. But, deep down, what she was feeling was intense relief.

"Woman," said Antonio, "woman… Paula."

# VI

Paulina's first memory was the waking in the night. The fear and distress of a child who is suffering and doesn't understand. The only thing she knew was that her mother was in pain. In those moments, she would loathe her father, and then during the daytime, she would love him again… And that was how it was, until there came a point when the only thing she felt for him was disgust.

These events began when they were still living in Asturias. From that time, she remembered a black village, a dark mist, a jet-black river flowing past the windows of the house. These were her only memories of the green Asturias where she was born. She had a brother then. A whiny child who died young… She remembered too, as if it were a dream, a short spell in Andalusia and a wonderful stay in Madrid, of a year or so, in Grandmother Bel's house. Eventually her parents made the move to Villa de Robre, and this arrival Paulina recalled perfectly, because by then she was ten.

Paulina's father was a great, ugly, hulk of a man, with a face that, despite its resemblance to a Mexican bandit, was not unattractive. Slanted eyes, a big drooping moustache and a cigarette hanging permanently from his mouth. The ash would fall onto his shirt collars and the lapels of his jacket. When he was in a good mood, he would tell dirty jokes and guffaw loudly. When she was young he treated her with great affection. When he lifted her up she could smell the tobacco and alcohol, and feel his prickly moustache. Then, Paulina grew up and the father's feelings turned to disappointment that she wasn't a boy. Up until then he had harboured the hope he would still have one, and it hadn't mattered too much.

"With a boy, you can teach him things. What the hell does one do with a girl who isn't even pretty? Nothing in this world scares me more than a spinster."

Paulina's mother was a skinny, embittered woman. Consumed by jealousy, she was constantly coughing and her eyes were red-rimmed with her constant weeping. The church was her one source of consolation. She would spend every afternoon there and a good part of the morning. Paulina got sick of hearing the priests' advice to her mother, resignation, resignation, resignation… They said she should give thanks to God that she had a good Christian husband, who had attended the nine First Fridays and would not die in sin because God is merciful, especially if she were to show resignation.

Paulina's house wasn't very clean and tidy, what with her mother being out so much. Paulina would often have grubby knees. Her mother didn't consider the idea of washing oneself to be very saintly… "Those are pagan ways," she would mutter when Paulina reminded her that when she lived in Grandmother Bel's house she would have a bath every day.

"Typical of my mother... she always was a show-off."

Isabel, Paulina's mother, usually wore black or purple clothes, impregnated with a smell of sweat mixed with incense. Paulina began to associate being religious with a love of dark colours, a vile smell, and sickly white flesh enveloped in thick clothes and deprived of sunlight.

When Paulina grew up she stopped believing in all those things that adults tell children: the story of creation, the New Testament, the tales of babies delivered by storks and the three kings bringing gifts of toys on the sixth of January. Once she had let go of all these things, she began to detest the clergy who had advised her mother to resign herself to her fate while heartily slapping her father on the back, those same priests who would come to their house on Sundays, after high Mass, to eat rice served by Leonela, the plump, curvaceous, rosy-cheeked maid, acquired on their arrival in Villa de Robre. Those priests who would gossip about the landowning Nives family, about Señor and Señora Nives, who were so perfectly well-matched. Those priests who were so fat and shiny and blond they appeared to Paulina to have been scrubbed with soap.

There was one image that Paulina could never erase from her mind. It happened on the day they arrived at their new home in Villa de Robre.

Isabel, Paulina's mother, looked happy. It was heart-warming to see her smile, because she never did... Every time Don Pedro agreed to extricate himself from his current romantic entanglements and move to another village, Isabel believed that, at last, she would find the happiness she had dreamed of as a young bride. But Paulina was too young to remember other house moves and was surprised and delighted with this unexpected, happy turn of events.

Paulina had been exploring the house, a yellow-painted chalet, with two covered balconies, of green wood: one above the main door, overlooking the street, and the other over the small vegetable garden and orchard that belonged to the property. The house was newly-built; they were the first occupants. It smelled of paint, of lime, of brushed wood. There was a bare wood staircase which led up from the hallway to the upper floor. Paulina climbed it, enchanted. She nosed around the bedrooms, which had the beds already made up… Her father had come from Madrid with the furniture a few days before she and her mother had arrived. They even had a maid, whom Don Pedro had employed. Paulina had often been surprised when adults saw her huge eyes and decided she must be a sad child. She liked cheerfulness, she needed laughter. That day she was in her element because she had come into a recently painted, happy house, in a village full of the mooing of cows and the joyful chime of bells in the distance. It was a village of stone houses, of slate roofs and of fair-haired people and fair-coloured animals. A storybook village.

Paulina didn't know anything about Villa de Robre; nothing of the rich landowners' comfortable life, nothing of the Nives family's influence in the region, nor had she heard the village latest, that an Austrian musician and two writers from Madrid were guests at the Nives house… She didn't know that the landowners and their sphere formed a kind of aristocracy politely considered separate to the newcomers the mines had attracted to the area a few years previously. The miners were just passing through. She—a tall, skinny girl with thick, black plaits bouncing against her back—had been spotted on her way from the station to the village and had been judged to be, along with her thin, dark mother and her noisy father, "just passing through."

It was a beautiful summer in Villa de Robre… Paulina had stepped out onto the orchard balcony and was looking not at the vast landscape, but at the paint on the handrail, which was still soft in places, which meant she could roll it into little balls. As she leaned down letting her plaits dangle over the balustrade, she was delighted to discover a nest among the leafy branches of a tree… The tree with the nest was in a neighbouring orchard, which was huge and lush. One corner of the green balcony protruded over the wall of this adjoining orchard. In the distance, she could see a stone house…

She was gazing at these new discoveries when she heard her mother's voice in the small orchard and looked downwards, because the cheeriness in her voice touched Paulina in a way she couldn't describe. Her mother, stood beside Don Pedro, seemed enraptured by her surroundings: the fruit trees, the sky, the lofty, far-off mountains.

The maid, Leonela, was pulling up vegetables from the ground and Paulina's mother was pointing to them admiringly.

"Look how fertile the soil is! You'll never regret coming here, Pedro."

Don Pedro was chewing on his cigar. He was smiling.

A while later, Isabel was bustling around in the top floor of the house. As she arranged the sheets in the drawers, she even sang softly to herself in a strange, hoarse voice. She called Paulina and asked her with unusual gentleness to bring her something she needed from the kitchen… Some time later,

Paulina had forgotten what she was to find in the kitchen, but she bounded down the steps eagerly.

On entering the kitchen, she was met once more with the sight of Leonela's large behind, accentuated by a tight skirt. The maid was crouched down, as she had been in the vegetable plot, this time in front of a cheerfully burning fire of rush broom branches. Don Pedro was beside her and just as Paulina peered in, he pinched the girl's buttocks, while he whispered something vulgar in her ear. She straightened up letting out a stifled laugh. In that moment, Paulina saw in her father's face a kind of panting desire, something bestial, that made her turn on her heels and run away.

From that time on, whenever Don Pedro subjected her to one of his many tremulous lectures about how she should behave, or forbade her from doing something, Paulina always experienced the same wave of disgust, the same desire to vomit. In her mind, she would always see that ridiculous face, coloured by the glow of the fire, and feel utter contempt.

The same year that they arrived in Villa de Robre, Isabel's cough became more sinister. They decided the little girl should go to Madrid to stay with Grandmother Bel and study at high school for her bachillerato. It would be better that she didn't spend all her time with her invalid mother.

"That girl is plain and she'll never marry," was Don Pedro's constant refrain. "She'll be better off studying something, so she can earn her own living, if I die."

Paulina grew up obsessed with becoming the absolute opposite of her parents. She didn't want to be weepy or sad or dress in drab clothes, like her mother; or be outraged by everything she read or heard as her mother was. The fact was that in her mother's own life truly indecent, awful things were happening, while she spent the day doing the household accounts and fretting about the price of lentils and beans. Between coughing fits, she would mend enormous piles of old clothes… and swelter in the kitchen on Sundays preparing a meal that would provide her only feeling of satisfaction in the week, and then only if the guests complimented her over and over… In contrast to this image of her mother, Paulina held up that of Señora Nives, wife of the cheese and butter factory owner, the woman they called "the foreigner." She was tall, blonde, knowledgeable. Once Paulina began spending more time in Madrid than in Villa de Robre, she began to appreciate Mariana's sophisticated taste in clothes. Once a year, the Nives would take a trip abroad… In the distant past of Paulina's adolescence, Mariana Nives had been her idol.

But above all, what Paulina wanted more than anything else, was to be nothing like that vile man with his vulgar tastes, her father. His hypocrisy and vanity made her furious. All that effort to make himself look like a good man, the tremble in his voice when he told an edifying story, his attendance at church, none of which prevented him from being a pig. Worse still, he forced Paulina to attend, yet he wouldn't allow her, or her mother, to watch—"because it's not for decent women"—any of the theatrical productions that came to the village in the summer, whereas he was first in line to flirt with the actresses.

This hatred would have been further enflamed if Paulina hadn't lived in Madrid and her father hadn't allowed her to study at the Institute and then at the University, which meant that his authoritarian repression was confined to those dreadful summer months in Villa de Robre.

She loved and admired Víctor because he seemed to her the opposite of Don Pedro. To her Víctor was a refined, incredibly sensitive, decent man, who tried to be supportive and didn't hide behind religion. "All that stuff, Paulina… How could you possibly imagine it's true? Do you imagine a devil with his little horns, a heaven full of saintly old biddies playing the harp?… No; I don't go to church. The church is old and corrupt, and pointless."

Since she had grown up, Paulina had been on the receiving end of a couple of slaps from Don Pedro, when she started laughing in church at the priest, in his sermon, blaming all the world's ills on the indecent way women dressed. This priest was one of those who, when he came to their house, only wanted to talk about two topics: how to grow his small capital, and good food. He baptised the children of the rich differently—using a Latin that sounded different—to the children of the poor. Paulina heard that, on hearing about her father's lurid exploits with the women who washed the coal, his only comment was:

"He's a man, Señora, he's a man…"

The comment had been addressed to Paulina's mother. As he stood at the pulpit, describing the women's short sleeves and painted lips he seemed to tremble with indignation. Paulina began to laugh so much it brought tears to her eyes. She had to leave the church. Don Pedro followed her outside, gave her a couple of good slaps that put a stop to her laughter and sent her back into the church.

For Paulina, the church came to represent a kind of let-off for all the males in the country, for all their uncouth behaviour, while apparently demanding nothing from them; for her it was old, corrupt, and evil, and her youthful self was desperate to fight against it.

Paulina's enthusiasm for Mariana Nives, despite never having spoken to her, was well and truly cemented when she learned that as well as "the foreigner," she was known as "the atheist." Her husband, Miguel Nives, a left-leaning man who had a great deal of political clout in the village, didn't go to Mass either.

# VII

Above the vineyards of Cascabelos, the skies were clearing. The pleasant smell of summer, combined with the freshness of the rain, was invigorating, perfect.

"We'll have to go back soon," Paulina was worried. "I don't know if I'll get a ticket for Madrid; you know what it's like at these smaller stations."

"Don't worry, I've got friends at the station on this line, in Ponferrada. We'll get something. I'm good at this stuff. Don't worry… I'm going to call and find out what time the train goes through. I can do it from here."

At the roadside, a café-bar was opening. The owner greeted them cheerily, his eyes on the big American car.

"Señores, what can I do for you?"

He had meat, ham and eggs, local fresh fruit, wine… Yes, he had a room at the back, a dining room, where the lady and gentleman could relax…

Antonio asked to be put through to Ponferrada station. They told him the exact time the express train would pass through.

He gave his name and asked for his friend in the ticket office.

Paulina touched up her lipstick as she listened from the small dining room.

"You can't get us a sleeper cabin?… No?… Yes, man, yes… you can, yes you can… There, that's more like it. Go on, I'll pay double for it."

Elated, he announced to Paulina that she was to have a single sleeper cabin for Madrid. It felt good that she'd witnessed this proof of his ability to get things done. He'd so often heard her praising this quality in Eulogio.

Paulina brought his hand to her cheek, a gentle caress… Suddenly they realised they were hungry. The excitement had given them an appetite. Paulina, however, was thoughtful.

"What will they think in the castle, about you sneaking off like this?"

Antonio was annoyed at Paulina for bringing this up. He was all too aware that he would have to creep like a coward—trying not to make any noise, and feeling that bizarre, childish dread—into a house where they had never asked him to account for his actions. For now, he simply shrugged and caressed Paulina's anxious eyes with his own.

"Bah, who cares what they think. Do you think they're even capable of thought? They're all asleep at this hour."

"But Rita…"

"You know she sleeps with her mother. I'll tell her the storm gave me a headache, that I went out for a walk… Then it got late and I didn't want to go up and wake them… Sometimes that's what I do. And this time as well it'll be true, more or less."

Paulina, without knowing why, felt very alone, as she listened to this man-child invent his excuses. She felt she was far away, absurdly drawn into something, a liaison, an affair, that didn't belong to her. She sighed.

"Take Rita to Switzerland."

Antonio remembered he'd teased her. Tonight, he felt good, resigned.

"It makes no difference, Paulina, you know that… There's nothing to be done."

"But try… If you convince her, if you go with her, she'll go."

"And afterwards?"

They were very close to each other. Everything seemed very intimate and easy, when they were so close.

"And afterwards, if she isn't cured, we'll wait… We absolutely must, Antonio. You must remain by her side; and then I'll try to revoke my marriage, you know it's only civil… And if I can't, it doesn't matter, we'll leave. If you want to, nothing else matters."

"Miguel?"

She became unsure again. She stared at the door. Without looking at Antonio.

"I won't lose him completely… I'm sure… I'd be more likely to lose him if he ever figured out certain things, like he could have done in Las Duras… I'm sure an amicable separation is better for children than parents who don't love each other, and have become embittered."

"And if Rita is cured…"

"If Rita recovers," Paulina's face was expressionless, "then you must choose between an old woman and a girl. I'll accept your decision."

Antonio watched her thoughtfully, and then pretended to feel sorry for her, a teasing pout on his lips.

"And what will you do until then?" he asked.

"I'll sort out my life, my conscience, my… pride, yes…"

Antonio gazed at her. He found her face extraordinarily attractive, its slender shape, the silk kerchief at her neck, the big, weary, black eyes, the pretty, soft outline of her mouth.

"Why must you go, Paulina? Why?"

An anxious look crossed her face.

"I've told you; I've already suffered too much in my life. I don't want to make others suffer. That's the last thing I want."

As she spoke, she found herself wondering, appalled, whether perhaps what she was saying wasn't entirely true, whether perhaps her running away wasn't so selfless, whether perhaps she was leaving because she felt entirely alone, and she had inside her a deep desire for much more love, understanding, and togetherness than Antonio could offer. As Antonio observed her face, it seemed to him rather gaunt. Overly serious.

"What was Mariana saying about you being obsessed with some skulls and nuns or something?"

Paulina didn't understand at first. Then she gave a little distracted smile.

Antonio began to feel uneasy. Happy that she was with him, but sad. He topped up her wine glass.

"I like to watch you drink. Come on. Drink."

Paulina drank and smiled. She took one of Antonio's cigarettes.

"You'll buy me some later, for the journey."

"Yes, my love, I'll do it now."

He felt different to the man he'd been only a short time earlier, when he'd been scathing towards Paulina, in his mind, branding her a slut. Now, he loved her, loved her tenderly. He had often experienced these abrupt changes in his feelings towards her, but he'd never felt his affection for her as strongly as in this moment.

They were alone in the small room. A window looked out over the yard belonging to the bar owner's small house. Through the closed window, they could see two or three tables covered with oilcloth, as theirs was. An ancient gentleman's bicycle, which looked like it was held together with wires, was leant against the wall. Light filtered in through the open door along with hearty smells from the kitchen, the voices of the locals in the bar and gusts of cool air from the road and the fields.

Paulina attempted, for a moment, to imagine the lives of these men whose voices, with the twang peculiar to these parts, drifted into her ears, and who she guessed might exude the same smell as the kitchen, with its notes of alcohol and tobacco… She failed. She very rarely thought about country people's lives. She had no inkling of what went on in their heads… Somebody was laughing, talking about birds. A man was saying that the post had been delayed because the bus driver wouldn't leave his house until he'd got the cages of his fifty birds spotless and fully stocked with food.

Someone turned up the radio and the conversations became unclear again even though the men were raising their voices. Paulina felt Antonio's fingers gently stroke her hand.

"You've never told me how you ended up in prison, Paulina."

They'd been eating together but separately, each lost in their own thoughts. On a small plate that they were using for an ashtray, Paulina's cigarette was burning down, leaving a snaking pile of ash and a yellow nicotine stain. Paulina looked up from the cigarette-shaped ash she'd been examining distractedly.

"What makes you think of that now?"

There was a tenderness in her voice; she imagined it was because that was where he'd got to know her, as a boy. Visiting her in prison.

When the Nationalists entered Barcelona, the lawyer Andrés Nives, who had fled during the period of Red domination, had returned to the city, too. Eulogio had written to Mariana from France, to ask her to contact Paulina, who was due to give birth around that time… Mariana charged Andrés, a relative of hers, with contacting her daughter-in-law. It took him a long time to track Paulina down. Two or three months… It turned out she was in prison with her child, who had been born there. Andrés Nives set about proving Paulina innocent of all political charges. He demonstrated that her father, a mining engineer, had been murdered by the Reds. He accelerated her hearing and she was freed. But Antonio had got to know her through the grating in the visitors' room. He'd always told her that he remembered her being very pale, smiling, with very short hair. The young Antonio had never come across anyone like her; an extraordinary woman, completely different to the others beyond that grating, amid the hubbub of the rest of the prisoners and their visitors.

"I'm thinking about it because you were talking about suffering. Yes, you must have gone through so much and you were so brave, but you made it seem unimportant. I still remember you laughing when you told me about your adventures in the women's prison. You were always laughing… But you never told me how you ended up there."

Paulina frowned. She glanced at him.

"It's private. It's part of mine and Eulogio's story."

Antonio felt a sudden stab of jealousy. He smiled.

"Your famous love for Eulogio! Well, you've used that against me enough. But… It was never the same as ours, was it?"

He said it softly, wanting to shame her a little. Feeling shame himself.

Paulina glanced at the watch on Antonio's wrist.

"It's very late, my sweet. We should be at the ticket office in good time before the train arrives… Let's go."

They stepped outside to a starlit sky, a veil of wispy cloud drawn across the sparkling dots of light. A blanket of low-lying mist was caught up in the brambles at the edge of the road. They could hear countless dogs barking. The scent of bramble blossom, of small wild roses and vine leaves floated in the air. Antonio put his arm around Paulina's shoulder. It felt good being like this, together, quiet. Or it did to him.

"Tell me you didn't love Eulogio like you love me… You can't have… It was something else."

Paulina moved away a little. For the first time, she felt swept away by a cold tide that left no room for any warmth towards Antonio.

"It's always different. One can't think about what it was or wasn't before… Yes, it was something else."

Her voice was oddly serious and she neglected to say whether she had loved Eulogio more or loved him less.

In the car, Paulina contemplated Antonio's profile resentfully; his sticking-out ears, his eyes like two dark narrow slits.

"Who is this man, what I am doing here beside him tonight?" The question was absurd and this minute was absurd. A minute loaded with discontent. As if everything she had suffered and enjoyed because of this man had been condensed into one spark of bitterness.

Just then, it was as if her life had come to an end, and that time was a clock with no hands and she could place those hands into another moment, a moment where she didn't even know Antonio's name. Where everything in her life responded to her personal, free, and spontaneous way of manifesting herself.

# VIII

The year was 1936. On 23rd January Paulina turned twenty. She had a somewhat wild look about her then. The wild look was mainly due to her hair. She'd always had a great respect for it, and until it was forced on her in the prison for hygiene reasons, she had never had it cut. She'd imagined she would always wear it long. She was proud of it: when it was loose it reached below her waist. Nobody had hair like that back then and people thought it strange. She would wear it in a single thick plait that fell over her chest like a shiny, silky, living thing.

In May 1936, Paulina was awarded her degree in mathematical sciences. Grandmother Bel invited Víctor to a family meal to celebrate. There they talked, very seriously, about the young people's plans. Paulina was to return to Madrid in October to study for her teaching exams.

"And you, my son, it's high time you sorted your life out, you're thirty years old…"

Víctor claimed he was determined to get a job and that he was even ready to officially communicate his intentions to the dreaded Don Pedro Goya, given that Paulina's mother had died some years previously… Yes, it was time to think about getting married.

Grandma Bel made the sign of the cross on her granddaughter's forehead, and with a benevolent and condescending smile, gave permission for Víctor, by himself, to escort Paulina to the Estación del Norte, when she left for the holidays.

The engaged couple kissed on the platform.

"Here," said Víctor, "is a good place to do it. Nobody knows if you're my wife or my sister…"

"That's ridiculous, Víctor. Are you serious? What does it matter what anybody else thinks?"

"Nevertheless…" Víctor had acquired a strangely conventional manner since he'd decided on marriage. "Nevertheless, we live in the world and…"

Paulina burst out laughing. That started him laughing. She made him promise over and over that he would do less talking for hours on end in the café with his friends and get a job. "I'm going to work hard, you'll see."

A while later, standing on the step of the train carriage, she waved goodbye to the tall man with a kindly expression, whom she thought she would marry. Víctor's hair glinted in the sunlight. She was smiling at him, believing that this must be true love. She would have been horrified if someone had told her then that Víctor would come to mean nothing to her, that she would forget him without the slightest regret, that she would even forget the shape of his features, in time…

It was then that Víctor felt a weird, powerful urge to run after the departing train in pursuit of the girl. He held back, surprised at himself and his stupid instincts. He held back, laughing at the ridiculous idea that she was escaping him. They never saw each other again.

Paulina found an empty compartment. The thought of going to her father's house—more neglected than ever since Isabel's death—was as abhorrent to her as ever.

For her the village was mind-numbingly dull. She didn't understand the beauty of the countryside. She was made for the city, for its liveliness, its intellectual preoccupations, its intense, nervy and even—for her—entertaining political life, in which she would have taken an active part if it hadn't been for Mama Bel, who was desperately afraid of student strikes, of the police and of the word socialism, which Paulina loved so much.

Paulina liked the city views, the houses with their thousands of different, unexpected, hidden lives. She liked the night in the city, its river of lights, the advertisements, the car headlights, the cafés full of people chatting animatedly, debating, buzzing until the early hours.

She closed her eyes, lost in her thoughts. A passenger who had placed a newspaper on the seat opposite Paulina, came in from the corridor and sat in his seat, without her noticing.

Paulina remained like this for a good while, her eyes closed, frowning slightly, thinking her own thoughts. She was sitting with one leg crossed over the other.

Nothing was further from her mind, in that moment, than any desire to be provocative. However, opposite her, or to be precise in the seat opposite her, on the other side of the carriage window, Eulogio Nives sat and marvelled at her beautiful, shapely legs. He had always rather liked this girl, the engineer Goya's daughter, although he didn't know why, given that she was ugly (or at least he had thought her ugly until now) and as his mother said, not very elegant, twee almost, with that ridiculous plait... Ridiculous?

Her legs were feminine, young, well-made. Her hands, smooth, her lips unpainted, a youthful, natural pink...

The setting sun was pleasantly warming the compartment. It was empty apart from Eulogio and Paulina.

Paulina opened her eyes and gave a start when she saw Eulogio Nives sitting opposite her, smiling.

"I hadn't realised it was you who'd come in earlier."

"I know Paulina... You didn't say hello."

Eulogio was ugly. He had a big nose, his bright blue eyes, round like his mother's, were somewhat bulging. His mouth was small, although when he smiled it revealed very white teeth and the canines of a young wolf. He was tanned by the sun, and wore an impeccable summer suit with no tie... It showed off his broad shoulders and the strength and grace of his sportsman's body.

Paulina had the impression she was seeing him for the first time. In fact, it was the first time she had seen him without thinking of him simply as Mariana's son... Paulina took a packet of cigarettes out of her bag. A treasure she kept carefully hidden from Mama Bel.

"Do you mind if I smoke?" she asked foolishly.

Eulogio laughed.

"Of course I don't mind if you smoke."

"Do you want one?"

"No, I hardly ever smoke. A friend of mine, you know him, Pepe Vados, says it's a women's weakness."

Paulina was intrigued.

"My father would be astonished to hear that."

"Yup."

"He despises my father," thought Paulina, "he's not scared of him like Víctor; he looks down on him."

After this short conversation, they remained in silence watching the stations rolling by one after the other. Those two hours were the strangest of Paulina's life. She didn't know what was happening to her, she smoked now and again, sometimes she closed her eyes or half-closed them… He was watching her, or reading a newspaper, sometimes gazing distractedly at the scenery.

"He's thinking of me, he's thinking of me, he's thinking of me."

The wheels of the train chanted the words. Paulina's brain hammered away. Her whole body was magnetised by a light, smooth, exciting electricity. She couldn't think of anything else.

Suddenly, Eulogio leant forward in his seat, looking at her. She, without thinking what she was doing, held out her hands. Eulogio took hold of them and for the first time, Paulina felt his strength pour into her. A deep magnetic current ran between them, and she felt as though something was drawing her outside of herself, absorbing her, drowning her. She didn't know how their lips had come together. There had been hundreds of kisses in her life and yet it was the first time she had been kissed, that she had kissed…

It was hard to open her eyes again to the faded upholstery of the train carriage, scorching in the afternoon sun. Several outraged, furious raps sounded on the window, from the corridor. Eulogio and Paulina turned around. The door was open and a large severe-looking woman and—partially hidden behind her huge bulk—a young man all in black, stood in the doorway watching them. The woman was also wearing black. Her face was sweating, flushed from the shock of having stumbled upon that kiss, and she was wearing a hat with a gauze veil.

Eulogio turned red as a beetroot. Paulina too. The woman came in huffing and puffing, muttering under her breath and settled herself down defiantly next to Paulina. Her son—the young man was evidently her son—sat down opposite her and hastily opened a newspaper.

"Let's go, Paulina," said Eulogio.

He stood up and took her hand to pull her up. He led her out of the compartment and found another with seats free. Paulina waited for him there while he went back for their cases.

They weren't alone again during the entire journey but Eulogio sat next to her. They didn't talk as they sat beside each other. Their bodies had a special language, as old and as young as the world, like the spring, like the simmering heat of summer. Paulina wanted him to take her hand again. He didn't, but she knew that he wanted that too. Sometimes they looked at each other, and laughed.

It was night-time when they reached León, where they were due to alight. Paulina had planned to carry on to the village on a bus that left very early the following morning.

"I've got my cousins waiting for me with their car," said Eulogio. "I'll give them the slip and go tomorrow with you."

"No."

"No?"

She didn't know why she'd said it when spending hours in León with Eulogio seemed like a perfectly wonderful idea. But she was certain that saying it was the right thing... It wasn't the same firm, clear certainty she had about such things when she was with Víctor, but...

"No, Eulogio. You go with your cousins. I'll go tomorrow on the bus… In any case, we'll both be in Villa de Robre tomorrow."

"And your house has an orchard that borders mine."

Paulina blushed in surprise. "Really? The house I can see from the balcony at the back? Can you believe I never realised that? I've never seen you or anyone from your house there, and the main entrance is so far away…"

"Well I've seen you lots of times. Lots of times, in the summer, reading on that balcony."

# IX

And that's how it started… The madness, the burning desire, luminous pain, dark joy…What could she call it? Over the last year, Paulina had forgotten it. Over the last year, it had turned to dust, but it was alive, burning inside her and inside Eulogio, inside the two of them.

Back in June 1936, that love changed the way she saw her house when she arrived home. Leonela, her father's maid, who attended to all his needs, was waiting for her in wary silence, as usual. The woman's face, like a red moon, made her giggle. Nothing could make her cross that morning.

The summer was arriving fast that year. The apple trees were still blooming in the orchard, it was true, and the house smelled of honey, but all the trees were full of leaves and sometimes they cast hard shadows, because an early heat thickened the blood.

When she boarded the train in Madrid, Paulina had planned to berate Leonela over her neglect of the house, force her to do some work, at least, as she had done the previous summer.

When she arrived in Villa de Robre the following day, she'd changed. She didn't feel like getting angry or arguing.

"You look almost pretty, daughter. You should watch out…"

Don Pedro observed her from the other end of the table during their first meal together. The tablecloth had holes in it and was covered in stains several days old. The crockery didn't match, the dirty walls were in dire need of a coat of whitewash, even more dire than last year, when Paulina had screamed and shouted so much… Now Paulina was smiling at her father. Not at her father exactly, but at something far beyond him, a ghost somewhere behind him. Don Pedro almost turned around to look. But he didn't. The only thing behind him was the door to the kitchen. A horrible stench of cooking oil would escape through it into the dining room whenever Leonela forgot to close it, which she always did.

The two dining room windows were ajar. It was midday. Sunlight streamed in, along with the buzz of bluebottles and the smell of pure countryside.

Don Pedro was fat, fatter than ever, and always in a gloomy mood. His hair was turning white. His fingers were dreadfully swollen and he looked dishevelled. There were soot marks on his shirt, and the collar, too, was black with the coal dust from the mines. He hadn't bothered to change… He didn't crack jokes anymore or roar with laughter as he once did… When he finished the meal, he belched and began, slowly, to clean between his teeth with a wooden pick.

Paulina left him alone and, like ten years previously, when she'd arrived at the house for the first time, bounded up the stairs and ran to the orchard balcony. The house she sought was there, half-hidden by the spring foliage. She was so overcome with emotion that her eyes pricked with tears, and a thousand expressions of love, of the kind she'd deemed too ridiculous to apply to Víctor, flocked to her lips as she thought of Eulogio.

The strip of Eulogio's orchard she could glimpse from her balcony stood deserted under the white midday sun.

She spent the afternoon enveloped in a curious and until then unfamiliar kind of suffering. Was she, after all, the only one experiencing that rush of love. (Men, they say, are always willing…) But she knew this wasn't true. She was sure of Eulogio's feelings, even though not a word had been spoken.

It was a long, slow afternoon… Divine too. She wandered through the rooms as if she were sleepwalking. She thought she must have a fever… Leonela came in from the street as night fell. She was very shaken up.

"Didn't you hear shots?"

Paulina looked at her in surprise. She'd heard nothing.

"There's been shooting, all hell's broken loose. They'd come to hold a rally. It was the miners who started all the trouble."

Leonela was shaking. She only calmed down when Don Pedro arrived home, safe and sound, at dinner time.

Don Pedro snorted at Leonela for worrying and placed a pistol on the table.

"This, old mother hen, is to give you peace of mind… And if you think they'll try it on with me, well, listen, anyone looks them in the eye and they shit themselves, bunch of layabouts… But if one day they do turn up, this," he shot a glance at the weapon, "will have something to say as well. I won't be slaughtered like a lamb, and I won't be like that fat, fawning, bootlicker Nives either…"

It was a moonlit night. Paulina spent a long time shut in her room but when the house fell silent she ventured out onto the balcony that overlooked the orchard. Then she "felt" Eulogio. She felt him so physically, it almost frightened her. She was buzzing as if an electric current, a gentle hum, was passing through her body; she felt that hum in her blood, the same as she'd felt it on the train.

She peered out at the shadows. She couldn't see a thing. For a few moments the orchard, the stone wall and the trees were like silver waves on a black sea. She blinked. Her eyes adjusted to the moonlight. Then she heard a faint whistle and the young man's silhouette emerged from the shadows into a pool of light. He gestured for her to wait and she watched him hoist himself up onto the orchard wall like a new, athletic Romeo.

At one end, Paulina's balcony jutted out over the wall and Eulogio, standing on top of it, could hold onto the wooden spindles of the balustrade and lean in. The boy's head reached level with the floor of the balcony. And so Paulina, by lying down, could bring her face to the same height as his. It wasn't a very comfortable position to speak or to kiss. But this is how they spoke and kissed over several days, when there was no other way. Here they arranged dates for walks in the countryside. Almost always into the woods, at the stone cross. If Paulina, whose father kept a close watch on her, was unable to go out she knew that Eulogio would do his tightrope act to reach her.

For Paulina, it was a June like no other that she could remember. Filled with the most flowery splendour, the most solemn beauty. She felt as one with the whole of nature, the warm rain, the sun, the agile grace of the animals... Eulogio didn't want to be her lover. Paulina, who didn't realise that, deep down, she wanted this, didn't know either that he was tormented because his mind, used to order and discipline, was telling him that he must not let himself go with this girl, whom he loved, but could never marry.

Eulogio worried when he learned of Paulina's intense admiration for his family. Gradually the young woman confided all the impressions she'd gathered as a child… How several times she had stood in the alley by the Nives mansion listening to Mariana playing the piano, how she admired Miguel's attentiveness towards his wife, and how she loved to see them always together, and know that they had been away together, and that they always spoke the truth.

"That especially… They don't try to look better than they are, they give when they believe it's deserved, they don't give gifts, they don't use weakness or sin as excuses, they always do what is right."

Eulogio swallowed. He loved his parents very much, but Paulina idealised them, and so he couldn't admit that they would never welcome her into the family, and that he didn't think he was brave enough to face his cousins' mocking looks if he were to marry a girl with no dowry, "an unknown." All the Nives were familiar with Mariana's plan: she had one son only, but that son, whenever he married was expected to bring in a wife who doubled their capital… Eulogio couldn't tell Paulina that while his parents might have very generous thoughts towards the whole of humanity, what they valued most was their luxurious lifestyle, and that they sacrificed everything for this… Paulina grew accustomed to Eulogio's silences, which would end in kisses when she was speaking.

They would fall into each other's arms almost without meaning to, as soon as they found themselves alone, among the trees or out in the hot sun. It was as if they were magnetised one for the other… It became easy to talk less and less. Paulina was no longer fixated on her great, vague political ideals, since Eulogio had told her that he didn't have any. She knew that Don Miguel Nives was affiliated to the socialist party. Her father had talked about Miguel Nives's politics in front of her, branding him a coward. For Paulina, Don Miguel was an idealist, like herself. She barely knew him but his kindly face inspired her affection. Eulogio appeared to be completely ignorant of his father's political ideas. Or at any rate, didn't share them.

"Look, I'm not on the right or the left. I stand for myself, for my work as an industrial engineer and that's all. This winter I'm going on a trip to Switzerland and to Denmark to learn about things that interest me…"

Religion didn't matter to him either. He liked the ideas of the Gospel and thought it the most sublime thing in the world, without seeing its divinity, but he didn't have a phobia of the Church like Paulina.

"No, no; you're wrong on this; I've never met these awful priests, or these demented pious women. I grant you they do exist, but why should that affect me being for or against the Church? I haven't met any saints, and I don't deny their existence either… All I know are decent people whose only fault is that they don't quite manage to live by what they preach."

And with these words all Paulina's most burning issues were swept away. She forgot about them completely. She thought of nothing but Eulogio, day and night; she was completely obsessed.

At the beginning of July, he told her he had to go away. Paulina was scared.

"Don't go crazy, woman, I always go to the coast for a fortnight. This time I've been invited by my uncle, one of the many, who's spending the summer in Santander; anyway, I'm not going until the fifteenth, and I'll be back by the beginning of August. Then they'll be staying a few days with us."

Paulina knew that the Nives were a big, powerful, close-knit family who were always visiting each other and helping each other out. Eulogio didn't tell her that his relative, a high-ranking army officer, stationed in Barcelona, had recently married a very rich widow. This lady had two daughters who were very much to Mariana's taste, pretty girls with handsome dowries. Mariana had said to Eulogio that if he fancied either of them as a fiancée she would be a very happy woman. The boy knew that he would find neither of them attractive while his head was clouded by the idea of Paulina, but he also knew that if one day he could forget her, he would eventually marry a girl of the kind Mariana favoured… Nevertheless, he continued to poison himself with the frenzied passion he felt for Paulina. Whenever she didn't turn up to their trysts, he felt sick. Mariana observed him with irritation and a contained resentment.

"I can't wait for you to go on this trip, son… I've never seen you look so unhappy as you have this year, don't you think, Miguel?"

This was all Mariana allowed herself to say. Between the two of them she and her husband had agreed to turn a blind eye to this silly love affair to avoid it becoming something more virulent, and they were biding their time in the hope that the boy would get bored before long. They were keen for him to be off to Santander.

Contrary to his body's desires, contrary to his feelings of lethargy, Eulogio, too, wanted to leave. He needed to breathe, to think. With Paulina, he couldn't.

He left on 15th July. Three days later Paulina received a hastily written letter informing her that he'd arrived, and heard the news that civil war had broken out.

After that events succeeded very rapidly. A wave of insubordination, shouts, chants, and madness began to take over the village. On 22nd July, the workers from his own mine took Don Pedro prisoner and locked him up—along with the parish priest, the curate, and two or three right-wing activists—in the village prison. Leonela, desperate, went to see him and took him food. They told her that he'd fought like a devil, but that now he had been "tamed" and was playing cards with the priest.

Paulina didn't leave the house. Nobody bothered her. She knew that Miguel and Mariana hadn't been harmed. However, the castle belonging to Count Vados de Robre had been seized. Fortunately, neither the Count nor any of his children were at home.

Paulina, shut up in her house, was living a nightmare. She wasn't properly conscious of the political situation of the country. She thought only of Eulogio, day and night, as ever. She assumed that one day her father would be freed… The only thing she worried about was what had happened to Eulogio. For this reason, she listened to the radio non-stop, trying to extract the truth from all the contradictory news.

Now she felt compassion for Leonela. The big woman wept constantly while she ran around the village, pleading on behalf of Don Pedro, to anyone she thought might have the authority to help.

"I saw that big pot-belly Don Miguel Nives. He told me to

'relax,' that nothing's going to happen. What a…"

She burst into tears when she reached the point of having to insult someone. Paulina didn't cry… But she was being driven mad with worry, not for her father, but for Eulogio.

One day at the end of July she arrived at the large studded door of the Nives mansion. She dared to let the bronze knocker fall two or three times against the door. She couldn't bear not knowing what had happened to him.

An old servant opened the door. In fact, she didn't open the door, she opened it a crack, poking her angry nose through it.

"Please, I'd like to speak to Señora Nives."

The old woman looked her up and down.

"Wait here."

She closed the door, leaving Paulina in the street. She waited… The sun was shining; she felt her hair burning in the sun and her hands cold and damp. She waited for a long time. She imagined that Mariana would come out and burst into tears on seeing her. She imagined that she would invite her in and that she would show her Eulogio's room and even portraits of him as a child. Her heartbeat echoed inside her skull.

Eventually, the old woman reappeared.

"Señora Nives is not at home to visitors."

After this announcement, she closed the door again, denying Paulina the chance to ask after Eulogio. The old woman would know if the parents had received any news in recent days. But she wouldn't have told her anyway.

Paulina carried on living in her house like a sleepwalker. She would eat what Leonela cooked. She didn't dare go out. She didn't receive any correspondence from Eulogio… During the time she'd been back in Villa de Robre she'd received half a dozen letters from her former boyfriend. They remained un-opened. She'd had neither the desire nor the strength to write back to him and so his letters had continued to pile up, waiting for the day when she would know how to explain things to him. It didn't seem like the right moment now, either. She didn't do anything all day, but her thoughts were filled with one obsession, and Víctor represented a very distant figure in her life. It felt completely absurd now to think that she'd once considered marrying him… She hesitated to touch the envelopes that bore her name, written in green ink in Víctor's ornate hand. She never did learn of their contents. Nor did she burn them; they remained forgotten forever on the chest of drawers in her bedroom.

On the first day of August they shot Don Pedro along with all the other prisoners. Leonela saw his body, and arrived home in a desperate state, her clothes torn, pulling at her hair in an astonishing and spectacular show of grief. Then she insulted Paulina, calling her a bad daughter. Paulina listened without defending herself. The insults, she felt, were deserved.

The following day, Leonela left the house, taking an enormous trunk with her and Paulina, for the first time, felt afraid. Nobody had turned up yet; it hadn't occurred to anybody to ransack the house… But it could happen at any moment.

During the night, if it rained—and that summer it rained on quite a few occasions—if the wind rustled the leaves of the trees or caused a window to bang shut, it terrified her. One night, the breeze was blowing papers around in goodness knows which room in the house. It sounded like footsteps or whispering. Paulina was too scared to leave the bedroom.

She had some food in the pantry and there were still some

vegetables growing outside. The gardener who tended to the little plot of land with Leonela's help had not reappeared. It was as though the entire village had forgotten she existed. She was glad. The apples were almost ripe… She nibbled at them sometimes, savouring their bitter flavour. She wouldn't die of starvation even though she never went out. She kept the doors bolted. She was overcome by a kind of numbness. A world without Eulogio seemed absurd and meaningless to her. There were times she believed that the revolution had been started to take him away from her forever, and although she waited for him every minute, she couldn't snap out of her stupor. She spent so much time on the balcony, staring into the orchard, that her eyes were seared with the distant image of his house.

One night she began to feel that pull of her blood—that extraordinary current as if she were connected to the fluid of another body—that announced Eulogio's presence.

"I'm going crazy," she thought, "I'm going crazy. That's it, I've gone crazy."

Eulogio wouldn't come back before things had calmed down, she was certain, it was impossible. The life she was leading was enough to drive a person insane. She didn't even know how many days had passed since her father's death and Leonela's departure… Even so, she peered over the balcony. It was a dark, warm night. Somewhere a storm was brewing.

As she leaned on the handrail, she heard a familiar whistle, and her ears began to buzz. A few minutes later, she was crying, her face pressed against Eulogio's. After a few moments, she noticed that he was dressed in military uniform.

"My uncle has done me a huge favour, he's made me his aide. I'll have to go with him to Barcelona, but it means I've got a safe pass to take my family to Santander... I can even requisition a car right now if I like. I came by motorbike, you see. But I can't persuade my parents to leave. They're convinced that nothing will happen to them even if the fascist troops ride in. I'm worried about them, because..."

Paulina waited. As he was speaking, Eulogio realised that whatever happened he wasn't leaving without her by his side.

"Paulina, if you're not afraid to come with me, tomorrow morning very early..."

"Afraid? Afraid to go with you?" She began to laugh softly.

They set off on the motorbike at dawn. As they passed the cemetery walls, Paulina closed her eyes. It wasn't until many years later that she allowed herself to think about her father's death. The death of Don Pedro remained buried inside her, trapped and forgotten by the arrogance of youth in one of those dark pits that, years later, if uncovered, poison the soul with the smell of rotten corpses.

Paulina would remember a wonderful trip. She guessed she must have been exhausted but she didn't recall the tiredness. On the first night, something happened that to Paulina was full of mystery and joy. As night began to fall, on the outskirts of the village where they had planned to sleep, they spotted a large house, silent and closed-up, surrounded by farmland. They thought it would make more sense to spend the night there. But the silence as they approached the house unnerved them. They walked around the side and found an unlocked, empty stable. Above the stable was a hay loft, half-full of newly cut grass. A step ladder looked to have been abandoned mid-task.

They waited for a long time, eating their provisions outside and taking a good look around. Eventually they felt satisfied that the house was abandoned, at least temporarily, which to Paulina seemed a stroke of luck. They decided they would rather go up to the hay loft than try to break the lock. And that's what they did.

They slept wrapped up in Eulogio's blanket, in the cut grass, inhaling its smell deep into their lungs. For the first time Eulogio had her completely to himself. Neither of them understood the reason for their mutual magnetic attraction, that human fulfilment. They were bursting with happiness. For Paulina, it seemed too much: being young, loving each other, belonging to each other, nothing standing in their way… Something like Adam and Eve must have felt in the Earthly Paradise, she thought.

In the morning Eulogio held Paulina's hair in his hands and it slipped through them like dark water. He couldn't believe he had ever wavered, had ever thought he could leave her.

"I could never be with another woman after having been with you."

"I know one thing: I know I could die now after experiencing such happiness. It would be worth the price."

Eulogio laughed.

"There's nothing to pay," he told her.

Paulina spent her honeymoon in Santander. Eulogio introduced her to his uncle and aunt as his wife. She and Eulogio felt confident in the knowledge that they had become one in flesh and in thought for ever. "For richer, for poorer, for better, for worse"… When Paulina thought about it, she felt a happiness so intense it almost hurt. They had given themselves to each other; they hadn't talked about formalising the arrangement legally, but they both knew they would whenever they had the chance. In any case, whether they did or didn't seemed very unimportant at the time. Paulina spent blissful days beside Santander bay. From the hotel at night, her head resting on Eulogio's chest, she could hear the boat sirens. The sand on the beaches, the silver summer rain, the changing colours of the sea, the seagulls, the green mountains, all this created a symphony of her good fortune, completely separate from the war. Eulogio was her security, her happiness, her reason for existing.

Their arrival in Barcelona, in a small, very unstable plane, was a new and exciting experience for Paulina. She felt as though she were skating through life, enjoying every minute by Eulogio's side. With him even death had no meaning. She imagined absolute oblivion, nothingness. And it didn't scare her.

Once in Barcelona, Paulina didn't see Eulogio's family again.

"My uncle found out we lied, and got very angry. I told him we're going to get married anyway, as soon as we can, but he's furious. He'll get over it… It's better this way. We'll have more time on our own."

Paulina didn't mind the isolation, although she felt it when Eulogio's duties meant he had to spend several days at a time away from her… But for her it was enough to know he was safe, in the rear-guard, and above all to know that there was no one else but her in his life, that the two of them shared the same small, confined paradise.

Sometimes she surprised herself… Her heart was filled with joy as she wandered through the streets of a city that the war had lent a lively, almost triumphant air! The Hunger Years had not yet arrived and Barcelona was bursting with life, with sensual happiness, its moist air scented with sea, sun and pine trees; its inhabitants had that thirst for pleasure, that carefree mentality so peculiar to wartime… Paulina couldn't comprehend that Barcelona was also a city in mourning.

Paulina learned to understand Catalan. The lady who ran the boarding house where she and Eulogio stayed for the first few months taught her how to cook delicious fish… The landlady—a plump, neat woman, reserved yet kind—enjoyed the company of this young couple, seemingly so untouched by the worries that overwhelmed everyone else in the world at the time.

Paulina delighted in the word happiness, wrapped herself up in her own selfishness to savour it at every moment in her spirit, in her body.

One day, around lunchtime, Paulina was wounded, in a quite absurd way. Hearing screams and gunshots in the street, she had leaned out of the window, but she never got the chance to find out what had started the skirmish… She heard another horrible scream behind her—in the dining room of the guest house, in an old, narrow street overlooking the Ramblas—and found the landlady on the floor, having a kind of fit… At the same time, a painting on the wall quivered as a bullet whizzed across it, and the next second she began to tremble, too, when she felt something tepid and red drip into her right eye, and minutes later, a stinging sensation on her scalp… The bullet had grazed her head. She laughed, in fact, when she told the story, it was so surreal.

Eulogio listened to her account that night, with that distracted look of his, that slight squint, an expression he wore when he was concentrating hard. Two days later he came home and told Paulina that he'd found a nice, quiet house in the San Gervasio district.

"A comrade has offered it to us. He's a poor man and he's frightened his two dotty old aunts might die of starvation. I've promised him that while we're in the house, I'll take care of their food, and in turn he'll convince them to accept us as house guests. He's told them we're very important people and if they don't take us in they'll be shot forthwith."

And so began a new period in Paulina's life, a very strange one, during which she often felt that her happiness must resemble that of a woman from the Far East, desperately in love, jealously locked away... She saw no one but the old lady owners of the little house and Eulogio... She only went out for walks or occasional trips with him... Whenever they began to run short on food supplies, Eulogio would sort it out. Paulina never found out what scrapes he'd got himself into, but he'd always arrive home with potatoes or coal or sugar or oil.

"This is my war," he used to say laughingly.

The Señoritas Martí, who owned the house, kept themselves to themselves, and despite the food provisions, viewed Eulogio and Paulina as intruders. They believed the couple's presence in the house had been forced upon them, imagining Eulogio as an evil Red, one of the Republicans' top brass, and a murderer. His heavy footsteps—which caused the antique console tables to shudder and threatened the fragile embroidered cushions, china dogs and lace that adorned the house—terrified them... Their petrified expressions, petite figures and quick, lively movements—plus they even had tiny moustaches—indeed all their mousey attributes led Eulogio to christen them "las señoretas ratonetas," a nickname he reserved for private conversations with Paulina.

Even after all the events that later ensued, things that would utterly wreck that period for Paulina, her memory of the sisters' pointy little noses endured, along with that of a striped restaurant awning rippling in the sea breeze in La Barceloneta, and the view of the city from Mount Tibidabo; all these pieces fitted together to form a souvenir of Barcelona… A city that was different to any other, and that without Eulogio would have made no sense at all.

For six months, Eulogio was on the frontline, in the south. Paulina accompanied him, living in a village jam-packed with refugees; strange, dirty people. But for her the only thing that mattered was to be near Eulogio. She was pregnant and so they got married, in a so-called "military" ceremony. After they returned from that trip, Paulina suffered an early-stage miscarriage. She was surprised at how upset Eulogio was and at his concern; he asked the doctor if it meant that she wouldn't be able to have any more children. And so, when Paulina found out that she was with child again, she was overjoyed. Eulogio was thrilled and took great care of her.

They had arrived during the worst moments of the war, and yet in the Señoritas Martí's house it was as though the twentieth century hadn't even begun. Paradoxically, Paulina would always recall the years they spent there as a haven of peace… The sirens and the rockets, and the distant rattle of machine guns seemed to belong to another world. Paulina, when she looked back on her life, could never associate images of war with that small, narrow, two-storey house and its tiny garden where a handful of dusty plants grew. The window of Eulogio and Paulina's room, on the top floor of the house, looked out over the garden. They could see a stretch of mostly empty street, too, and beyond that, a wall covered in flowers, which looked like it bordered a large estate.

The only home that Paulina remembered as her own in her

entire life was that little house in San Gervasio. The whole of the top floor was hers and Eulogio's, and Paulina kept it clean with the help of a very old maid that the Señoritas Martí had known for ever. The maid, Nuri, wore her hair in an enormous o-shaped bun that reminded Paulina of a tortell, a cream-filled Catalan pastry. Paulina suspected that the "tortell"—that time had not turned grey—was filled with something other than Nuri's hair. They communicated through Paulina speaking half in Catalan and half in Spanish, and Nuri in a language she had invented especially for Paulina. The only thing Paulina understood clearly was a kind of refrain, which advised that a "dona" or lady should keep three things clean, her "peus" or feet, her "cap" or head and her… Paulina was at home. Between them, she and Nuri had the kitchen gleaming and had planted lettuces in a corner of the garden. Nuria had got it into her head that the old ladies were Eulogio and Paulina's aunts, although of course she knew full well they weren't. Still, she referred to them as "las tietas"…

Years later, Paulina would recall that homely period as a special, warm, happy time, in which she and Eulogio were so good together, a simple married couple in love, who even looked after their two frail old aunts… One thing the Señoritas Martí absolutely forbade the couple to do was step foot in their bedroom or in the other few rooms that they reserved for their own use.

Paulina used to cut back the dusty ivy that grew around her window and covered the entire façade of the house. It was an old plant and seemed to have adapted to the neglected, dirty garden. On the ground floor, it had completely overgrown one of the living room windows. Eulogio offered to cut it away to free the window, but the Señoritas Martí looked at him aghast.

They were appalled by Eulogio. One time, he'd even climbed up the wall of the house, clinging on to their celebrated ivy, and into their room. In the summer, he would go into the garden to shower, wearing nothing but an old pair of underpants. He would wash himself with the hose and, on his way, give the plants a quick water and show off his athletic physique with gymnastics displays. The Señoritas Martí would observe him from the window, their tiny eyes glistening. As Eulogio carried a rifle and pistols the señoritas assumed he spent his time perpetrating "orgies of killing." The one thing they were grateful for was that he never brought friends back, nor did he partake in behaviour any more scandalous than the showers or the constant kissing of his wife.

One day, however, Eulogio did something awful. He decided to open the dark, mildew-ridden living room on the ground floor, and sit down at the señoritas' piano.

"This old thing needs tuning, ladies."

The señoritas looked at him indignantly; no one had touched that piano for years. A sea of porcelain figurines danced on the lid as Eulogio's fingers bashed at the keys.

Paulina, seated beside Eulogio, was amused by the outraged expressions on the sisters' faces. The braver of the two (also the tiniest, with the pointiest little nose and the brightest eyes) was Conxita. She approached Eulogio, squeezing carefully between the plush, red chairs. Eulogio raised his smiling face to her.

"Do you like Albéniz, Señorita Conxita?"

"Let me tell you something," the little old lady's voice quivered… Eulogio stopped without shifting his gaze from the keys.

"You can't fool us with your piano playing… Those fingers are not a pianist's fingers."

Eulogio examined his strong, square hands.

"What's wrong with my fingers, my dear ladies?"

"You can mock us all you like, sir, but the fact remains that every one of your fingers is a centimetre too short."

Paulina and Eulogio laughed at this, not realising that it was an act of retaliation, of supreme bravery, with a secret, mysterious significance, which completely eluded them. Conxita's underlying message to Eulogio was that as far as the sisters, daughters of a music teacher no less, were concerned, Eulogio was not only a murderer but an uncivilised oaf, and they would never be taken in by his purported passion for the ivories.

People were saying the end of the war was in sight. Eulogio, certain that the Nationalists were going to win, was now happy that his parents had stayed in Villa de Robre, which had been taken at the very beginning, in 1936. The news that Don Miguel had died didn't reach France until the war was near its end.

The "señoretas ratonetas" would gaze in terror at a sky crisscrossed with planes, flames, and bombs. Yet their hearts beat with hope. Paulina was preparing a trousseau for a baby who, if it were a boy, would be named Miguel. The Señoritas Martí, begrudgingly, were helping her ready the trousseau. She couldn't help but laugh, because she hadn't even asked.

Eulogio was worried. A crease had appeared, like a shallow vertical cut, between his brows. But outwardly he was optimistic and told Paulina that, when the time came, his uncle would have a private plane take the whole family to France.

"We'll be in Paris in less than two hours, Paulina. We'll get in touch with my mother and she'll send us money and we'll stay there for a few months, until things settle in Spain..."

When the time did come, Eulogio's uncle sat down at the desk in his office and shot himself.

Eulogio stayed away from the house for a day and a night; Paulina was out of her mind with worry. Of course, she was used to him staying away for several nights at a time when he was on a mission, but he would always tell her… The entire time she was expecting a knock on the door of the little house in San Gervasio, someone asking for him or bearing bad news. She didn't know a single number she could ring. For the first time, she realised how isolated she was.

Eulogio arrived at dawn, after a horrific night. Paulina was in bed but awake, so she heard the faint squeak of the garden gate and peered out of the window. When she recognised Eulogio, she thought she'd collapse. But once he was in the bedroom, beside her, it struck her that she no longer knew him, that in a few hours he had become another human being. The young man's face was gaunt and angular like a wolf. There was a feral gleam in his eyes when he gave her the news.

"The worst thing is that they made him do it. They made him kill himself."

"They? Who?"

Eulogio looked at her with tiredness in his eyes and a glimmer of contempt too. Paulina realised that, although he'd deliberately kept her at a distance from his fears and from the realities of the war, despite this, he resented her ignorance. She vaguely knew that communists and anarchists had been fighting in the streets. She knew that there were bands, divisions, plots everywhere. But if Eulogio was a simple soldier, an aide who didn't belong to a specific party, he had no reason, in her mind, to get so excited. Eulogio used to say that as soon as he arrived home he forgot that entire sea of mud and blood… And for the first time, since they kissed on the train, Paulina found she was the object of neither his desire nor his sympathy. "I'm very tired."

The dawn light was beginning to creep in through the window. Eulogio took off his boots, undressed, and fell asleep the moment his head touched the pillow. Paulina, beside him, watched the dawn break, watched the morning light up and a thin veil of winter mist turn the sky pale.

The next day, he asked her for a list of their food supplies.

"We're leaving, you see? I arranged everything yesterday. Tomorrow, before dawn, a car is coming for me. I'll take my uncle's widow and his daughters to France. It's something I have to do, and believe me, I will get them out of here safe and sound."

Paulina nodded.

"I'll get everything ready… But we can't take all the food. We'll leave some for the poor ratonetas, won't we?"

Eulogio, for the first time since that early morning, seemed to sense her at his side. He took hold of her wrists and pulled her to him.

"No…"

"No?"

"Paulina… Can't you see it's impossible? The food, the soap, the small amount of coal we've got left, all of it's for you."

Then he explained that she had to stay, that she couldn't put herself through such a journey.

"You don't know what's happening out there on the roads. There are hordes of people running. There's shelling. Goodness knows if we'll have to ditch the car and continue on foot… Nothing will happen to you here, Paulina. As soon as I arrive in France I'll write and ask my mother to fetch you. Then we'll be together again…"

The words sounded reasonable; she was convinced. They were expecting the baby at the end of March or the beginning of April, and it was half way through February.

Neither of them got even a moment's sleep that night. It went by so slowly and yet so fleetingly, as they lay beside each other, their eyes wide open. Paulina could sense her hand close to Eulogio's. For years, she carried with her the memory of the light brush of their hands, along with the memory of her own tears, falling from her temples onto the pillow.

At dawn, they heard the automobile come for Eulogio. They said goodbye in the bedroom. They couldn't bear to part.

She looked out of the window. On the other side of the garden was the old, flowery street, quiet as if sleeping… There were many like this in the area. She saw Eulogio turn back towards the front gate to say goodbye to her, and she saw his determination as he got into the car, which after a few minutes started up with a terrific roar and a rattle of metal plate that sounded as though it might shatter into pieces in the middle of the road. Paulina remained at the window for some time. It seemed to her that the sky, as it cleared, was reddening, not only because of the sun, but because of the blazing fires. She felt Eulogio's body next to hers as though he hadn't left, as if he were there with her. It hurt.

"Other women have suffered infinitely more than you and endured it with much more courage," said the Señoritas Martí when they saw her weeping the following day.

"Others have lost their husband and their sons in the war, and not because they've had a car come in the early hours to take them for 'a spin.' What on earth are you complaining about, you selfish, spoiled creature?"

The ratonetas, seeing her without Eulogio, felt very brave, but their words comforted her. She was sure that, in a way, the old women were right, and her happiness, during that time of great suffering for everyone, had been something akin to a robbery.

A few days later the Nationalists arrived. The Señoritas Martí, having reflected on Eulogio's alleged activities, felt it was their duty to denounce Paulina. And so, finally, she experienced the hardships inherent in war, and gave birth to her child in prison.

# X

The calls of frogs and crickets filled the air. A summer symphony. The moist, sated earth was opening its burrows, and a thousand tiny creatures were announcing their existence in a murmur that grew to a crescendo like a magnificent concert.

Antonio stopped the car again in the middle of the road. He was frowning.

"I don't get it."

"Pardon?"

He saw the fear in Paulina's eyes. It made him angry.

"Tell me, did you love that puffed-up, fat bourgeois like you love me? Did he make you lose your head, like I do?"

Paulina glared at him.

"No… Our love was young and pure… I didn't need to fight against my better self to love Eulogio. My love for him was simple. But you, sometimes I detest you."

"I'm delighted to hear it. The feeling's mutual… Is that why you're leaving?"

Paulina was silent for a few seconds.

"No…"

Now Antonio turned his face away slightly, his expression cold. Paulina recognised that look.

"Are you still going to lie about what your body desires, about what really makes you happy?"

"What are you saying?"

"I'm saying that, if I wanted to, right now…"

Sometimes men's words have a cruel sting.

"Take me to the train, Antonio."

They could hear the frogs and the crickets again, as if at some point they had stopped singing, quietened by the lovers' attraction for each other. Eventually Antonio spoke. Hands in his pockets, he threw his head back against the seat like a spoilt child and fixed his gaze on the roof of the car.

"Explain something else to me. Why was Mariana talking about my mother-in-law's influence on you, and the nuns…? I always found it odd, your liking my mother-in-law. You can have absolutely nothing in common with her and yet you were always together…"

There was a smell of new leather, of dark intimacy. Antonio's voice had a childish, slightly bored, resentful tone.

Paulina was tired, and had been resting her head against the seat, but she sat up to look at Antonio when he spoke, and as he talked she began to feel irritated.

"Why is my friendship with Blanca so strange? You know better than anyone what happened when my child was still-born, and I was seriously ill… Mariana is decent, organised, and many other things besides, but she is squeamish about anything natural. Mariana would prefer babies were delivered by storks. She can't deal with the crudeness of certain things, she finds it all rather distasteful… It was Blanca who cared for me, stayed with me, watched over me for hours. And all of it as discreetly as possible, so Mariana wouldn't get cross. I came to realise that Blanca was a wonderfully good woman. She's not a pious woman in the same way as my mother. Nothing shocks her, she sees everything through pure, clear eyes; one instinctively feels one doesn't want to hurt those eyes… I've always thought that I was an appreciative woman. But Blanca, how have I repaid her? Going after her daughter's husband. You said it yourself. Forgetting everything, trying to obliterate the memories of that dark, unhappy period through joy, oblivion… This isn't me. This isn't who I am. How many nights have I lain awake? And when we went to Las Duras, and we were hiding from the child, when I looked into your brother-in-law José's eyes, they reminded me of his mother's… And I, having ranted about rotten, corrupt people concealing their weaknesses beneath the cloak of religion, I found myself hiding mine under something else: my outspokenness, my boldness… Then, Blanca took me to see those barefoot Carmelite nuns. She said it was a special privilege to enter their convent, because it was new, and so people were allowed to visit for a short period, until the time came for it to be closed forever… That was a very peculiar experience. Yes, very odd. I only went to make your mother-in-law happy. I've always found nuns rather annoying. I've come across religious orders who simper and fuss while underneath their habits, they hoard money, they despise the poor and flatter the rich, and that's not all… Anyway, everyone knows that."

Now, Paulina began to speak more slowly as if she were remembering.

"But these women are incredible. It's not that their convent is poor, it's that it *is* poverty. They have no electric light and the rules don't allow glass in the windows. Each nun has a whitewashed cell with a bed of wooden boards and a straw mattress. There's not a single chair in the entire convent, they all sit on the floor, even to write or work. The crosses in their cells are made from two simple sticks of wood... Everything is affectingly simple. They grow vegetables and, in the garden, they have their own cemetery. They accept the alms people offer them and they don't ask for anything... They sew their own clothes, and they all have the same clear eyes as your mother-in-law; I've never seen such cheerful faces, nor heard such joyous laughter... Many of these nuns come from rich, aristocratic families. They're from a world of privilege, a world that I know a little, from a distance, and that I know is littered with stories that make our affair seem like childish innocence... And yet, it can also produce people like these. A prudish middle class can produce them too. And I was amazed to meet among the nuns a serving maid who'd entered the convent at the same time as her mistress, though now they're in different convents. I asked the nuns why they live there, why they punish themselves, and why they're so content... They told me they live in penance for the entire Church and that they're so happy because they're certain that by obeying their Mother Superior and following the rules they are doing God's will... Personally, I think it's nonsense... But I can see that these women have something I don't at this time in my life. I can see that they're following their consciences. And although they believe blindly in a load of claptrap, like the devil, for example, they're not stupid. The Mother Superior herself appeared to me to be a highly intelligent woman... No, I've never met anyone like them... Is it weird to feel so moved by them? You've laughed at me too many times when I told you I was in torment. You don't know how true that was..."

Paulina was silent for a few seconds before she went on:

"That's what I'm drawn to the most, what strikes me... the joy... I've known so many people, usually malicious and spoilt, who are always laughing, apparently leading an incredibly wonderful life... And with all of them, behind the façade, there is a kind of desperation, or emptiness, or incessant need not to be bored. They can never be without something to do for even a second, or be quiet for a few hours, all through this fear of boredom... I've known so many people who create problems out of nothing, invent tragedies to make their lives more interesting... I don't know of one person who could be profoundly happy and hide it; nor anyone who fakes happiness without eventually being found out... I tell you, Antonio, the Carmelites' happiness is something very serene, deep, true, impossible to fake... And, poor women; I'd always thought of the contemplative orders as useless, absurd and scary, but I found myself envying them.

"This morning I went to the cemetery... I was desperate... We hadn't spoken for three days... I thought your car would be there at the bend, before the cross, like it's been before. It's true we hadn't arranged to meet, not at all, but... It wasn't there... I felt a rush of loneliness. And then, Antonio, I felt a need for revenge, a desperate need to wander the roads in search of you like a madwoman... I remembered my father, the poor man, as I often do now, since I found out that I too can be ruled by my body, and I too can desire something that torments me and sullies me and debases me... I can find excuses for myself, like him... Sometimes I think I'm very much his daughter, that I'm very close to his bones. Do you understand? That's why I go to the cemetery on the days I don't meet you…

"This morning I met your mother-in-law at the cemetery. She goes often, to change the flowers for her dead. She says it brings her immense peace…

"I was going through a bad time… Yesterday you were unbearable. You made me feel so cheap. You know how you like to sometimes. Perhaps you have a right to, I am… Not as much as you, but I am…

"Blanca came towards me, calling me with her smile… I couldn't resist her smile this morning. She looked like an innocent black fly among the bluebottles, the butterflies, the flowers… She couldn't imagine the crazy thoughts going through my head.

"The mother superior told me that you went back to see her again… If you could only see, Paulina, how happy it would make me if God enlightened you (you know the special way of talking Blanca has). You are better than you think; and if only you could see how different suffering would be if you had the refuge of God…"

"Her words meant nothing to me but you'll understand that the last part worried me. I stopped your mother-in-law with a smile.

"What makes you think I am suffering?"

"Anyone who is not with God suffers much." I laughed and shook my head. I was thinking of Mariana.

"Even my mother-in-law? You surely don't think my mother-in-law is sad? But she's not a believer."

"Blanca looked at me with that strange serious expression of hers.

"If you weren't so absorbed in yourself you'd realise that Mariana too suffers and almost always because of very small things."

"I thought about my mother, always involved with the church, always sighing and mean-spirited.

"I've known very religious people who were always suffering."

"That's different…"your mother-in-law said in that way she has, stubborn as the sea. "One day you'll understand. We're all praying that one day you'll understand."

"All?"

"Yes, the Carmelites, me, and a thousand others you don't even know but who dedicate their lives to praying for people who are like you, blind…"

"Can you believe this simple, and in a way absurd, conversation really left an impression on me? Yes, that's when I decided. Every hour that passed, the idea that I had to leave got stronger and stronger. I don't want to be worse than before, Antonio. I don't want to give in to this law that says that the older we get, the worse we become… I don't have the option of confession where I can go and tell someone my sins and… I've only got myself…"

Antonio had listened to Paulina's explanations with a smile on his face… Eventually the smile began to hurt, as uncomfortable as the smile on a mask.

He lit a cigarette, wanting to cast light on Paulina's features with the match. Her face too resembled a small mask… With only the bright shining pools of her eyes showing through.

The odd thing was that he didn't feel strong enough to deny what Paulina was saying. He sensed that she was sincere and that her words were expressing an inner struggle. Even so, for a short while he tried to persist in thinking that Paulina was vulgar and a liar. He looked at her out of the corner of his eye and saw a woman exhausted, her body slouched in the seat… Then he leaned closer to her and without speaking began to caress her hair, with an affection that seemed to become ever more urgent.

Then he began to talk, to try to persuade her there was no need to be afraid. She hadn't done any harm to Blanca, for the simple reason that she didn't know anything… Nor to Rita. Rita didn't suspect a thing… Nobody, absolutely nobody had even an inkling about their affair… But yes; maybe, after all, this trip to Madrid, which would take Paulina far away from the in-laws and Eulogio and everyone, would turn out to be for the best.

Antonio would visit her. Everything would be easier. Paulina was to write to the post office in León, and every two or three days he would go and collect the letters…

He was convincing her with his voice, enriching it with spiritual tones that he thought he'd lost. Behind this weak and distraught Paulina, he was seeing the pure and disdainful woman of times gone by, the one he could never attain.

"I'll always love you, Paulina. You've been my destiny in a way; don't forget… Don't pay attention to the clumsy things I say. The important thing is that I love you so much…"

Antonio's voice was kind, deep, protective.

His pleading began to have its effect on her. She needed this feeling of being loved and fulfilled. Her soul wasn't made for emptiness and sadness. The man noted how her petals opened, noted how her pride fell away and the powerful feelings in her body, aroused by so many recent memories, flooded into her at the slightest touch of his hands. He didn't want her to see the faint, satisfied smile on his lips and he concealed it in the descending darkness.

For a long while they remained there listening to the chorus of a magnificent August night in the countryside, boundless and beautiful. A magnificent night that the rain had refreshed, but that once more, was exhaling its vital warmth.

Paulina felt as though she had split from her own body. Her mind was whirring with a line from a book she had recently read: "Sex and death: the front door and the back door of the world." It seemed to her that the author had encapsulated the secret of existence in one single sentence. Its author was Faulkner, the great American novelist, a favourite of Antonio's.

"Death and sex"… As the years passed it felt to Paulina that the key to life could be expressed in these two words. Where everything came to an end, and where all the turbid poetry of existence was born.

She realised with painful clarity that she would never be able to forego the dark and brutal desires that, simply by living, she had awoken in her body. She would never return to that time of innocence when she'd declared: "I'll never love another." She knew now that she could, and she could live without Antonio's love, given more time or less time, with more suffering or less suffering… But, who would she love? She could understand everything except emptiness. Only death could derail her from the course that had been set… Leave Antonio, rid herself of the nightmare of loving Antonio… and inevitably, start over again. A different happiness, a different chain, different desperation, different love…

"You'll have to kiss me here, Paulina. We shouldn't kiss each other goodbye in the station…"

"Why must life be so complicated, Antonio? Why do we make it so complicated? Sometimes it's impossible to live with the toughness and the strength that one longs for in youth… Why do we exist like this, in misery and longing? Why can we have no happiness except for these fleeting moments of abandon, of pleasure followed by darkness?"

Antonio smiled as he put his hand to Paulina's lips. After he had silenced them, he kissed them.

# XI

Antonio arrived at the castle close to two in the morning. The storm, on its way through, had wiped the sky clean. He saw the tall ridges against the stars and the crisp outline of the still sleeping village. The slate-covered rooftops were like sheets of old, smooth silver.

The castle walls, silhouetted against the night, held a special charm for Antonio. He felt an owner's pride when he looked at them. He had bought those history-filled stones when he married. It had been worth it, although he wouldn't truly own them while his parents-in-law were living.

The story of the Count and the Countess, like a nineteenth-century vignette, made their son-in-law smile thoughtfully.

He was imagining Blanca, just out of school, as she appeared in a photograph he had seen: a girl with a round, naïve face, her hands resting on a vase on the landing of a grand staircase. The suitability of a marriage match between the two young people had been agreed upon by their families. Blanca had barely been introduced to the then handsome Alfonso before she duly fell head over heels in love with him.

Alfonso was the second son of the Count of Vados de Robre, and Blanca was also second best of a noble family.

Alfonso had wanted to become a friar, so he said, but no one, not even the monks at his school, had taken him very seriously. He was a young lad of nineteen, very spiritual and melancholy, extremely pious, his eyes always cast downwards, and he was horrified when he saw the plump and cheerful young woman his parents had in mind for him to marry… Blanca, on the other hand, was determined she was going to marry Alfonso, or die trying… With the whole family's support, she succeeded. And not long after, Alfonso seemed almost to shake himself out of a slumber, and began to fall in love with his wife, letting his religious zeal fall by the wayside. He began to enjoy the parties given by the entertaining but not particularly intellectual society they frequented, which was almost entirely composed of relatives of varying degrees of distance and of varying levels of wealth and titles. His overriding passion was for the theatre. He rented boxes in the two or three that were fashionable and he liked to show Blanca off in them. He also wrote poetry, but he wore an embarrassed grin when he talked about it. He felt it was a weakness in a great gentleman to lower himself to honour Poetry with his pen… Because, naturally, the Count subscribed to the rather un-Christian idea that a title gave him a sort of superiority over other mortals. Precisely because of this, he was kind and protective towards anyone who wasn't lucky enough to count among their personal belongings one of those moth-eaten old honours.

Blanca, after her marriage, slowly evolved in the opposite direction to Alfonso. Gradually, when the affection between them became solid and blissful and firm, Blanca began to occupy herself less with her handsome Alfonso and became less interested in parties and swanning about, gradually withdrawing into her home. Her current state was very like a nun's vocation. Blanca felt happy now living permanently in Villa de Robre. Alfonso, not so much, although he didn't have any choice.

The married couple, economically speaking, relied on Blanca's dowry. On their marriage, they had something like the amount of money that a hundred or so middle-class families, if you added it all up, would usually have to live on. It wasn't too much, barely enough in fact, for the lifestyle they were expected to adopt, and it dwindled to very little, because of the unsettling presence of the old Count of Vados de Robre, an aristocrat who had spent his whole life joyfully frittering away money and even at this stage was desperately frittering and gambling. Whenever he felt that "needs must" he would dip into his children's fortune. The land from Blanca's family had to be sold off, one estate at a time, because of that plundering pirate. The old gentleman's last act was an edifying death, performed with great panache as he threw himself onto a bed of ashes to receive the last sacraments, leaving behind mountains of debt and—because the eldest son had died—the title of Count, plus the castle to Alfonso and Blanca.

The couple pampered their children, providing them with every luxury; governesses and tutors, good schools... but in a rather haphazard fashion, which resulted in a somewhat chaotic and calamitous upbringing. All their hopes rested with the eldest boy, José. Following the new modern way, this boy and his brothers wanted to study for university degrees. José became a forestry engineer. He was handsome and very attractive, and though his character was marred by certain strange ideas, his parents imagined that he would make an extraordinary marriage match. The war scuppered those plans, when incomprehensibly José felt called to the priesthood… During the war, two of the Count and Countess's sons died, and Joaquín—the next eldest after José, and at the time a medical student—married a little bourgeois girl named Ana María. Secretly, the family considered this marriage a worse tragedy than the deaths of their heroes.

The Count and Countess had one other remaining son, Luis, a career soldier, who made up for these disappointments with the marriage match of their dreams. As for Rita, the youngest in the house and the only girl, an auspicious match was made with Antonio Nives, who though he hadn't a single drop of blue blood, was not only very rich, but extraordinarily generous. The family agreed that they would find him some good qualities. He was handsome, he was elegant, the Count found he had similar interests to his own. Possibly he read too much; Rita said that he read an almost excessive amount… But Blanca remembered that José, as a boy, had also read a lot, and now was turning out perfectly: into a saint.

So, to sum up, the history of the Counts—much like that of certain kings—in the end was the story of the marriages of their children. Blanca used to say:

"I do worry when I think of all the silly ideas we entertain; chasing after money and noble lineage and that sort of thing… But everything has its good side. Luis with his marriage has been able to help José with paying for the reconstruction of the parish, and Antonio, indirectly, too…"

Curiously, the origins of Antonio and Rita's marriage could be traced back to when the country was at war… During the civil war, Blanca, who used to have a genuine dislike for Mariana Nives—to the point of needing to accuse herself of such, repeatedly, in the intimacy of the confessional—became great friends with her. This is how it happened:

For the Counts' firstborn José, who during the summers of his youth in Villa de Robre would while away the hours at her house, Mariana had become confidante, intellectual patron, and the object of his admiration; the woman was indifferent to any kind of gossip. The truth is that, according to him, she was the only person with whom he could exchange ideas and books. When he wasn't chatting with Mariana or reading, he would set off into the wilderness, a rucksack on his back, with his friend Eulogio. The two lads liked hunting and simply hiking through the countryside. They were close, united in their love of exploring. The two of them liked the forests of Las Duras so much it determined José's career.

"There is no god but Nature and Science," José used to say to annoy his mother.

Only Blanca knew the details of her son's gradual conversion and calling to the priesthood… But when Blanca became friends with Mariana, José was at the battlefront and no one knew of his vocation.

One simple event occurred. When the Nationalists entered Villa de Robre, Miguel Nives was imprisoned, judged, found guilty of numerous crimes committed in the village during the period when he was in the highest office, and he was unceremoniously shot.

The Counts, who were in San Sebastián, came back to Villa de Robre almost immediately after the village was liberated. Blanca learned that the woman she called her "enemy" and for whom she prayed every day, was going through a dreadful time. She was told that the village boys had painted insults on the walls of Mariana's home and that someone had even dared to throw stones at the house. Since the shooting of her husband, two days earlier, Mariana hadn't been out. None of her relatives were in the village at the time, and none of the well-to-do people in the village had been to visit her.

Blanca went.

She had never seen inside Mariana's mansion, but that day she swept right in, right past the stunned old serving maid and held out her arms to Mariana, who had become lean and drawn from shock… Blanca did this in such a kindly way, with so much clumsy affection, that Mariana didn't feel any resentment towards her and very soon began to feel quite protective of her… Over the ensuing days, and following Blanca's example, the house thronged with belated visits…

Antonio's family—his father, his stepmother, his two half-brothers and he himself—had moved to the Nationalist zone. Frequently, during the three years the war lasted, they were sent to spend long periods in Villa de Robre, in Aunt Mariana's house, and while there he was forced to play with that silly, cry baby, as she was then, Rita… But Antonio, who underneath had always been a bit of a snob, liked the fact that Rita was the daughter of a count and countess and lived in a castle. Even now this snobbishness floated over his other qualities, like oil. Secretly he dreamed of persuading the Counts to pass down their title to Rita, and he would indulge them, watching them live out their lives, with the curious sensation that they were big kids, living in utter bliss. As time went on the Count recalled more and more poems and songs, and became more affable and protective with everyone. As for the Countess, with her chapel, and her Masses held in the house, in Antonio's mind, she lived in an alternate rose-tinted universe. Neither Alfonso nor Blanca seemed to him to be too worried about Rita's illness. They didn't realise how serious it was, and perhaps this did the girl good. Yes, Blanca devoted herself to Rita, and spoiled her, but that was what she'd always done. And the truth is, Rita would get quite bored with the stories of saints that her mother liked to tell. Except that this gentle boredom, when she was so weak, was exactly what she needed.

As for the castle's other inhabitants, Joaquín and Ana, they tried to go unnoticed, saving their money like little bourgeois in case one day they were forced to leave the place. They were completely different from the rest of the family.

"It's as if," the Count would say, "our flock of swans had adopted a gentle, tame duck."

Joaquín didn't find his father's inspired comparison very funny.

Now, the castle lights were all out, and the garden filled with moist air and peacefulness. Antonio parked the car in the garage and slowly crossed the garden towards the house. In the chapel, behind the stained-glass windows, he could see a faint glow. Maybe it was the tabernacle lamp. His parents-in-law paid for—with Antonio's help—an old, toothless chaplain, while their son played the missionary in his own country in the humid forests of Las Duras.

Antonio grimaced at the thought. He yawned.

"It takes all sorts."

A while later he climbed into bed, in the single room he had occupied in the castle since Rita's illness. He fell asleep, exhausted, with an expression on his young face that gave him a strange look of suffering and innocence.

Rita woke up agitated.

"Mamá…"

She switched on the bedside lamp. The bed next to hers, dark wood with tall columns, was empty, untouched. It had been left as the maid had prepared it, with the cover turned back and the voluminous nightdress folded on the pillow.

Rita thought she'd heard footsteps on the terrace a moment earlier. She listened carefully. Gradually her ears began to pick up the unsettling crackle of woodworm. She recalled that spiritualists believe that this crackling sound is a manifestation, like voices, of the dead, and she bristled with fear… Sometimes she had dreadful visions. At night, she thought she saw membranous wings and the devil in a corner watching her, laughing.

She remembered that her mother had told her that for most of the night she would be holding a vigil for the Blessed Sacrament, and began to panic.

"If you need anything, ring the bell. María knows…"

"*If I need anything!*" She felt a vague resentment. In that moment, she was completely oblivious to the lengths her mother had gone to for her, to Blanca's complete dedication to her.

That, after all, she felt, was natural, something that the woman owed her for the simple fact of having carried her in her belly. She was her flesh… She felt deeply jealous when she cast her mind back to the days when Paulina had been dangerously ill, when Blanca used to spend the night at Mariana's mansion, and she, her daughter, had been forced to make do with the housemaid or her sister-in-law Ana… Antonio didn't want to be by her side. That was another source of anxiety. Something she felt but didn't show, though it weighed on her. Antonio wasn't born to be a nurse. He used to say it himself. Blanca, yes. Blanca had been born to care for others, but she didn't see her, Rita, as important. She neglected her… But how much concern, by contrast, she showed for that despicable woman, that Paulina, that rude old hag, who seemed to have a gift for gathering everyone expectantly around her and her cigarettes! What Rita really couldn't stand about Paulina was the way she smoked, her sometimes lopsided smile when she was smoking. Or at least a smile that left its mark on Rita, like a slap, like a hot iron, one time when she saw it directed at Antonio…

"That Paulina is a vicious, evil woman."

She'd said this to Antonio one afternoon.

"Yes, you could be right."

Antonio had answered yes, he had said she was right, although he was attracted by Paulina too. Simply by looking in the mirror, comparing her face with that woman's, Rita began to calm down a little, but… It was like a nightmare. Every time the woman appeared with those pure black eyes, with that look, as if, inside, she was laughing at everyone, Rita's heart would race with revulsion.

The darkness was intense. The lamp on the bedside table gave off a halo of light. Large shadows remained in the corners. Rita began to cry. To her mind, Paulina had everything a woman could want from life. She'd enjoyed a love affair on her own terms, during the war, but afterwards had been welcomed into her husband's family home like a daughter; she was impertinent and disdainful towards everyone, even though she was treated with nothing but kindness and smiles by the rest of them. Even

Rita's mother worried about her… Her mother, who was capable of abandoning her to look after that common slut.

Tonight, fortunately, she wasn't looking after anyone else, but in the chapel. If something happened, she could call the housemaid, and if necessary she could send someone to fetch her mother. For a moment, she was tempted by this idea. Then, all her suffering poured out like the tears of a child.

"I need *you* here, not María," she thought, picturing her mother. "I'm frightened… You shouldn't leave me… You, of all people, shouldn't leave me. Not you… Everyone leaves me."

She turned the light off again, distraught, sweating in fear. Her mother was a woman who took her devotion to the church too far. She was selfish, in a word. Yes, a selfish woman.

In the chapel, Blanca was kneeling. She was overweight and from time to time her knees would ooze pus. She had one of the nasty abscesses now, but she'd stopped noticing it. She had been drowning in a kind of agony ever since she witnessed Antonio leaving: "He's going after her." "Dear God, let her see the light."

Blanca was always astonished—and upset—by how much her eyes could see through the people around her.

"Why can't I have Rita's innocence, Joaquín's disinterest, Mariana's wilful blindness?"

She had been asking herself these questions for a long time, since she first became aware of the dark love affair that was unfolding between her son-in-law and Eulogio's wife. No one else saw it. Only Blanca. The others were absorbed in their own problems, they were blind to it, believing the world centred around them, but she, Blanca…

Blanca's prayer was very pure, very simple. For years now she had lived only for God and had observed, without surprise, without judgement, the things that happened around her. In fact, she saw them with infinite compassion.

That night she could find no relief through immersing herself in the great flame of love that sustains the world and that she knew. That night she felt only unbearable suffering. She pictured Paulina's black eyes, when they'd met in the cemetery. The eyes of those who choose damnation, she supposed… As if from far away, she remembered Antonio and Rita's wedding day, when she had felt an ominous sadness that she'd kept to herself, amid the general cheerfulness.

"Dear God. Enlighten her."

She wasn't thinking about Antonio. She didn't know why but she was only thinking of Paulina… Perhaps because she had been brought up with the idea that women are the cause of all evil. It is the women who lead men "into temptation."

Or perhaps she wasn't thinking of Antonio, because it wasn't the selfish reason of her daughter's earthly happiness making her pray. It was simply that she had glimpsed a soul at a crucial moment. She would never be able to explain what exactly had made her kneel before the tabernacle to pray for Paulina, and why she had frozen like a statue in the attitude of prayer when she heard Antonio arrive, why she fell asleep on her knees, why she woke up in anguish and why she had remained there praying, until the sun had fully risen.

"Enlighten her."

When they saw her at breakfast looking hollow-eyed, stiff-limbed, washed out, Blanca's family were undecided as to whether to scold or ridicule her.

"You shouldn't overdo it," said the old, toothless chaplain, when Rita told them all about her mother's night prayers.

Blanca began to blush, laugh it off and protest, as usual.

Antonio, eating his boiled egg at the other end of the table, looking bad-tempered and frowning, glanced at his relatives, as if afraid they might make some comment about his nocturnal outing.

No one was worried about that, not even Rita. All the morning's comments were about Blanca's innocent obsession with praying… Antonio relaxed. From his vantage point at one end of the table he began to imagine the people at the other end as puppets on strings, getting all worked up about meaningless nonsense.

"Most people, don't understand what life is."

This profound realisation gave him a wise, mocking air, like an owl. Poor Blanca, for example, would never know true human passion, she would never have raced through the night, like him, to taste those acrid, burning sensations, she would never guess that the passionate love that bound him and Paulina to each other had blossomed here, under her nose. And the rest of them? Joaquín and Ana… Were their lives even worth living?

By the time he had finished the boiled egg, Antonio was convinced that of all the characters who inhabited this castle, there was only one worthy of note… one, who beneath the surface of ordinary existence, flowed like an underground river, leading a turbulent, torrid double life.

*"Vigils for the Blessed Sacrament!… Dear God, they've been discussing whether that wretched Blanca had or hadn't the right to pray all the hours she wants!"*

*"Why do they waste their time thinking about stuff like that?"*

"You shouldn't overdo it, you shouldn't overdo it. Overdoing it, my dear, doesn't help at all, not at all…"

Father Pérez's kindly voice hung in the air amid the aroma of coffee and roses, scents that were beginning to attract flies.

PART TWO

# I

It was like a cradle. Clickety-clack, clickety-clack, clickety-clack…
A rhythmic, monotonous movement, deeply monotonous.
Something was holding her, enveloping her, rocking her in
her sleep. Something that, in the end, had woken her.

She was on the train. She had undressed, put on her pyjamas
and crawled between the sheets in a train bunk… That was
where she had woken up.

For a few moments, she luxuriated in the sensation of being
rocked on the wheels, her body fully stretched out, comfortable.
Through the slats of the blinds she could see a faint light. She
guessed it must be dawn. She felt hot… She threw off the
blankets.

Then she pulled herself lazily towards the foot of the bed,
lying on her front, and resting her head on the pillow that she'd
thrown down there during the night, drew the blind to a sight
of such pure, serene beauty that it left her smiling quietly to
herself for a long while. Absorbed. Someone had wiped away, as
if with a sponge, the previous night's torment when, worn out

and tearful, she had climbed into bed. Now she wasn't thinking of anything at all. Her head, her body, all her senses, were serene in this pure moment of awakening.

The countryside was yellow and scorched. A yellow world. An immense, smooth plain, entirely different to the landscape she had left behind a few hours ago.

Larks were taking flight among the stubble on the fields. Not a single human being in all those miles of the meseta, stretching as far as the eye could see... A lone tree in the far distance. A telegraph pole, a cairn, all neatly, sharply drawn against the dawn sky.

Paulina imagined herself walking, as tiny as an ant, between the furrows of the yellow and brown grassland, inhaling countless aromas of common herbs, dried in the sun... She was familiar with the scents of lavender, thyme, rosemary. She knew that at this hour, before sunrise, one's body, invigorated by the crisp, pure air, wouldn't feel tiredness no matter how far one walked... A long way off, mountains loomed like blue shadows.

The hills of León were far behind her. Life... The fervent, vulgar, petty intrigue that was life, was far behind her. The pain in her body and in her soul, far behind too. Everything was behind her, except for the immensity of the earth and high above her, the pure sky.

A humble cottage, seemingly clinging onto the plain, almost fused to it, between the huge sheets of the firmament and the earth, stirred her emotions as the train passed by... High above that wretched human dwelling the last star was shining, ennobling it with a flickering poetry.

Paulina felt a fleeting, fanciful longing to live in that earthen house, with its tiny yard of piled-up stones and dried mud...

To live in a place like that, surrounded by vastness, forgotten and alone forever.

This strange idea came to her as if with a deep desire for peace. No. More than that… It was a desire to savour, quietly and without interruption, the peace that had begun to flow into her. Because, like a slowly rippling tide, peace was flooding into her soul. It was a divine sensation. Half sat-up in her bed, not yet dressed, she was transported by this sensation, absorbed in the spectacle of the plain.

She saw the browns and yellows of the dry earth in August. She saw a reddish glow, deepening, spreading, ever more spectacular across the sky, surrounded by small, golden clouds, like flames, on the horizon…

She imagined the cold, sweet song of the first birds, and the chill morning air… And all these things remained in front of her eyes, igniting her senses, while she felt she was seeing all the spaces of the world at that hour: the wide, solitary spaces of the plains of the entire earth and the wilderness of the great mountains; tall, blue, dusted with snow. And the warm seas that, at that hour, were swelling with sun until their beauty bubbled out in silver-coloured patches, in a thousand mirrors of light, in a gentle untouchable, quivering mist… She imagined, too, the cold seas, with their great shadows beside the rocks, and the foaming spray of their surf, and the creatures in the depths, displaying their colours, their life, so far from human view, yet perfect down to the last detail of their colouring and their impulses and their instincts.

Paulina's heart, too, felt mysteriously united to that of all the men and women in the entire world, with their capacity for harm and destruction and that other capacity too, that other thirst, that other quest that can sometimes become lost… The quest for love. She saw how she herself, and how all men, including those who deny it, those who turn their backs on it and, frustrated, disguise it as crime, are searching for love. Sometimes they search for it with the simplicity of animals, sometimes with pain and blindness, and sometimes with a hatred of its allure and of its name.

Sometimes love sounds beautiful to them, they believe it will be an infinite sea of breaking waves… But then men get waylaid by any small puddle of glinting water and never reach it. Human beings love these puddles, they drown in them, lose themselves in them, die in them, a few steps away from the murmur—further away, more difficult to reach—of that immense sea of love, which exists, which waits.

Paulina, lost in thought, slowly lowered the blind. The train whistled as it pulled into a station. She had no need now to look out to the plain. It was as though the beautiful dawn had remained within her.

While she washed and splashed cologne onto her short black hair, the mirror above the sink reflected her slender image, but she wasn't looking at it. The great tide of beauty that in the morning had begun to fill her spirit was flooding ceaselessly into her.

Now, the sense of the full beauty of the world became purer and more complete to her… She saw the towns where human beings suffer, crammed together, desiring each other or hating each other, refusing to see what they truly crave, even when they're killing each other, the only thing that can fill the void, love. She saw the pain of the many, the pain that was so pure, so cheerfully offered by her Carmelite friends. A pain that reaches its object of love… And she felt that many other men are conscious obstacles to their brothers feeling and contemplating the love they need, and she felt that these men were helped by a spirit of cowardice and evil. Hers was the intuition of those human beings who are living channels through which love flows and bears fruit, and these men and women are the ones whose lives are entirely complete, even if outwardly they may be ugly, poor or sick; their human life is fulfilled in the same way as the flowers are fulfilled when they produce colour, scent and then become fruit, and as the lowly plants in the Castilian countryside are fulfilled, by their invigorating, pure smell.

Soon, she became aware that all this was pouring into her spirit in bright rivers of understanding that were in no way sentimental, otherwise they would have drowned her.

She was smiling, calm. With all that inside of her or enveloping her. She caught her own reflection, and became conscious that she was applying lipstick in the bathroom mirror, steadying herself as the train rattled along. Her eyes were deeply serene. A serenity she hadn't experienced for many years.

"What's happening to you Paulina?"

She asked the question tenderly, half-aloud, to her reflection in the mirror… But, in fact, materially, nothing was happening to her. And absolutely nothing was happening around her.

She turned back towards the window and opened it, feeling on her face the fresh smelling air, the breeze from the speeding train, the chirping of the birds, the vivid colours of the sun-drenched earth merging into each other in the glimmering dawn.

"Love," noted Paulina's soul, "love is something beyond a minor passion or a great one, it's more than that. It's what transcends this passion, the good that remains in the soul, if anything does remain, when desire, pain, anxiety have gone. Love is like the harmony of the world, just as serene. Like its vast beauty, which is nourished even by deaths and separations and illness and pain… Love is more than this harmony, it is what sustains it… Love gathers up into itself all the harmonies, all the beauties, all the aspirations, the tears, the shouts of joy… Love decrees the immensity of the Universe, the laws that are mathematically the same for the stars as for the atoms, those laws that, occasionally, amid his pitiful babbling, man discovers.

"Love is God," Paulina realised, "God, that immense blazing hearth of happiness and goodness, in which we find ourselves, become fulfilled, the hearth towards which we are drawn, to which we are free to go, and to which we do go, if we don't tie stones around our own necks."

Paulina's face was almost contorted in concentration. She was watching the approach of a tiny village, sketched in China ink on the morning sky. An earth-coloured collection of houses, a bell tower, and at the top, a stork's nest. The bells were ringing and, as the train came closer, she could hear them.

All at once, she felt a surge of happiness. Much more than this. What she felt was too vast to fit inside the narrow confines of the word happiness: it was Joy.

For the first time in her life, Paulina knew joy. Something indescribable had happened to her, something was happening to her that was outside of everything she had experienced in her life thus far…

As if an angel had grabbed her by the hair and had whisked her off to the edge of the narrow horizons she had always known, and had torn those horizons apart, showing her a chasm, a dimension of light whose existence she could never have even suspected... The dimension of life that is confined by neither time nor space and that is the golden, the impassioned, the astonishing, the immense dimension of Joy. The Why of the Universe, the Glory of God. Joy.

Until this moment, Paulina had never understood what Heaven meant. True, she hadn't wanted to imagine it either, and the childish words men used to explain it had made her laugh, conjuring up ridiculous images in her head... "Little angels playing the harp," "quietude"... And she felt that if she ever tried to explain it, her explanation, too, would be childish and incomplete. As if someone wanted to convey the concepts of colour and light to a person who had been blind from birth—that's what her explanation would be like for someone who hadn't yet understood. But she immersed herself in the mysterious and peaceful yet fierce understanding of the hearth of joy to which, miraculously, man has been called. The Blazing Hearth of Love that has given the human soul this spark, this dissatisfaction, this yearning...

"My God," said Paulina, "My God!"

And for the first time ever, these words were not a mechanical habit, they were full of reverence and meaning.

Nothing was happening to her. Her nerves were calm, her body at peace, while that profound wisdom entered her spirit... And it was, at the same time, the understanding of God, Infinite Happiness, Eternal Love, towards which our entire life tends, for Him that we exist, for Him that we grow, love, suffer, desire and shape ourselves... And she could feel, too, this same infinite God entering her soul to kindle this knowledge within her... And yet, more than that, the certainty that God himself, He who waits and calls, He who enters into the spirit and captivates it, God, shows us the path of this desire… God has given himself to us as a human word. With the body of a man. Living God and Living Man, to spell out the secret of the Universe in the language of men.

She felt the one God as a flash of light that calls and creates. She felt God, who enters the soul, the Holy Spirit. She felt God, the Way of God Himself, the conductor of all life, from the yearning the Holy Spirit places in it, to the Blazing Hearth of Joy, God the Son, Christ.

Feeling is an inadequate word; but, today, I can find no other in my language to describe the blessed and gentle state that allowed Paulina to know these things. She wasn't rooted to the spot or enraptured… Nor was all this a fleeting experience; it was an understanding, pure and simple, that remained inside her while outwardly she continued with prosaic tasks such as arranging the clothes in her suitcase and trying to close it without her hands shaking.

For her it was effortless to feel flooded with this Faith, comforted by this absolute wisdom. It was as if only in this aura of love, of understanding, of faith, could she live… It was natural to her, like the air she breathed. In the same way that breathing and crying are natural to a new-born baby, though the journey from the mother's placenta to the outside world remains an extraordinary thing.

A few minutes after closing her suitcase she looked at it, bewildered. Then, slowly, she came to, and she knelt on the floor of the rattling train and gave thanks to God for the Life that was coursing through her. Thanks for everything that had prepared the way for her rebirth into the light, for the long and painful gestation of her soul, that for her had been effortless. Thanks for this new life that, undeservedly, this morning, this very morning, was being given to her by God.

She heard the waiters from the dining carriage ring a bell in the corridor, announcing breakfast was served. Paulina smiled, surprised to discover from her expression when she lowered her hands from her face, that she felt hungry. The impression of birth, of natural and clean life still enveloping her, she peered into the corridor of the train, her face radiating happiness. In the corridor, she crossed paths with two or three people, and greeted them with a light-filled smile… Then she found herself in the restaurant, in front of the first breakfast she would enjoy in the company of God. She didn't give or say thanks with words, as—and this was already forgotten—her parents would but, deep within her spirit, Love continued to feed her flame.

At Paulina's table, sitting opposite her, a short, bald, grumpy-looking man was clearing his throat. She began to smile dreamily. The man was intrigued, his eyes lit up a little, and he made a vague attempt to flirt with her. He was perplexed when Paulina didn't answer him or indeed seem to notice him at all. Paulina was now gazing out towards the landscape, nibbling her bread and butter, with the same warm, intimate happiness on her face, as when she had looked at him a moment before.

"Important events always seem to happen to me on the train." She thought this, but was ashamed of the thought. The love she felt towards Eulogio could not even come close to this other Love that filled her. Something else, another dimension… Nothing… She was in another world, a serene dimension… In another world, the same as the enraptured anguish that had filled her a few hours earlier and as her gasping words in the arms of a man.

She looked in her bag for the packet of cigarettes. The gentleman, eagerly expectant, lit Paulina's cigarette. He murmured something she didn't quite catch, but she recognised the arrogant, bestial expression on his face. The man, in that moment, looked sadder and dirtier to her than a pig in a pigsty. She felt sorry for him… She stood up.

Besides, she wanted to be in her compartment, to return to her blessed solitude. She understood how incredibly lucky she was to have the luxury of being alone. She knew that the same thing would have happened to her even in a crowd, this advent of Love. The Joy inside her didn't fade even for a moment. She understood that what was driving her life and was blossoming inside her was something that could find its way into any human life whenever it pleased… She understood that it was a force that was more vital than seclusion, more powerful than the attraction between the sexes, hotter than an inferno… She knew all this, but she was happy to have, right there at that moment, an individual cabin, a place where she could close the door, and smoke quietly on her own.

When she remembered the story, that Grandma Bel had told her so many times, of Saint Paul falling from his horse, struck down by the love of Christ while he was pursuing him full of hate, Paulina began to cry. She had received her Christian name because she'd been born on the very day the Church commemorates this event… Slow, joyous tears trickled down her cheeks.

She was so innocent, she was so utterly ignorant of the mysterious, personal and extraordinary adventure of a human life in a state of grace, that she imagined, as did the other Paul, that her faith in this immense discovery she had made would remain forever unshakeable.

The landscape had changed. She looked on with infinite calmness and wonder. The train was travelling through the gorges of the Guadarrama Sierra. The window revealed patches of yellowish green, brown, black on the rocks. Down below in a small valley, two bulls, motionless, black, glistening, surrounded by white doves, seemed straight out of a Picasso painting.

A couple of hours later, the train was whistling through the vast sea of track at the approach to the Estación del Norte. Madrid, shining beneath a liquid-gold sun, welcomed Paulina, thirty-three years old. Newly born.

# II

Paulina received the following telegram: "Go see Father Pedro González. 109 Pardiñas. Great friend José. Happy. Blanca."

That was it.

Four days previously, Paulina had arrived in Madrid. She'd asked the taxi driver to stop at the Puerta del Sol, on the way to her house. The hoses were working; the fountains were working, the morning was still young but, even so, Paulina's throat and nose had felt dry… The sky was already an intense blue. The traffic officer was chasing the butterfly-shaped shadow cast by his brightly coloured sunshade. The square was torn apart and dusty with the never-ending summer roadworks.

Paulina went into a tobacconist's, bought some paper and an envelope, and right there wrote a brief note to Blanca, telling her that, suddenly, she had found God, that she understood the happiness and the heroism of the saints, and that she wanted to give her a big hug. Carefully, she affixed a stamp to the letter and put it in the postbox in the Calle del Carmen.

And it was done. It had been an impulse. She smiled as it

occurred to her that she could never have imagined, the previous day, that the first person she would write to on her arrival in Madrid, before anyone, would be Blanca. Before changing her clothes, taking a shower, resting. Before anything.

It was years since Paulina had done anything on impulse like a young girl. She hadn't done anything like that since she lived in her grandmother Bel's house.

That day, while she was travelling in the car, towards the house where she had lived for the whole of the previous year, she remarked in herself a new way of looking at the world. As if she were discovering a panorama, a city, a neighbourhood. Like in her student days when her friends in the faculty used to organise daytrips to ancient, magical cities, that appeared to them to exist, with all their history, purely for them.

The taxi drove up the Calle de Alcalá, moving away from the centre, until they reached one of those areas where the city widens around the bullring in Las Ventas. Following Paulina's directions, the car went up a street that hadn't yet been modernised, bumped over the cobbles in the narrow road, raising a fine, dry dust into the air, and pulled in beside some old, run-down shacks that were all crammed together. On the door of one of them, there was a sign painted in black letters: "Wines."

The taxi came to a stop.

"It's across the road," Paulina said softly.

It didn't make any difference, in any case. The street was so narrow... Opposite the bar stood, between two empty plots, a tall, spindly house, which seemed to have been abandoned there, like the funnel of a run-aground ship. Though the house was relatively new, it was already sad and listless. Eulogio and Paulina had rented a furnished flat on one of the upper floors.

Paulina could hear drills boring into the morning. When she stepped out of the car she understood why: in one of the adjacent plots, a team of workmen were laying the foundations of a large building.

The heat was already intense. The sky was clouding over with a light veil of hot, grey dust… The concierge handed her the keys to the flat, eyeing her with an indecipherable smile.

The woman, who was deaf yet chatty with a somewhat inquisitive air, judged everything she saw without listening, perhaps because of her physical impairment. Her eyes came to rest on Paulina's cheekbones and the faint hollows beneath them.

"Well I never, you don't look at all well, Doña Paulina!"

Paulina who had left that house feeling bloated, old, and sad, and who was returning with the feeling of floating on a golden world, as light as a feather, couldn't help laughing.

"Such a shame," said the concierge, "such a shame… It's the babies of mothers who could have given them a good life who die. Whereas, well, in poor Doña Luisa's case, none of them die."

Paulina hadn't seen her premature baby, the one who had been stillborn last spring, and she didn't feel great pain at its loss, so she felt rather confused by these words of condolence. She acknowledged them, however, before heading up to her flat, which smelled of mothballs and had all the wooden shutters closed. Only the kitchen window didn't have shutters; it looked out over the patio—a wide channel that, until another house went up, had beautiful views over the neighbouring plots of land—and sunlight trickled down over the bricks and seeped into the hallway bringing a sense of solitude, of summer.

She'd barely stepped into the tiny hallway of her flat when she heard wailing from the floor above, the small attic apartment where Luisa, the neighbour she knew best, lived. The noise, too, was familiar. There was always one of Luisa's five children crying.

It was as if nothing had changed since March when she left the house... Except that now the encroaching sun was threatening to heat up those fragile walls so much the house would turn into an oven. Back then, those same walls had struggled to protect her from the cold... And except that she, Paulina Goya, was a different woman.

Her white wool coat was draped over her arm. She let it drop as if it were something dangerous, it was burning her... There were places where people would be glad of a coat in August!

She began to turn on the taps in the house, simply to hear the gurgle of water. She opened the windows in the main bedroom, and the sun and the dust streamed in from the street... She recalled, as if it were ancient history, the anxiety she had suffered months earlier, and how during that period she used to lie in that bed until midday, immersed in a weird lethargy, in an atmosphere of sadness and endless apathy. How the sweat under her arms would turn cold and she'd have a bitter taste in her mouth, while some common, unscrupulous maid, would have the run of the house, and even steal from her.

She recalled Eulogio's exasperation the day he arrived home for lunch and found her still in bed. The servant had run away, taking the best sheets with her. The fire had gone out, the furniture was thick with dust... She hadn't even called for breakfast when they didn't bring it to her. Nothing in the world had mattered to her in those horrible months. Eulogio had shaken her, that day, in frustration.

"I don't need a servant, but what I do need is a wife who keeps an eye on the house, who pays attention, who knows what belongs to her, who helps me."

"Find yourself a new wife. I'm not like that. I don't want to be like that…"

How different Eulogio was, over that year, to the boy who had fallen in love with her and whom she had loved, and how different, too, to the calm, self-confident man she had left behind in Villa de Robre.

Perhaps he too had found a very different Paulina to the one who had laughed so readily, who had been so perfectly suited to him in body and mind, whom he had left behind.

Life together, almost from the moment Eulogio stepped off the plane in Barajas airport and approached the group who were waiting for him nervously, impatiently… almost from the moment he embraced Mariana, and made a great show of lifting Miguel into the air, not turning to meet Paulina's fearful gaze until a few minutes after that, yes, from that point onwards everything had been difficult.

They spent the first night in a hotel in the centre of Madrid, and once they were alone together they couldn't figure out how to speak or act around each other, and the result was a strange formality between them. Only Eulogio had managed to say something pleasant.

"The boy is even better than I'd imagined. He's magnificent."

Paulina had given a little laugh.

"You mean he's like you… No?"

The irony was lost on Eulogio.

"Exactly… He's a real Nives."

What had Paulina expected? She remained awake that

night, desperately lonely. It was like the last night she had spent at Eulogio's side in Barcelona; at dawn, she felt the same burning, wet sensation as her tears rolled down from her temples to the pillow. But now she was alone. Eulogio in the other twin bed was sleeping soundly, exhausted.

The following day Eulogio began to go through the figures, and in less than a month he had found them a cheaper apartment to rent. Paulina had walked through the door as if it were a prison. She was repelled by the traces of other people's lives. There wasn't a single detail of the décor that she found pleasing.

"I can't live here. It's horrendous."

Eulogio had been angry.

"Maybe you think this is the height of luxury for me. In any case, you've lived in worse places, I think, and for a while we're going to have to adjust to what I earn."

"I can work."

"You've got work. You've got a house to look after, that's enough."

This was all reasonable. The devastating thing was Eulogio's tone. He would stipulate every tiny detail without ever asking Paulina's opinion.

He moved Miguel to a different school, and criticised his upbringing. He overruled Paulina in front of the boy.

Paulina, her nerves already fraught, was close to the edge. She would scream. She would fly into rages. Eulogio would shrug his shoulders.

"It's women's troubles... Come on, son."

And the boy would take his hand. Proud of that authoritative, calm man he admired. One day Paulina heard him say:

"Mamá spent the whole morning crying."

"Did she? What was the matter with her?"

"Nothing. Just women's troubles… Nothing to worry about, father."

Paulina thought about leaving that house and never going back. But she thought it from inside a kind of nightmare, without the strength to follow through with it. She didn't have the energy to do anything. Only to resist passively. And so, she had stubbornly refused, again and again, to get married in the Church, without a thought to whether this was good or bad for her children.

After her failed pregnancy, when she caught a serious infection, Eulogio stopped insisting: "We must be wedded in Church"… Now he would say simply: "I'm not going to force you, but think about it."

"If I ever marry," Paulina said now, alone, "it won't be to you, my friend."

"If I ever marry, it'll be to a younger man. A man who knows that even though I've been through years of suffering, I still haven't lived, who knows that I need to discover the joy of life. A man who doesn't obsess about his financial assets, but knows how to spend them cheerfully, fearlessly, imaginatively and most of all youthfully."

That was what she had once thought. She almost felt it now. Except that she couldn't express it clearly, because she was too steeped in this blissful feeling to wish for any more, or to desire any kind of revenge.

And so, surreptitiously, like an old ache, the memory of Antonio crept to the surface. However, since this depended not on her will, but on the joy and perfect peace that had been given to her, Antonio disappeared again beneath the intense and joyous bliss from God, which continued to breathe in her.

She put on an old dress and an apron and began to scrub and wash down the flat, and she caught herself singing. It had been years since she'd carried out these menial women's chores with cheerfulness. As the dust disappeared and the floors gleamed, the unpleasant memories trapped within those walls began to disappear too.

Sometimes she would stop mid-chore to reflect, dazzled, on what she believed. She would turn to God, lift her heart to Him, ask Him what He desired of her, of the poor woman that she was, for that is what He called her. She forgot to eat lunch, and in the afternoon, went down to the street to buy some fruit… and a catechism of Christian doctrine.

Seated on the floor in her hallway, in the coolest corner, she read with her entire soul that afternoon.

The noises from the house, the maids singing on the patio after siesta time, the whimpering and the racing around in the top flat, the relentless, dusty, racket of the drilling in the street, and the shaking of the entire house as result; all this formed a kind of backdrop of sound. In the hallway, the orangey light slipping in through the cracks, through the parched closed doors, formed what looked like a campfire. Paulina was sat at the far end of the corridor, like a Moor, parched too; the backdrop was unimportant and would have remained the same if Paulina had been sad or tired or if her soul had been dry like her nose, because of the change in the weather.

Never had anything appeared so luminous to her, never had simple questions and answers been shrouded for anyone in such delicious scent and emotion as each phrase, every response in that Ripalda children's catechism was for Paulina…

It seemed to her that many years previously, when as a young girl, she had prepared for communion, she had recited these words—so profound and so full of extraordinary beauty and absolute sense—without giving them any significance. She saw her young self, bored, swinging her small body, playing with her plaits and singing in a nasal voice:

"I believe in God the Almighty Father." Now, she was in tears.

"Cry baby," she said to herself after a while, "Cry baby." She smiled, wiping away her tears.

When evening fell and the swallows' shrill cries rang out above the street, now sated with sweet air and cool blue shade, Paulina looked out of the window, and listened to the shouts of the boys below as they played in the still warm dust.

The old ladies had set out their chairs and their sewing baskets on a large patch of land they called "The Beach" because they claimed there was a breeze that blew through, making it cooler than anywhere else… Paulina watched the throng of children and women who had all planted themselves in that spot, not all that different effectively, when it came to the crowds, to a fashionable beach.

Relatively near her house towered a huge block of flats, a monstrosity, its symmetrical windows, open all hours of the day. From every window of that great hive, from every flat in the house where Paulina lived, the same song rang out: the evening radio program was deafening the world… Madrid was lighting up into the distance. A thousand dots of light, beneath the leaden sky, the heaving, weary August sky. Before the stars, a sea of electric lights.

"My God," thought Paulina.

God took her by the hand and it was as if she were flying.

She understood the mysteries of the sky and the earth, without the need for explanations. It felt to her as though the Mother of God were smiling down on her life… She knew that a long line of people who had come before her were helping her and hoping she would help them too. She knew that she must kneel before a confessor, as Christ had invested in some men, his priests, the immense and tremendous power to forgive, and he asked this simple gesture from whoever was able to do so, to earn his forgiveness. Confession was, in fact, the gesture whereby a person confesses their love and seeks to rid themselves of everything that might prevent them from attaining it.

Paulina stayed up until the early hours examining her conscience. She recalled her entire life. She became aware that she had never made a proper confession, that she had always been indulgent with herself, since she was a girl. That she had never paused for a moment to consider what an incredible thing the sacraments are, and the sacrifice of Mass and who was being sacrificed… It seemed to her too that her Christian family hadn't really taught her the more profound aspects of her religion, that they had simply filled her head with moral precepts, which she hadn't understood at all until now, because, in truth, their only meaning was that they led to Love.

She fell asleep fully dressed, kneeling on the little rug beside her bed, and she woke up with a start a while later. She turned out the light and remained there observing the beautiful and profound stars, in the awe-inspiring, mystical Castilian sky, on that August night. She contained her thirst, because in that year the Pope hadn't yet given the dispensation that water doesn't break the fast… and waited for the morning.

When she arrived at the church her knees were trembling.

It was quite early, and she, without knowing why, was convinced that she would be the first person to enter the place of worship, but the Mass had started much earlier and several altars were already lit. Mass was being said at three altars at once. She was confused. A priest climbed up to the pulpit and began to pray, in a loud voice, a rosary… Paulina knelt in a corner in the shadows. She closed her eyes behind her clasped hands and her feelings of confusion disappeared. All that remained was the solid, firm conviction of what she should do in that moment.

When she looked up she saw one of the confessionals had a light in it. Inside a grey-haired priest was reading his breviary. Paulina approached and knelt in front of the wooden grill. The light went off immediately.

"Father, it has been many years since I confessed…"

Paulina said the words so quickly and in such a faint whisper that the priest didn't hear her. She repeated it.

"I see, my child. And what made you come?"

"I didn't use to believe, now I do… I am convinced…"

The priest showed no sign of surprise, asked a few questions, to help her, and eventually Paulina remembered everything she had thought about during the night.

"As a child, I detested my father… I never confessed…"

At this the priest did seem surprised, and said something to the effect of there were sometimes things that one didn't even know oneself, but Paulina felt that something very dark and painful had been cleansed, and afterwards she spoke of her antipathy towards everything clerical and "obscure," and he listened to her in silence. One by one she ran through all the commandments and was shocked to realise she had violated almost all of them by violating the first one or by not practising it…

Suddenly she became aware that her knees were hurting. She was no longer trembling, she was calming down. She made a mental effort to remember things more succinctly, not in a vague way, as she had been thinking about them the previous night, and she began to talk about her love life.

The story of her love affairs took her longer than she'd thought it would. It was complicated. First, she spoke about Eulogio, and the confessor told her that if social or family circumstances required them to live together, he could give her absolution, provided that Paulina was prepared to accept a complete separation of their bodies, until either the marriage was blessed or until she could break off all social ties with the man.

Paulina promised, certain, absolutely certain of herself and her desire.

Then she spoke about Antonio. She thought she saw the priest take out a handkerchief to wipe his forehead… Or maybe she was imagining it.

"No," she told herself, "it's just hot"… But she found it distressing to have to offload her miseries into the ears of this innocent man.

The case of Antonio seemed to be much more serious. It was double adultery. She had to distance herself from Antonio.

The difference between the confessional and life is that in there you can't dress things up. Paulina couldn't explain anything about what Antonio's love had meant for her, or that it had followed a period of utter emptiness, sadness, and illness… Now nothing remained but the repulsive skeleton. In the very depths, the truth.

Still, something was unsettling her, like a reptile, a worry, a doubt.

"But if his wife dies, and I'm free…"

"I cannot give absolution if you speculate on such things."

At that moment, Paulina felt an unbearable pain, a pain that wasn't sentimental in any way, but a pure pain, as her joy was pure when she thought of God. The pain of seeing herself deprived of that love, of that presence.

"I repent with all of my heart, everything which offends and has offended God in my life. I promise."

Antonio was nothing. A tiny idol formed of mud, a whim, a miserable puddle of water beside the immensity of the sea… There was no doubt.

She came out of the confessional feeling not only the sense of certainty and happiness that had filled her the entire time since the previous dawn but also a deep restful feeling in her body and her mind.

She lost count of how much time she'd spent in the church that day, after taking communion. In the portico, she noticed a large woman dressed in brown breathing a little agitatedly and staring at her.

There was nothing appealing in the woman's shining face, nor in her sweat-drenched clothes, but Paulina looked at her with a cheerfulness and a peacefulness that the woman found disconcerting.

Paulina never knew that the woman's problem had been, since quite some time earlier, that she couldn't work out if Paulina was wearing stockings or not, and that she had been waiting for her in the portico to find out for sure. Paulina's eyes had distracted the good woman from her purpose to such an extent that, once she realised, it was already too late.

Paulina was on her way home, her heart radiant, her legs stockingless… Later that afternoon she saw a sign on the church door prohibiting this very thing. She put it right straight away.

When Blanca's telegram arrived, all of this had already happened. Paulina was receiving Christ every day, in her body and in her soul. She lived in a strange kind of seclusion inside her small flat. She hadn't seen anyone since arriving in Madrid. She was soaking up catechism… She felt so far removed from everyday human life, that when she received Blanca's telegram she considered ignoring it at first. She had everything she needed in this great wave of gentleness, in her profound exaltation.

But perhaps it was time now to speak to someone of her joy, to communicate it, to share it. Maybe Father González would help her understand what God wanted of her when he raised her out of her woes and her anguish, to the unimaginable heights of this great happiness.

109 Pardiñas turned out to be a friary. Father González wasn't one of the friars, he was a priest, but he was living in their community. He was an enthusiastic priest, an educated, decent, and spiritual man.

Paulina didn't know this when she knocked at the door and a monk came out, dressed in black with his eyes cast down towards the tips of his large, scruffy boots. She felt excited at discovering things that were totally alien to her previous life.

"Are you the lady who telephoned this morning? Come in. Don Pedro won't be a moment…"

He left her in a gloomy room that smelled of bleach. She could hear boys laughing and looked out of the window. Some novices were playing ball in the building's large central patio.

Paulina stepped back from the window ledge and sat in a hard chair with a black back. The room was furnished with many such chairs lined up against the walls. The ceiling was very high and it was chilly. There were enormous, extremely poor quality lithographs of the Sacred Hearts and the Holy Family on the walls, as well as a portrait of the Pope and another of the Head of State.

Paulina wondered about the life of a boy destined for God almost since infancy. A few days before, she would have thought of this as an unimaginable absurdity. Now she knew that if God wished it, a child could feel the secret of the universe inside himself.

She stood up nervously when a tall priest came in, a priest who though he looked nothing like Pepe Vados and was much friendlier, nevertheless very much reminded Paulina of him.

"I've just received a letter from Blanca," he exclaimed. "Welcome, Paulina."

Paulina's heart was bursting. She couldn't explain that current of kindness and brotherhood. She realised that the man dressed in black, whose gaze—the gaze she now recognised as a secret symbol of purity of spirit—was so clear, and Paulina's eyes, which weren't yet as clear as his, lit up and sparkled with happiness… That this man, who had studied the science of God, had left behind all worldly things for God; and was God's priest… And she, a woman who had glimpsed the world of the supernatural for the first time… that the two of them, who had never met before this moment, loved each other deeply in the love of Him who had called them both.

Father González was smiling, looking at Paulina as if enchanted by her.

She told him that if it were necessary, right then, to proclaim the existence of God and the truth of the Church, from a public square, she would do it. And if it were necessary to be burned alive, she would let herself be burned.

Father González believed her. He believed her absolutely. What Paulina was saying was true. Except that—he said—she needed to strengthen that faith, that love. As soon as possible.

"You're in luck, could you begin a week of retreat tomorrow?… We don't normally hold spiritual retreats at this time of year, but there is a group of ladies who are very keen, and they've asked me… it would be perfect for you. It would be a recap of all the fundamental truths of religion."

Paulina nodded. Then she became a little scared. She'd been given the address of a convent… What was she going to do in a convent? Convents are austere places. Nuns are shocked by everything… Would she be given enough water to wash herself? All this raced through her mind, but she said simply:

"Father, I've got habits… I smoke a lot."

"Well, don't forget to take your cigarettes. It is precisely when doing these spiritual exercises that nothing should distract us from our thoughts. We shouldn't change any habits if denying ourselves might affect…"

Don Pedro didn't even smile when he saw the distrust in her eyes.

*"Smoking isn't a sin, and I'm not prepared to give it up to please some fusty old ladies… at the same time, obviously, I don't want to impose my habits on them either."*

This is what Don Pedro read in Paulina's eyes. For him it was of no importance.

Nevertheless, Paulina was afraid when, the following day,

she arrived at a large house, several storeys high, near where she had lived as a girl with Grandmother Bel. The front door was closed. She knocked and a young woman with a pleasant smile came out.

"Is this the place?"

"Yes, this is it."

Paulina dismissed the taxi that had brought her. The young woman took her suitcase and spoke to another girl with blue eyes and prettily styled hair. She couldn't have been more than twenty years old.

"We're giving you a room with your own bath, it's always more comfortable. And as you're new… Anyway, as you can see we've also got showers with hot and cold water."

"Is it very expensive?" asked Paulina.

The girl smiled.

"I don't believe so. It depends on what you can afford. Often it costs nothing… Our job is to make sure these houses are clean and tidy for the retreats; we have people come from all social backgrounds. Of course, as well as that, we do have other duties and there is always the apostolate…"

"You? But what about the nuns? I was told this was a convent… Where are the nuns?"

"I'm a 'nun,'" said the young woman. And she burst out laughing when she saw the astonishment on Paulina's face.

There followed a few days and nights of remarkable stillness and goodness. Blue and golden days, in the chapel with its smell of wax, a chapel decorated with the utmost liturgical sobriety… Nights of pure, deep silence, with the parched smell of the little garden floating in through the window.

She learned to live in a house where Christ was truly in humanity and divinity, hidden in the Eucharist. During that time, she listened to the clear, pristine, sincere words of the love of God.

She understood—And now how well!—hell, that deprivation of love, to where the idolatrous adoration of one's own misery leads; and even that physical suffering of hell. She understood how hell is chosen by an act of free will. She understood the amazing mysteries that God has revealed across the centuries… And during those few days, it occurred to her that the only thing that had prevented her believing before, in something that now appeared blatantly obvious, was a lack of basic intelligence.

Father González had suggested she buy herself a missal, a small book that contained the Gospels, the Acts of the Apostles and the wondrous Epistles.

Living with God, in absolute silence, made her joy even sweeter, like a treat she'd been given. The absolute peace of the house on its own would have done her good, she thought, even if those meditations on eternal truths, made by a man who loved God as Father González did, hadn't interested her quite so passionately.

All this did not stop her from stifling a giggle when she found herself, at meal times, in a pleasant little dining room, among ladies dressed in mourning clothes, whom she didn't know and who seemed to sigh more and more as the days went by.

It was a rather childish laugh. It reminded her of occasions when she hadn't been able to control her laughter in class, in her student days. There was nothing in particular about the ladies. It was only that their demeanour, their eyes cast downwards were as alien to Paulina as if she'd fallen onto another planet.

In the breaks, she would go to her room and, with the window open to a little garden, she would smoke… She would leave the ashtrays full of butts.

Nobody seemed bothered or shocked.

Don Pedro González presented the meditations, taking the theme of the Mass. Paulina, awestruck by so much beauty and so many deep mysteries, so exquisitely expressed, thought to herself that if, when she was a child, an assistant priest had read the daily Mass from the pulpit in Spanish, and had taught her to follow it, she would have attended the Sacrifice with greater interest. But instead, as she recalled it, the cleric had often diverted attention away from the wondrous miracle taking place on the altar, to comment on this or that behaviour he disapproved of, almost as if rather than Catholic priests, the preachers from her childhood had been Protestant pastors.

Paulina learned so much in that week! Now, her state of being was not the same as during the first three days when she had felt enlightened from within. But an ember of that love, felt with such certainty, of that supernatural understanding, helped the effort she was making.

She understood, above all, the Church, and the great work of the Church, that over the centuries brings together all the men that form the mystical and total Christ. She understood how the Church takes the word of God, guards it, interprets it helped by the Holy Spirit, and how human life, with its vicissitudes through the years, only gains greatness through the struggle, advancing little by little in its quest to attain Life in God. She understood how sometimes we waste time on silly things that are not important to man's purpose or even put obstacles in its way. How sometimes sinking to the depths of sorrow and misery is the way, our pride broken down, we begin to distrust our own strength, and turn to God.

Yes, she felt she'd understood all of it, like a very diligent pupil in class.

The first day that she was leafing through her missal—which smelled new—it fell open at a place that seemed to her to explain the Church's ever more complete interpretation, as times progressed, of Scripture and the word of God.

It was a passage from the Prophecies, which are read on Holy Saturday. A section from Isaiah, which she marked with a red pencil so as not to forget it.

"… For my thoughts are not your thoughts, neither are your ways my ways, says the Lord. For as the heavens are higher than the earth, so are my ways higher than your ways and my thoughts than your thoughts. For as the rain and the snow come down from heaven, and return not thither but water the earth, making it bring forth and sprout, giving seed to the sower and bread to the eater, so shall my word be that goes forth from my mouth; it shall not return to me empty, but it shall accomplish that which I purpose, and prosper in the thing for which I sent it."

When Paulina stepped outside, after those mystical few days, it seemed to her that she could smell—as she walked along the pavement shaded by sad, stunted trees—the flowers and the pristine chapel, and feel the peace emanating from the smiles of those nuns dressed in lay clothes, and the silence of the house of retreat… She was a woman without a cloud in her soul.

She hadn't seen fit to confess her old sins again, nor her peculiar situation, and so on the last day, at the end of the spiritual exercises, she had confessed to a collection of ridiculous wrongdoings, one such being that she had sniggered to herself about the devout ladies in the dining room.

"In my head, I called them 'snooty old witches.' That's what I thought whenever I saw them."

"And did you not think about what they might have thought of you? Yes? Good… Now, seriously: don't trust your new-found optimism. Don't think that you'll always have this feeling of absolute faith, of joy and grace… A time will come when you'll doubt everything and you'll despair. Continue then at the feet of Christ; that will be the moment God tests you. Steel your-self now."

This might seem strange, but Paulina found his words very difficult to comprehend.

"But Father, how could I doubt what I know, absolutely, to be true? Once you know, then…"

She went out into the street with that confident smile… Although, of course, slowly, that breath of light that she'd felt over these few days, even more gently than on her arrival, had been fading away. It had left her changed. Infinitely enriched, certainly. Like a river that, after returning to its source, leaves its banks loaded with seeds, life-giving soil and moisture.

Paulina inhaled the burning air that rose from the pavement and the tortured city trees… She noted that she was simply a poor woman alone, and not the martyr or the saint that she was prepared to be, that a few days earlier, she had imagined she would be.

*"This is what Father González was trying to tell me…"*

Nevertheless, she believed. Her faith was immense. For the first time, now that the mysterious light in her mind had gone, she had faith. Faith is being in the dark, and believing in what you can't see or feel.

# PART THREE

# I

Ssss… ssss… ssss.

"Saturday," thought Julián, "Saturday."

The hiss of the gas torch. Martín, dark as a gypsy, narrow face, hooked nose, was wielding the flame. Good hands, slender, a light touch. The master said that Martín showed promise. He was very young, only fifteen years old. Julián's eyes drove into him like ice picks.

Julián's station was opposite Martín's, at the table set up for four operatives, and he watched him, a faint grin playing on his lips. In the spot next to Julián, an earnest man, with a blond moustache and a friendly smile, was working. He was the workshop owner's right-hand man, and had worked with him since before the war. And the boss's place, next to Martín's, was empty… It seemed all the emptier because when Don Paco was there he filled it with his enormous belly.

Julián spun around on his stool and took out a cigarette.

"Haven't you got anything to do?"

The moustached employee was talking to him.

"Right now, I'm having a fag."

"The next job is to turn this silver into fine thread. You've used the wire-drawing machines before…"

"Yes," said Julián.

"You can get on with it then."

Julián smiled.

"What's the hurry, Don Alberto?  Don't be like that. Let me smoke the ciggie, man."

It was an odd situation with Julián in the workshop. His position wasn't entirely clear; he'd come in almost as a friend of the owner, as an apprentice, of course, but unofficially. He was a shirker who preferred to watch the others work; he'd apply himself when Don Paco was there, but the minute the fat man left, he wouldn't lift a finger.

Light and dust poured in through the large, clear-glass windows of the little basement workshop. Everything was clear, clean and simple, nothing hidden from view. There were three or four canary cages. Whenever the blowtorch stopped, the birds would create such a din with their chirping that sometimes you couldn't hear yourself think.

Julián, blue eyes flecked with yellow in a handsome, fine-featured face, was taking it all in. He smoked, hands in pockets, sensing Martín's admiration and his resentment, too. Martín wasn't so fond of Julián since he'd been "going out" with his sister…

Clouds of tobacco smoke rose in the already warm morning air, mingling with the dusty rays of sunlight that spilled down from the basement window to the table.

"Saturday," he thought. "It has to be next Saturday."

If he'd closed his eyes, the word Saturday would have been

plastered in bright letters across the deep, black, cavernous space behind his eyelids. But he wasn't closing them. He was looking at Martín, unaware that his conceited little smile showed on his face, and that he was staring.

Julián had curly, chestnut brown hair, white hands, and his voice was breaking. He would lose the plot if anyone, because of his delicate looks, called him queer. He could time a punch perfectly. He wasn't delicate then, he was very strong.

He wore a fancy tie that looked like it was covered in sparkling snakes. His overall was undone at the front, and the tie glinted in the sun. He had unfastened the overall to put his hands in his trouser pockets, his jacket was hanging up in the other room of the basement.

"Saturday." The word was like a mantra, sounding over and over his head.

The door opened and the workshop owner appeared, clutching a drawing. He was a huge man, with at least four chins, bald and red-faced. He was wearing an enormous ecru-coloured work apron, tied at the back.

"Let's go, let's go son, get to work," he said, looking at Julián. "What am I going to say to Señora Nives when she comes back after the summer. I'll have to tell her you're a waste of space."

Señora Nives, Paulina Goya, his mother's former tenant, had recommended Julián to this small workshop in the basement of the house where she lived. She'd seen the sign "Apprentice Wanted" stuck on the basement window and had gone in straight away to say hello and have a chat with the workshop's fat owner.

Don Paco couldn't have cared less what Señora Nives, his neighbour from the floor above, thought. He'd given the boy the job because she happened to come in at the right moment, and the fact that the boy had got into some trouble in another workshop might even prove useful. It was more convenient for Don Paco to give the boy a year's trial, unofficially, so he could get rid of him if he reoffended, than take on some good-for-nothing he didn't know who might pull some dirty trick, and then he'd have a load of hassle with the union if he wanted to fire him, like last time…

Señora Nives had turned up one afternoon last winter, wrapped up in her large overcoat, her face pale from the cold, and told him vaguely that she was acquainted with the family of a boy who had already begun to learn the trade in another well-known workshop.

"He fell out with the owners, I don't know why… And now I'm sure he would want to carry on working. It's no good for his mother, having him at home doing nothing, and she's a poor widow and such a good person. I lodged in her house for many years… When my husband was in America," she added hastily, looking strangely flushed.

Don Paco was a well-mannered man and smiled pleasantly at his neighbour.

"Well, nothing to worry about; you tell the boy and his mother to come see me any evening after clocking off time in the workshop: tell them they can pop up to my flat, eh?"

And that was the end of Paulina's involvement in the affair.

Just as Don Paco—having dug a little deeper into what happened at the previous workshop—had decided to tell Paulina they shouldn't come after all, the mother and son appeared at his home… The boy's misdemeanour had been too serious.

He'd falsified an invoice, and he'd done so with some nerve. A former client of the company had called to ask them to send her bill because she was going away for the summer. The boy took the message and told no one. He made a copy of the lady's invoice, which had already been drawn up, and paid himself a tidy sum. A few days later, when the workshop was ready to ask for payment, they found the lady had gone away. They didn't think anything of this and didn't discover the truth until the summer season was over. The boy, Julián Mateo, had carried on with life as normal, going to the workshop, only taking a few days off mid-summer, a special request his mother had made for him, because a friend, an old classmate, had invited him to the mountains… That's what they said. After the summer holidays Julián's workmates had been surprised to see him looking paler and more hollow-eyed than ever, and they made fun of him when the boy explained that the water in the mountains hadn't agreed with him.

Obviously, no one had pressed the matter, or given it a second thought, but when the robbery was discovered, the police investigated this "summer holiday in the mountains." The little angel had spent his holidays in houses of ill-repute, splashing his cash all over the place!

Don Paco had felt his ears turn red and was considering having it out with Señora Nives for recommending such a piece of work to him.

"And why is the boy not in juvenile detention?" he'd asked Julian's former boss.

"Man, we felt sorry for the mother… Well, you'll see. She gave back the whole amount that was stolen, and apart from that, the boy is very young, he has aptitude, and up until then we didn't have any complaints at all. The temptation must have been too much. And he'll probably never do anything like that again in his life… but…"

Don Paco was relaying all this to his wife, the same winter evening that he'd heard it. His wife was shaking her head, horrified.

They were both sitting with their feet tucked under the heated night table; María, the wife, was knitting and frowning in her usual way. She made a sour comment about their neighbour.

"I bet it was that Nives woman upstairs who recommended that piece of rubbish to you! You know her maids steal from her and she hasn't even noticed? The husband seems like a real gentleman, but as for her she's a disaster, an absolute disaster, I tell you… That poor man…"

Don Paco didn't know then—or even now, this summer— that one day, a long time hence, he would remember his wife's idle chatter, and that the table top's thick green reflection, the smell of chestnuts roasting on the coals, the yellow lamplight, the newspaper crossword he was struggling to decipher, the closed wooden shutters on the balcony, the curtains drawn against the icy cold of the street below, the click of his wife's knitting needles; all these things, much later, would reappear in his mind to torment him.

Back then, he yawned.

"Tomorrow I'll call the lady to say I don't need the boy, and that'll be an end to it."

He could have done it right then, but he was feeling too lazy. Slowly he took out his tobacco pouch and began to roll a cigarette. He didn't feel like traipsing through the dark, cold house to reach the telephone.

"The truth is," said his wife, "when I hear what boys are like nowadays, I think it's a good thing not to have had children. A lot less trouble!"

Don Paco's wife said this all the time. She wanted her husband to agree with her, but he kept quiet when she brought it up. He was quiet now too.

That was when the couple had heard a shrill ring and looked at each other.

The wife had a hunch.

"Aha… Here they are!"

"Are they?"

"Yes, you'll see! The mother and her precious child, the ones you didn't want to meet. It'll be them, you'll see… Speak of the devil."

Don Paco had felt emotions that were now forgotten but would reemerge in the fullness of time; the first was great irritation at the thought of a red-eyed widow in a veil, whom he would have to let down… He heard footsteps echoing through the house. His wife showed them into the small sitting room which must have been freezing cold, as usual, and uncomfortable, its furniture covered in a wine-coloured fabric and that unmistakeable smell of moth balls. His wife appeared in the doorway, closed the door behind her and approached him mysteriously. This also surprised him and even more so when he felt her stale breath on his face as she whispered to him.

"Watch out for the mother; if I'm not mistaken she's a 'fallen woman'… and I'm rarely wrong… She's got that look."

This was the last thing Don Paco was expecting. He felt a twinge, a sort of faint shiver run through him. Not entirely unpleasant. "Fallen women," "wicked women," "lost women," he'd always thought of them with pity and sympathy, and even with a little reverence. He couldn't help it. His house was full of reproductions of paintings by Romero de Torres, featuring dark-haired, dark-eyed women in low-cut attire, that for him were a kind of sublimation of that mysterious and attractive world. Unconsciously he cleared his throat and fixed his tie.

"Bring me the other jacket."

He'd suddenly realised that he had on the old, shabby one he always wore in the house.

His wife didn't answer but hobbled off to the bedroom, eventually coming out with the new jacket, an expression on her face that her husband tried not to notice. Don Paco stood in the doorway of the small lounge, now a vast expanse of ocean.

Things like this, small things, determine other things, and later these things mysteriously become entangled. Perhaps Paulina Nives's meddling hadn't contributed as much to Julián Mateo's ending up in Don Paco's workshop as his wife's whispered words, "watch out"…

Amalia, Julián's mother, was a tall, striking woman, and that afternoon was dressed in an astrakhan fur coat which, though it was somewhat threadbare, she wore to stunning effect. She had on a hat, gloves and a full face of makeup. Her yellow eyes would well up with tears or, just as readily, she would burst into laughter revealing a fine set of teeth, which gave her a youthful appearance. Julián appeared very young and very inoffensive in his black coat, and the overall picture of the mother and son was confusingly different to the one Don Paco had been expecting. The woman launched herself at him with her hands stretched out before he could open his mouth to speak.

"I'm so happy, so happy it's you, that my little boy is going to work with you! Paulina is forever talking about you… Saying what a kind person you are… What an honourable person you are, and how if it were her own son she couldn't want for a better job than in a workshop like yours. Of course, she's saying this to make me feel better." Amalia wiped her eyes with a handkerchief, hastily pulled from her pocket. "She knew I wanted the poor boy to study for a profession like all the men in our family! But when I became a widow, as you can imagine… things happen." Amalia put away the handkerchief and smiled. "The only thing that consoles me is this, that he's with you now, a true gentleman who'll be able to appreciate my little Julián's education.  Perhaps I shouldn't say this, but he's been a pupil at the most expensive school in Madrid…"

Don Paco, somewhat bewildered, cleared his throat. While Amalia gabbled through this speech, barely pausing for breath, he too had done things… He had greeted her in stunned silence, shaking her hand, and afterwards had collapsed into a cold armchair, where he feared he may have to remain, finding himself rather wedged in. The boy, dressed all in black, had something of an angel about him, a naivety, an innocence in his pale, round face. He was sitting politely in a chair, and held a grey hat in his gloved hands. He hadn't even taken off the white scarf. He looked like a mannequin.

"Señora… I don't know what to say… The truth is, this afternoon, I made enquiries at the workshop where your son worked last year…"

The woman's eyes widened under the brim of her hat. She wrung her hands.

"Oh wicked, wicked woman!"

Don Paco, taken aback, looked towards the boy, who continued to smile inanely while his mother again pulled out the perfume-drenched handkerchief before bursting into tears.

"I never thought Paulina would be so wicked as to talk about the other workshop! To think that I took her in like a daughter when everyone else had abandoned her! To think she could spread such slanderous rumours about an innocent child!"

Don Paco cleared his throat again.

"No, the truth is, Señora Nives didn't tell me anything. She simply told me that he had worked in another workshop and I made enquiries. They told me bad…"

Amalia stood up, and Don Paco began to panic as he realised he might have to stand up too. He decided to remain seated and gestured to Amalia to sit back down; with a gesture not unlike that of a drowning man.

"Señora; I'm explaining the situation, but I haven't said that I won't take your son on a trial basis, for a season! I'm not saying anything terrible; calm yourself, for goodness' sake…"

"But, Don Paco! The thing is my son won't go somewhere if people are going to think badly of him! The thing is that my boy, so you're aware, took that money when I was in a lot of trouble. He did it to help me out! The poor child told me he'd won the lottery! And the truth is, I can't let them cast aspersions on him. If you have children, you'll understand my situation, a woman alone with an only child. You see, when he was growing up, he had every luxury, he was used to seeing me treated like a queen while my husband was alive, and now…! Honourable work, yes to be sure, but work all the same, a lady like myself, friendly with all the ladies of the aristocracy, with all the best people in Madrid… Do you know what my close friend the Duchess of Cascojo did when she heard about the other workshop? Well, she never used them again, she was so outraged by the way they treated my son. And she'd gone there because of me, of course. Because, thanks be to God, I get on very well with, I mean we're very close, and…"

Don Paco was already beginning to like Julián's mother, and when she casually dropped a string of highborn names he began to feel a certain amount of respect for her. By the end of the conversation, it almost seemed as if Amalia were doing him a favour by entrusting her son to him.

That evening Don Paco had a heated argument with his wife and said something very unpleasant to her, that one day he would live to regret.

"I'm taking the boy on because it suits me, you silly old fool! I'll keep him on for a year unpaid. And if he oversteps the mark… He'll be out on his ear… And if I make a man out of him, well it'll be a good job done. Do you understand?"

A few days later, Julián started at the workshop. Don Paco observed him patiently. He was an easy-going, calm lad, somewhat lazy and a touch vain, but affable and cheerful, with good hands. He soon became firm friends with the young apprentice Martín, whom he kept spellbound with his tales of his life among the aristocracy. Later they became less close. Other than that, nothing of note happened in the small world of the workshop. The important thing was that the boy was useful and did his work. It's true that he spent a couple of hours a day on his other job—fitting locks, he said—that way he made a small amount of cash to help his mother.

Unconsciously, Don Paco treated him with a certain indulgence that stemmed from knowing he was on good terms with several affluent families… This was true. One private client had come to him through Amalia. But the first day they met was forgotten by then, and Don Paco, whenever he wanted to encourage Julián, would always mention Señora Nives: "What am I going to say to Señora Nives who recommended you?"

Julián, on hearing these words, threw his cigarette to the ground and went over to the wire drawing machine. Sometimes he felt as though he was suffocating in a fog of tedium.

Martín had taken his foot off the pedal and was wiping the sweat from his brow with a handkerchief. It was going to be a swelteringly hot day. The birdsong and the sunlight already streaming down the wall seemed to simmer. Julián started up the wire drawing machine and thought about a swimming pool. He had been to a swimming pool not long ago, with his girlfriend Paloma, Martín's sister, but he hadn't enjoyed the experience. Firstly, he couldn't swim, and the other thing was that Paloma was dreadfully plain and he couldn't feel proud of her body, it was ugly. If anything, he felt ashamed of those rolls of dark-skinned flesh that bulged out all over her… He wasn't thinking about a swimming pool like the one he'd seen in real life, and where he hadn't played a starring role, but like the one in the film he'd watched the previous night. A swimming pool fit for a millionaire, where stunning women emerged from the water to smile at him and sit beside him.

"Careful!… Good!"

Don Paco was inspecting his work. Julián found himself frowning as he worked on that stifling summer day.

The clock hands began to turn unbearably slowly. Julián, too, was working slowly. At one point, he walked lazily to the bathroom and came back with his hair combed and dripping water. He leant down to Don Paco's ear. Don Paco glanced at the clock, shaking his head, not pleased.

"All right then, you can go. But you know next week there's to be no leaving early. Next week we have enough work for all the staff and more if we had them."

Then the word Saturday returned for a moment to Julián's brow. He made an effort.

"Next week, if you want, I'll even do extra hours… You know I'm always willing to do whatever. Don't you Don Paco?"

"All right, all right… You're a crafty monkey, you are."

Martín, watching in silence, swallowed with an obvious movement of his Adam's apple.

Julián raised his eyebrows, smiling.

He stepped outside into the sun-filled street. A drill was opening cracks in the road surface. Workmen were shouting to each other across mounds of earth and rubble. The bar across the road cast a thin strip of shade. The swallows were screeching. Julián sheltered in that shaded strip with his hands in his pockets. He was careful not to brush his smart beige jacket against the lime-coated wall. Everything about him gave off an air of a "refined" young man, as his mother thought him, or "distinguished" as he thought himself. He was well-groomed, had an attractive physique, and although occasionally he had a few of those damn spots, like most young men his age, he considered himself good-looking. Women liked him.

"I'd like to know," he thought now, "how my witch of a mother managed to pay off the other workshop. She's got money hidden away. She makes me work like a slave, but she's always got a bit coming in from here, a bit from there… And when the pressure's on, a stream of cash pours in from somewhere. Well, I need money now. I'd like to get shot of Paloma. But I need her, for her rooms…"

Julián's mother rented out every possible room in the apartment they were living in, which was large and had an old rental contract. At one time, she'd cooked for the tenants. Now she rented out the rooms with access to a kitchen, and put a lot more into her work buying and selling dresses. She bought them from Madrid's high society ladies, millionairesses, who in one day would lose at cards the sum his mother could earn in a month from her commissions, more even, but who delighted in taking twenty-five pesetas from poor Amalia. Then, Amalia would call on the ladies she jokingly referred to as "the substitutes," ladies of a different kind… the high-class hookers. She would sell them the clothes… Amalia was fond of the aristocratic ladies whom she, with a rather old-fashioned Gallicism, deemed "chic." She enjoyed gossiping about their lives, as if they were her best friends. Julián himself had been regaled with all sorts of colourful stories… Julián believed his mother when she talked about these close friends of hers; she would drop their first names or their titles into the conversation, with a note of familiarity that was very convincing. One thing she told Julián was true; the ladies loved a good haggle with her over their last year's dresses… But the funniest thing was that she'd already heard the juiciest titbits about these ladies, from the "substitutes," who'd heard them via the men.

"The richer they are, the tighter they are with money, son," Amalia would explain, not without a certain respect.

If there was one thing Julián wasn't, it was stingy. Money was for spending, for enjoying… You only live once. That was his philosophy. Nothing like the workshop owner's. With his smock, choosing to live in that house, with the money he must have squirreled away in the bank. People like that… Slash… You cut their throats. Slash!

The boy glanced up at the house, shaped like a ship's funnel. A tall, narrow, grey-painted house, with screeching swallows flying in circles around it.

"Now's the time, in the summer, when it's noisier and the flats are empty. There won't be another chance like this. But I need cash to prepare the job."

The ground floor of the house was empty all day. The only person still there from the family was the husband. He made his money on the black market. The family could go to the countryside… The first, second, third and fourth had people in, as did the attic… The attic you could say was full to bursting, with that maggots' nest of little kids belonging to the office clerk.

"That's what my mother would happily have turned me into," he thought now, a bitter taste in his mouth, "an office clerk. Drooping shoulders and a maggots' nest of kids. No thanks."

The job at the first workshop had been down to Rosendo, another paper pusher, who wanted to marry Amalia, otherwise, his mother had wanted him to sit the exams to become a bank clerk.

He put a cigarette to his lips and lit it. Then he put his hands back in his pockets. That was how he liked to smoke.

The attic was no problem. It was useful to have the extra noise, with the kids. Although there was plenty of noise with the roadworks.

Could he get himself a passport? No, it was very dangerous. Too dangerous. He'd stick it out. Nobody would be able to accuse him if he did things properly. Afterwards he'd bide his time. But, all things considered, the passport wouldn't be a bad idea. No, caution. If he could manage to carry on as normal… But now it would be much harder. A lot harder…

The annoying thing was being underage. He'd have to get a fake passport. In theory, dealing with the questions is fine, but when it comes to it, people can't handle it. They spill the lot. But, "I'm a lot smarter than everyone thinks, damn it."

The fifth floor was empty all summer. This was a stroke of luck that he should take advantage of. Empty. A kept woman, a kind of second wife to a gentleman who wasn't satisfied with the one home. The mistress had two or three children, and lived almost like a prisoner; she never went out. Except in the summer when she went to the beach with her children.

The sixth belonged to the bosses. They didn't have any servants. The woman could manage the shopping and housework perfectly well herself. Luckily. There was something rather bourgeois about her, though she was very well-dressed. Julián had studied this lady's entire life. Her comings and goings. The time she spent alone in the house… She had a cast in one eye. That didn't stop her glaring with the other one, the old witch.

The seventh floor, between the "masters" and the overcrowded attic, was also empty. The seventh floor belonged to the Nives… Julián had been startled a few days earlier, when he thought he'd seen Paulina. It was in his interest that Paulina's flat was empty. Essentially, the whole thing relied on those two floors, the fifth and the seventh, being empty. The best time was midday.

He asked the concierge:

"Has Señora Nives come back?"

The concierge, who fortunately was deaf, asked him to repeat the question twice, and then replied:

"Yes, she was here for a few days. She's gone again. There's no one at home now."

Time to seize his chance. Everything was falling into place.

He was smoking like a chimney. A tiny dark-eyed boy in scruffy clothes was watching him smoke admiringly. Julián noticed, and for the boy's benefit, but without looking at him, began to exhale smoke from all over. Nose, ears, eyes… He was very good at these kinds of tricks. The small boy was open-mouthed.

After a short while, Julián grew bored of being watched. "Someone might notice me and…" His shirt clung to him with all the sweat. Now he knew how careful he had to be so as not to leave any evidence behind for the police.

When he came to the corner, another disagreeable surprise was waiting for him. Paulina. There was no doubt. He knew her perfectly. She'd lived in his house for many years. And by the look of it, she had regained her good looks. Her youth. She was walking down the sunny side of the street, wearing a straw-coloured jacket and carrying a small bag, as if she had been on a short trip away. She looked lost in happy thoughts.

"Julián," she said kindly and almost joyfully, when she saw him.

"How are things, Paulina?"

Julián showed off his best smile. He knew how to keep his thoughts hidden and how to lose well.

"On your way home from work? Yes? I'm so pleased. One of these days I'll go and see your mother."

Julián, inside, very deep inside, swore at her. He kept on smiling as she moved away. Afterwards he realised he hadn't asked her if she planned to stay in Madrid for the whole summer.

# II

Antonio's yellow car drove past the cemetery gate on the road from León, raising clouds of dust behind it. So much dust that Blanca, even with her veil, was momentarily blinded and began to cough. Her eyes followed the car. Antonio hadn't stopped when he saw his mother-in-law. He'd kept driving down, towards the valley, as if it were of no consequence, even though he knew how much walking tired Blanca.

It was hot. An August heat. The cicadas were singing. It had been several days since the last storm and the air was full of an angry humming, of flies, beetles, dust, pungent smells which seemed to emanate from the hard leaves of the trees.

Blanca was sweating.

Her attire was most unsuitable for climbing up to the top of the graveyard, dressed as she was all in black. She always wore black, in a strict, never-ending mourning since the war, and a black gauze veil covered her face.

Fortunately, the cemetery keeper provided her with all the flowers she could want for her dead, and Mariana's too. He also made sure she could place a few flowers on the engineer Goya's grave, a common grave he shared with various other villagers, and on his poor wife's grave, which had been very hard to find.

Blanca's mind was filled with serene thoughts during those moments spent in the garden of grass and light, where Villa de Robre's dead lay sleeping.

Life was buzzing around her. Small lizards scuttled over the cracked, fallen tombstones. Large butterflies fluttered through the air. The days when it had rained, especially, it was a lively, intensely exciting world. Blanca was astonished by all the different colours of grasshopper: green, blue, reddish brown, striped… She was amazed by the dragonflies clustered on the pylon by the entrance, where she changed the water in the jugs.

It was more than a graveyard; it was teeming with the lives of countless tiny creatures, and Blanca liked to pray there, too, for the souls of her dead, and she venerated their decaying bodies that would one day be resurrected in glory. Blanca knew that even when this cemetery no longer existed and the dust of the dead had spread to all corners of the earth, every atom of this dust would be reunited and the material regenerated on the last day of Humanity.

Now Blanca, as she left the cemetery behind her on that suffocatingly hot day, was thinking about her daughter Rita, who certainly was fated to die without knowing anything of life, and who didn't wish to prepare for death. She couldn't even bear to speak of it. She would yawn and get bored as soon as prayers started. All she wanted to do was go for walks with Antonio, make plans for the "future," invent new interior designs for her flat in Madrid or think about restyling her outfits or playing cards. Since finding out that Paulina had gone to Madrid, Rita had become more animated.

"She's not very nice that Paulina, is she Mamá?"

*"My goodness, she knows,"* Blanca was thinking. *"And why wouldn't she… when Antonio hardly bothers to hide it. He scurries off like some small animal to whatever he desires. And Antonio is everything to her… While I… why am I conscious of these things, of so many things?"*

A few months earlier Blanca had tried to sound out her friend Mariana, by asking her about Paulina.

"Do you think the girl is happy?"

Mariana, who had just finished proudly recounting a business negotiation with one of her tenant farmers—the most astute man in the area—during which Mariana had countered all his little tricks one by one. Mariana, who had just finished impressing Blanca with her business acumen, when it came to the question about her daughter-in-law, raised her eyebrows in surprise.

"Happy? Of course she's happy… I'm not saying she hasn't been through a lot. She had a bad few months when Eulogio was in America. And I confess there was a time when she wasn't my favourite person. But I've made up for it. And I don't mind telling you so. When I saw that she was going ahead with the child on her own and she paid back, to the last centime, the money I lent her when she came out of prison, my dear, I changed my mind about her. It's true that Eulogio could have made a better match, but now as it's turned out, I'm very content."

Blanca sighed. She had asked about Paulina's well-being, not Mariana's. It was always the same. Mariana had no idea of the sentimental drama unfolding in her own house. Blanca clearly recalled her own son José's verdict on the woman, back when José spent all his time in Mariana's house, when in Blanca's imagination, Mariana was dangerous, and morally detestable: "I'll never meet another person with such an untainted view of those around them," said José. "She's simply not capable of uncovering any kind of indecent behaviour, at least not of a sexual nature, the kind that mothers fear most."

Despite all this, Blanca could not comprehend how her intelligent friend Mariana didn't suspect a thing when it came to the amorous liaison between Paulina and Antonio, or how Eulogio was so calm. Her own son Joaquín, Alfonso… Well, Alfonso was usually away with the fairies, but… It's true that people look at everything from their own perspective. Humans observe other humans, finding in others their own hidden flaw that at some point begins to eat away at them. Those that crave luxury see luxury, the greedy, hidden money; those that are in love suspect others might find the same reasons to love the object of their love. Simple people don't understand that a person can be good and bad at the same time, and so they always look at them one-sidedly. And Blanca viewed all this through her eyes which were not dazzled by any hidden desire, and didn't understand that spiritual beings, like artists, see beyond what others see. Artists, because they are interested in everything, delving into everything, transforming everything. And because they can. People like her, because they have transcended all human interests and so view life from a universal standpoint, as if from on high. But if anyone had explained this to Blanca, Blanca would never have understood. It would have been far too complicated for her.

This morning she was worrying that she knew too much, and that perhaps her knowing these things stemmed from some terrible wickedness in her nature. "It can't be true," she had thought many times. But it invariably turned out that the horrible and repugnant thing she had discovered was true.

"Antonio didn't see me, what bad luck," she murmured to herself that day, on the dusty road home from the graveyard.

But she knew that, actually, he had seen her and that he hadn't felt like stopping the car. She didn't want to admit it. "He'll have been on his way back from the mines... He said that one of these days he was going to visit the mines, that he needed to for his book. That one time he had gone, and had been shocked by a vision of hell, those sweating, half-naked men in the deep galleries that echoed with the sound of explosions, the beams of light from their hand-held lamps like tortured souls in the darkness. Yes, he'll have been to the mines"... But she knew that he'd been to León and that whatever he'd intended to do in the town, he'd failed. "The poor man is desperate," she thought then, more sincerely. "He must have heard nothing from Paulina."

Blanca hadn't heard anything from Paulina either since those joyful few lines, which she believed were an answer to her night of prayer. She thought that Eulogio shouldn't give up on his wife, he should go and fetch her, love her a little more and... But better, perhaps, that she spend a little more time far away from here, away from the sceptical and elegant Mariana, and above all, far away from the madly egotistical Antonio, and gradually she'd forget, now that she could understand the dreadful consequences of the love affair.

When she arrived at the village, she was tempted to slip into its cool streets, rest a little in Mariana's house. She would invite her for lunch, Mariana managed her house impeccably.

Everything was pleasant, spotless, and organised in the manor house. Mariana would be pleased to see her; she could even take a siesta to avoid the bother of walking the mile or so to the castle in full sun, and call home to say that she wasn't coming. Then she decided against it. She had felt a little awkward in Mariana's company since she'd been keeping Paulina's secret. Mariana would be stunned when she found out about her daughter-in-law. Her daughter-in-law's unbelievable conversion.

And when it came to these kinds of things, as with the others, Mariana was innocent. Perhaps the idea was unsettling, but Blanca became quite anxious as she imagined Mariana's astonished expression on hearing of this "hysteria," which she would find incomprehensible, and then would come the assumptions and the suspicions.

"Paulina wasn't quite right after her illness," she would say eventually, with confidence. "We'd noticed she was acting rather strangely. I'll never forgive myself for letting Blanca get so involved, when the poor girl's nerves were so fragile…" And, of course, she would look at her, at Blanca, reproachfully.

It had been Mariana herself who had called Blanca, when Paulina developed complications, including a fever that Joaquín, Blanca's son, tentatively diagnosed as "brain fever." Mariana, who was finding all this very disconcerting, began to regret bringing her daughter-in-law to the Villa de Robre mansion, and remarked to Blanca: "Perhaps the sanatorium in Madrid would have been a better idea… I… in our family we're all so healthy, we're all mentally strong, and these delusions my daughter-in-law suffers, I must admit I find somewhat alarming. Sometimes she says terrible things about Eulogio… Don't listen to her. You know disturbed people often attack those they love most. Any psychology text book would tell you the same."

Blanca remembered Paulina's illness, her contact with a sick, sweating Paulina who, in the grip of her delirious fever, would scream that she didn't want to die. She seemed like a woman in agony.

"I still haven't lived. I need to know why so many things have happened. I need to know. I can't die like this, without understanding…"

When she was gravely ill, Blanca had called a confessor. Mariana couldn't refuse to have him in the house. She didn't refuse. She received him politely. It was Paulina who had flatly rejected him.

"No, Father. I don't need it… What for? Even supposing that I had to answer to God. When something has felt wrong to me, I haven't done it. As for the things I think I've done well, why would I confess? My only regret is that I haven't done any of the things you would call sins. Yes, I regret everything I didn't do. In the name of what didn't I do these things? In the name of absurdity. I believed in love… Absurd… No. One should never, ever deny life as I've denied myself. Grand words… Love, duty… I only regret what I haven't lived."

It had been a terrifying scene: the woman with her swollen face, red with fever, trembling—in a room that despite efforts made to the contrary, reeked of sickness—her white teeth gleaming as, laughing, she showed the priest the door with a trembling hand. They had to get the confessor out of there.

Of course, while she appeared lucid, Paulina wasn't quite thinking rationally at the time, but still Blanca had been struck that a person could regret not having done bad things. From then on, she had paid close attention to her. On a physical level, she'd watched her progress, improving little by little. When Paulina showed her kindness and gratitude, she had tried her greatest resource, the lives of the saints, which she read to her during her convalescence. She had failed. How Paulina would laugh when one of the saints' stories described the phenomenon of levitation or other such ostentatious miracle… "Absurd," would be her verdict, once again. She would ask Blanca to excuse her while she cried with laughter. Then that thing had started, that madness with Antonio. Blanca imagined or wanted to imagine that the love between them was no more than a torment of the mind. But she could "see" this torment. It was so clear… Now, since Paulina had left, Antonio had made two trips to León and had come back furious from both. One of them was this morning. Not that he'd said he was going to León. But Blanca "knew."

She arrived at the castle feeling almost liquefied, her clothes drenched, though she had taken the short cut over the Roman bridge. She felt her gauzy veil sticking to her face. It was gone lunchtime. They were waiting for her anxiously, because most of the family were hungry, but it hadn't occurred to them to go and look for her.

"Come on old girl, where have you been?… A woman's place is in the home… You know the saying," said the Count cheerfully.

"Mamá," screamed Rita.

She turned around startled, swiping at what her daughter

was pointing to, an insect as hard as a scarab beetle, pink and gold like a jewel.

Antonio said: "Man, I had one almost exactly like that on my neck when we went on that dreadful expedition to Las Duras with Eulogio. It was gold and green. They're obviously sociable little creatures; do you know what they are? They're pretty, especially when they're not landing on you…"

No one knew what the shiny flying insects were called. Not even Joaquín.

"Joaquín, you should know; you're the resident scientist…"

"Who? Me? I find keeping up my knowledge of human anatomy too hard, let alone beetles…"

"I suppose Father Pérez has had lunch," said Blanca sitting down to the table.

"Yes, Mamá… Don't worry. Say Grace, Papá… Father Pérez had his lunch as usual in his room."

Father Pérez had no teeth and had to have special meals.

The Count blessed the family table. Blanca, who had barely had time to hastily wash her face and hands, was feeling over-heated and dirty. The hum of summer filtered in through the half-lowered blinds. The dining room, a great glass-panelled circular room, was very beautiful.

Antonio's face was pale and ugly, his eyes two slits of ill omen. Blanca thought that sometimes it was as if Antonio's pupils ran the whole width of the narrow slits of his eyes, rendering them completely black. This didn't bode well. Suddenly, he raised his head and said, quite naturally:

"I'll have to go to Madrid this afternoon."

There was a silence. The Count continued enjoying his pasta greedily, and Joaquín and Ana didn't look up from their plates.

Only Rita and Blanca stopped eating.

"Why?" asked Rita.

Antonio looked at her and frowned. His face was broken up by the stripes of shadow and light from the blinds. "I need to go."

Rita's eyes filled with tears. Antonio ignored them. He carried on eating. But after a few minutes he couldn't ignore them anymore. Rita pushed her plate away and began to sob loudly. There was a small commotion. Everyone joined in. Antonio protested several times, impatiently…

"But don't be silly, come on, but…!"

Afterwards, he went out into the garden slamming the door behind him. His mother-in-law went out after him. "I'll tell him… I'll tell him now…" Blanca was thinking. But she couldn't utter the words she had prepared. Her strength was improvisation. Antonio was already coming back, she saw him coming through the rose bushes, with almost the same excitement as a hunter who has spotted his prey… She didn't need to say anything; he spoke first.

"I'll bow down to that spoilt little girl and of course I won't go, if she doesn't want me to. But you must agree this is unacceptable. If she doesn't want me to, I won't go to Madrid, or anywhere else. But one day I'll have to go. Because I need some information for my book. I don't think you want a man to do nothing, sit there twiddling his thumbs all blessed day long."

Antonio's book! Blanca didn't understand a thing about books, but she was sure her son-in-law was never going to write one. From time to time he would read the family a few complicated, disjointed paragraphs, and that was it; but in any case, this book was the constant, ridiculous cover for all his little schemes. Blanca was flushed. With a curtness that was unusual for her she said:

"You all go after what you desire, and you want it straight away." It was a timid protest, but Antonio turned on her.

"Did you not get your chapel? Didn't you desire that and now you have it? Were you not happy your daughter married me, to have your chapel, your plaster saints and your chaplain?"

He didn't wait for Blanca to answer, and left her, drained and sad, among the flowers teeming with buzzing bumblebees.

# III

"Listen to me, Paulina. I know you don't believe me now, but you may encounter setbacks in this new life of yours. I'll always be available to help you."

These were Father González's words that morning. Paulina, bewildered, hadn't taken them in. Now she thought that Father González was worried because she hadn't appeared stupid to him, but her confession had been that of a stupid woman. And she hadn't uttered a single word about her problems.

"I've never explained my problems to anyone. And, what's more, I know exactly what I must do… I'd already confessed. That's enough."

She said it out loud. Sunlight was seeping through even the tiniest cracks between the joints of the wooden shutters and warming the thin walls, in such a way that the darkness was becoming tinged with red and it was like being inside an oven. As soon as she'd arrived home, Paulina had stretched out on the bed, and was lying quietly, unmoving, her hair soaked with sweat. Despite everything she felt an urge to talk, to explain herself, just at the point the moment to talk and to explain herself had passed.

It was as she left the retreat and her eyes were bombarded by the harsh colours of summer in the city, and her ears by the noise of the streets, that it struck her that she hadn't spoken for days, and she felt a desire to do so. Not, of course, a desire to explain her problems, but her spiritual discoveries… To pour them into ears where they could fall like seeds, pour them in so they could grow among people whose spirit was awakened, but who didn't yet know the great truths, the amazing beauty, the meaning of life hidden behind such an unenticing exterior: the obscure, distant world of the Church, with its pious women, its nuns, its prosperous convents, its sermonising about modern ways.

She was engrossed in this wish, walking from the Metro station towards her house, when she bumped into Julián. He had an incredibly smug, foolish grin on his face. Paulina shuddered. And she felt suddenly ashamed by the nonsense she'd spouted to the priest, who had given her so much of his valuable time, when she hadn't wanted to waste hers explaining her affairs… "I thought 'snooty old witches'… Father González will think I want to pass myself off as a silly schoolgirl."

Her overheated and dusty flat, with its sad, neglected air, did nothing to improve her mood; part disappointment in herself, part desire to communicate with another human being.

There wasn't even a letter waiting for her. Nothing. A mustiness, a smell of mothballs, of loneliness… Then she remembered Concha and Rafael and decided to call them. She'd had no news of them for nearly two years, but they were a likeable couple and full of intellectual curiosity. She'd met them in the distant past when she'd been going out with Víctor, and they would come to his intellectual gatherings in cafés. They were studying philosophy and literature back then and had progressive ideas. They were married before the establishment of the National Movement and Paulina lost touch with them, like she had with so many other friends, because they'd moved out to the provinces.

Because of the war, Paulina had spent many difficult and lonely years in Madrid—in the boarding house run by Julián Mateo's mother, Amalia—but one day she'd run into Concha and Rafael again by chance. Paulina's life changed hugely when she re-entered their orbit. Concha earned her living as a journalist, Rafael worked in an office and had gained a reputation as a poet. They confessed to not having a centime between them, but that didn't stop them enjoying themselves and having a busy social life. Their get-togethers were famous... The couple would use all their ingenuity to decorate their house as if for a carnival and the guests would arrive with bottles under their arms. Once they'd been there for a while, all the partygoers would have drunk a considerable amount and be feeling euphoric. They would all talk about whatever they felt like. They would criticise the establishment or the establishment-to-be and embrace all the novelties that a life among the intelligentsia entailed: the latest forms of art, the latest philosophical theories... Concha and Rafael's friends made themselves feel intelligent simply by constantly meeting up to criticise or accept as they saw fit. Their motto was "a short, intense life." By intensity they meant being interested in everything they saw. They assumed it would be "short," because when it came to eating, and the hours they kept, they flouted all the rules of healthy living... As well as their own meetings, the couple would attend whatever ambassadors' cocktail parties, or banquets for foreign scholars were taking place in Madrid. Concha used to say that this was part of her work as a journalist. In fact, they were so engaging, holding forth about so many things, and joking about so many others that Paulina had begun to find them serious and oppressive.

When Eulogio came back from America he wanted nothing to do with his wife's friends. He found them ridiculous. Paulina had stopped seeing them entirely.

That morning when her house had seemed so gloomy after the retreat, Paulina dialled the couple's number… Luckily, they were in Madrid, and they invited her to have an aperitif at their place, with enthusiasm. They were sorry they couldn't invite her to lunch because they were invited somewhere themselves. "Ah," they said. "We've moved to a new apartment."

Now Paulina was sweating out the alcohol she'd ingested on their cool terrace, and was feeling dreadful. Her friends, it turned out, had settled very comfortably in a large flat. Chatty, as ever, and kind as always and yet, utterly transformed. They had found some obscure money-making scheme, but this wasn't what interested Paulina. The interesting thing was observing their inquisitive glances, their warmth, their wanting Paulina to introduce them to "that moneybags Nives you've married… You kept that quiet…"

"I'm a business man now too, as it happens, Paulina. Don't be embarrassed about your husband's fortune; it's not a bad thing," said Rafael.

Paulina didn't know how to begin to talk about the feelings she was having. It seemed that the couple's interest in spiritual discovery had dwindled now that they were living comfortably.

Paulina drank and listened to Concha's chitchat and her

malicious gossip about people she didn't know, until eventually she could get a word in to explain her new outlook on life. The only possible salvation in life.

"I think we're going through an era of absolute paganism," she began. "Everything you're telling me now, we've read about in the time of decadence, of pagan culture… If there's nothing more than trickery and cruelty, robbery on a grand scale and an unbridled sexual obsession…"

Concha interrupted her, annoyed.

"You sound like a puritan, my dear, but honestly there are a few things you need to know about Catholicism. I tell you that there's never been the devotion to the Church there is now, and I tell you too that Rafael and I are convinced that it's dreadfully antisocial not to be fully behind the Church. I won't say we've been converted. That would be ridiculous, given that we were baptised when we were born, but we practise publically like most of our friends… There's none of this paganism you mention; and the fact is that no form of entertainment or way of life is incompatible with godliness. You have a strange way of looking at things… If you give it some thought, it'll take away your fears about religion."

Concha's speech in defence of religion had made Paulina's head swim, even more than the drink. And so, as she lay on her bed in the burning midday heat, the woman's face—small, apelike, hair styled in the latest fashion, her dressing gown in the style of a white sleeveless tunic, gold sandals and painted toenails—span around her… Yes, spinning around her brain along with the serene, sad face of the priest and his words and her own silly giggles while she was confessing. "I thought when I saw those ladies: 'snooty old witches'. It wasn't funny. Not funny in the slightest. Concha wasn't funny either… It can't be true that of all our friends the only one who has been estranged from religion has been me. Something isn't right, something doesn't fit here."

She hadn't been able to tell Concha that she was a believer. Concha irritated her more than those prudish people who are shocked that a Christian woman like Santa Teresa could walk barefoot. "A new life," said Father González. "You don't need to change a single thing," said Concha. Now everything that Paulina thought about was irritating her, and once that wave of happiness, serenity, and goodness that had enveloped her over the last few days had passed, she was feeling uncomfortable, as if she didn't fit in anywhere. Her eyes closed with the heat. She fell asleep. A few minutes later she woke up startled; someone was at the door. In her dreams, the bell bored into her brain.

"Don't be alarmed," the concierge said, studying the dress that Paulina had just fastened. "I've brought the things you ordered from the shop. There was no one here when they came so they left them with me, and look… The ice is melting in this bucket. Also, I forgot to give you the letters that arrived while you were away…"

The concierge went right through to the kitchen with the delivery. The letters, which she left on the kitchen table, were crumpled. She'd taken them out of her pockets and they smelled vaguely of fish. Paulina glanced at them, without touching them, while she was talking to the woman. There was one from Mariana and the other must be from Blanca and two, definitely, from Antonio.

"Go on with you, don't tell me you're cold. If you're feeling cold you must be really sick," said the concierge as she eyed

Señora Nives, who had shivered and whose face was unusually pale. Paulina could see the inquisitive eyes, the mouth adorned with its curly strands of moustache.

"Is there anything you need? You sure?… Right!"

"Go," said Paulina, "I don't need anyone."

She'd meant to sound polite, but somehow it came out as if she were ejecting the woman, who tutted resentfully. To tell the truth, she was ejecting the woman. That morning she had longed for someone to listen, but not her.

It was five in the afternoon and the heat in the house was relentless. Paulina wished night would fall so she could take the mattress out onto the balcony and sleep there, in the fresh air. Time was ticking by so slowly and it felt like a thousand hours had passed since daybreak.

She was worried, frowning. The smell of the coffee she'd prepared permeated the room. She wasn't hungry, but she needed to drink coffee so she could smoke. Her throat felt dry.

The telephone began to ring suddenly, in the small dining room, and Paulina felt a huge rush of emotion, so intense that it took her a few moments to go to it. A woman's voice on the other end of the line began to chatter.

"Paulina… Is that you, Paulina?"

Paulina gradually calmed down, disappointed.

"Yes, Amalia, it's me."

"Ah! Well, you weren't saying anything!… My little Julián told me that you were back, that he met you this morning, and you know how fond of you I am; so I'm calling to see if we can arrange a catch up. What is it, holidays over?"

"I… don't know… It depends," said Paulina stupidly, realising that at that precise moment she herself had no idea.

"I understand, Paulina; you never did give much away, my dear. Do you remember when you lived in my house? Who would have thought that in the end the mysterious Señor Nives would appear? By the way, what was it, in the end?"

*"What was it? Eulogio? Who is Amalia talking about? Eulogio doesn't exist; or at least not the one I was waiting for."*

"I don't know what you're talking about…"

"The child you were expecting, woman… Was it a boy or a girl?"

"It died… I think it was another boy. Yes, it was another boy."

Paulina sounded relieved and distracted at the same time.

"Jesus, you really are a strange one, sweetheart. And how are you, happier now or are you as low as you were this winter?"

"I don't know, Amalia."

"You don't know? I have to say you are the most unique person I've ever known. Yes, yes, and given that I've known a lot of people in my life, from the upper classes to… Anyway, all kinds of people. And little Miguel? Still not very affectionate?"

*"I don't know,"* Paulina was about to reply, when it occurred to her that it would be an absurd response and she smiled at Amalia's tone. If a person adheres strictly to the truth every time they answer a question, a conversation can become a game that makes no sense at all.

"Miguel is very well. How are things with you, Amalia?"

"Well, my dear, I've got my cinema in the evenings, and my friends, and my dreams… My son won't let me marry Rosendo, but I think we'll persuade him in the end. The boy loves me too much, that's what it is, and he's jealous of Rosendo, but in one sense, he's right. Rosendo (between you and me) is a decent man, but he doesn't belong to the same social class as we do."

It was Amalia's eternal topic of conversation. She could go on for hours, tirelessly, poring over the same subject.

Paulina gently lowered the receiver, resting it on the small table. Amalia's voice kept on relentlessly, churning out story after story, most of them made-up, and Paulina smiled distractedly at the chatter. Amalia had been very kind to her when she had arrived from Barcelona, Miguel in her arms, all those years ago. Paulina would never forget it.

Amalia's home was dark, damp and sad—a lower-ground floor in a mansion house in old Madrid—a place that was highly unsuitable for a little boy like Miguel... The lightbulbs in the apartment were always too weak, and the guests would stumble along like ghosts through a maze of corridors, but in spite of all this, Paulina had lived there for five or six years, not only because the rent was ridiculously low, but also for the simple reason that to her Amalia seemed like the friendliest, most optimistic woman she had met since the utter carnage of the war.  Yes, Amalia's smile had lifted her heart. Because Paulina, imperceptibly, gradually, had become used to the curtness back then, when people wouldn't say excuse me when they bumped into each other in the street, but would simply glare. Back then you'd see many men, women too, standing all alone on the pavement and gesturing, talking to themselves. And all the talk on the trams, on the Metro, in the parks was driven by an obsessive hunger... Talk filled with desire, the talk of ravenous wolves...

Amalia had told her immediately that she would, through a friend, get Paulina's ration card sorted; that this was no problem, and that there was always a solution... When she came into her life, dressed in one of those kimonos she always wore in the house, with her cheerful bustle as she walked, her hair full of little papers and her inexhaustible chatter, it was a huge relief for Paulina. Amalia told her straight away that she loved children, and Miguel, so blond and healthy made her happy; she told her that if Ernesto had lived, she would have had six children and that that divine little creature would always be well looked after in her home, even if his mother went out to work. And Miguel had held out his arms to her with complete confidence…

Now Paulina picked up the receiver again because there had been a small pause in the torrent of words. She panicked.

"So, Paulina, I asked you what you thought."

"Ah, perfect… that's perfect…"

"*Maybe that was completely wrong… It's ten past five already… Poor Amalia!*"

"Yes, clearly; that's what I think. My son is at the workshop on a trial basis. He complains and he's right, because even with a trade you can't make enough to live on, or with a career either, we're all agreed on that, because this is what he says about Rosendo: I'm not throwing away my youth to become a boring office worker like him. Wasting all the hours in the day working and not earning more than enough to eat badly, and not to be able to get married. Because, of course, the boy, in a way, is right in not wanting me to marry Rosendo, because poor Rosendo doesn't earn enough to support me and I would have to keep working…"

Paulina put the receiver back on the small table and Amalia's words continued to pour out unabated in that same haphazard way. Paulina sighed quietly and settled back on the arm of the chair, beside the telephone. She debated whether to light a cigarette or not. Amalia's boy, "Juliancín," was a halfwit. The woman had made enormous sacrifices to send him to the best schools in Madrid, but he didn't manage to pass his bachillerato in any of them. Paulina had taught him maths and knew what that "extraordinary" brain—according to his mother—was capable of. There was one time only when that boy had surprised her with a clear logic, when she was giving him one of her pep talks, a longer one than usual.

"I don't study because I don't want to die of starvation," was the astonishing conclusion Julián had reached one day, when Paulina had tried to pin him down. "If you're so clever,"—Julián used the informal "tú" with Paulina, even though his mother Amalia addressed her politely as "usted"—"and you live like Cinderella, like my mother says, and Pili, in number three, who's really stupid but, according to my mother, can afford a grand lifestyle, then I don't want to be that clever…"

When Julián shared this with her, Paulina wasn't sure how to respond. It was true that Paulina's existence at the time took courage and was exhausting. She would get up at night to correct the pupils' homework, and from all those years ago she could still remember the yellowish glow from the lightbulb, which she would pull closer to the table in her room with a system of weights, or, when there were restrictions, the white pool of light from the oil lamp on the exercise books; and the feel of the new dawn rising as she finished her work and turned off the artificial light… The dawn in her room in the boarding house was a grey stain behind the barred window that looked out onto a patio. If you went right up to the glass you could see a grey wall as well, and the grey creatures of the earth, the rats, scurrying between the stone floor of the patio and the sewer… She would get up at that hour because she dedicated the mornings to her son and spent every minute of them with him, always in the fresh air, and in the afternoons, she was busy, in the early part of the evening too, teaching classes. Her only friend was young Antonio Nives, who now and again would come from Barcelona to see her and take her out to dinner, or would accompany her—with the inevitable presence of the little boy—on her morning walks, to "educate" her on his latest literary and artistic discoveries… It wasn't a very appealing life, obviously, in the eyes of that plump, lazy boy who was constantly regaled with tales of the aristocracy, but had grown up among poor people obsessed by their desire for material pleasures, and for whom certain precious gifts in life—like the pure joy that Paulina felt in fulfilling her duties despite Spartan conditions, in Eulogio's love that she sensed deep inside—would be incomprehensible. She couldn't tell him that in her opinion poor Pili, a manicurist with a married lover, led a life that was base and stupid and deeply sad, and that she didn't covet in the slightest Pili's fancy watch or her fur coat, and that the very reason one studies and trains is to reach this level of detachment. "Paulina… Hello?… Paulina?"

Paulina picked up the receiver, startled. "I'm here Amalia; I don't know what happened there."

"Yes, I think we got cut off… Did you hear what I said?"

Paulina was cautious. "I think so…"

"I was telling you about the boy's future, my son's. What I'd like to do is set him up in his own jewellery workshop, but it costs so much! It's frightening, don't you agree? And to think how well off we used to be; if Ernesto were alive there would be no problem at all…"

Paulina had become so accustomed to hiding her smile when Amalia prattled on about her Ernesto, that she kept a straight face even now when her vivacious friend couldn't see her.

Don Ernesto, through his wife's fantastical imaginings, had succeeded in dying twice. When Paulina arrived at the boarding house, the portrait of Don Ernesto, adorned with black ribbon, presided over Amalia's room; the good man was, in his widow's imagination, a paragon of perfection. Even in his death throes he had been exemplary, giving advice to others, praising his wife… But she, the poor Amalia, had fallen victim to some unscrupulous villains who had robbed her of her son's inheritance, taking advantage of her innocence… "Ah, but I am in litigation, my dears, I am in the middle of litigation. My friend, the Countess of Parrilla is assisting me in this matter. Soon, God willing, I will once more live in the manner to which I am accustomed…"

Amalia spoke so convincingly that one had no choice but to believe her. She herself believed everything she said. She believed she was a gorgeous woman, who had many suitors, among whom she preferred the kindly office worker Don Rosendo, but even this part of the story was tragic because of the difference in their social standing… She believed her son was a loving, angelic little boy and the fact that he was always swearing and didn't study was simply proof of the child's genius. She believed that her home was a palace, a little shabby perhaps, but with a lick of paint would be a magnificent chateau. She believed that in times gone by the boarding house's dingy, ramshackle dining room had been a ballroom where she and her Don Ernesto had thrown lavish parties…

When Don Ernesto, looking exactly as he did in his portrait—with a shifty expression and tiny piggy eyes—turned up one afternoon with two suitcases, Paulina almost screamed. She had opened the door and was the only one at home…

This apparition was however too real to be a phantom. Paulina calmed down, though her calm state ended when Don Ernesto, his breath reeking of wine, told her she was a cutie.

Once inside the house, the man headed straight for his bedroom, burst out laughing at the black ribbons on his portrait and began cursing. He took over the house… Amalia, when she arrived back a little later, threw her arms around his neck and said he was a rogue for letting her think he had perished in the war. Don Rosendo, the food supplies clerk, turned grey, almost as if he were the one who'd died, and he tried desperately to catch Amalia's eyes. The following day he moved out of the boarding house. And Paulina, a short while later, did the same… Paulina decided to look for some sunny rooms in a private house, because Miguel was getting older and she was earning a lot more with her classes. But most of all, she didn't want to have to put up with the boorish and philandering Don Ernesto's impertinent remarks, or listen to him rowing with Amalia, or vomiting in the middle of the night after his drinking binges, or the insults to his wife, that the boy Julián had learned to imitate.

Barely a month after Paulina left Amalia's boarding house, the infamous Ernesto really did die, rather improbably from indigestion, because of a bet, according to Amalia over the telephone, between shuddering sobs. Paulina, on her way to the funeral parlour, was still unsure if she'd heard the story correctly, or if Amalia, confused by yet another of her husband's tricks, was exaggerating again.

In the same way that she clearly remembered, from her time in that dark house, how it felt to work until the small hours, and how it felt that in room number three, Pili and Amalia were always whispering about clothes, second-hand jewellery, and other things they were embarrassed to talk about in front of her, the day of the wake, too, was forever engraved in her memory. She had gone to offer her support to Amalia… It was a cold winter's day, and the sky was opaque and hard like emery rock. Leaning against the doorway of the fruit shop, next to the house, stood Julián, smoking. The boy's attitude was one of supreme disinterest, complete indifference. Paulina thought: "*Amalia must surely be making it up. Don Ernesto has gone off with that foreign woman who took him to Tangiers during the war.*" (Because this was Don Ernesto's version of the first time he died; a version that in Paulina's mind seemed quite as fantastical as Amalia's.) Julián, who was friends with the fruit seller's son, disappeared inside the shop when he saw Paulina, through the small, dark opening behind the bunches of bananas, the shelves of apples, pears, and late grapes… There was no one there, when she peered inside.

Paulina went into Amalia's house and this time was met with real death, an actual dead person—who had barely lasted two days of battling the chronic indigestion caused by thirty platefuls of "calamares en salsa verde"—and his widow who tearfully declared that there had never been a man like Don Ernesto, such a gentleman, so refined, so well-mannered. And now he had died, at the very point when he was in litigation over the large family inheritance…

It was a strange day for Paulina, in that gloomy house, listening to the chorus of lamentations, sincerely expressed by various strange friends of Amalia, and to the understanding silence of Rosendo, the family friend; small, round, kindly, taking care of all the arrangements for the burial.

"Paulina… Did you say something?"

"No, Amalia; I'm listening."

"Yes, my dear; well don't despair about that thing…"

Paulina was startled as she came back to the black mouthpiece of the receiver.

"What thing, Amalia?"

"The thing with your son… You say that I've brought Julián up badly. Yes, yes; I know you've been saying it, though not to me… But look, I, at least, have a loving boy who'd do anything for me, and you, my dear, with your harsh punishments and the high expectations you have of the boy, are paying for it now… Of course, poor Miguelito, how can he trust you? And he'd be right not to, even if you are sorry."

Paulina was puzzled, until she remembered that this was another of Amalia's favourite topics; Julián's upbringing. She'd guessed that Paulina, in the past, had been frustrated with the boy. "*But, where did she get that idea about Miguel? Did I tell the woman some nonsense last winter? Last winter I was a horrible, mean, bitter woman.*" She sighed.

"Amalia. It's so good of you to have called… I've got things to do now and you too; I don't want to hold you up, I know you're always busy… Yes, yes… I promise I'll come and see you some time soon. Yes, I promise I will."

She put the phone down with another sigh of relief and smiled… She could almost see the receiver vibrating still with Amalia's babbling chatter. Her coffee had cooled a little. She poured herself a cup, thoughtfully. The letters were on the table, open. The smell of fish from the concierge's hands lingered, and Paulina pushed them away so she could drink her coffee.

She'd read all the letters, but she had only really taken in Antonio's. Antonio expressed his feelings better in writing than he did in speaking, and she could sense the suffering and desire in those lines. In the second letter, he announced he was going to phone her: "I'll go to León at daybreak so I can call you at home before nine." It was today that this call was to have taken place. The phone must have been ringing pointlessly, while she was listening to the last Mass of her retreat.

"I have to write to Antonio. I owe him an explanation."… Despite her long conversation with Amalia, Paulina's alarm clock showed only five thirty. The minutes fell, heavy like drops of lead.

"I should go out. I should look for Father González, or at least go into a church, or, simply, go for a long walk and think about the letter I must write."

Behind these thoughts there was another worry that she didn't even want to articulate, but that was there, deeply real.

"And if he calls now, and I'm not here again?… He'll think something's happened… he'll come…"

As time went on she felt more and more anxious and less and less capable of escaping her anxiety.

She began to walk up and down the small corridor that led from the tiny hallway to the bedroom, as she'd sometimes done when she felt distressed in the days when she and Eulogio used to quarrel.

God came into her mind, often. She told herself that she didn't want to offend Him in any way, thinking of Antonio. But her strong feelings, lying dormant for a few days, were seizing hold of her imagination.

"*Can thoughts be brought under control?*"

Her mind began to play tricks on her; she could see Antonio in his car, on his way from León, his disappointed face when his calls remained unanswered…

Finally, she called herself to order. The afternoon went badly. The Gospels were waiting… She wasn't sure she wanted to open them. She felt all prayed out. It was an odd feeling of detachment after the exaltation of the last few days. Eventually she opened them: "If thine eye offends thee pluck it out." It was too harsh. She lost patience.

As the sky began to fade, like it did every evening, and the iron railing on Paulina's small balcony turned black, as the first star floated on the hot breath of the city and the first shouts could be heard from the kids in the street, from the small children who'd been trapped inside all day by the heavy weight of the sun, Paulina looked out from that balcony, pale, parched, tired, and eager all at once.

# IV

It was midnight when the telephone rang. Paulina was beside it now. Gazing at the black telephone cradle… In the end, she'd settled herself there, in the little inner dining room, crammed with furniture, where the telephone was installed, and she'd sat in the small armchair that for the whole of last year had been Eulogio's favourite, next to the radio. It was strange to think about Eulogio now, in that chair, with that look he had, like he was a thousand leagues away, frowning, smoking his pipe… One of the pipes he brought back from America. He'd acquired the habit of smoking over there.

Paulina put the radio on very quietly… She didn't want to think. She let the music and even the toothpaste adverts gently lull her.

She told herself softly, "I'll go to bed…" But she didn't.

When the telephone began to ring, it was as if her skin was being torn from her nerves. She had been waiting for hours. It felt like the sound was killing her.

"Call from León."

Several distant voices. Laughter. Snatches of other conversations, other lives… And at the same time, a throbbing in her arteries, her veins. A throbbing in her neck, behind her ears, behind her eyes, blinding her… In those seconds she clearly pictured León's strange cathedral, with its towers of differing heights, swifts circling, she pictured the San Isidoro Pantheon, one of the places she loved most in the world—she had sensed the poetry of those Romanesque arches when she was a little girl—and that Antonio, he said, liked so much because Paulina liked it, and he spent a whole afternoon there like a refugee thinking about her, when Paulina was convalescing in Mariana's house after her serious infection… All this in a second, suggested by the word León. She also imagined she could see the less poetic telephone building, which she knew well. A phone booth. Antonio's worried face. She knew how his lips looked in that moment. His voice, from far away:

"Paulina, at last… Why weren't you in this morning?"

Paulina shouted, wanting to shorten the huge distance between them.

"I hadn't received your letter."

She couldn't hear properly, there was a buzzing on the line.

"I asked where you were."

"In a convent, I'll tell you all about it later."

"In a… what?… I don't understand, I don't understand…"

Paulina shouted eagerly, wanting to calm him down.

"I'll tell you all about it, I'll write to you…"

And, suddenly, his voice could be heard clearly. So clearly, that she had the feeling Antonio was by her side.

"Antonio, something huge has happened, something absolutely extraordinary for me, I've been converted."

Antonio shouted:

"I can't understand a thing, you're talking nonsense."

She could feel the irritation in his voice. The wire all those miles away was buzzing.

"It happened on the train, in a flash. I was converted…"

"Paulina!" his voice sounded desperate. "I don't know if you're mocking me or I just don't get it."

There were noises on the line. Paulina felt a nervous urge to laugh, relieved of an enormous pressure, and at the same time as soft as a sponge, steeped in a ridiculous tenderness.

"Antonio, I'm going to write to you, straight away."

"No… No, Paulina! I haven't been able to until now, but tomorrow I'll come to Madrid… Tomorrow without fail, eh? See you tomorrow."

Paulina hung up. She could feel the entire weight of the warm night, of the day spent worrying, on her shoulders.

And she could feel too the joy, black, heavy joy like storm clouds. Magnificent joy, loaded with hidden anguish, but irresistible, so irresistible that at times her eyes filled with tears. She needed Antonio's desperation. She needed the exasperation in that beloved voice.

"This joy is not a sin, it's not a sin," she told herself. "I can't help it."

It occurred to her that the only difference that existed between her former life and now was this bringing the word sin into everything. This thought brought with it an odd sensation of weariness.

She stepped under the cool shower, humming to herself. The air was so dry and burning hot that she put on her nightdress over her wet body. "It'll help me to sleep."

"I can't control my joy," she told her conscience once more.

All the windows and doors were open to let in the cool air. The three bedrooms, the dining room, the kitchen… The clear, blue, dusty night rushed in, carrying with it the open, light-filled windows of other houses. And behind the windows, people living their lives: men in their shirt-sleeves or pyjamas, women with bare arms…

Just then, as she turned out the light to go to bed, Paulina noticed that she was envying herself. She was envying the woman from another time who would have indulged wholeheartedly in the pleasurable thoughts flooding into her. She felt she was being hypocritical and panicked. She quickly crossed herself and threw herself into bed as if into the sea. She fell asleep, exhausted.

The following day, she didn't go to Mass and missed that great miracle, that immense wonder of her daily communion.

# V

The telegraph boy was dragging his bicycle over the dust-filled potholes, bouncing it over the stones. He was hot and he was irritated. He'd been on this same street corner when he'd been given the wrong directions and ended up going around and around until finally he'd found the house. It was the right number. It had to be this one.

As he stepped into the cool, dark entrance, he nearly collided with a rather effeminate young man, who smelled of pomade, coming out of the small side door, the one that led to the basement.

"Do you by any chance know a Paulina Nives?"

The boy raised his eyebrows.

"Nives? You bet I do, I'll take the telegram up myself."

"No," the telegraph employee was firm. "All I need is the floor. The good lady concierge must be deaf."

"She is deaf," replied the other lad, inexplicably pleased about this. "The Nives live on the seventh floor. Do you want me to take you up? I'm a friend of the family."

The boy from the Telegraph Office bristled and studied him closely. "Man, I said no, thanks a lot."

He was on the point of opening the lift door when a whistle from Julián held him back.

"What?"

It had occurred to Julián that he absolutely had to know what was in that telegram. He needed to know if Paulina would be in next Saturday, if she was going to stay on, pointlessly sweltering in Madrid while her husband was in the country, or if that slip of blue paper would at last summon her back to the village she should never have left.

Fleetingly, he wondered if he could bribe the lad to let him read the slip of paper. He concluded immediately that this was a stupid idea. The delivery boy's honest, serious face, his intellectual expression, with his cheap wire-rimmed glasses didn't lend itself to bribery, at least not just like that, on the first try (in Julián's mind everyone had their price), and anyway, if he did accept, it would end in a punch-up later… He had five pesetas at the most in his pocket. In any case, his friend the concierge would tell him. His mother didn't have the knack!

"Nothing, my friend, nothing, don't look so cross…"

The boy from the Telegraph Office banged the lift door shut and went up to the seventh floor.

A young woman with black hair, dressed in a white blouse with colourful embroidery and a coral necklace, opened the door. A moment later, when the woman was eyeing the telegram apprehensively, and holding it in her fingertips, like an old lady, the telegraph boy realised that despite the blouse, the slim figure, the head held high, the woman wasn't young, as he had first thought. "She believes she is, which isn't the same," he thought distractedly, with a vague sense of being deceived by poor Paulina who, completely oblivious, was looking in her purse to find a few coins for him. The vision of those too black eyes stayed in his mind for a few seconds. Then, moments later, he forgot them.

Afterwards, Paulina stood alone in the apartment, holding the telegram. She hadn't received many telegrams in her life, and the few she had received had been very important… Leant against the front door, she folded the blue slip of paper, smiling at her own nervousness. She didn't need to open it or read the signature to know who it was from… It was from Antonio. And it didn't have a signature. Why would it? It didn't need one.

"Rita worse. Trip impossible. Desperate. Will write. Awaiting news."

Paulina remained there for a few minutes as she was, leant against the door, her mouth part-open in an odd expression. Then she recovered herself. The world, after having surged and ebbed away like a sparkling tide, flowed back to her once more and flooded into her, leaving her as she was, her stature and slenderness and summer outfit all the same. Her hands had the same gentle shape, and she noticed the warmth of her palm, the one that was crumpling the slip of paper.

The noises in the house… A canary chirping vociferously from somewhere around the patio. The noises from the street… A rag-and-bone man calling out. Summer. Solitude.

For the first time since she'd arrived from Villa de Robre she felt profoundly let down. She'd imagined she would spend the day with Antonio. A completely innocent day, of course. A day like when he, as a young lad, used to travel up from Barcelona and come to meet her at Amalia's old house.

She and Antonio would have gone out to lunch in one of the restaurants on the outskirts of the city. Everything would have gone smoothly, well… They would have talked and she would have told him all about her wonderful adventure. Paulina had been imagining that conversation as a goodbye… Not a goodbye forever, necessarily, but until such time when the two of them were free. What she felt obliged, absolutely obliged and willing to do was to risk Antonio's affection for her. She knew that she had to do it.

"As for me, I… I…"

She felt as though the flame he'd ignited in her when he was a young man would never die. A few days earlier she would have been able to see his affection as trivial, completely ridiculous even, when considered in relation to God… But now she felt small again, human. Everything around her was regaining its importance. And God existed, and God entered men's hearts, and God loved enough to become man and suffer for love and she knew this, but… The exaltation was over.

She didn't understand anything of what had happened, she couldn't make sense of it, and she felt almost resentful… What? Didn't God know who she was, she Paulina? A poor woman, a miserable woman even. Why had He come to her to then abandon her? More than anyone, He, her Creator, knew that she wasn't capable of understanding nor of loving if He didn't place this understanding, this love in her heart. Her capacity was only small. It was for things that were immediate, close by… Of course now she knew that beyond all the senses and experiences there is another experience of Love, but she didn't feel capable of attaining it, of trying to attain it.

She desired happiness too much. She wasn't afraid now to

be happy, like when she was a girl. Now, she was afraid to let happiness pass her by. She needed it, it was hers, this small, nearby and understandable human happiness. It belonged to her, she'd earned it by suffering so much pain already.

After these reflections, she imagined herself for a moment as a hard, haggard woman, yearning for pleasure that was carnal, no matter how she tried to dress it up. And it was terrible to feel like this after having believed she even deserved the revelation of Heaven.

Sadly, feeling strangely humiliated, she sat down to write to Antonio.

She sat at her son's desk and turned face down the blown-up photograph she and Eulogio had taken in Barcelona, in the garden belonging to the "ratonetas."

She chewed her fountain pen. She was finding it very hard to put her feelings down on paper… But above all, the miracle on the train, from this distance. In the end, she wrote it down simply:

"Suddenly I believed. Without any room for doubt. In everything. In God. In the Church. In the Virgin Mary. In the Communion of the Saints. In everything.

"They say this is a very special grace. I even thought that it was an answer from God to all the desperate questions I had last year, when I was suffering so absurdly, so wretchedly, and with no apparent reason… I thought that God wanted to give me the joy of the Saints for ever and ever. And if the Saints are always full of joy, then surely there is no reason for me to tear myself into shreds… But now I've lost the joy, and I'm suffering again because of you.

"Now that… I assure you this isn't a figment of my imagination or a delusion or anything. What I had was a realisation of the truth, that has now faded, but has left me with certainty… What I don't understand is why it has happened to me and not someone else… But they say you shouldn't ask God why… That we are like tiny children before his designs; we do not know… We cannot understand."

After writing this letter with its theological digressions, she remained pensive for a while. A soft sadness descended upon her. A sadness like fine dust.

In the afternoon, she received another letter from her mother-in-law. Mariana was surprised at her ingratitude, surprised that she hadn't written even a few lines.

Paulina could picture Mariana perfectly. She could see her, a faint frown on her face, inspecting her beautiful house, checking that the "Frigidaire" and the water heater that allowed hot baths at any time of the day were working correctly, gauging through narrowed eyes the effect of her new curtains and trying to understand, on seeing how perfect all this was, why Paulina should have left the comfortable paradise she'd created for this horrid little apartment, practically out in the suburbs of a scorched Madrid.

"It's all very well leaving like that, doing your own thing, but surely you could have shown a little courtesy towards a person, like myself, who has gone out of her way to give you every comfort."

Next, Mariana told her how excited Eulogio was about both the factory and his plans for exploiting the forests of Las Duras, in collaboration with the priest from Peña Robre. Long-term projects, of course, but that really seemed interesting, as they wouldn't only help the locals, as was José's wish, but would be of great benefit to the Nives themselves. Eulogio sent his regards… Inside Mariana's letter there was another one from Miguel, very short and very sweet. Miguel had good handwriting, round and clear. He told her that he'd added to his collection of insects, he'd been given the loveliest little puppy, and he wanted to see her.

Paulina was touched because in all the sentimental commotion she had left him to one side. And looking after her son was a clear task that God had entrusted her with… But, did she merit it? She felt a pang of humility. She thought she didn't deserve to shape her son's spirit. Mariana, though an unbeliever, with her practical nature, her integrity, and her kindness, would be a better influence in the child's upbringing. She herself was a weak and strange woman. A woman who was incapable of living up to what was expected… Incapable.

As these doubts played on her mind, her face in her hands, she suddenly remembered a book she'd read about Luther, whose theory was that man is incapable of lifting up what he has put down, of going back along paths he has already trod. In his opinion everything must be done according to God's grace and man's free will serves no purpose.

An odd memory haunted her, of the three photographs that illustrated the book on Luther. The first, a photograph of a painting of Luther when he was an Augustinian friar, with an anguished face, rather austere, beautiful. The second was of a portrait painted in the times when people were convinced that man could do nothing to modify his nature, not even to gain grace: a comfortably off bourgeois, bon viveur, a little like Amalia's husband. Then, in latter times, bloated, almost monstrous.

She pulled herself together. She answered the letters quickly, and taking Antonio's with her too, went outside. She posted them. Then she went to find an air-conditioned cinema and spent a few hours dozing and forgetting her own problems immersed in a film in which the unexpected event of a murder unfolded against the icy backdrop of the South Pole.

When she came out she realised that nothing she'd left outside when she entered the cinema two hours earlier had disappeared. Not even the heat. All the heat, with the lights and the coloured signs on the Gran Vía, hit her in the chest.

On her return, the concierge handed her a parcel. Father Pedro, as usual, was sending her books. She now had a collection of books he'd sent, which all dealt with conversions to Catholicism, conversions of people from the modern day, famous people in the arts, science, philosophy... And a magazine with an article marked with a red pencil.

She didn't deserve all this, in her opinion. She'd like to have broken through her own reserve, run to Father Pedro and tell him what kind of person this woman really was, who a few days before, had assured him that she would be willing to burn for her faith.

But the books were there, they accompanied her. She read until the early hours. She felt she was accompanied by all those who like her had found, after many years of distance or denial, true faith.

They were good, even extraordinary company. Many of the converted came back to the Church after a desire for God based in Protestant doctrine, but others, like Paulina herself, had been "caught" by God's grace in one fell sweep... Sometimes, in a curious way like Pitigrilli, who wrote of cynical grace and who found God after attending séances and realising the falseness of such a path.

Gradually the reading calmed her soul. She was sure that all those men and women must have experienced struggles, anguish, setbacks. "Why would you be any different?" they asked her. "What have you done that God should choose you, lift you up in flight, and that you should no longer feel pain or earthly desire, like a blessed one? Will you not know hardship too?"

It was a beautiful night. The stars flooded in through the open balcony. Not even the little bedside lamp could diminish their brilliance when Paulina put down the book for a moment and looked upwards. She felt enveloped in mystery. Propelled by something bigger than her own desires. When she lowered her gaze from the night sky, Paulina's hands, holding the book, appeared too soft, pale and needy, and she averted her eyes.

Two things in particular made an impression on Paulina. One, the story of Edith Stein, an atheist of Jewish origin, Husserl's secretary, and a philosopher herself. This woman was an extraordinary intellectual, who discovered the truth one night while reading Santa Teresa. She discovered it with such certainty that shortly afterwards she entered a Carmelite convent. The other thing that Paulina found intriguing—because she couldn't help but connect it to her memories of the Luther photographs that had fascinated her a few hours earlier—was the illustration for the article that Father González had circled in red.

It consisted of three photographs of a remarkable French convert, who died at the beginning of the century in Africa: Charles de Foucauld. The first was taken in his youth as a chic Parisian. When they used to call him "Fat Foucauld." Unsurprisingly there was something weak, cynical, and slightly unpleasant in this bon viveur's expression. The second photograph dated from immediately after his conversion. An interesting face, revealing a man's struggle. The third, in his later years: his face more spiritual, more severe, intelligent and, one could imagine, kind. The face of a saint.

The following day, Paulina went very early to church. In the confessional, she accused herself humbly of having indulged in evil thoughts. She took communion and remained there weeping for a long while, her face in her hands, without knowing why… Then she was quiet for some time, in the peaceful church full of murmuring old ladies, full of shadows and the smell of incense. She was still, as if waiting, as if longing… Nothing. Nothing happened.

# VI

The girl began to laugh like a horse. She wasn't pretty, but she was well-dressed. She crossed her legs with an easy confidence, she smelled delicately sweet and she whinnied. She was very young.

Julián had sauntered up with a supremely confident air, but it was a feigned confidence. He wasn't fooling anyone. It hadn't gone down well. At least, his friend Arturito wasn't impressed, and the girl carried on laughing while she showed off her tanned legs and face, her lovely, lightweight, cool summer dress.

"I'm sweating," thought Julián. He imagined he could smell his own sweat, and as he did so the back and collar of his shirt began to feel damp.

"So, my man." Arturo didn't offer him a drink, but the silence was becoming intolerable. "So, my man, see you around."

Arturo and the girl were being fanned by the rippling orangey shadow cast by the seat awning.

Julián knew he needed to collect himself, gain some time. His smile was waxen, and his voice quivered foolishly.

"I've got a bit of business, my friend, a tidy bit of business, and as soon as I saw you I thought to myself that's
my man."

He said this almost with a wink, attempting to convey his
meaning subtly to Arturo. But his attempt failed.

"Me?"

It was clear from Arturito's face that the word "business"
meant nothing to him.

The girl whinnied again, her teeth gleaming.

Arturito's face too was tanned by the sun at the beach. A
clean, fresh, beige-coloured suit. A gold watch. A Longines...
His dark chestnut brown hair fell in tight curls.

They'd been classmates studying for their bachillerato at an
exclusive school, until Julián had been forced to leave. A year
previously they'd bumped into each other in a night club. It was
during the brief period when Julián had been flush with money
and had been cheerfully spending it. Arturito had recognised
him and given him a hug and asked him to lend him a thousand pesetas for a bet. Julián had given it to him immediately.
He'd not seen him again, and for months he'd been thinking
to himself that those thousand pesetas were his security. He
needed that money.

An almost abject fear, a mixture of respect and an anxiety
he felt at not knowing how to behave among such a rich family, in Arturo's father's magnificent house, had prevented him
from daring to knock at their door, but he'd called his friend's
house on the telephone at least ten times. He'd only managed
to catch him in once. It was before the summer, and Arturo
had begged him for more time, until after the summer break.
It was impossible right then...

Arturo had been in Madrid for two weeks now. Julián knew this and had been keeping his eye on him. Every day he would wander the streets where he lived, and suddenly, almost unexpectedly, he'd come across him this morning, sitting on the swing seat beneath the coloured awning, beside a little table right there on the Calle Serrano, with the girl-horse who was giving Julián such a hard time. But he couldn't let Arturito get away. Especially not now, he was thinking, when the thousand pesetas were integral to the success of the job. If he could even lend him more… But at the very least he must have what he was owed.

He noticed a little open-topped car, parked right by the pavement.

"Is that yours?"

The girl-horse neighed again. It was weird how much that whinny startled him.

"He means the 'cockroach,' Arturo!"

"It's Mari-Carmen's."

Mari-Carmen had a glass in front of her, a half-drunk cocktail, and Arturo another glass with ice and lemon floating in it. It was hot as hell. Julián, without knowing why, didn't dare wipe his forehead with his handkerchief. A waiter came up to them.

"We're leaving," said Arturo suddenly, a challenge in his eyes. "You having something?"

Their glasses were almost full. The malicious intent was clear. Julián could have turned his pockets inside out, and he still wouldn't have unearthed a single coin. He smiled, trying to keep his cool. Just then, a tremendous rage made his hands tremble.

"Man, thanks a lot, I'll have a cocktail with you if you insist."

Another hideous whinny. Julián's yellow-mottled eyes fixed on the girl. Now instead of feeling afraid of her laugh, he felt a rush of confidence. She approved of his retort.

"Say yes, baby, say yes… This one's a dreadful cheapskate… By the way, what's your name?"

Julián blushed. This had never happened to him before, but at that moment he felt ashamed to admit his name was Julián Mateo. He stuttered without producing any sound, pausing on the first syllable, which he couldn't pronounce. It was very odd.

"It's the same as that idiot in 'La Verbena de La Paloma': Julián," Arturo told her.

"No way!"

More laughter.

Julián felt a furious desire to grab the girl by her hair, to possess her, to beat her. Sometimes these brutal animal urges took hold of him. He took out his packet of cigarettes with sweating, trembling hands.

"Yes, thank you," said the girl.

Julián hadn't offered. There was only one cigarette in the packet. The young woman took it calmly and while Julián, his throat burning, struggled to ignite the match as it slipped between his soft, wet fingertips, the girl took out a tiny lighter and lit it herself. The waiter appeared with Julián's cocktail.

The boy hated his own body, sweat pouring out of it like water from a jug. He could feel his feet sweating in his white canvas rubber-soled shoes. It was revolting.

Arturo looked at his watch.

"We have to go."

"I don't," said Mari-Carmen; "I rather like Julián."

"Well, I'm off then, honey…"

Arturo made as if to stand up, his almond-shaped eyes with their thick curly lashes staring intently at Mari-Carmen. She stayed sitting as she was, comfortable, relaxed, and smoking. The face was ugly but the body was very young and slender, a very nice body. Slim arms, deeply tanned. Julián hated her carrot-coloured hair, but overall, he'd have liked to have her as his girlfriend.

"Okay, I'm going."

Julián reacted. He had never stammered until today, but his voice came out high and squeaky. This made him feel so ridiculous that green triangles were dancing in front of his eyes. However, he stood up too.

"Hey, man, by the way, can you give me back the thousand pesetas? I've left my wallet at home so it would be really handy right now…"

"You're crazy, my friend."

Arturo's voice was cold; he looked at him like he was an animal.

The liquid from the cocktail began to drip from Julián's armpits, his feet, the back of his neck. He felt sopping wet like a snail.

The neigh again. He couldn't stand it. His furious expression when he looked at the girl made her laugh even more. People at other tables were starting to look at them. A ridiculous little hairless dog started barking.

Arturo turned to leave and Julián caught his arm. Arturo had a round face with small, pale features.

"Your hands are sweating; get them off my jacket."

The voice was so calm that Julián obeyed. He became aware of the silence from the neighbouring tables. The waiter was moving around nearby.

"Either give me back the thousand pesetas, or pay for my drink and tell me when you're going to pay me back."

"All right, the joke's over, yeah? When have you ever, in your shitty little life, seen one thousand pesetas? Loser."

Arturo was serious, raising his voice.

At first, Julián was so shocked that his stomach hurt, as if he'd been punched.

"The joke's over, yeah? Just because I felt sorry for you and I let you sit at our table, doesn't mean that you can scrounge money off me, you miserable…"

Julián raised his fist. The punch missed, because Arturo twisted his body out of the way, and Julián found himself trapped after crashing into a woman's chair as he tried to run after Arturo.

"Put it on my tab, Pablo."

Arturo's shout. A wink of his curly-lashed eyes, a wink to the waiter. A hum like a beehive as the engine of the "cockroach" fired up and the laughter of Mari-Carmen, who'd jumped in at lightning speed, were the last Julián heard of the pair.

"Go on, go on; off you go lad; go."

He was thrown out. He could hear murmured conversations behind him.

He imagined all those girls like Mari-Carmen, young and tanned, all those ladies and young men sipping their aperitifs, making snide comments at his expense.

All the noise of the street at midday crashed down on him like a wave. The car horns. The trolleybus. The bicycles. The people. He caught his reflection in a shop window. Looking back at him, yellow eyes in a pale face. A twisted tie. A shirt drenched in sweat.

"Saturday," he thought, "Saturday."

The word had been his talisman for several days now. It was the name of a day of the week. A name that had been gradually taking shape in his mind. Now it worked for anything. To calm his anger. To slow his beating heart too.

In the evening, Julián climbed the narrow concrete steps, behind Paloma, his girlfriend, the sister of the workshop apprentice Martín. Slim, dark Martín who kept watch on them whenever he could.

Through the windows on the staircase you could see clothes hanging in the enormous patios of the monstrous concrete block of flats, and views of the countryside. Colourful, patched clothes. Yellowed sheets, like the old sails of a ship.

Paloma was small, plump, provocative. She awoke filthy instincts in many men. She was twenty but she looked a few years older. Men liked her, but Julián observed her thick calves with a kind of disgust.

"So, here we are."

Paloma inserted a key in the lock of the peeling, chocolate-brown painted door.

"This is it…"

Now Julián didn't mind wiping the sweat from his brow. As soon as he was inside the house, he took off his jacket. Paloma had said:

"We'll have the place all to ourselves. The whole family are going to Toledo after lunch, to my brother Toribio's wedding. They're not coming back until tomorrow night."

"And what did you tell them?"

"That we've got masses to do in the workshop, that I've got a night shift tonight and overtime tomorrow, and that if I don't do it I'll get the sack."

She burst out laughing at her own joke. Julián carried on drying off the sweat with his handkerchief. Paloma opened the window and a fierce yellow light streamed in from the fields. The flats were surrounded by countryside.

"I'd gladly take a cold shower," said Julián.

Paloma's laugh didn't have any effect on the boy. The memory of that neighing laugh this morning came back to him vividly. It was painful, like a thorn deep inside him. The flash of her large, dazzling teeth.

"Come; here's the shower sir… Your bath sir, if it pleases you…"

The shower in the house was positioned directly over the bowl of the toilet. Julián looked at it, stunned.

"But, what on earth…?"

"Yes, sweetheart; another of the little jokes they play on us poor folk… The builder was supposed to put in a shower and a loo. As you can see he had a brainwave, and this little beauty occurred to him. At first the toilet didn't even have a proper bowl; we put that one in; there was nothing but a hole in the floor. Clearly, that was his roundabout way of telling us we were pigs… Well, that's precisely what he meant. He meant for us to wash ourselves in our own filth. Obviously, now we wash in the kitchen, in a tub. But if you fancy it…"

Julián slowly rolled up his shirt sleeves. He took off his tie. As he gazed out of the window he saw a strange, beautiful Madrid, an unfamiliar Madrid, in the distance, turning orange in the sunset, its skyscrapers and its roofs and the trees in its parks drawn in black like a charcoal sketch.

Paloma was bustling about in the kitchen, which was very

small and was separated from the lounge-dining room by an open archway. She'd turned on the light that hung down from a wire, floating like a tiny sun in the warm air.

"All this is going to end. I swear it ends Saturday."

Julián was turned towards her, looking at her with his yellow eyes.

"What's going to end?"

"This… Showers over toilets. Damn poverty. The laughter of those rich whores. And this…"

He indicated their surroundings, not thinking Paloma might be hurt. "This" wasn't so bad. The house was spotlessly clean and far more pleasant that Julián's own. The kitchen taps shone, the walls had a just-painted smell, the curtains crackled with starch. Besides those rooms, there were two bedrooms. One very ostentatious master bedroom. It had everything: a mirrored wardrobe, a dressing table, a small wingback chair. A crib by the bed, a faint smell of talcum powder… Over the bed, a crucifix.

"My sister Patro's bedroom."

In the small living-cum-dining room, a "drinks cabinet" which when opened revealed Martín's divan bed… Another bedroom, with a large single metal-framed bed where Paloma and her mother slept. On the walls, framed pages from almanacs. A chest of drawers, a coat stand… And all around, the haunting yellow countryside, which was beginning to darken.

"What's this about Saturday, Julián? What are you going to do? You know while I've got money…"

Julián did know. He knew that Paloma was mad about him. He wanted to be free from Paloma and her money. He'd set her up as a prostitute. It's true she was up for it, and when he met her, she was already not the innocent girl her family thought her. But Julián had convinced her to leave the workshop and spend her free time doing something more productive. ("Who's it going to hurt, silly? I'm not bothered and I'm the one who'd have a right to complain…")

Paloma brought her daily wage into the household, the same as if she were still going to the workshop, and the rest of her earnings went straight to Julián himself. "What are you going to do?"

Julián smiled. He looked almost like a decent boy, an innocent lad. He was younger than Paloma.

Paloma laid a white cloth on the table and lit the dining room lamp. She began to place little dishes on the table: olives, anchovies, cold meat slices. Julián grazed distractedly.

Her dark, needy eyes drank him in. Julián, to her, was a handsome boy, with a softness around the contours of his face. Nothing more.

"Don't worry so much… I've not kept it secret from you. I've been waiting for this. It'll be eight days from now, next Saturday… You'll hide the jewels for me. They're worth over two million… You know Don Paco goes out for lunch on Saturdays, that's the time to do it. Don Paco said it himself: 'We'll have over two million worth in the house next week.'"

Paloma's chest was heaving. It was funny because her name suited her, she looked like a puffed-up pigeon.

"You don't know what you're saying."

"I don't know?"

The yellow eyes looked at her.

"I don't know? If I were someone else I'd have no need of anything… And I understand myself… Or don't you know?"

Paloma was quiet. She believed blindly in Julián's stories of rich, distinguished grand ladies who were keen to look after the boy in the same way she did. To marry him…

Night had fallen and the lamplight illuminated the window boxes full of geraniums, outlining them against the black. As Julián looked out at the darkness, he felt a rush of excitement like being at sea. The city was like a port beheld from a boat. He could hear the waves rolling in.

From the city streets beams of red, green, and yellow projected into the sky: advertisements.

"This town is full of things I want," said Julián.

He didn't say that among these things he desired so much were women who were different to Paloma. Women like Mari-Carmen, even with her whinnying, that unpleasant, obsessive whinnying that really got under his skin.

"I've got it all worked out. I've been thinking about this for months. No one will catch me out. I'm cleverer than the police… How do you think I coped before?"

When they sat down at the table, he was affectionate with Paloma, caressing her and gazing into her eyes.

"I need you to get me a pistol."

There was a silence. Paloma was very dark-skinned. When she was emotional, her face seemed to become rounder and to take on a grey tone.

"I beg you, Julián, don't take it. Take the mask like you planned, stun the old lady… whatever you want. But don't take the pistol."

Her eyes were wide in terror. Eyes made wider still with charcoal.

Huge moths began to fly in through the open window,

attracted by the lamp. It was like a night in the countryside. Julián was no longer sweating. He went on:

"It'll be a stroke of luck if the neighbour upstairs has flown the coop by Saturday. Then it'll be nice and quiet."

# VII

Paulina had argued with Father González. Father González was smiling as he observed her glittering eyes, her angry, pursed lips…

They were in a very clean and sparse little office. On the wall were garish lithographs of the Virgin Mary gesturing to her heart, and a Crucifix.

"Yes, Paulina, you're right. In these particular cases, you're right. What are we to do? Many of these failures are the fault of people who could put them right, yet simply criticise them. A mystical guilt… I agree with you that some charitable institutions have lost their way over the years and aren't what they should be. They have stagnated, the blazing fire of God's love that produced them has been forgotten. Nevertheless, there are so many others that do marvellous work. Right here in Madrid, I can point you towards the Cottolengo organisation; you should visit the Sisters of the Cross, who give up so much of their own lives to care for the poorest, sickest invalids, washing and scrubbing their houses when they can't even drink a glass of water in those houses for fear of infection. These women only sleep every other night…"

Paulina made a gesture as if to brush this off.

"Yes, I know; I know ten or twenty more. But it's not about isolated acts of heroism. If overall these people from the larger religious orders especially, those who have contact with the public, acted in the way they should, ordinary Spanish people would not be forgetting their Catholicism…"

"Clearly there is much to be done, Paulina. This is the Pope's message to all of us. Christ is counting on you for this renewal. Why don't you join Acción Católica? We must unite."

Paulina sat up at the edge of her seat.

"Father, I don't think it works… At least not here in Spain. It isn't effective in its current state. You say Acción Católica is a movement of lay people who are supposed to live normally, carrying Christ in their lives, through their kindness, their generosity towards others, when they're out for a walk, when they're working, when they're dancing… Teaching Christ's love through their example and their smile. But the reality is, at least in Villa de Robre, where I've observed this phenomenon to some extent, that none of this is happening. The poor creatures who've signed up (the women at least) are practically nuns. They wear strange clothes. They're forbidden countless things that are perfectly healthy and lawful. It's becoming yet another religious order, while claiming (which is the bad thing) to be a lay organisation. The impression they're giving is that anyone who wants to be more involved with the church must be a very odd individual in the first place."

Father González was distracted. He looked at his watch.

"All right, Paulina… Truthfully, I don't recognise what you're describing. I'll introduce you to some ladies from here, from Madrid, wonderful people who are members of Acción Católica and who aren't at all prudish or odd, I can assure you. Acción Católica carries out very effective pastoral work. It gives its members excellent religious training."

"Yes, it does that, yes; but the Pope's idea…"

"Forgive me, Paulina; I must attend to my work now. Precisely because of everything you say and for many other reasons, there is so much to be done. Another time I'll tell you how you are indeed needed among the ranks of Acción Católica and so forth."

Paulina kissed Padre Pedro's hand.

She'd always said, on seeing other people kissing priests' hands: "I'll never kiss a man's hand." But those anointed hands that were raised every day to a living God, inspired a respect in her now, a deep reverence.

Paulina felt despondent as she left. She hadn't explained anything about her life to Father González, nor had she asked him for any advice. She didn't wish to anymore. There was only one day when she had wished to… The Commandments were emphatic in her case, there were no doubts to clarify. This priest only knew what Blanca had written to him about her: that she was married to a cousin of Blanca's son-in-law. That she had been an unbeliever and had recently converted. Also, Blanca had explained to Father González how she herself had been praying the entire night of Paulina's conversion. This revelation had affected Paulina deeply, immersing her fully in the true, astonishing mystery of the Communion of the Saints.

Father González had put her in contact with some of the people involved in various charity boards. Paulina had asked him to do so. She wanted to let go of the resentment she'd felt towards devout women in her childhood, especially now that, in fact, she owed her faith to the prayers of a devout woman. She had met some rather peculiar people and many good people, too, who were pure and gentle and brave hearted. What a strange world! But she felt lonely even among all these people who had welcomed her so kindly…

She felt lonely, perhaps because she couldn't throw herself into it like the others. So, the faith of those women, their pure eyes, their desire to do the right thing, and at the same time to not deviate one iota from what the priests, who were practically leading them by the hand, told them; all this made Paulina feel as uncomfortable as when her old friend Concha explained to her that everyone was Catholic in Spain, whatever kind of life they led, and that was all that mattered.

Paulina found herself wandering past villas and gardens in the Colonia de Viso area of the city.

"All I do is criticise," she told herself with a wry smile. She broke off a sprig of honeysuckle that was overhanging a garden wall and attached it to her jacket.

She felt desperately lonely. "Dear God, please don't leave me."… What was it like? What was that emotion like, that beauty, those extraordinary heights that had enabled her to understand she was more than an intelligent animal, understand the world that exists outside of space and time, that is ours, that has been given to us…? How could she get that back…? How?

She was sad and tired. "Am I mad?" Sometimes she asked herself, "Am I mad?"… Every day she took communion, knowing that Christ was in that piece of bread. Knowing it, but unable to feel moved.

It wasn't so hot now, as she arrived home mid-afternoon. Two days previously, when she'd heard the rainfall during a light storm, she'd thought about Villa de Robre, when the water had come down in sheets, and the smell. There was no mud left now in her little street. Only dust. She was tired from the long walk. She felt a deep sadness.

As she turned the corner into her street, however, she forgot that she'd ever been unhappy. The entire street was taken up with Antonio's car. That great big, unmistakeable car.

She almost sprinted to the house. It was ridiculous to rush like that, she knew it. She had to disguise her feelings. "I can't throw myself at the door like this."

The concierge was sewing, sitting in a small low chair, with two or three women gathered around listening to her. She began to smile the moment she saw Paulina. Paulina wasn't the owner of the huge car with its sparkling windows, but the concierge, once she realised she was related to him, became much friendlier. The same had happened when, a few months earlier, she'd come out of the house in the company of Mariana and Antonio.

"Doña Paulina, your brother-in-law is upstairs. He seemed to want to wait, so I gave him the key to your flat."

Since a few days previously when Paulina had lost one of the keys, she always left the remaining one with the concierge.

She nodded. It always made her nervous when people called her Doña Paulina; but what could she do?

Standing in the lift she felt shattered. Shattered. Her legs weak. She knew now why she'd been sad these last few days. The root of her sadness was that she'd been trying, and she was trying, all day long, never to think about Antonio. And she felt empty without him. God, it seemed, had also left her, and she felt she was without Him too.

She almost didn't dare knock.

Antonio was behind that door, laughing. She'd forgotten how young Antonio was. She looked at him. She wanted to take in those features that she knew so well. For a few moments neither of them spoke.

"I've been wondering about this awful flat. How have you managed to live here?"

"I've lived in worse places, you know I have."

"*Where have I heard that before? Like that, the exact same words…Ah!…Eulogio. I mustn't think of Eulogio now, how stupid.*"

"Yes, but…"

Paulina's face was very different to that of the woman who'd spoken so seriously to Father González, criticising the Catholic institutions of her country. Paulina's face was cheerful, an orange tinge reflected from her linen dress.

"You've been living here… You didn't even get rid of the little vase of fake flowers in the hall."

"I haven't got rid of anything. When a person truly has no real desire to live, the objects around her don't matter at all. Last year, when I came here, I was half dead… And this time I haven't bothered about it either… Come, let me show you. I'll give you a tour. I have some lovely wax fruit in the dining room, it even has little tiny flies on it."

"I've seen it."

But they walked around the dining room. It was a stuffy room, with a stained-glass window. Two sideboards, some chairs and a table with an imitation wood veneer. The small armchairs next to the radio and an ugly cubist style lamp.

"You lived here…"

"No; essentially the person who lived here was Eulogio; he used to sit over there," she pointed to the small armchair, "with Miguel. He'd smoke his pipe, talk to the boy or listen to the stock prices or a concert on the radio…"

It was an unfortunate choice of topic. Antonio felt excluded from a world with that man living in it. Suddenly it was as if his cousin Eulogio were between them, with his broad shoulders, his bright blue eyes, his intense maleness. A powerful masculinity. It seemed to infect the entire house.

"I," Paulina was saying, "was mainly in this little corridor here, pacing up and down, thinking about how I could leave Eulogio, end the miserable sham our love had become; but feeling too sick, and trapped by my unborn child, to do anything. It's dreadful to be tied to a man who treats you as if you're not capable of rational thought. He was so condescending, as if I were straight out of school and knew nothing of life…"

Antonio was frowning. He could only ever remember Eulogio being courteous towards Paulina. Quite indifferent yes, luckily for him. But so what if Paulina was wrong? He wasn't going to be the one to tell her. He said:

"You need to try to get that divorce. When did you marry?"

"In 1937."

"Where?"

Paulina told him the name of the village.

"It was a military marriage," she added. "Either a captain or a major married us, I've forgotten which."

She remembered, too, the beach by the village, and the line of agaves in bloom, its flowers like small yellow trees, separating the sandy beach from the path that led to the house where she and Eulogio were lodging, and the fear when, one night, a guard stopped them as they tried to walk along the shore, and then Eulogio explaining in his calm voice. The wedding day had been quite an occasion. Several officers were married at the same time. The major… Or the captain? wrote their names down, they signed.

Then they all had a meal. Eulogio was the only private among the newlyweds and this was the cause of much laughter. Paulina remembered too the faces of the other brides. Nearly all of them were from the village, very cheerful girls, animated by the party atmosphere and the free-flowing wine. Nearly all of them had perfectly vacant faces. It was almost funny…

"Forget about all this," Eulogio had said to her; "you and me, we're different."

Paulina was about to confide, at this point in her train of thought, that Eulogio had said they were different from everyone else. And she'd felt the same. But it was all nonsense. Antonio was looking at her with the face of a hopeful child. The expression that touched her the most.

"Paulina, many of those marriages weren't even registered. Are you sure yours was?"

"No, I'm not sure… But I think Eulogio asked for a certificate and… He asked for it shortly before I went to Villa de Robre."

Paulina looked at Antonio, very serious, her eyes wide. Antonio was so tall she had to tilt her face to look at him.

"Antonio, I'm thinking about how Eulogio never mentioned the certificate again and since then has kept insisting we marry in Church."

Antonio took out a notebook and wrote down the information that Paulina had given him.

"I'm going to ask for this certificate."

They didn't dare say anymore, they were so excited. It seemed possible that if Paulina were legally free, all barriers would disappear… "*Which isn't true, but yes some of the difficulties would have disappeared*," Paulina thought to herself, wildly. Her mind seemed to be whirling around like a butterfly, as if her thoughts were frightened that someone might catch them, while she continued to show Antonio around the house.

"This is Miguel's room; this is the box room and the maid's room… When we were lucky enough to have a maid. This is the main bedroom. What do you think of this?"

She was pointing to an enlarged photograph, with an oval frame. The wedding portrait of the owner of the furniture. She'd been widowed and had rented out the flat exactly as she'd furnished it when she got married.

The portrait, undoubtedly, had been deliberately left behind in pure hatred. It was of a somewhat mature lady, dressed in black with a comb and veil, feet conveniently positioned to show little lace slippers, mouth in a half-open smile which looked forced, most likely through having to hold it for the photo. From her right hand hung a bunch of flowers. Holding her left arm, a little old man, with a mischievous expression, who'd only lived six months after the event… This work of art was signed by a photographer from Madrid and the date was recent.

"That could easily have been our grandparents' generation, in any village."

"Look, Eulogio felt uncomfortable every time he came in here… Do you know why? Because this little old chap's eyes follow you around. Eulogio 'felt' something without knowing what. I used to laugh to myself when I saw Eulogio turning around to look, puzzled, unaware it was the dead man watching him. You can understand my reluctance to take down the portrait. Now that I'm used to it, I'm almost fond of it."

"Paulina."

Paulina felt, simply on hearing her name, an emotion that she hadn't thought she'd ever feel again. A twilight glow washed in through the kitchen window like a red sea. It rose towards them in a long tide. Reflections flickered on Antonio's excited face.

"You know… you know…"

He didn't say any more. Paulina knew. She knew that he truly loved her now, almost as he'd loved her as a boy; that now, if he could, he would marry her.

"To travel with you, Paulina… We could go wherever we wanted. I haven't even realised until now how wonderful it is to have money, to be able to do so many things. Paulina…"

She put a finger to his lips.

"Remember. I wrote to you…"

"But that's all nonsense. Nonsense… Anyway, what does it matter, if you believe? Believing is good, our religion is a beautiful thing… What?… I'm not an atheist; I'm more Catholic than you are. I go to Mass every Sunday. Every Sunday, do you hear me? I wouldn't miss it for anything. But I wasn't born to be a saint. I'm an ordinary man… Who are we hurting with this? Rita will never find out… She's extremely sick, you know… Now it's she who's asking me to take her to Switzerland. I've come to prepare for the trip… I only have a few days, no more than a few days to say goodbye to you. As for the rest of it, you're surely freer than you think. And if not, at least as far as the church is concerned, you're free… Who would you be harming? Your son? I can assure you that's not the case. I don't want children with you, I just want you. Your son would have a godfather who, if he doesn't squander his fortune himself, will make him an heir."

Paulina felt a kind of tickle in her throat. A nervous laugh. A silly laugh. There they were, she and Antonio, in the doorway between the bedroom and the corridor, with the red light, darkening now, as if dying on the floor…

"Like a fairy tale."

She began to laugh, to laugh in that silly way. She moved away from Antonio. Her nervousness had brought tears to her eyes; she wiped them away. Antonio sensed her stiffen, felt the coldness in her voice.

"Get out, Antonio."

Antonio looked at her, furious.

"Are you mad?"

He caught hold of her shoulders. He turned her towards him.

"Do you think you can treat a man like this, like you're treating me? What kind of men have you known in your life?" She shook him off.

"Go, Antonio; you can't be in the house at this hour of the night; I can't have you here anymore…"

"If this is a game…"

He tried to see her face. It was difficult in the dark. She turned a switch and the floor filled with sad yellowish trickles of light.

Antonio's lips were twisted in a strange grimace. He looked at her with disgust,

"Do you know what you look like? A hysterical prude, that's what you look like."

He felt shocked and foolish at the same time. This woman with her evasive gaze, her pursed lips, had nothing in common with the woman he had loved for her sweetness, even when she refused… Could this be the same woman whose memory had turned his body into a living mesh of desire? She'd been looking at him for a minute, while she'd been speaking to him, looking at him with a longing that had made him take her hands. He had felt those soft, trembling hands on his own cheeks before she'd rejected him in this absurd way. She looked ugly, in that light he could see dark shadows around her mouth. It meant nothing. Her trembling fingers on his face meant nothing. She wasn't looking at him now. She was staring at the floor, she was rigid.

Paulina lifted her eyes, filled with darkness, towards him.

"The thing is… Antonio, I'm not a hypocrite. I never do things when I think I shouldn't."

Antonio began to laugh in her face. He swore at her and left, slamming the door on his way out.

<h1 style="text-align:center">VIII</h1>

That was the start of an unhappy night for Paulina. A distressing night. She took a mattress out onto the balcony and spent most of it out there, smoking. It was her favourite place. She should have explained to Antonio that she was living there, in that place, now, in the summer.

How could she have rejected Antonio like that? She'd been so cold, so hard. "It's because I don't know how to be flexible… I give my whole self or I break," she thought.

Beneath her, on the small balcony of the flat below, Julián's "masters" were chatting. The neighbours had turned the room where Paulina had her bedroom into a dining room.

"Why don't you get rid of the boy? He's bone idle. Alberto says he's dragging the other apprentice down."

"It's a trial period… You let me handle it. I'm not risking anything. The boy is clearly shaping up and he's capable…"

"There'd be no shortage of others with better track records… And that reminds me, I don't want to be home on my own with that case of jewels midday Saturday… I'm too scared to have something that valuable in the house when you're not coming back for lunch."

"Come on, woman, stop your moaning, what's going to happen in broad daylight, in a mere couple of hours, even if I'm not there. We're not taking it to the bank for just two hours..."

The woman was preparing a gazpacho with ice. Paulina couldn't hear what the couple were saying. It didn't matter to her, nor did she think anything could matter. She heard the lady go out onto the balcony for a moment. She could also hear the ghastly cricket desperately rubbing its wings together in the tiny cage the couple had hung from the balcony.

"Cree... cree... creeee..."

It was an artificial countryside down there below the balcony. A dusty countryside.

*"Who am I hurting? I'm hurting myself... Before, I'd decided to abandon my own child for Antonio... Now it seems I'm only afraid of hell... Of course I am. Not one false step... 'Hysterical prude!' He's right. He's right... I sought him out, it's true... And now I'm leaving him. He'll go off with some tart, or any woman that opens her arms to him... A better woman than me, who doesn't ask anything of him."*

She got up from her mattress. She turned on the light to look at herself in the wardrobe mirror. To see the woman that Antonio loved, and she tried to convince herself she was irreplaceable to him. "You, as well as simply being you, as well as giving me these special moments, you are my adolescence in all its purity and all its murky depths." She marvelled at this passion she had doubted so often. She realised that she didn't have the right to reject what her entire being was open to and longing for. "No," she said to her reflection, "no."

She turned out the light so as not to see herself and re-membered the last words Antonio had spoken to her and, even worse, the look of disgust on his face. She felt herself sinking into an overwhelming sorrow. Nobody knows, after all, which look will one day mark the end of love. Perhaps Antonio had felt inside himself that ice that means the end of love, that renders the loved one unimportant, even hateful, a stranger to us, full of flaws, intolerable.

Paulina could feel herself sweating with anxiety. She stood up several times and went into the house, towards the telephone, only to return to the mattress without having touched it. She was aware that this toing and froing was absurd. Eventually she dialled Antonio's number. No one answered.

She went into her kitchen. She left the tap running. There was no ice in the fridge and she wanted to let the water run cold. She was thirsty. Not hungry, no; but she was thirsty.

She noticed a dark figure in the window overlooking the patio, in the flat above her. It was her neighbour Luisa, the office worker's wife. She smiled and waved at her... The dark figure remained motionless. It was only then that she realised that she was in darkness and Luisa couldn't see her... She didn't feel up to turning the light on, although she knew that her poor neighbour, who she'd been friendly with back in the winter, now shyly avoided her. She must find her much changed... Mariana had taught her to dress well. She had persuaded her to get herself a collection of summer dresses, once she'd recu-perated, and she'd gone along with this. She was very happy to look pretty for Antonio.

While she felt an unexpected stab of pain at the thought of Mariana, she realised that her thoughts would inevitably keep coming back to Antonio. It didn't matter where they began. They would end with him…

She turned on the lamp in the dining room. Spread out on the table, her now quite extensive collection of Catholic books. These were the only books she had in the flat. She picked up the Gospels. The book fell open on Saint Matthew.

"*Or how can you say to your brother, 'Let me take the speck out of your eye,' when there is the log in your own eye? You hypocrite, first take the log out of your own eye, and then you will see clearly to take the speck out of your brother's eye.*"

She closed the book hastily. It brought an odd image to her mind. Herself, while she sat, very erect, at the edge of her seat, smiling with superiority and becoming indignant as she criticised the Catholic organisations.

"Nonsense," she said out loud, despairing. "None of it makes any sense…"

It was a miserable night. She barely slept. The neighbours' cricket made a never-ending racket. She felt as if she had gone insane.

At seven in the morning she dialled the number for Antonio's house. No answer.

She was wearing a light dressing gown over her pyjamas. Madrid seemed to be sleeping beneath the early morning sun… A fresh breeze, a scent of pine, blew through the house making a door bang.

From the window, she could see the luminous sky and the Guadarrama Mountains, beyond the immense white swell of the peaceful houses and the rooftops of the city.

In the stillness, she could almost hear the neighbours breathing, tired after a long night. A great crash of water from the flush of a toilet in one of the flats seemed to cause the fragile walls of the entire house to tremble. The swallows were already screeching…

She called Antonio's house at eight, with the same disheartening result.

At ten Antonio called her. Paulina hadn't dressed. She felt limp. Her head ached. Her hands were shaking as she picked up the telephone.

"You weren't at home? I…"

"The flat is closed up; I'm in a hotel… Why? Have you been calling me? I've been such a brute! I didn't mean any of it. So? Paulina?"

"Come and pick me up."

"Really?"

"Yes."

"Throw a few things in a bag… We'll go somewhere. What day is it?"

"It's the beginning of September, Thursday I think…"

"We've got until Monday. Would you like to see the sea?"

Paulina hadn't seen the sea for years. Yes, she liked the sea…

Three hours later they set off, in the big yellow car. Paulina looked very pretty, her eyes sparkling. She'd dressed in white and was wearing a red neckerchief, which suited her.

"I'm not going to spoil things with regrets. I want these to be the most wonderful days of our lives."

It was a beautiful day, the windows of the houses glinted in the sunlight. As if they'd already arrived and were beside the glittering Levantine Sea.

"I'm not going to think about anything," Paulina spoke again, "nothing at all."

Antonio looked at her tenderly. He loved her. This wasn't the cruel game from those days in Villa de Robre. It was much more than that now.

"Then don't think, my love… Let it be true." A few minutes later they were heading out of Madrid.

# IX

"Saturday," he thought, "Saturday."

The word kept repeating in his head. He couldn't stop it, even though Saturday was finally here. The die was cast. Fortune had been kind to him with Paulina's trip. The concierge had told him that Señora Nieves had mentioned she'd be away until Monday… He had no excuse not to go ahead.

Money can get you anything… Anything. He once heard a lawyer say; "When some poor devil rips off a bank for a small sum, the bank has him put in prison. When someone cons millions out of the banks, the banks team up with the fraudster…" Paloma's role in the affair was essential. Afterwards, it would be wise not to rush, to go slowly. Once the jewels had been sold, Paloma would get a share of the proceeds and he would leave for America. Money can get you anything… Travel, false passports, smiles, everything…

Ssss… ssss… ssss.

Martín was on the bellows again.

The work, the exquisite morning light, so pure as it flooded in and bounced off the newly washed floor tiles and the white walls. The birds, too… It was like a strange dream, the innocence pervading those objects and living creatures.

That morning Julián had downed a shot of bootleg liquor with churros, when he came out of the Metro, near Las Ventas market. He had observed a bustling, humble humanity going about its business. An ants' nest of women with their shopping bags. Men, unshaven, in a hurry, taking the tram from opposite the Plaza de Toros. The beauty of the morning had surprised him, as if it were something he'd never seen. The well-watered grass in the little gardens around the Plaza was bright green. The bullring itself, red, circular, monumental stood out against the clear blue sky. There was no suffocating August heat now. At least not at that time of day.

Looking towards the East, from that same spot, he'd glimpsed on the horizon, beyond the fields, the walls of the cemetery, and the huge cypresses inside that immense city of the dead… Julián made the sign of the cross. He was superstitious. He didn't want the dead to bring him bad luck.

There was no going back now… What? Was it so hard? He'd seen in the cinema every day how easy it was to do a robbery. And if you had to kill someone, then you did it. Killing people is very easy. He'd seen millions of deaths on film. It was simple: a shot, the other person brings their hands to their heart, their eyes widen, they collapse, not even any death throes. The old lady, snuffed out…

His thoughts startled him. No, that wasn't the idea. A robbery, nothing more. Go in with the key, catch her in the middle of her siesta and knock her out… But if she saw him, he'd kill her. He wouldn't tell Paloma this, but that morning, he was a man prepared to do anything.

Afterwards, when he had money, no one in the world would be able to catch up with him. A few days, or rather a few months, of nerve-racking pretence and that was it… To start with, he was thinking of coming down with an illness. Saying he was sick. Curiously, as it happened, he was having cold sweats and feeling uncomfortable.

He was sure that at two in the afternoon nobody would see him go in. He'd tried it out a few days in a row. Not one single soul had seen him. At that time of day, the concierge was well ensconced in her den. It was still extremely hot in the middle of the day.

Now it felt weird to be doing his normal work. He had cleaned some silver powder with a magnet and was shaking off the iron and steel filings. Little Martín, with a blowtorch, working with his foot on the pedal and his hands pushing the metal through. Martín was an idiot. He was content to be in the workshop.

Content! "The truth is I've got no complaints, working for Don Paco." Well, the people that are content, can stay content… Now, he didn't believe Martín was quite so innocent. Martín must have filthy thoughts and greedy desires in his dark head, just like him. Life boiling up inside him. He too would want women and comfort in time… It was only that he was too weak to take it. Martín would never be as bold as he was. Too bad for Martín. There are two types of people in the world, those who take and those who let others take from them.

A dusty beam of sunlight shone down onto the table. And in the sunlight, the workshop tools… He looked at them anxiously. An enormous mandrel for watch bezels: a huge iron bar in the shape of a sugar pestle, good for striking a blow. He imagined a head cracking, splitting open. He averted his eyes… The files, the scissors, even the smallest mandrel for the rings… Everything took on a sinister air that morning, seen through his eyes. Especially the two metal files, one large and one small. The very tools that Don Alberto was now using to do some buffing.

He turned towards him.

"Hey, kid, what's up with you?"

"The thing is… I'm not feeling good. It's true, Don Alberto. I didn't want to say, in case no one believed me."

At that moment, Don Paco came in and before the boy could say a word he noticed his appearance.

"What's wrong man?"

His face was pale and sweating. Dark circles under his eyes.

"I'm not well. I think I'm coming down with a fever."

"For once I think you might be telling the truth. Go on, get out of here. We'll manage without you."

It was true. Maybe it was the liquor, the cold churros, or the image in his head: the old boss lady's skull split open like a fruit.

He had to sit down for a moment, his knees were trembling.

"Yes, I'm going, I'm very sorry… when there's so much work to do."

"We'll manage," said Don Alberto, who had never liked him.

Julián left the basement, after throwing up in the toilet. "Hell, I'm worse than a pregnant woman." He could almost hear the woman-horse from the Calle Serrano laughing, and a fury took hold of him. It fired him up.

Finally, he left the workshop via the main entrance to the building. As he passed through, he overheard the concierge gossiping with the woman from the lower ground floor, newly arrived back after the summer break. He listened carefully as was his habit.

"Well, yes, Doña Amparo, there's something odd going on with that rich brother-in-law. And if there isn't already, well, you mark my words… I tell you, there's something fishy about this latest little trip."

Julián wandered around the streets for a while, turning things over in his mind… The tenants were already returning from the summer break. But the biggest stroke of luck was that the ones on the fifth floor had gone now that August had started. And Paulina…

He arrived back at his house, picking his way through old Madrid's narrow twisting streets, as if in a dream. His large, cool house, with its smells of food ingrained in the wooden stairs, holes worn in the middle from so many feet traipsing up and down… An ancient, indescribable smell, of stew bubbling on the stove. A smell of two centuries of "cocido madrileño," lingering in the air.

"I'm not feeling well," he said as a greeting.

Amalia panicked.

"I'll call Don Enrique right away and ask him to see you. Let me see… You don't look like you've got a fever."

The sleeves of his mother's kimono were flapping about. She smelled of perfumed soap. She'd just had a wash.

"Don't be stupid, Mamá… It's only a headache. I don't want to see Don Enrique or anyone else. I want to go to bed, so if you can leave me in peace…"

Afterwards he calmed down a little. The darkness in his house appeased him. The apartment had two exits and his room was near the service door for which he had a key… Those corridors, of wood or old broken tiles, the faint smell of latrines from the patio, mingled with the very different, enticing one from the kitchen, where there was always something good, appeased him. There, in that house, he'd always felt like the master.

His mother set about putting him to bed herself, as if he were still a child. She seemed to enjoy having him unwell, at her mercy.

*"If you gave me all the money you've got hidden, the money you find when you need it, if I could have my car and my tarts, as it should be, I wouldn't have to do any of this."*

He looked at her with uncomprehending fury. Of course, he believed what he was thinking.

"Right, bring me some tea and some aspirin, but then let me sleep… Even if it's five in the afternoon, if I don't call you don't disturb me, all right? Don't disturb me!"

Then he imagined the girl-horse's face, if she could see him having tea and aspirin, and raged silently. Eventually he calmed himself… with his watch.

He had climbed into his large and comfortable iron bed. The window that overlooked the patio was half-open. A tiny amount of light trickled in, and by this light he could see the shadows passing over the roof. He could trace the irregular shape of the roof, of the room that wasn't quite square but had an awkward wide angle in one of its corners. The pieces of furniture didn't fit properly, even though there was plenty enough space for them… The modest, high-footed wardrobe, on top of which his mother stored suitcases and baskets, with the large mirror, which, annoyingly, was reflecting the tiny ray of light from the patio… The old chipped washbasin. The coat stand, heaving with clothes that smelled faintly of his own sweat. The entire room was impregnated with his sweat, his tobacco smoke. It always smelled vaguely of him.

Tick, tick… Tick, tick.

The watch had been a gift from his mother a year and a half ago when he started at the first workshop. It wasn't the type of watch he would have chosen himself. He liked showy things; gold, enamel, sparkling jewels… But it did its job. Alerted him.

He got up from the bed for a moment. He prepared the keys. It was ridiculous, but it had to be done. He'd stolen one of the keys from Paulina when she came to visit his mother. The other one was from Don Paco's flat… It was a curious thing that all this, the "idea," had been taking shape in his mind since that day in the spring when he happened to find the boss's keys on the floor. The latchkey to the flat had come loose. Instinctively, Julián had kept it.

"You haven't seen a latchkey, have you? It's the one to my flat. Damn it! At least we've got three… Keep a look out when you're sweeping, eh?"

Now Julián had added Paulina's to his collection. That was good luck indeed.

He lay down again, fretting about the creaking bed springs. With his eyes open, looking up at the ceiling, he began to think. Don Paco's flat was imprinted in his memory. He had studied Paulina's which was identical. After the entrance, on the left, the kitchen. On the right a small bedroom, box room, and further along, the dining room. Then, a kind of a T-shape. On the right of the cross, the child's bedroom. On the left, the main bedroom and opposite that, the bathroom, which also opened onto the patio. The dining room must communicate

only with the ventilation shaft through which the lift came
up, behind the stained-glass windows. You could hear the lift
going up and down from there. The box room, which was also
the maid's room in Paulina's house, had no direct ventilation,
only the door to the corridor and its fanlight… The layout was
different in Don Paco's home. He remembered that they had
the small lounge-diner in the room where Paulina had her
bedroom. When he'd gone up to the flat with a message, the
boss lady had left him standing in the hall. In Paulina's flat,
there was no curtain between the hall and the small corridor.
In the bosses' flat, there was a fancy red curtain. One time he'd
gone up to look for the box where they kept the jewels. Peering
round the curtain, he'd seen how the old woman went into the
dining room. No, into what was the dining room in Paulina's flat.

Tick, tick… Tick, tick.

It was only twelve o'clock. Twelve o'clock. Thinking about
things is worse than doing them, much worse, he thought. Only
the day before he'd seen a film. Five deaths in five minutes…
One of the guys who… no sweat… that was the way to do
it… And, they were Americans. He never understood why in
American films there were guys who, even when they knew
they were murderers, the police couldn't catch. He wished he
could go to North America…

He rolled over in bed and sighed.

Then, part two. Getting out of the place… The metal box
full of jewels, wrapped up in paper, an ordinary little package…
First, he'd thought about leaving it in Paulina's flat, and going
back for it another day. But why would you trust that crazy
woman? And what if she decided to come back earlier than
she'd told the concierge?

In the end, he'd decided he would meet Paloma in a bar on the Plaza de Manuel Becerra. She would put the package inside a shopping bag. Probably best to keep things simple. A taxi would be too dangerous… Hard to know the best thing to do. They might have to improvise…

Tick, tick… Tick, tick.

It was one o'clock… The bosses always had lunch at one o'clock on the dot. The woman would be eating by herself. He could picture her with her neat, grey hair, her wide hips, her waddling, unsteady gait, one eye cloudy, the other sharp as a tack.

An oily smoke filtered in from the kitchen through the chinks in the door. One or other of the guests "with kitchen access" must have burnt the oil… He heard Amalia's footsteps. A timid knock on the door.

"Can I get you anything, sweetheart?"

He swore loud enough to blow the house down.

"Can you not leave me alone for once, damn it! I told you I want to sleep until five…"

The footsteps receded. Timid. Forlorn.

Deep down he was happy. She wouldn't disturb him again. At five he would be back already… A perfect alibi.

Afterwards he would say goodbye to his mother, when the time was right. In fact, in his mind, she was the cause of all his pent-up resentment. She had brought him up to expect a life that she didn't then provide. Such good schooling, with boys who had so much more than him. She would put a bit of money in his pocket so that he wasn't "worth less than the others," but then, when it came to it, the time in a man's life when he really needs money, when he starts to enjoy women and entertainment, quite naturally… Then what had his mother done? Got him a job in a workshop, what a joke!

He dressed carefully. He was wearing a blue-grey, pinstriped suit made from a washable fabric. If, worst case, he did get blood stains on it, his mother would wash it. He would tell her he'd had a nose bleed… Or whatever. She would swallow anything. In any case, he trusted her. Even if she suspected something, she wouldn't tell, even on pain of death. "*It's her duty, after all, to protect me,*" he thought.

Everything went smoothly when he left the building, via the back door. He made sure to lock his room with a key. It was a nuisance having to take the key with him, hidden in his inside pocket, because it was old and heavy… In his hand, he carried a rolled-up newspaper concealing a sand-filled sock, which he intended to use to knock the woman out with one hard blow, and the silk mask. He'd stolen the sock from a clothes line. He didn't want anything to lead back to him.

The concierge of his building was never in her hovel until six in the afternoon, at the earliest… Now, as usual, the dark, empty hallway protected him. The sun made him squint. A beautiful blue sky shimmered above the narrow streets… He could almost have been in a peaceful old town in the provinces. There was a slope at the end of the street, like climbing a hill. The brilliant thing, for Julián, was that no more than a few steps away were Arenal, the Puerta del Sol, tons of noise… People spilling out from the pavements, cafés and crowded shops.

The Metro, jam-packed too. He moved as if in a dream. Squeezed among the disgusting, overflowing throng of humanity; a cattle fair. He, in turn, squeezed the package under his arm… The Metro was fast. It spewed out crowds of people. It spewed him out, along with many others, finally, at Ventas. He started walking, and walking… It was very sunny. He didn't notice.

In the films, of course, it looks better. No sweat dripping from your forehead. Jangling nerves. Tight throat.

He forced himself to enter the house. As he'd expected, there wasn't a soul to be seen. The heat was overbearing; he was glad of it. His shirt was completely drenched. "*They won't call me a coward after this, to hell with them…*" And after going through this agony did he really have to share with Paloma… with Paloma, who was sitting pretty in a bar on Manuel Becerra…?

He stepped into the lift and pressed the button. No sign of the concierge. And then he stopped thinking and concentrated on the word: "Saturday, Saturday, Saturday"…

He wasn't conscious of how he'd arrived at the small landing at the top of the stairs or of how he had sent the lift away. Only that he was there. He wiped away the sweat… He could hear a deafening thump: his heart beating against his ribs.

Silence. The sound of children's voices, far away, deepened the silence. He had to make up his mind. He put his ear to the door. Nothing. Not even a whisper… Nothing.

"*When have you ever seen a thousand shitty pesetas in your life, loser?*"… "*You are what you own.*" He unwrapped the package. He left the paper on the landing. Paper makes noise.

The whirr of the lift. It was coming up. If it carried on up past this floor and he was seen, it was all over. He was gripped by a curious, paralysing panic… Silence. The lift stopped at one of the floors below him. It was going down.

Strangely the shower head above the toilet popped into his head at that moment and, for some reason, it soothed him. The man who'd done that was just as much of a thief as he was, and he felt calm… People would bow down as he passed.

He composed himself. Still no sound whatsoever from inside the flat. His hands had stopped shaking. He placed the sock on the floor and put the mask on. A laugh escaped him. He felt renewed, completely relaxed. He had to admire himself, his remarkably cool head.

Picking up the sock, he inserted the key into the lock. He went in.

They were lying on the beach. They would drive to long, wild stretches of coast, far away from the villages. They took provisions with them.

Paulina watched as a burning mist rose from the sand, like a new tide of gold rushing in from the silvery grey midday sea. Beside her, Antonio gazed at the same spectacle… A serenity, a calm beauty in the scorching air. The seabirds seemed to dissolve in a haze of shimmering heat. Wet bodies dried quickly.

"I wish I could stop time," said Paulina.

# X

"I'm going to ask you something, Señora. I'm going to ask you not to complicate things. The concierge says that you went out with your brother-in-law…"

"With my cousin."

"With your cousin, in the gentleman's car, and you maintain that Señor Nives only accompanied you as far as Atocha station… Why don't you tell me the truth? I don't believe you have anything to do with this, but if you stop lying to me, everything will be a lot easier, you'll save me wasting my time with a lot of boring rigmarole, until eventually I find out what you know…"

The scene was playing out in her house. And the pleasant young man, with the furrowed brow, about the same age as Antonio, was a police officer and he was taking notes. The police officer, as it turned out, was not very threatening. In fact, he had a very sensitive manner. He was talking to her almost as if she were his mother.

Paulina felt her throat tighten. "*They'll definitely interrogate*

*Antonio as well… Rita will find out…"* The young man with brown eyes looked at her again.

"I know you're finding it difficult to decide how much to say… but I assure you that nothing that isn't directly connected to the case will be made public. Nobody will ever know what you tell me tonight. Think about it: if we're forced to investigate ourselves it will be much worse. Much less discreet. You see… The murderer had a key to your flat… or… it was opened from the inside. That's where he was hiding initially…"

The police officer, this youngster, certainly wasn't an old hand at the job, but he'd recently completed a law degree, and he was intelligent. He talked to Paulina in the only possible way. He felt sorry for this woman with her unreadable, pale face. The concierge had been very willing to chat. She had told him that the woman suffered with her nerves and that lately she'd taken up religion. But there were certainly no hysterics now, simply silence. The young man waited patiently. He asked her permission to light a cigarette. Paulina watched him place his note book and pencil on the table in the small dining room and begin to smoke, while he stood and observed the woman's proud profile, her sealed lips, out of the corner of his eye. But he could almost hear the beating of her heart. When she covered her face with her hands, he spoke again.

"Señora, it's as I said. I have no interest in breaking up a family… I know you are married and that you have a son. I know that up to now… anyway, you've never told me anything about yourself… I understand that it's hard for you to explain where and with whom you were on Saturday… But if you don't tell me I'll have to find out for myself, and you'll have to declare it officially. I'll ask you the questions myself."

"Will I have to give the name of the hotel I was staying in?"

"Yes, Señora."

When it was over, Paulina felt wiped out. The man was thanking her, putting his notes away. He almost seemed to want to carry on chatting.

"Go. Could you please go."

The young man looked at her, a little hurt. He couldn't understand her being so proud at a time like this. He spoke to her coldly afterwards.

"I'm not interested in your personal life, Señora de Nives. The only thing I'm interested in now is checking your statement is true, and if I can confirm that the key was a matter of chance I won't bother you again…"

Paulina, nevertheless, felt a violent hostility towards the young man who had treated her in such a gentlemanly way. She was surprised by her reaction. The loathing lasted only a few minutes, but the feeling of fury towards him sent a tremor right through her.

"Please go away," she said again.

Once she'd heard him leave, and for a while afterwards, her entire body trembled.

The murderer had remained hidden in Paulina's flat for some time. He'd washed in there… The crime had been horrific. The woman fought back. They struggled… He had smashed her head against the wall, and struck her multiple times about the head with a sock filled with sand. More blows, with the iron hook from the kitchen, when she was already unconscious… But the woman hadn't died; she was beyond saving, but she hadn't died straight away.

It was the husband who had discovered her at four in the afternoon, and the man hadn't even made it to the telephone. When he was found, his face was grey; he was in almost as bad a state as the poor old woman lying by the bed. All the furniture had been thrown about... And for a small amount of money and a few pieces of jewellery belonging to the deceased... That was it. There was nothing else in the apartment that day. The precious stones from the jewellery they were working on had been taken to the bank at midday. The poor woman, as if she'd had a premonition about the danger of having them at home, had insisted...

They'd caught Julián a few hours later despite his mother swearing blind he hadn't moved from the bedroom. He'd been seen leaving, with a package under his arm, at half past two in the afternoon. By someone in the bar over the road.

After a few anxious days locked inside her flat, like a prisoner, though no one had put any restrictions on her freedom of movement, Paulina decided to visit Amalia. She did it once she was sure that details of her private life were not going to be made public. Antonio hadn't come to see her, but they spoke on the telephone. At last, he was allowed to leave for Villa de Robre to fetch Rita, and Paulina felt sure that the family wouldn't hear the story.

Amalia was exactly as she had been at her Ernesto's funeral, wrapped up in a kimono, in her gloomy rooms, in the depths of a murky sea... She was surrounded by the female contingent of her guests and several women with made-up eyes, who all looked remarkably alike.

"They're all blaming him, but it was that little whore, the one they're saying was an accomplice, she's the one that did it.

He didn't move from here, I've got witnesses. Paulina, give me the name of the best lawyer in Madrid…"

For Paulina, ever since coming back from the beach, the world had felt like a hideous nightmare.

And then, Amalia turned on her.

"You, all you do is blame me, for the way I've brought him up. All you do is criticise… Help me at least, at least give me the name of a good lawyer who can prove this is all lies, and won't think I'm guilty, because my little boy has done nothing…"

Paulina told her that she was totally convinced that even if it turned out that Julián was responsible for the atrocity, Amalia was in no way guilty, nor did she intend to reproach her for anything; she wasn't in a position to reproach anyone for anything. This reasoning didn't calm Amalia. Paulina went to the pharmacy to fetch the medication that the doctor had prescribed, and then slept next to the poor mother that night and, the next day, she did indeed take her to see a renowned criminal lawyer.

"I'll study the facts and I'll see whether I can take his case… Unfortunately, the facts are very clear."

Those were dreadful days, enveloped in a suffocating clamminess. For Paulina, ever since she had spent time in one, prisons filled her with dread, as did trials, police officers, lawyers…

Sometimes, Paulina would close her eyes and picture the luminous Mediterranean Sea… All that belonged to another planet. Antonio was in Villa de Robre now. Soon he would come with Rita and the Countess, but they'd agreed not to meet when he was passing through on his way to Switzerland.

On one of those afternoons when she was living in a daze, she came back from Amalia's to see a light in her own flat.

She went up with an acute sense of trepidation. She was conscious that she was scared of everything these days. Her nerves were permanently on edge. Everything made her anxious. The lift seemed to be travelling up more slowly than usual, as if the world were paralysed or slowed down. She didn't know what she would find inside the flat...

From the landing at the top of the stairs she could hear a dog barking. She didn't understand. When she opened the door, she came face to face with Miguel, who threw himself at her with a happy shriek. The barking went crazy around the mother and son. A golden cocker spaniel puppy was getting very excited, his soft, furry ears flapping about.

"What a racket," cried Paulina, "what a racket! You rascals you... My darling... Miguel...You're so big! My darling..." And then she began to cry.

Eulogio appeared in the doorway of the dining room, in his shirtsleeves, very tanned, with his pipe in his hand.

"I came a few days earlier than planned because of the crime. It must have been terrible for you... They must have been giving you a hard time."

"It's been awful," said Paulina.

She felt exhausted. The little dog began to play, chewing on her shoes, as soon as she sat down. She looked at it, nervously... Gradually she calmed down. She realised that for the first time in many years she'd felt a real, spontaneous urge to kiss Eulogio. It was ridiculous, but Eulogio made her feel calm even about her dealings with the police. Nobody else in her life had given her the solid feeling of security that this man provided. She held his gaze with a grateful glance which he accepted with pleasure.

Paulina was aware of Miguel beside her, strong and healthy,

his hair even blonder than before, yet the warm, homely normality his presence hinted at seemed out of her reach.

"My poor Paulina!" Eulogio's expression was concerned, "you don't look well."

"Mother," Miguel was saying, "Papa says that if you don't want to stay here this winter, they'll put me in the new church school near Villa de Robre and I can study for my bachillerato there."

"And would you like that?"

Miguel laughed.

"Oh yes, yes I think so. Anyway, for this one," he looked lovingly at the dog, "the country air is healthier."

Dinner was cheerful, light-hearted.

"I have a few things to tell you later," said Eulogio, in a good mood.

In front of the boy he spoke only about the factory, saying it could be quite profitable, if managed well. And Mariana had offered him a very generous deal.

"And what's the news on Las Duras?"

"It's so exciting! You've no idea how much work Pepe is doing there… I think he's a real live saint. What he does for those people! They're falling under his spell. And the other thing is the faith he has… It's infectious."

"Don't tell me you've caught it!"

Paulina asked him in a jokey tone.

Eulogio paused a moment before smiling and answering no.

After the boy went to bed, taking the dog with him to his bedroom, despite Paulina half-heartedly protesting, and then insisting this must be the only and last time… Eulogio explained what he had been patiently waiting to tell her about: Mariana's indignation over the bouts of mysticism which seemed to be breaking out all around her.

"That's why I was laughing when you asked me about Pepe's infectiousness… For my mother, it's like a contagious disease, with Blanca being the worst culprit. You should hear the way she tells her off, and Blanca's face, almost contrite… Poor Mamá, she's totally in shock about what's happened to you. So, what is going on?"

"It's true," said Paulina.

But she didn't say any more. She didn't feel strong enough to go over again what she had felt in those moments. It was almost as if she hadn't felt it… But, she had. She had. How powerfully and how extraordinarily clearly she had seen things then! There were no illusions. She had *known* things, then they had been erased. But she had tasted a different life. Yes, a wisdom.

"I'll be here for a week. Then I'm going back… You let me know what you decide."

"I'm in such a state… Would you mind, Eulogio, if I stayed here a short while longer? I'll look after Miguel. He can go to school as normal. Then, after a while, I'll write to you."

Eulogio leaned forward, looking at her. He said jokingly:

"I'm guessing now you'll definitely want to get married in Church."

Paulina felt her cheeks redden. She was in the ugly little dining room in the flat, sat opposite Eulogio, with a cigarette between her fingers. The window was open to a tiny internal patio. The lamplight shone boldly in her face. She swallowed.

"I think… I think I don't want to get married, Eulogio."

She waited. She listened to the beating of her heart. It deafened her, as if it were sounding inside her ears.

Eulogio emptied the bowl of the pipe into the ashtray, with sharp, strong, taps. He looked at her. Eulogio's eyes betrayed all the expression his face did not. Their colour was changing. Now they seemed almost black. He narrowed them slightly.

"I understand, woman… What you went through last year was terrible… It's because of that, isn't it?"

Paulina held his gaze, very calm now. When she remembered how much she had wept here, in this very flat—with this man who had become a horrible stranger—sick, drowning in a cold grey loneliness at this man's side, she looked him straight in the eyes.

"Yes, Eulogio, it was bad. I'd imagined that you and me, what we had, still existed and…"

Eulogio picked up another pipe. He would always have several on the little table, within easy reach. Paulina was struck by how quickly the house had filled with him, with his tastes. He took out the tobacco pouch and began to fill the bowl with the aromatic tobacco mixed with honey.

"I know…"

He lit the pipe, drawing on it gently. He lit another match. Slowly the tobacco began to glow red. Slowly… Eulogio began to smoke. He seemed to be looking over Paulina's head. He seemed to be thinking of far off things.

"However," he said after a while, "we have a son…"

"This isn't a barrier for me, Eulogio. The boy is older now. It won't do him any harm to live some of the time with one of us and some with the other. It's worse to live with parents who don't get on… Also, I know what I'm like. I can't live in the country."

"I've come back to you, for the sake of my son," said Eulogio firmly.

"And I waited for you, for you yourself, if you must know." After a short time, Eulogio stood up.

"This conversation is painful, Paulina. It's starting to get ridiculous... When two people have as many things in common as you and I... It can't all end in a few words: 'we've had enough now, it's over'... No, that's not how it works. I also have to let go of certain things, to love you as a wife."

Paulina remembered Antonio. Intensely.

"It's useless," she said.

A few moments later she stood up and began to busy herself in the flat. She made the bed in the maid's room. Eulogio saw this.

"I'll sleep here, Paulina, don't worry."

"As you wish."

Paulina left him settled down next to his radio and went out to her mattress on the balcony. The nights weren't as hot now. She pulled on a jersey. She thought for a long time. She heard a knock on the bedroom door. It was Eulogio.

"I wanted to say goodnight..."

She got to her feet, surprised. She could see the solid bulk of Eulogio's figure in the shadows. He could only see Paulina's outline, silhouetted beside the iron railings of the balcony, in front of a newly emerged gigantic moon.

"I've been a coward. I didn't tell you at the time, I thought I wouldn't have to, but I need to tell you... You're freer than you think. Completely free. Our marriage was never registered. We're not married in the eyes of the law, or anyone's eyes."

Paulina's deep sigh carried through the darkness. For some time neither of them moved or said anything. Eventually, Eulogio walked away.

During those few days, Eulogio lived in the flat, and they were perfectly friendly with each other, comfortable even. Miguel felt happy to see his parents like this, content, or so it seemed to him. Paulina accepted money from Eulogio to buy school equipment for Miguel and winter clothes for herself.

"You don't have to... I'm thinking of starting up my classes again, you know?"

"It's fine, woman, that's up to you. As I said you're completely free, but you can accept something from me in good conscience. After all, didn't you look after the child all that time I was in America? I could only send you pitiful amounts of money... Now, the house, the child, I want to provide the money, and you, you know, use it as you see fit. I'll have very few expenses in Villa de Robre..."

The night before Eulogio was due to leave, Paulina, unexpectedly, asked his forgiveness in a timid voice. She had come into the flat looking pale and anxious. She ate in silence. And now when they were alone she asked for his forgiveness.

"What for, Paulina?"

"I'm not the woman you think I am... I've not been as blameless as you think. It's very hard to say this, but I think it's the honourable thing to do. I don't want you to think you've lost a precious jewel."

They were sitting in the small dining room, having their last after-dinner conversation. Miguel had gone to bed. The conversation between them had become easy over those few days, more like it had been before their separation in Barcelona.

Eulogio flushed red under his tanned skin while he sucked nervously on his pipe. Eventually he looked at Paulina with kindness in his eyes.

"I don't want to know anything… Look, this stuff is unbear-able to listen to. It hurts me to hear it, even though I always thought it wouldn't affect me much… Because I've thought about it. I've also thought about the misunderstandings between us when I came back. We'd come to the conclusion it was all my fault but… Paulina, forget about what happened in the years when we were separated. Why are you thinking about it now?"

Paulina knew very well why it had occurred to her now.

"Blanca came to see me. She made me think about my own smallness… I don't know; she is such a good woman… I wanted you to despise me… Don't think again about marrying me. It's not a good idea."

Eulogio moved closer to her and tried to lift her chin to see into her eyes.

Paulina resisted. She didn't let him.

"Is that the only reason you don't want to get married, Paulina?"

"No… Even if you wanted to, even if none of it mattered to you, I wouldn't want to. But I don't want you to wish it either. Do you understand?"

"Not really…"

Eulogio was disappointed. Paulina too. She was disappoint-ed in herself for not managing to explain the truth. But perhaps she didn't even deserve to have the chance to unburden herself. Eulogio thought she was referring to the years when they didn't see each other.

"Paulina," Eulogio said eventually, "my wanting to marry you isn't about what you're worth or not worth. It's because you're the mother of my child, and because, apart from whatever madness or weakness you're talking about, you're the woman who sacrificed herself for my son. And no other woman I could bring into our house, none, could take your place, for our boy. That's the reason… just that."

Suddenly Paulina burst into tears and told him that in spite of all that, marriage was impossible.

"No! No more charades!"

Eulogio felt cold as he watched Paulina's tears trickle down her face and saw the way her nose reddened. He stifled a feeling of revulsion… He gave her his handkerchief because her own was drenched already.

"I'm starting to think, like my mother, that Blanca rather upsets you when she visits, my love…"

Paulina hastily dried her tears. She lit a cigarette and eventually, calm now, said something which took Eulogio by surprise.

"Yes, Blanca helped me understand many things. Many things… She is extraordinarily intelligent… In fact, it's more than that. She is truthful to her core."

Blanca was passing through Madrid. She was on her way to Switzerland with her daughter and her son-in-law. She had a lot to do in those hours in the city, but she didn't want to miss seeing her "miracle," as she liked to call Paulina. Having knocked confidently and contentedly at the door of the Nives's apartment, she was somewhat taken aback, because the extraordinarily gregarious woman dressed in red, kissing her on the cheeks, and treating her as though she were a very fragile old lady, was not the Paulina she'd been expecting. Of course, she couldn't guess at the thoughts hidden behind the smile, behind the furrowed brow, behind Paulina's warm greeting, but…

Paulina was thinking that this woman had just been with Antonio and that she would see him later and that she would talk about her to him.

"*A last goodbye, as we cannot communicate with each other for now. But he will hear my name. He will ask his mother-in-law about me. If I seemed happy, or… He will know something of me.*"

"My dear," said Blanca, looking at her with her deep, clear eyes, "you don't seem very happy… How can this be? Do you remember the letter you wrote to me? I carry it with me always…"

With a sigh, Blanca sank down into one of the small armchairs in the dining room. She was slightly concerned about how she would get out of it again. Blanca put her hand into her large black bag and held out the old letter to Paulina. Paulina, her hands trembling slightly, took the little note that she'd written in her state of euphoria in the Puerta del Sol. Barely two months ago… No, not even two months.

"I don't feel any of this now, Blanca… It's not that I've lost my faith, how can I explain? I know that God and His love exist, and yet… Now I'm at a distance, wrapped up in things here again. If you only knew, how horrific it's been. A kid I've known since he was tiny has murdered someone. He killed a poor old lady right here, in this house. How can God allow that to happen? These dreadful things happen and I can't find any explanation. Back then I knew everything, I know that I felt that everything was good, that everything had a magnificent order Heavenward, but now…"

"Now you must ask God to help you, now that he has opened your eyes, my dear. He has called you! Look inside yourself, see if you have answered his call. Talk to a priest; he will be able to guide you… You'll see, you'll recover what you think you've lost. And if you never recover it in quite the same way… but, inside, you'll become serene, if you allow the Holy Spirit into your soul, if you continue on the path of truth. There is no other: the path of Jesus, you know? Renouncing oneself, not living only for oneself. Taking the cross and following him…"

Blanca drank a glass of water that Paulina had brought her. Paulina, too, felt thirsty as she watched her drink. Blanca went on immediately:

"Personally, I'm convinced that if a person truly follows Christ, the rest will come by itself. This murder, all these crimes committed by people who have not found God… All this, sometimes I feel, Paulina, as if it pierces my flesh. I tell myself that *I*, I who know the Lord yet don't know how to teach Him, to show that He has come into the world, that He has said 'Love one another,' I, who do not know how to carry Him in my life, in my actions, in my love for others, I am to blame for those who don't have any references to know Christ as he truly is, who because of us, see Him distorted and twisted, and believe there is no salvation… Yes, my dear, you and I, all those of us who say we are Catholic, those of us who believe in the Communion of Saints, and yet are not as heroic or as pure or as good as He demands, we are to blame for this young boy losing his way… Has he seen a true society of Christians around him? Or has he only seen those of us who *say* we love God, but in practice, live our lives in whatever way we please?"

Blanca was feeling inspired. She wanted to share her fears with Paulina. Her fears about the obsession with material things that was everywhere now. The promotion of pleasure, power, money…

Paulina was ashen. She watched Blanca's innocent face talking to her and it felt as if, unknowingly, Blanca was accusing her directly. She, who had forgotten everything, had given in to absolute egotism with Antonio, the very day that Julián was committing murder. And committing murder simply because of that stupid desire for material things, money and the fleeting pleasure it brings, gluttony, sensuality, the golden calves, the idols we create.

Blanca tried to stand up but couldn't. Paulina helped her out of the chair. She couldn't speak to her. Deep in thought, she showed her around the tiny flat, in silence. As she was leaving, Blanca hugged her affectionately.

"Paulina, my dear, I want to ask you something: pray hard for Rita to have a good death, if the Lord believes it is better for her to die now than to live. But otherwise… pray that she lives, Paulina. I always hope for miracles. I am a great believer in prayer!"

Paulina nodded, promising she would.

That day was Eulogio's last day in Madrid. He had settled his affairs with Nives Enterprises.

"I cut my ties, Paulina. A man needs to find his own purpose in life. Sometimes one can lose one's way…"

He found Paulina very quiet and thoughtful. The conversation with Blanca had stirred Paulina's soul. Yes, she felt ploughed like earth, wounded, touched in the deepest part of her… And then, after dinner, she had felt that desire to be despised…

Eulogio took leave of her the next day with a quick kiss.

"You know what I'm hoping for, Paulina."

She shook her head.

"You have the right to be happy. If you met a good woman, do you think I would blame you? It wouldn't be difficult. In your village alone there are hordes of decent women… the sort of women you like, homely, without any will or judgement of their own, hardworking, nice and quiet, and most importantly, excellent mothers."

Eulogio cast a worried look towards the boy, who was hanging around nearby with the dog.

"Don't be silly, Paulina. You women always think you're the centre of the universe. A man can also live perfectly well without a woman."

# XI

Blanca, with her words, had done something akin to shaking a nest full of wasps over Paulina.

Now, Paulina's life would never be the same as before her intense experience, her enlightenment on the train. Her pagan lifestyle, clean and stoic of spirit and ruled by instinct, her desires sharpened by education, her feelings more or less developed… that life was over. It was useless to try to think any differently. She'd lost the innocent belief that she was always doing what she considered right. This judgement could vary slightly in her previous life, according to her innermost desires, and in fact had varied many times… Not so now.

Now she knew, without a doubt, that there are things that obscure the presence of God in the soul. Certain things kill and defile the soul. They rob God of the soul's song of glory.

Blanca's words had horrified her. Yes, it was all about those who knew Christ following Him, truly forming part of the mystical and whole Christ and revealing Him through their lives. What mattered most? Stealing, or fornicating, or killing?

All of them obeyed the same selfish impulse. Apparently, some things were more harmful to society than others... And always in a limited amount of time. In the long run, all of them were equally harmful, even to society... And in the eyes of God, perhaps she, Paulina, had committed greater sins than that murdering idiot boy.

Two weeks after her conversation with Blanca, Paulina received a letter from Antonio. She read it in the kitchen. It lay for a while on her cheap, chintz apron. The dog was circling around her, wanting to play, to snatch it from her. The letter brought back sun-filled days and spoke of many more carefree, happy days touring around new sites, marvellous places in Europe. Days that would soon be upon them. "Soon," would come the death of Rita, for whose life she had promised to pray. Paulina knew now that praying is not simply speaking empty words.

Paulina, pale, a weary expression on her face, pushed the dog aside, screwed up the letter and burned it.

Setting off on the path of Christ... Something that had seemed so easy, so easy in that first flush of spiritual awakening. How difficult, my God! How difficult when you had to start by tearing out that eye, that offending hand. Her heart. Her very heart.

She was in the kitchen of her flat preparing lunch for Miguel. The sunlight, spilling out over the kitchen tiles, softly flowing, already seeping in. A sparkling, joyful, end-of-October sun.

There was a knock at the door. It was Luisa, her upstairs neighbour, wanting to borrow an onion.

Luisa's story was distressing. The year before, they had often gone to the market together and Paulina found it hard to watch her choose, choose... the worst sardines, the gone-off fruit...

This was in the summer, when it was cheap. If not, there would be no fruit. And milk, only for the youngest children, unless it was the entire meal, cheaper than anything else… Paulina, wishing to help, would invite one of the children to have lunch with her almost every day. The clothes that Miguel had grown out of went to Luisa of course. She had done the same the year before that, too.

"The thing is, Paulina, my husband, poor man, works eight hours in the office. With all the 'points' for the children and then taking off the taxes and, in the end, the total, I'll tell you the real figure he brings home: one thousand nine hundred exactly, not even two thousand pesetas. The apartment, which is very cheap for what it is, costs eight hundred pesetas… Tell me, how do I feed and clothe seven people on that money? The 'Brothers' gave our oldest child a grant on top. But what about books? And shoes? Sometimes the child can't go because he doesn't have a coat, or he doesn't have shoes… In the office, they insist my husband dresses smartly, and if not, he'll be out…"

"Luisa," Paulina had said brutally last year, "don't have any more children, it's cruel." Luisa had blushed.

"It's my husband, the poor man, he hasn't got any will power…"

"But it's not about that, don't be ridiculous, woman, there are precautions you can take, and if necessary, well there's even… Look, Luisa, I can't bear to see you in that situation again. If something happens, you tell me, I'll find the money, I'll lend it to you and…"

Luisa didn't understand at first. When she did, her tone was icy.

"But Paulina, how do you think I was brought up? Don't you know I'm from Aragon? I really am religious. I don't believe only when it suits me and stop believing when it doesn't, and I will never refuse the children that God sends me. And what makes you think I could, that I could...? Really!"

Paulina had felt her hair stand on end, a feeling somewhere between admiration and horror towards this woman who was so primitive. Now, as she listened to those crying children, Paulina knew that Luisa was right. She bore her cross, heavy as it was, like so many men and women, knowing perfectly well what she was doing. Now she was smiling at her and saying goodbye with the onion in her hand.

"How's everything? How's it going with Francisco?"

Luisa laughed and said it was going very well, perfectly in fact. Paulina was smiling too as she said goodbye. The two of them were remembering an incident that had happened to Luisa the year before.

Luisa's husband, the man she always said was her "angel," that tall, skinny, slightly bald angel Francisco, with his sunken cheeks, who Paulina sometimes heard pacing and crooning while he rocked his children to sleep, and who, when he said hello on the stairs, looked about to expire, yes, one day that sad seraphim revolted. Luisa had come down to Paulina's flat in floods of tears.

"He's... dr... driving me insane..."

"Come now, woman..."

Paulina, who back then believed everything that happened to Luisa was her own fault, because of a blind stubbornness protected by the Church, and because she didn't heed Paulina's sensible advice, had listened slightly impatiently at first.

What had happened, it seemed, was that Francisco had begun to detest the grilled sardines that he used to eat for lunch and for his evening meal. Before, he'd been addicted to them. But lately, as soon as they appeared on the oilcloth-covered table, he would fix them with a frown that didn't bode well. Luisa, of course, didn't pay much attention to the frowning, or the shaking of the head. She served up what was cheapest. And that was that.

"But two days ago… when I take, as calm as ever, the dish of sardines to the table… Guess what he did… He stood up, and you know how tall he is… And he started to laugh, to laugh, like this, silently, with his mouth wide open; and as the poor man has so many teeth missing, it was quite scary… All the children, you see, Paulina, were silent, the poor little mites, their little napkins round their necks, not crying or moving, and I was silent too, in shock… And then Francisco goes and lifts the dish up in the air and smashes it on the kitchen floor. Then he punches me and insults me and tells me if I serve him those sardines again he'll strangle me… Ah, but I, Paulina, I stood up to him; I tell you I stood up to him, by our blessed Lady of the Pillar! No way was I putting up with abuse. He wasn't getting away with that. So, I stood up too and I started shouting like a mad woman and I shouted twenty thousand truths like punches, and I told him if he wanted to eat anything other than sardines, that he should earn it, that I ate sardines and his children ate sardines, well I had no choice. And he, Paulina, stormed out and slammed the door and…"

Paulina had stroked Luisa's bowed, weeping head with her fingertips.

"Well, he'll be back, you'll see… You were absolutely right."

Luisa shook her head.

"No, he's already back. Didn't I say this happened the other day? Now he's carrying on with the hunger strike. And so…"

"What?"

"It's not about sardines any more… I don't give him sardines now, so help me God. But whatever I give him, he barely touches. He says: 'A man who doesn't earn enough to eat, doesn't eat.' And he looks at me with those dead-lamb eyes… And I burst into tears… And that's how it is at every meal… And the children burst into tears too when they hear us. And he's wasting away, though he was so thin already you wouldn't think he could get any thinner, and… and…"

It was awful, but that day Paulina—she couldn't help it—had burst out laughing, while Luisa was telling her this; and Luisa too, between sobs.

A few days later, the seraphic Francisco gave in to Luisa's tears and began little by little to swallow his potatoes, his chickpeas… Not sardines. Luisa, during that time, let go of her sardine obsession. Paulina had said at the time that she shouldn't trust Francisco, that he might be an angel, but sooner or later he'd play another dirty trick on her.

"It's a well-known thing, Luisa, that every good husband's first duty is to annoy their wife. Otherwise, where would be the matrimonial cross that you talk so much about?"

Luisa was smiling, shaking her head.

"Oh Paulina, Paulina!"

Now Paulina was in a reflective mood as she said goodbye to her. "*I'll never be able to wish for sufficient strength to be a good Christian.*"

"*If I can't stop thinking about Antonio's wife dying so that I can have him, it's time I let go of Antonio.*"

This was a clear, a perfectly clear thought. There was no other side to it. Either stop thinking about Antonio or stop thinking once and for all that she believed in God and that the Catholic and Apostolic Church was the repository of the commandments and the powers of Christ.

At times, she was desperate. It was as if a demon were talking inside her: "*God has come to you, has shown himself to you so that you may condemn yourself. While you were carrying on innocently, in the tranquillity of your material vision of life, you were very rarely guilty. But now, now you reject the light, you say: I want hell. You choose it… You choose like Lucifer. God has given you so much freedom.*"

In the afternoon, she went out. Autumn was on its way. She walked through the streets that, now the summer was over, were teeming with life, and the air felt even crisper than in spring. The shop windows were lit up and tastefully dressed. The women were wearing the first tailored dresses and light coats of the season. All Saints' Day was fast approaching and there were many stalls selling chrysanthemums, dahlias and sea lavender. She wandered aimlessly, with frightened, anxious eyes. She stared at people as if she had lost something. She remembered she had found something more important than life itself, that summer, and that she had lost it… She had known the feeling of God and she had lost it.

She came across an ordinary church and stopped. An ugly, uninspiring building, behind a small fence. She hadn't been back to church since her outing to the seaside… Only on Sundays, since Miguel arrived, to accompany the boy. A hypocrite now, like so many others, like the ones she used to laugh at when she was a "free, pure pagan," but whom she now could understand… "At least, they try to encourage others in what they know is true but don't have the courage to live…"

On an impulse, she entered the church. She felt an urge. Yes… She felt it… She took off the scarf from around her neck and knotted it at her chin, covering her bare head, and went in.

The church was dimly lit. Just two electric candles on the altar, and the lamp of the Tabernacle. An old lady, whispering prayers. A young man, on his knees, with his head in his hands, praying.

The church was decorated in very poor taste. A lot of plaster and glitter. There were two huge pictures of the Sacred Hearts.

Paulina's anxious eyes barely registered this. The Sacred Heart, the conventional image of a Christ conceived according to utterly affected and absurd aesthetic principles, no longer seemed affected or absurd to Paulina. She was beginning to look to its deeper meaning. It is the so often repeated message of the love of God made man. The eternal message centred, above all in Christ's immense love. *"He who is too immense to fit into Heaven, was not afraid to be enclosed in a Virgin's womb."*… *"The Heart of Jesus is the door to that great blazing fire of Joy that I glimpsed."*

"My God," she prayed, "my Christ, Jesus! I know that you exist, that you have called me, that you want me to follow your own path of renunciation, your path to the happiness you have shown me, your path that, what's more, I know provides the only true and lasting happiness on earth… I know it's true, though I'm so far from that joy now. And that is how it should be. What did I ever do to attain it, even when I knew it to be true? I may never feel that joy again, but… I know it is not enough to see the happiness of Your light, that this alone is not enough. We must follow You, but… You must do everything. I ask you humbly, dear God, one small thing. Only that you allow me this, to begin, to wish with all my heart, unreservedly, to follow you…"

"That you allow me to wish… that you allow me to wish…" she repeated without realising, and she felt her hands were wet with her tears, which were large, clean and good.

It was difficult to desire to be with Christ when she knew that being with Christ would strip her heart of that cruel human bond, so painful, so dear; her love for a married man.

"Let me wish…"

At once, she felt peace. A soft, a gentle peace.

# XII

Antonio belonged to a generation of Spanish university gradu-ates who had begun their studies after the end of the National Movement. Among this young generation, there had been a resurgence of religious feeling. It wasn't that all the students were fervent believers, but the majority, the best, seemed to be, and it was fashionable to take issues of a spiritual nature seriously. Antonio hadn't thought about this fact very much, nor had he worried about it, until his half-brother Jordi—an infuriating boy whom he had just welcomed to Paris—informed him, during dinner, that neither he nor any of the other young men he knew took the question of religion seriously. They were all sceptics. Though Jordi's view could be somewhat biased, Antonio was inclined to believe him.

"The youth," thought Antonio, "always want rebellion, re-action. We were reacting against the pre-war climate of secu-larisation: this lot are perhaps reacting against an environment which is too much the other way..." When Antonio thought "we," he was separating himself absolutely from his brother who was five or six years younger than him, even though he in his time had been one of the worst, the most indifferent in his duty… Though not as indifferent as Jordi.

Antonio had come to Paris because his father had written to ask if he could meet Jordi—who would be staying for a few months—and guide him a little. The letter was a surprise, given that Antonio had always been considered more of a bad example. Old Nives must be having a lot of trouble with his brood, if he was resorting to allowing Antonio to influence his brother.

For Antonio, it was a huge relief to have a pretext to once more escape his duties as Rita's caring husband. "I'll bring you Christmas presents from Paris."

He intended to honour this and return laden with exquisite, expensive gifts. This was how he would compensate Blanca and Rita.

Clearly, he wasn't expecting his reunion with his brother to be such a cold shower. Or that the boy's superior smirk would wind him up so much. Jordi branded Antonio, and all his friends, naïve.

"I tell you who's here in Paris," said Jordi, "your old friend Torrent, the stuck-up one father used to hold up as an example. He's become one of those scruffy Bohemians, so I hear."

For Antonio, this was unimaginable. Torrent's family had pampered him, brought him up wrapped in cotton wool. As a boy, he would write ardent and hate-filled poetry, but purely from his imagination; he led a perfectly healthy, ordered life.

"Yes, yes…" Jordi's voice grated on him, "he discovered life a little late, but it appears he now wants nothing more to do with his comfortable home, or soap and water."

The more time Antonio spent with Jordi, the more he found him dislikeable. He was a calm chap, tall, with a beard, rimless glasses and a pedantic manner.

*"How did this twit persuade my father to let him drop his studies in Barcelona, evade military service, and enroll in a course for foreigners here in Paris?"* Antonio didn't have the strength to ask his brother the question. As they talked about the topics of the day he discovered that, despite Jordi's self-confidence, the younger man's intellectual zeal was superficial. When they lit a cigarette with coffee after dinner on the first evening, Antonio broached the subject of women, an obsession of his since he'd grown into long trousers.

"They're of no interest to me," said Jordi.

"Do you mean you're a virgin?"

Jordi reddened beneath his beard, but shot him a contemptuous look through his glasses.

"Don't be ridiculous. Women are fine for a while, but you can't deny that the classic falling in love has been consigned to history."

"What the hell *are* you interested in?"

"Me, nothing. I'm not interested in anything… Not enough to pay much attention, I mean. I like to live in the present, rack up experiences. Yes, maybe that's it…"

Antonio had recently returned from a getaway to Rome and had enjoyed himself like a young lad on holiday. After the emotional turmoil of the summer followed by the quietness of his life in Switzerland, he had excitedly made the most of his youth and his wealth in Rome. He'd arrived in Paris inclined to do the same, but his half-brother had put him in a bad mood. He was forgetting that he too, until very recently, had been miserable and hard to please, and he found his brother lacking in any youthful lust for life.

"You make me feel young. It feels as if of the two of us, the younger and the one who knows how to enjoy life is me."

"You're wrong. I've had experiences that you, at my age, never even dreamed of. At my age, you spent all your time writing romantic poems for your much older cousin… whereas I know everything there is to know about women, and they bore me. I've come to Paris to escape one of them, if you must know. Father thinks I'm in deep trouble and that he's helped me out. I don't see any trouble at all, but the whole thing was becoming a bit of a bore and in any case, I'm happy to have a change of scene."

It was through pure frustration and an effort to impose his authority that Antonio had decided both he and Jordi would go to bed at nine that evening.

"Tomorrow, I'll drop you at your lodgings, but tonight we're going to have some rest."

He regretted his decision almost immediately, but nothing in the world would have made him go back on it.

Jordi made no comment. After stretching and yawning like a monkey, he'd fallen asleep peacefully, while Antonio, annoyed at himself, read an Italian novel, while listening to the slow breathing of his brother, who slept on in the next bed, not disturbed in the slightest by the light from Antonio's reading lamp.

Jordi had succeeded in making him forget his desire to have fun. Paris seemed as distant from this hotel room as from Switzerland or Villa de Robre…

Antonio didn't manage to interest himself enough in the novel to unlock the secrets of a language he hadn't mastered. He'd bought it, in fact, to practise because his intention had been to make frequent visits to Italy while Rita remained in Switzerland…The encounter with his brother had put him in an unusually self-reflective mood, and eventually he lit a cigarette, turned out the light, and smoked in the dark as he thought about his life. Yes, it was useless and empty, but compared to Jordi's, he felt it was oddly beautiful. It was true he hadn't held down a serious job, but at least he'd tasted the good things in life. He'd explored the world of art. He was quite a connoisseur of painting, for example. He was keen on literature too, and there were exquisite things in the form of objects and architecture that could touch him deeply. Certainly, he had always pushed intellectual pleasure to one side if an affair that would satisfy his baser instincts had presented itself, however stupid and vulgar that affair might be. But at least he had a notion of what sin was, of morality, and he knew where the lines were. He might or might not cross them, but at least he recognised them… Jordi would see all this as overcomplicated and old-fashioned. As for love, for him only passion existed.

Antonio thought about Paulina and the flavour and beauty that she had brought to his whole life. The memory of Paulina grew huge into a tender, warm gratitude. Even now she was filling his life with motivation and beauty, elevating it. He was certain that he could be extremely happy away from her, like he had been in Rome for example; but he was equally certain that, inevitably, he would need her again.

Suddenly he longed for her with an extraordinary force. Paulina was something permanent in his life, something rare and exquisite that he should never lose.

"I'll marry her," he decided right then, with absolute conviction. "When Rita dies, I'll marry her."

He dismissed Rita's death; it was something natural and, though very painful, inevitable... And Rita, he knew deep down, had always been transient in his life. He had married her because she was beautiful, because she was the daughter of a fabulous family and because she was disarmingly honest and completely embodied the image that, unconsciously, a man carries deep inside, of the ideal wife. The strangest thing about his marriage was that he, the stronger personality, and the one who wasn't in love, had adapted himself, with an easy kind of mimicry, to Rita's tastes. They had lived a year happily caught up in a social whirl that didn't leave them time to think about themselves. They only concerned themselves with their clothes, their furniture, their cars, having the latest records... Antonio had felt proud of his wife's beauty and had even designed dresses for her. Their marriage had transformed him into an affected and vacuous man, fussing over silly trifles and vain as a peacock.

Jordi turned over in bed, groaning in his dreams. Antonio could barely make out his outline in the half-light.

"You are my conscience, little brother," he thought again; "I never thought this would happen to me."

He felt for an ashtray on the bedside table and as soon he'd crushed the cigarette butt, his hand groped around again for the packet of cigarettes and a lighter.

The memory of Paulina filled the room now, as if she were there. She hadn't replied to any of his letters since they'd separated in Madrid.

He had always written Paulina very long letters that she would usually answer with a few awkward lines, but it was a relief to have her as his confidant, his friend. She'd always been affectionate towards him, sharing the secrets of her mind long before she had given him her body.

"I'll marry Paulina," he thought again.

The three days in Alicante had been perfect. Paulina was both wise and naïve. It was wonderful to see how many of the things money could buy were entirely new to her, and the pleasure they gave her had been a revelation and a joy for him. It would be marvellous to travel with her... And he found himself moved by her fears concerning the religious revelation she believed she'd been through.

"I'm going to damn my soul because of you."

These words, coming from her, had been sincere. No one had been able to give him more than Paulina. No one could be a truer companion for him than she. He missed her, now that she was so far away, having made her suffer so for such small-minded reasons, that summer, treated her with disdain and criticised her, Paulina, who was the best part of him... It upset him to think back to the disastrous ending of the trip to Alicante, when there were all those police investigations. He hadn't behaved well towards Paulina, passing the buck like that. Clearly, he couldn't have compromised himself without compromising her... It had been a disagreeable and sordid affair.

For a few minutes, he tortured himself with the idea that Paulina would think badly of him when she compared him to Eulogio, who had come from the village as soon as he heard about the murder in the house... He hadn't been to see her, not even once! This train of thought culminated in a rush of loathing for Eulogio. Paulina's silence during all this time, could it mean that she'd decided after all to go back to the father of her child? He didn't think her capable of such stupidity. Paulina and Eulogio had nothing in common, not in their tastes, nor their feelings, not in any way. Their union had been a disaster.

What's more, Eulogio would never consent to a reconciliation with his wife if he had even the slightest suspicion that she'd betrayed him.

Antonio jumped out of bed to look in his luggage for a tube of sleeping pills. His head was burning and if he continued like this, he thought his head would explode. That night in Paris was turning out to be a dreadful night for Antonio.

He was distracted by the sight of his weary, sleepless eyes in the mirror above the sink, while he drank water to swallow the medicine.

As he got back into bed he saw on his watch that it was ridiculously early in the evening. In Madrid, Paulina would be still up… The need to see her became unbearable and before he fell asleep he knew that the next day he would buy a plane ticket to Spain. Even for a few short hours, he had to go to Madrid.

The concierge hadn't felt it necessary to leave her apartment door ajar. But as she was half-deaf, and on all fours underneath the skirts of her brazier table stoking the fire, she didn't realise that someone was knocking impatiently on it. Eventually, the door was unceremoniously pushed open and a gust of cold air, which the woman felt on her haunches, blew into the kitchen; the cat stretched, arching its back. The woman turned around then, annoyed, and banged her head on the table top in her haste to stand up. That bump terrified her for half a second; it made her remember the bloody events on the sixth floor, where the poor lady had her skull bashed in…

She was breathing heavily by the time she finally managed to straighten up, and her eyes came level with a man's thick overcoat. Raising her head a little more, she came face to face with Antonio Nives. She knew him well, but like the bump on the brazier table, the man brought back unwelcome memories. She eyed him so suspiciously that Antonio lost patience.

"I've been up to my cousins' flat and no one is answering the door. Do you happen to know if they've left Madrid?"

The concierge gave him one of her scathing looks.

"Only Doña Paulina is there. The boy left this morning to spend Christmas in the village. But that's not of any interest to you, is it?"

Antonio decided to ignore her impertinent tone. "And you don't know where my cousin might be this afternoon?"

"Yes, sir. Your *cousin* is in church. She's spending the day in prayer, God bless her. She's reciting the Rosary as we speak… Walk around the corner and when you reach the street that cuts across you'll see the Brothers' school. As soon as you pass the gate you'll see the church. You can't miss it… But if you want to save yourself the bother, if you come back in a little while, Doña Paulina will be back. They close the church at eight o'clock."

Antonio decided to go and look for Paulina. It had been very different last time, when he'd arrived from the village impatient, almost hungry for her. Now he noticed his emotions were calmer, deeper. Perhaps because two months had gone by and in that time, he'd taken his trip to Rome. Since then things had settled down, come back into perspective.

When he arrived at the church, he watched one veiled woman dressed in black after another slip out of its doors. They all looked the same to him. They would open the interior door of the church and for a moment a shaft of light would outline them. Then the door would shut again and they would come out into the dark grey air, moving away along the pavement or joining the other devout women who had come out before them. Antonio smiled in amazement. He couldn't fit Paulina's image with these women… Some men were coming out too, it was true, but there were a striking number of these dark female figures.

Antonio wondered if Paulina had bought a black overcoat. He had never seen her wearing a veil.

The night was humid and misty. The pavement he was walking on was very wet. Antonio opened the door of the church to let an old couple out first and saw the lit and practically empty interior… He decided to go in at the point half the lights went out. Perhaps it was a warning that they would be closing soon. One or two of the few remaining people inside stood up to leave.

It smelled of incense and even more strongly of humanity. The breath of the many people who had filled the church had loaded the air. Antonio noted with surprise that it was not only his world and Jordi's world that existed. All these people had other worries. "Old ones," he thought.

Then he recalled his brother-in-law José, and he began to think about the life of so many young men who dedicate themselves to the priesthood. It was another world, unknown to him, certainly.

He couldn't find Paulina behind the few black veils that remained dotted about the benches, over the faces of their owners. He had remained standing, next to the font of holy water at the entrance, because the church wasn't very big and he could take in all of it from there. Then he noticed Paulina, kneeling very close to him, her head in her hands. She wasn't wearing a veil at all, but a waterproof cap that matched her raincoat. She was still as a statue and didn't realise that Antonio had knelt beside her. He became impatient and tapped her on the shoulder. Then he saw her raise her head, startled, her fearful expression lingering, even after she recognised him.

"What? Aren't you happy to see me?"

Paulina turned to the altar and crossed herself hastily. "Let's get out of here."

Antonio followed her out of the building and they started walking side by side. Paulina was walking very fast and Antonio strode to keep up with her.

"Where are you taking me, Paulina?"

"I don't know," said Paulina confused, and smiled. "I don't know where I'm taking you. It gave me a shock seeing you."

"That's your fault for not writing to me. Your silence worried me... Now you see. I couldn't resist the temptation to come for a few hours. A flying visit. I'm leaving again tomorrow."

"You know very well I can't write to you."

"My dearest devout one, friendship is not a sin."

"Friendship no, but..."

Antonio's letters of course had been far more than simply friendly. He found the playful tone of her voice charming. There was none of the dry edginess Antonio remembered from when he'd arrived from Villa de Robre after what she called her "conversion." But she was suitably moved and nervous. He sensed she was trembling. He put his hand on her arm.

"I can feel your heart, like a little clock, under your raincoat..."

"Are you sure it isn't a real clock ticking? You're wearing a wristwatch..."

Paulina said this laughingly, as she gently removed his hand from her arm.

"Will I have to win you again every time we see each other? Don't you think that's a bit much?"

Paulina had picked up the pace again, almost running away from him, nimbly avoiding the stones and muddy puddles of the only partially paved streets.  Suddenly they came out into the Calle Alcalá and the people filling the streets—even in the part that Antonio remembered as being not too crowded—forced them to walk more slowly. Madrid's population was bursting at the seams, Antonio thought to himself. The city was growing too quickly. The trams, the lights from the shop windows, the rumble of human chatter, was deafening. It started to drizzle and Antonio had to concentrate so as not to jab anyone's eyes with his umbrella. Paulina was moving further away, two steps ahead of him. He had to run to catch up with her.

"Don't be ridiculous, Paulina, listen to me. We need to talk. Let's go to your flat."

"No."

"As you wish… Do you know you make me proud with your fear? I've got the car… Let's go and get it. I'll take you somewhere quiet and comfortable…"

"No. We're almost in Manuel Becerra. There are a few cafés in the square… We'll go to one of those."

Antonio resigned himself to following her until the street opened into the little square, which was better lit. Chasing her through the drizzling rain felt like a dream. Warm bursts of an aroma of roast chestnuts filled the air. The red embers in the brazier where the nuts were roasting and the smoke, billowing sluggishly out into the humid air, gave him an idea. He took

Paulina by the arm again and suggested they buy some of the hot chestnuts. Paulina smiled at him then with a confidence that she hadn't shown until that point, and the small purchase seemed to bring them closer. The old lady selling the chestnuts smiled at the two of them, while she counted out the nuts with her clumsy fingers, and for a few moments Paulina accepted the intimacy of him peeling the chestnuts and feeding them to her as if she were a child.

Eventually Paulina sighed, shaking her head as one does when one sees a child getting up to mischief. There was a dusting of fine rain on Antonio's coat. They were opposite a church, its façade covered in scaffolding, but no one was working there at that time of day. A flower stall, no one there either, covered with a waterproof sheet, the electric lights reflected in the umbrellas that crossed now and again, all of this had the same silent, dream-like feeling as the chase a few moments earlier. Paulina began to walk again, and as she passed the church she made the sign of the cross. Antonio smiled.

"You can't complain about a lack of churches to pray in."

"I've nothing to complain about. I'm living the most beautiful period in my life."

She had said this with such conviction that Antonio felt resentful. He forgot that he was a rational man who understood his own feelings and desires perfectly.

"Look, it's quite annoying to have come half way across Europe on a plane to see someone, and then to have that person decide to make fun of you and take everything as a joke."

"You shouldn't have come."

They carried on walking without thinking where they were going. They had already passed the square. Antonio carried the cornet of chestnuts in his hand as if it were a bunch of flowers. He stopped Paulina under a street lamp. It irritated him that her cap shaded her eyes. It looked like the oilcloth hats the fishermen wear in the North and it didn't suit her.

"Say that again, where I can see you."

"You shouldn't have come."

"If you can tell me in that same tone of voice that you have completely forgotten me and that I'm simply a nuisance to you, rest assured I will leave you in peace right now."

"I've been struggling to forget you for three months."

The pain he could see in Paulina's smile filled Antonio with a rush of tenderness. "*I will marry you,*" he thought.

"Paulina, I'll marry you, when…"

Paulina's fingers tightened on his hand to make him stop. Her gloveless hands were frozen.

"Look, let's go into the nearest place. Then you must go…"

Antonio watched as she pushed open the door of a café. Feeling crushed all of a sudden, he threw the cornet of chestnuts down on the wet pavement, and followed Paulina into the dirty, crowded bar: unshaven men playing craps, middle class families, couples. It smelled of damp overcoats and the smoke was so thick that they cut it as they walked through. The conversations, the noise of the coffee machine—which was drawing out a thick, dark, boiling liquid—the clink of teaspoons and a radio program; all this merged into a terrific din. The stale snacks lined up along the counter looked unappetising.

"It smells of everything minus the coffee, doesn't it?"

Paulina spoke light-heartedly. She had removed her wet cap as she entered the place and was looking for somewhere to sit in the heaving room.

Antonio hoped she wouldn't find anywhere, that she would eventually come to her senses and let him take her somewhere else. An unfamiliar feeling of sadness began to wash over him. But it wasn't an unpleasant sensation. Since the conversation with his brother, Antonio was noticing sensitivity in the same way others might notice a fever coming on. He felt proud of his ability to feel sad, to be in love with a woman unlike any other he had ever known. A woman who always made him uneasy. Paulina spotted a table that someone had just vacated. It was jammed into a line of them, in front of a red bench which ran the whole length of one of the walls. There was a very narrow space for them at the table. Antonio turned to excuse himself to a large lady, with a thick black moustache, who was stirring her milky coffee at the next table.

"Yes... Well, go on, love! What a mess! What the hell!"

"I'm sorry madam."

The lady hadn't registered Antonio bumping into her, or his apologies. Her exclamations, in a broken, bitter voice, were directed towards an individual who must have been sitting on the other side of her, obscured by her bulky form.

Paulina was laughing. She was looking at Antonio's suit— now that he'd taken off his overcoat—examining his tie and telling him that he looked very smart, the same as she might have told her son Miguel, but he, unconsciously, turned to look at himself in a mirror opposite them, which made Paulina smile. The café had recently installed lurid florescent lights which tinged their faces with violet giving the two of them a ghostly look. They laughed. Paulina's face was particularly severe. In that light she looked much thinner, but there was something else that made Antonio freeze. Now she did indeed look like the Paulina who used to think of nothing but Eulogio, who was indifferent to everything except her memories of him. It was a face chiselled by an obsessive love.

Antonio passed her his cigarettes and, without knowing why, felt relieved when she took one.

"What would you like?"

The waiter was picking up the dirty glasses from their table, and waiting.

Paulina didn't know what to have.

"A cognac? It's cold."

"Fine."

"Afterwards we'll go and have dinner somewhere nice. My plane leaves at eight in the morning. We don't have much time together."

"No, we don't…"

Paulina's voice began to make him feel confident again, and he placed his hand over hers, which trailed casually on the seat: it felt soft and limp in his fingers, but almost immediately she pulled it away.

"Antonio. I'm not going to have dinner with you. I want you to understand me. I must have, I absolutely must retain, the purity I now have in my life. The very least that God asks of someone who knows him, the smallest thing, the minimum, let's say, is that the person becomes pure and abandons sin…"

"Is it a sin for us to have dinner together?"

"Maybe not. But I have loved you too much for it to be okay."

"You have loved me… in the distant past, is that it?"

"And I do love you. It's not necessary to lie. But it is necessary that I never say that to you again."

"That's absurd and inhumane. And what's more, insincere.

Paulina. You know I'm an ordinary man, with the passions of an ordinary man, and I'm married to a dying woman. You have to understand that if Rita dies I will come and find you again, and you have to agree, without hypocrisy, that you will wait for me."

Paulina's expression was very serious, as if refocused, smoking, while the cognac was being served in small, crude glasses with a red stripe around. When the waiter left, Paulina continued to refuse.

"I can't think about waiting for you, Antonio. I can't tell you what I would do in those circumstances. I can't tell you anything, because now for me everything depends, on God…"

"You were telling me the same thing in September. Then, on the beach, didn't you also tell me that it was as if you'd woken from a nightmare to find your life was full of possibilities? Didn't you tell me that God cannot condemn true love, and that you felt so ready to spend your life discovering beautiful things, enjoying the company of other human beings, music, travel and all the good things there are down here, that God could only be content?"

"It's very easy to say these things, Antonio. It's very easy to conjure up gods from our own small, mean perspective. But the truth is that when Christ came to earth he showed us how to die on a cross to make ourselves divine."

"Do you believe that God wants only misfortune, and that a person who is happy and wealthy cannot find Him?"

"No. It's not that. I believe that He grants the only true happiness. But the path to achieve it is different to the one we follow to earthly happiness, the one we can see, within easy reach… Yes, it's a very different path. Sometimes one feels lost, unsure… But Antonio, I swear to you, you only have to give yourself with sincerity in communion with Christ, and He helps you…"

"If He helps you, he'll tell you that you don't have the right to deceive me, to abandon me with my lack of faith, my materialism and my despair…"

Antonio was looking at Paulina like a cat looks at a mouse. He liked it when she spoke to him in that spiritual way, because it suited Paulina, he acknowledged, even though he felt a little overwhelmed.

"The only way I can help you is to be completely honest. Doing what I believe I must do. Sometimes, when your letters arrive it's a shock for me and it distresses me, worse if I read them. But I almost always burn them without reading them, and I'm gradually becoming strong enough to do this, because the grace of the sacraments is so real you'd be amazed… Obviously if you go to communion expecting a miracle, but you don't show humility or ask for God's help to follow Him, you're not likely to feel any effect, but otherwise… My God! I don't know how to explain to you what my life is like now…"

"Won't you have a drink, Paulina?"

Paulina tried a little of the liquid; it tasted like a mixture of methylated spirit and varnish.

"You should see your expression, Paulina. That funny face you pull doesn't go with your mystical speech. Can't you see how comical it is, you telling me this stuff here, with all these people around us? Do you think a single one of these people thinks like you? Honestly, you're obsessed. I know how to bring you back to reality…"

"I don't want a pig's reality. I want a human reality. I've spent too many years thinking about my body, about its feelings, its desires, its emptiness. Now I must put it through something much greater than I've ever been able to see… Antonio, I was so proud when I didn't believe! I thought that anything I glimpsed or desired, I'd always get, whatever the cost. Suddenly I saw, with absolute clarity, the world of the spirit, and life in God… And I had to convince myself that I alone can do nothing…"

"You're contradicting yourself."

"No… No… If I ask for help, it comes to me in the sacraments. I have it right there. It's very hard sometimes, you know? But it's wonderful. It's like returning, going back upstream in years, in all the cynicism, all the dirt in your mind, to arrive again at the clean strength of youth… Yes, living this life is like sailing against the current; it's so hard, and that's why it's so wonderful."

"Paulina, let's go somewhere nice, somewhere without this door squeaking every time it opens or these mirrors making us look like corpses, or this noise. You might not believe it, but I like to hear you talk like this… It's so Spanish!"

Paulina looked at him surprised.

"Yes; if I repeated all this to a woman from another country, she wouldn't believe it…"

"I don't think we have exclusive rights to the saints or to true belief."

"But this mysticism… Paulina, a mother-in-law, a brother-in-law, and now you. Three mystics! You can't tell me that's not a good percentage for one single family… Come on, let's go and have dinner. Look, we can do something good. Dinner, a walk, all perfectly innocent… And before I get on the plane and you go to bed, we can listen to the first Mass together. Are you not tempted by the idea of catechising to me?"

"Don't talk nonsense! Let's go…"

Antonio felt disheartened when she stood up. This time she didn't forget her gloves. She took them out of her bag and put them on slowly, while Antonio watched her, without anger, or much desire either. It hadn't been simply Paulina's words, the sense of which he hadn't entirely followed, but her attitude, her way of saying things, including her gentleness as she said them, that had disarmed him in such a way that now he only wished to express his goodwill, wished that she would respect him as well as love him, that she would trust him. He sighed and gave her a look as if to say it was all fine, and Paulina rewarded him with a smile so full of affection that it seemed to melt his blood. It occurred to him that in his relationship with this woman it had always been the case that one of them held the sentimental reins, while the other submitted… His forehead creased into a frown as he thought about this while they made their way out of the café because, incomprehensibly, he felt subject to Paulina's will, in a way that he hadn't expected would ever happen again.

When they emerged into the misty street, they could breathe easily again. In the sky above them the clouds were dissipating and a few stars were shining.

"Paulina, promise me you'll wait for me until I know for sure about Rita."

"I can't… I can't promise you that…"

Paulina continued with that same firmness that Antonio found so disconcerting, because in his heart he was sure that she loved him. There was a warmth in her that responded to his plea. Intangible, but certain.

They walked side by side. Paulina didn't seem to be trying to run away. Antonio began to tell her about Rome, enthusiastically.

"If you travelled to other places in the world, you'd soon give up this hard-line Celtiberian attitude of self-denial… I went to visit some friends in Rome not long ago; they live in a palace that once belonged to a famous cardinal. The paintings that adorn the palace walls would make you blush."

Paulina was smiling.

"It would be hard to make me blush… And nothing of what you say will make me believe I'm inflexible. Exactly the opposite… I…"

"If everyone understood religion as you do, I can assure you, very few people would do it."

"On the contrary, if everyone had the determination to be faithful to their beliefs, the world would look very different. And I, personally, have been accorded such great clarity… When I think how many men, how many women must be circling around the truth, full of doubts, probably incredible people, and then I, when I was in a state of utter degradation, subject to an absolute materialism, I…"

"Don't be ridiculous, Paulina. You've always been a purely spiritual woman. You're… the most spiritual woman I've ever met. The peculiar thing is that you didn't have faith… What's happening to you is a natural consequence, albeit a rather exaggerated one, of your own character."

Paulina didn't want to talk about it. She admired the sincerity in Antonio's voice, and how he himself had forgotten the painful abyss of jealousy in which the two of them had been drowning a few months back, and that it was he who had provided Paulina with the exact measure of her degradation… with his contempt. But she didn't want to talk about that, nor about many other things that lay dormant inside her body.

"We'll go our separate ways here," she declared, "and… don't write to me."

They stood at the entrance to a side street. Through the gap, unfinished building works loomed in the half-light… broken walls, vacant lots, shadows… A stage set, mysterious, intimate. The yellowish light from a street lamp cast reflections in a puddle. Darkness was falling…

"I'm sorry. I left my car outside your door and it's still too new to leave it on the street overnight."

And so they walked, slowly, in silence, through the puddles and the mud, until they reached a lit-up area where they could see Antonio's car between the lights from the entrance of the Nives's house and those of the small bar opposite. Without knowing why, they had paused beside a fence, in the shadows. Antonio felt such a strong desire to kiss Paulina that it reminded him of the desires he'd felt as a young man, when she'd been out of his reach. Perhaps this held him back, and for a few seconds the two of them stood as if paralysed, feeling only that they were together somewhere in the world. Eventually the moment passed and Antonio held Paulina by the shoulders in a light embrace, as if she were a child. Paulina felt frozen in the darkness. She wasn't expecting him to speak. She couldn't. But his words rang out clearly.

"Goodbye! And remember that I came here to tell you that, whatever happens, I will marry you."

His words made no sense to her. She was struck by a presentiment that she would never hear that voice again, and for a moment she wasn't conscious of anything else.

Paulina stayed where she was, numb, not moving, while

Antonio walked towards his car, and she watched the red light at the back of the vehicle come on, as if in a dream, and as if in a dream, she saw the headlights light up a huge swathe of the night, at the far end of the street.

Antonio, dejected, started the engine and, after the car had disappeared, Paulina remained rooted to the spot, trembling, feeling the cold, wet night and the deep pain that, despite her new-found serenity and determination, ripped through her like a knife.

# XIII

It was Christmas Eve morning. A grey mist hovered over Villa de Robre and it was bitterly cold. In Mariana's small living room thick logs were burning brightly on the fire, even though the heating was on. When Mariana looked up she could see the orchard, filled with ghosts, grey mist, and reddish leaves blowing in the wind.

Mariana was at her desk, wearing the horn-rimmed glasses that she only put on to read or write. She was dressed well and her shiny, carefully styled hair went beautifully with her blouse, her mauve knitted cardigan and her skirt.

As Eulogio watched her from the door, he felt a rush of affection. He'd always known that he loved his mother; it was so much a given that he'd never felt the need to examine his feelings. It was only now, however, having spent this time alone with her, that he realised how much he really needed her. He watched her, pleased by her simple elegance and the fire bringing a warmth to her entire look. He saw her writing urgently, surely, at great speed, as she always did everything.

At the end she sighed, after signing, like someone finishing an important work, and looked towards the orchard again. Eulogio laughed.

"Might one ask to whom you were writing?"

Mariana took off her glasses to look at him. "Ah, it's you, is it?"

She observed him with the same thoughtful expression that she always wore now when she looked at him. It irritated her slightly that Eulogio, who had been working very hard all season, spent his free time eating too much. He was putting on weight.

She sighed and turned back to her papers. The fire crackled. She began gently tapping the desk with the horn rim of her glasses… "Well, son. I was writing to my ex daughter-in-law… You know she and I have been writing to each other a lot and lately, even about her mysticism. I was writing because I'm delighted that she's sent Miguel to us for Christmas… She says she's done it for me, because this will surely be the last year she'll spend with the boy… Isn't that touching? I have to admit that Paulina might be mad, but she is sincere."

Eulogio approached the sideboard where his mother kept drinks and nibbles for aperitifs. That day it was spilling over with nuts and sweet and savoury treats.

"And…" Eulogio was filling a small plate with these as he spoke, frowning, "how is this the last year Paulina will be with the child? She hasn't deigned to communicate any of this to me."

Mariana's chair creaked as she turned around quickly.

"Eulogio… Don't eat that rubbish, man… Look, I'd even prefer you had a whisky from the bottles Ramirito gave me than see you chugging snacks like a priest… Your wife has decided she's going to become a Carmelite nun and meanwhile you're determined to give yourself a canon's belly… Crikey, it's revolting!"

Eulogio laughed, but at the same time he did fetch the bottles of whisky his mother had mentioned. Suddenly, he stopped and looked up.

"What did you say, Mamá? I didn't know… Did you say Paulina wants to become a nun?"

Eulogio's smile was more pronounced, only not as sincere as before. A smile that the flickering firelight transformed into a grimace.

"Yes, my son, yes… She's written me a load of gibberish, the kind of thing Blanca would come up with, explaining that the love of Christ means sacrificing oneself, surrendering oneself entirely, darkness, poverty, and love."

"What… Let me see…"

She looked down, putting her glasses on again while she searched through the desk. A beautiful grandfather clock, with a gold metal pendulum, decorated with arabesques, was ticking melodiously, and from time to time, its entire case would creak, as if there were spirits hidden inside. Eulogio began to pour whisky into his glass. He rang the service bell.

"Look, here it is, son… You see? I wasn't too far off the mark… 'Darkness, poverty, and love. And how I believe so firmly, dear Mariana, in the power of prayer, and I know that my direct action in the world will not be enough, I think the best thing I can do is to pray day and night for all of humanity and offer the sacrifice of my body and my separation from those I love, in the joyous knowledge I am doing it all for God.'"

Mariana paused. Eulogio was open-mouthed. A maid came in, one of those that Mariana was good at breaking in, and who, once broken in, would leave for Madrid. Eulogio cleared his throat.

"Bring me soda and ice, Rosalía."

The woman left the room. Mariana corrected him:

"Eulogio, her name's not Rosalía. She's been in the house for a month and…"

Mariana took her glasses off again. She stood up, looked at Eulogio out of the corner of her eye and noticed he looked nervous, bewildered even.

The maid returned almost immediately, her hands, holding the tray with the soda and a tiny ice bucket, were visibly trembling. Mariana observed her manoeuvres with a critical eye. The girl was moving things around so that Eulogio could reach them easily. Then she left, her cheeks noticeably redder than when she came in.

"Well," said Mariana, when they were alone and she saw that her son was stirring his drink very deliberately, frowning somewhat. "Well… One can't say, despite everything, that Paulina isn't being reasonable… True?"

"Reasonable?" Eulogio took a big gulp from his glass without waiting for it to cool. "Mamá, you call that reasonable? You?"

Mariana began to tap the floor with her foot.

"Son… Don't be ridiculous! I can't be held responsible for everyone around me going mad… Or do you think like your crazy friend Pepe Vados that it really is all my fault? Did I tell you the story your friend Pepe told me? He clearly said it to wind me up, but it's funny in a way… He says that during the war they had a little chaplain in their regiment and this fellow was an absolute disaster. One of those people that make you want to vomit. He used to get very overexcited and scream and shout, the only thing he wanted was to cut off heads, he thought he was as much a soldier as the rest of them and even got offended if anyone called him 'Father'… But then in the mornings he would put on his vestments and celebrate Mass.

"There, in that company, it seemed Pepe Vados was the chaplain (I say chaplain in the ideal sense, you know?)… Pepe, as you're aware, has always been a wonderful man, it's not a recent thing, not at all, his whole life he has been exceptionally sensible and honest… One day, Pepe goes and starts insulting this little chaplain, for whatever reason. In fact, Pepe says he had begun to loathe the man. And he even shook him.

"'It would be better if you stopped this farce of a Mass you perform every morning and demonstrated some Christian charity during the day, you miserable…'Well, I don't know if he called him miserable or some such thing… Don't laugh… I think Pepe was totally in the right, and then he tells me he gave the chap a lecture using all my arguments about corruption in the Church and he was listening quietly to it all with his head bowed. Pepe says the chaplain only disagreed with the bit about his Mass being a farce, because he said it wasn't. He admitted he was a miserable wretch, but said God turned up anyway in the bread and wine… So Eulogio, listen, because this is where I come into the story. Pepe says that from that day the chaplain began to change, to change… And that it wasn't simply an act, and Pepe also began to change his opinions, as the other man improved. Eh? What do you think? Do you know what Pepe concluded? Well, he says to me: 'Mariana, your own arguments opened a man's eyes to his faith… I transformed when I saw the change in him… Basically, Mariana, it's down to you that I'm a priest.' So, what do you think of your friend's story? It's quite funny. I said to Pepe: 'No my friend, you owe this honour to having inherited your dear parents' feeble brains…' And there we are, the jokes I share with your crazy friend… But, do you want to explain to me why the devil you're looking at me as if I were the cause of Paulina's delusions?"

Eulogio took another gulp. He began to feel somewhat better.

"Mamá, if you say that it's reasonable for Paulina to become a Carmelite nun, I suppose I'll have to accept it and believe it too, but I think… I feel that my wife, that… really, that Paulina… that…"

He began to laugh, a little confused. Mariana came closer to him.

"But, you great oaf, why would I think that was reasonable? It's absurd. But, given that these absurd things are happening, what I think is reasonable is the second part of the letter…"

Eulogio began hastily filling his pipe.

"This second part, Mamá, you haven't told me what it says. It's a small detail…"

"Ah, yes, of course… Look…"

She put the glasses on and rummaged through the desk to find the letter, written in Paulina's tall, straight hand.

"The biggest sacrifice is to separate myself from the boy, but I have decided, dear Mariana, that I can leave the boy completely in Eulogio's and your care. I know that the boy's upbringing will be my great gift to you. I know that no one else would look after my baby with such tenderness and refinement as you, and that you would not stop him practising religion…

I know you too well not to be sure of this. All this, obviously, if my idea becomes a reality and I see if it is truly God's will. If so, and if Eulogio marries again, which he should, because he is young and needs more children, I beg you, Mariana, to have Miguel stay with you."

Mariana's voice let the words fall like dry leaves or like large, slow droplets or like ink spots, something black and cold and weightless, which seemed to pool on the floor as soon as it fell.

"Well, well, well..."

Eulogio didn't say anything else. After a while, he repeated: "Well, well, well..."

He felt a strange pain rippling across the muscles in his chest. He couldn't draw on the pipe. He began to waste matches trying to light it.

Mariana folded the letter and, for the third time, took off her glasses.

"This, my son, is what seems reasonable... Paulina understands, correctly, that the boy is much better off with me than with her. And I, as you know, honour my commitments... Tonight the boy will go to midnight Mass in the castle. Because of this, I've agreed that we'll all dine there, although Ana can't really cope... At least I'll be there in good time to manage everything."

Eulogio felt a pleasant warmth spreading through his body, after downing his third whisky. He crossed to the window. The whisky didn't only perk him up, it made him see things as better than they were... The orchard, dappled with light amid the last leaves slowly falling from the chestnut tree, took on a fantastical beauty as he looked on from the warmth of the room. Far beyond, at the end of the garden, he could just make out a small house, between the now bare branches. A balcony that seemed as if it had never existed. The sight of that balcony, in the grey air, in the distance, caused Eulogio neither pain nor happiness. Except for an acute sense of the fleeting nature of life. If it weren't for the fact that he had a son, that balcony could have been erased from the landscape, almost unnoticed.

The dinner in the castle was a success. Everybody knew the success was down to Mariana. She prepared the wreaths, the tree and even the nativity scene. Nor did she forget to send a long affectionate telegram to Switzerland, to send Christmas wishes to those who were, in a way, exiled. Fortunately, Rita seemed to be improving, according to the latest news.

Miguel played with Joaquín and Ana's little ones. He was better looking and taller than Joaquín's boy of the same age. This filled Mariana with pride. She'd smiled when she heard Miguel's dismissive comment in response to the other child boasting about his castle:

"Okay yours is a castle, but our mansion, even though it's not a castle looks nicer and is much warmer."

"Mariana, my dear friend," said the Count, "we must thank you and our dear Ana for this joyful evening, when so many loved ones… including some… (the Count who, glass in hand, had stood up during dessert, was looking at Eulogio) inexplicably… Yes, they are absent… inexplicably…"

The Count was a little merry, and his speech was a little faltering, but he hadn't lost his aristocratic manners.

The large table was beautifully laid by Mariana with the Count and Countess's best china, but there was too much space at it, even with the various children seated there. At the head of the table sat Father Pérez who had led midnight Mass and was now smiling kindly at everyone. Mariana, despite all her energy, felt strangely melancholic as she listened to the Count. Joaquín and Ana shifted about nervously during those few seconds when Alfonso's gaze rested on Eulogio, whose complexion already reddening from the plentiful food and drink, deepened still further… Paulina's name hovered in the air like a sword above all their heads, and none of them knew what to do with themselves.

The Count, however, after pausing over the word "inexplicable," turned towards a portrait of Blanca hung above the fireplace. A very young Blanca dressed in a ball gown, depicted by a second-rate painter, was unrecognisable.

"The best and most innocent of wives… and the daughter and the son-in-law… And the sons who died, and those who are far away… All this inevitably causes us great sadness. You will remember, dear Father, dear friends, dear family, the carol that I propose, in a few minutes, the children sing by the manger.

*Christmas comes*
*Christmas goes…*
*And we will go and*
*We will not return…*

As the Count recited the carol, and attempted a tune, his oldest grandchild and Miguelito Nives, who had been kicking each other under the table, burst out laughing. One of them choked on a mouthful of champagne. This broke the tension. Everyone stood up to admire the tree and hand out small gifts to the children. After singing a few carols, they all gathered around the fire, which Eulogio, rather stupefied by the wine, found unbearably hot. The older children (the little ones and Father Pérez had fallen asleep) were causing havoc running around the house, happy they had special permission for that one night.

Joaquín Vados brought out his little car to take the Nives back to the village. They had barely taken their seats when Miguel fell asleep, leaning against his grandmother.

"It's all been very pleasant," Eulogio said to Joaquín.

The car was very small, and Mariana heard him knowing that Eulogio felt obliged to say exactly the opposite of what he was thinking.

Mariana suffered the uncomfortable drive along the pot-hole-ridden road in silence. She had felt so happy while she was making all that effort preparing the spectacular dining room and the tree, busy, in other words; but now, with a strange sadness, she was wondering whether it was all worth it. She'd missed Blanca, and she was surprised how much. Her naïve, goody-two-shoes friend, who to Mariana had become indispensable, had unknowingly saved her life once. Blanca never found out. No one would ever know. It was a secret that Mariana intended to keep forever.

Mariana looked back calmly on the day when, after her husband Miguel had been shot, she'd decided to take a whole pack of Veronal sleeping pills before bed, and never wake up.

She didn't recall feeling any fear, rather a kind of painful astonishment that her life's work had been pointless. She had believed that the farmers, whom she had spent so much of her time, money, and enthusiasm on, had adored her. She had thought herself dearly loved and respected by all these families

in the village who had always seen it as an honour to be invited
to the manor house… And then during that terrible time, she'd
heard songs alluding to alleged indecent behaviour and orgies
in her house, the walls of that same house were pelted with
stones, and one morning insulting slogans were painted all over
them. And nobody had called round to offer support… Of the
servants only old María remained, and Mariana wrote a letter
to Eulogio recommending her, in case he ever returned to the
village. During those desolate days, the image of her happy,
wonderfully successful marriage was erased too. Her husband
Miguel, the peaceful, good-humoured and obliging Miguel,
had not been able or had forgotten to tear up some letters
which, when she was sorting his papers, she was forced to read.
They were letters from different women, from various years,
and from the dates, Mariana realised that, without a doubt,
that man, her husband, had cheated on her from practically
the beginning of their married life… Until almost the day he
died. And his lady friends were no better than the lower-class
women the engineer Goya had so scandalously flaunted, much
to Miguel's disapproval!

Mariana destroyed all this proof of how low her life had
sunk and readied herself to disappear. The only thing bothering her was how to fill the empty hours between putting
her affairs in order and going to bed. She hated inactivity.
She didn't know how to be alone, and she didn't want to rush
things… She wanted to do things properly, so there would
be no chance of being saved. María, the old servant, who was
hanging around her, as if she could sense something amiss,
wouldn't dare go into her room once she had closed the door
to go to sleep…

When the doorbell rang, and eventually, after a quiet discussion with old María, Mariana watched an emotional Blanca sweep into the house with her arms outstretched and tears in her eyes, and heard her blurt out that she'd dared to come because her son José loved Mariana so much, and Miguel and Eulogio Nives, too, and that she was there on his behalf, though she had so often wished to know Mariana better herself. When this happened, when Mariana felt all that warmth, generosity, and heartfelt affection, something clicked inside her. Something told her that life would go on, and that she, Mariana Nives, had a duty to carry on living it with her head held high, defending what was hers, defending herself, hoping that those who behaved so despicably would realise what a grave mistake they had made. She needed to convince this Blanca that she had found a friend who was worth having, who wasn't a wreck, but a woman with integrity, exactly as Pepe Vados himself had described his mother.

After Blanca, all the village families that she had ever had any dealings with, one by one, came to offer their condolences. Every single one of them…

Now, Joaquín's car headlights were illuminating the cold, milky night. Mariana was caressing the sleeping Miguel's soft, straight hair. It seemed to her that only one's children, one's flesh and blood, make the effort of living worthwhile, compensate for it, fill it. Because of her excessively selfish affection for Eulogio, and doubting she could love any future offspring as much, she'd decided one child was enough, but now she would have loved more grandchildren. She thought about Paulina alone, in her horrible flat in Madrid, wallowing in her madness.

"Paulina must be thinking about us, at this hour," she said

out loud.

Nobody answered. As the little car approached the edge of the village, the beams from its headlights cut across a thick flutter of white butterflies. It was snowing in Villa de Robre.

Once the third Mass had come to an end, Paulina went out into the street. Everything seemed illuminated by the fire burning brightly in her veins… What a tremendous thing it was to understand Christ's message, the Birth of the Lord… It was turning her life upside down, inside out. God's message and the warning he gave when he was born a poor man and a child, abandoned like the gypsies under the bridges, that if ever a man should feel he is superior to others because he possesses honours or material things, he cannot do so if he believes that Christ is the Lord.

People were pouring out of the churches into the street. Many windows had lights in them, and Paulina could hear shouting and the deep hum of zambomba drums. The stars were out; it was one of those crisp, winter nights in Castile when the sky glitters high above you. Simply to look at the sky was to fill the soul with cosmic wonder.

The crowds spilling out of the churches mingled with the masquerade. Groups of drunken revellers carrying tambourines, zambombas, and some wearing masks, were shrieking. It was a howling, mournful and wild joyfulness, like something from a Solana painting. Paulina, happy to have arrived home, went into her house. All the apartments seemed buzzing with life. As she entered hers, she heard laughter from the flat above. She was happy. Luisa's parents had come from their village, laden with food, even an enormous turkey, for the Christmas festivities.

They'd asked her to celebrate with them. She'd excused herself, citing a prior engagement.

She did have a commitment… She couldn't quite explain the commitment she felt to being alone, feeling the strong, warm joy of God, alone on the family night, the night of togetherness and love. "Solitude with you, my God. With you who have been born man and been alone. I love this miraculous solitude."

She hadn't even turned on the light, but the small flat appeared illuminated… She laughed when she realised she'd forgotten to prepare anything for dinner. That very morning Father González had banned Paulina from considering life in a convent. At least… for the next half a dozen years, he told her, she was forbidden to think about this desire.

Paulina, thinking about it now, didn't really understand this obstacle to her zeal for perfection, for self-sacrifice, for love. She knew that the deep joy the Christmas liturgy had awakened in her spirit would soon pass and that the bad days—when temptation and letting go of virtue seem easy—would come again. A convent, too, was a kind of safety net! But Father González didn't take her vocation seriously.

She wrapped herself up in her overcoat and tied a scarf around her head, knotting it under her chin, so as not to feel the cold. She stepped out onto her small balcony. The city was like a muted tide of lights and over there, to the north, Paulina could see the white peaks of the Guadarrama Sierra, shimmering below that other wave of thousands of incandescent, bright worlds that carried one's imagination upwards. The quiet air froze the face with an intense cold that Paulina didn't feel for a few minutes. She let herself be transported by the wonder of the night, and forgot everything, simply breathing in the height and beauty that rendered her almost weightless, that consoled her, and the same as for the blessed of the Apocalypse, seemed to wipe away all the tears of her life.

# XIV

"The death sentence." "That boy Julián, he'll get the death sentence." A silence, then the same voice: "That's the way it has to be… Otherwise, it'll set an example, and we'll be in big trouble."… "These murderers are all very brave when it comes to killing, but they're very keen to save their own skins."

Paulina could hear the words but couldn't see who was saying them. She heard them one day on the tram. The rain trickled down the windows of the vehicle. She watched the grey water. A few drops fell into the carriage, slipping through the gaps around the edges of the windows. Paulina didn't turn around. She shuddered as if freezing droplets had slipped down her back beneath her coat too. In the winter rain and ice a new house was being built. The old, grey, tall, tube-shaped building where Paulina lived was now propped up against this new house, and seemed to have lost its character.

Finally, on the first day of March the new house showed off a small flag on the rooftop, indicating the building had reached its full height. Soon they would be inserting glass into the windows. The street hadn't been tarmacked; it was all mud and stones, and in the small bar opposite trouble still broke out from time to time. There were no birds now in the basement of the narrow, grey house. The smell of medicines seeped out from the small closed windows. The basement had remained unoccupied for a while, but then it was rented out as a storeroom for chemical products.

The flat where the crime had taken place had new tenants. Don Paco had left, to the delight of the landlady, who put the rent up. The rooms in that sixth-floor apartment were now occupied by a noisy family, who by a curious coincidence also kept birds. When it wasn't raining they would hang four cages from the patio walls. They also had a parrot, but this love of animals didn't make them peaceable in the slightest. The couple (two huge, hot-blooded specimens of humanity) would have fights. The mother-in-law—her mother—would fight with the brothers-in-law—his brothers. The two kids would fight too, but nearly always out in the street where the family had usually sent them. The boy who lived on the seventh floor, Paulina's son, Miguelito Nives, was fascinated by these lads, smaller than him but fiercer. Whenever his mother left him alone for a few hours, he would slip down to the noisy flat with his dog, Capitán, who was made very welcome and could bark along with the general hullabaloo without anyone even noticing.

The boys from the sixth floor were allowed to jump on the beds, which filled all the rooms. They were allowed to climb inside the messy wardrobes, and one time they tied up their grandma; they tiptoed up behind her, gagged her, and bound her to the little sewing chair. The good woman, it must be said, let out a torrent of swear words when they took the gag off, but she couldn't even be bothered to lift her huge behind off the seat to give them a smack… Sometimes the little ones got a slap and unfailingly a string of swear words, which they would answer in kind, but they also received kisses, stolen from their aunties in the corridors, and shrieks of delight. They were happy children. Miguel felt a real thrill when he was with them, possibly because his mother had completely forbidden him to be friends with them. For Miguel the smell of sweat, of the men's tobacco and the women's cheap powders, of the food, all of which seemed to impregnate the neighbours' flat, was the smell of mystery, of happiness and even of homely warmth.

Señora Nives, Paulina, was gaining a reputation in the neighbourhood as a devout Christian woman. She kept herself to herself as she always had, though she smiled more than the year before and her step was livelier, more confident. A reputation as a devout woman was not a good thing; it created an atmosphere of veiled hostility, hatred even, the kind of hatred that simple people feel towards things they are incapable of understanding. The deaf concierge loved to spread juicy gossip nonetheless about this proud woman who lived alone and devoured the saints. The women from the sixth floor would glare at her suspiciously whenever their paths crossed. Luisa's impassioned defence of Paulina was no match for the concierge's sly smile. The husband from the sixth floor, who liked a gossip as much as the women in his household, decided that the best thing would be to tactfully question the boy. But Miguelito turned out to be a quiet child, who didn't seem to understand any of the questions about his family.

The winter was slipping quietly away. Paulina had mapped out a very busy program. She had done this painstakingly, precisely, as she used to timetable her study when she was a girl, and she followed her plan to the letter, as she had back then. "Fight the imagination with occupation." Imagination was restrained, overcome. Eulogio sent enough money from the village for her and Miguel to live in reasonable comfort, but Paulina allowed herself no luxuries, except for dressing well. She didn't have a maid and what's more, she taught classes. She liked to afford herself the luxury of donating money to good causes, and she liked this to be money she'd earned. "A principle," she thought smiling to herself, "that my mother-in-law would always have approved."

As well as these occupations, Paulina was ever more eager to learn about the great mystery of religion that had changed her life.

Paulina's spiritual life had been calming and stirring in precise cycles during those months. She almost never indulged in festivals of sensorial enjoyment such as Christmas. Most of the time—she thought—spiritual things are somewhere inside, feeding and strengthening themselves, and strengthening life. Like the heart. We're not always thinking about it, but it beats rhythmically and pumps fresh blood through our arteries.

Paulina, busy with her chores, felt like a very ordinary woman, except that she was certain that she was turning her life into something meaningful. Separating from Antonio had been painful, but she knew it was the right thing and she felt happy that she'd done it. She felt a sense of the purity of her life, and of the truth within her. The truth that a body accustomed to pleasure can be reborn and a broken will can rebuild itself and a cynical outlook can purify itself… God was among men until the consummation of the ages and always gave himself to good will and humble desire.

Paulina was living her life completely inwardly, but she was barely aware of this. She didn't usually go to any kind of shows, or look up any of her old friends—though she had so hated Eulogio for the loss of them—and she read very few books which weren't treaties on prayer or theology. It wasn't that she thought any of those things were bad or inappropriate, it was simply that she was so fixated on the one essential topic, that everything else appeared cold and without perspective… Child's play.

She wasn't at home much. She was out more than a society lady, travelling from one end of Madrid to the other to listen to religious speakers she thought good. Now and again, she would spend an entire day on a spiritual retreat in a convent. She could do it on Sundays, because Miguel's school organised outings to the mountains, and the boy always went.

The only event of note—comical and unpleasant in equal measure—that occurred that winter in Paulina's outer life was bumping into her neighbour from the sixth floor on the stairs one evening when the government's electricity rationing was in force. Paulina was going up in the dark when she heard someone strike a match, and over the banister of the stairs, where they turned a tight corner, practically up against her own face, appeared her neighbour's, as ugly as a cathedral gargoyle, with his faun-like, gleeful expression illuminated by the small reddish flame. The man, before blowing out the match, extended his arm and held it very close to Paulina's surprised face; he must have seen something that made him utter such a vile curse, followed by such an outrageous flirtatious remark, and all of it so unexpected, that Paulina started laughing, regretting it bitterly half a second later when she found herself in the arms of the huge hulk of a man, who smelled of dirt and tobacco, and was trying to rub his unshaven cheeks against hers in the darkness. There was a quiet panting for a few seconds. She poked her nails into his eyes and he released her instantly with a curse, even stronger and more spontaneous than the first.

"Bible-bashing, damn whore…"

Paulina arrived at her door trembling with rage, and in spite of herself, with laughter too. But more anger than laughter, although the man's face, in its ugliness, was so funny, and those curses so splendid in their spontaneity. She was sure that the man wouldn't have dared do such a thing if she'd been living with Eulogio, and this riled her most of all. The cowardice of others, feeling defenceless against this thuggery.

The day after the incident she'd gone to see Father González again to try once more to persuade him that she needed to enter the convent.

"A woman alone, in an environment as unsuitable as mine, where it's almost impossible to meet people, because of my personality. And the fact that I'm not interested in anything but the pursuit of God."

Father González told her that one had to find God, simply, in the life one had been given.

"You have other duties. You told me at Christmas that your marriage isn't recognised as such, that you are a free woman… But, why don't you marry the father of your child, my dear? Has he refused?"

"No."

Paulina felt desolate in the cold visitors' room in the convent where the priest received her, a bare lightbulb giving light to them both, and the priest, unwell, with a scarf around his neck, his voice hoarse, pacing around the room as he spoke to warm his feet, rubbing his hands, which had turned blue.

"Father, you can't imagine the hate and the loathing that an attachment with no love at all, no understanding, inspires. Can God want me to base my entire life on a lie?"

The priest looked at her with a concerned expression.

"No, not that… But you have obligations. Being afraid of life is not a good reason to enter a convent. Christians should be in love with life. Don't you understand? With real life, and all its heroism and struggles."

The visit hadn't calmed Paulina down, or consoled her.

Sometimes Paulina—who had forbidden Miguel from having anything to do with the sixth-floor neighbours—happened to witness the family's activities from the window overlooking the patio. Sheets being shaken out, insults flying from the windows. The man of the house, usually hidden away in the bathroom, would lean—always bare-chested despite the cold—out of the patio window, a cigarette hanging from his big mouth. One time he spotted Paulina hanging out some clothes and gave her a wink after rolling his eyes and clasping his hands together in a comic impression of prayer. Paulina slammed the window shut angrily, but couldn't help smiling at the thought of his clown's face. The family, bursting with noise, with enthusiasm for everyday life, had a roguish charm that, of course, had much to do with their vitality. The wonderful Amalia had possessed a similar kind of charm, at one time; because Amalia, over these few months while Paulina had been feeling invigorated, had begun to fall apart and no longer seemed the same. And even Luisa, with her kids, her Francisco, her troubles, had a bright flame inside her that in Paulina—one day she suddenly noticed it—had gone out. Perhaps such a huge effort had exhausted her. It was as if everything in her had dried up, except for her thirst for learning, grasping ideas, and for divine knowledge.

These thoughts went through Paulina's mind on the first day of March as she made her way home. It had rained that morning and the streets were impossible. The workmen who were finishing the new house had constructed a bridge over the mud with some planks. Paulina was crossing it when suddenly she saw her gargoyle neighbour coming in the other direction. Her nemesis… Paulina threw herself into the mud and her shoes sunk right in.

The neighbour came to help her, because she seemed to be stuck. She fled.

"Hey, crazy nun lady, you'll get soaked…" the man shouted. It was a curious coincidence. The mud had a good smell, an eternal smell, even in that street. The soft sky, with small white clouds, the hint of spring in the air, none of this moved Paulina. Once more she wondered, in the curious yet detached way in which she now observed herself, if she would ever again feel a simple, tender, emotion.

The next day was the first Friday in March, and Paulina, who the previous month had begun the devotion of the nine First Fridays with Miguel, felt an unfamiliar emotion when her son flatly refused to get up at dawn to go to church with her.

When she went in to wake him, Miguel had yawned, raking his fingers through his blond hair. His dog, Capitán, lying at the foot of the bed, sat up alert, ready. Miguel's eyes looked almost black, serious.

Later, Paulina thought that perhaps the boy had been awake for a while, waiting for her arrival, but at the time she didn't realise.

"Set the alarm for quarter to eight, Mother; then I'll have plenty of time to get to school."

"What do you mean? Aren't you coming to Mass?"

"No."

Paulina was disconcerted.

"You know it's the First Friday, don't you?"

"Yes, but I don't want to go; I want to sleep."

It was the first time in his life that Miguel had dared to express a decisive opinion to his mother. For a moment, Paulina felt real fury. The boy had turned to face the wall and had his eyes closed. His mouth wore a somewhat superior and arrogant sneer that Paulina recognised as her own. The dog, Capitán, lay down again at the foot of the bed with a sigh. Paulina took hold of Capitán by the collar and pushed him out into the corridor.

"I've told you a thousand times, I don't want dogs in the bedroom, do you understand? If you bring that animal in here to sleep one more time, he's out of the house."

Miguel didn't answer.

Paulina came out onto the street upset and trembling. A memory came to her, of herself looking at her father in the same way that Miguel had looked at her this morning… It was getting light. She was so on edge even the shadows in the street irritated her. She didn't dare receive communion without confessing her bad mood.

Holding her head in her hands, she couldn't focus on the idea of God that morning. She could only think about Miguel. Perhaps she hadn't thought about him enough, though she'd kept him by her side all those months. Could the boy be unwell that morning? Miguel was never unwell, he never worried her. She always imagined she could leave him alone to take care of himself. But now…

On her way home, her pace quickened. An extraordinary spring light rose from the street as if bursting out of the ground itself. Paulina felt as though she were walking on the light as she hurried through the streets, urged on by a strange fear that Miguel would escape her.

Of course, he was at home, and not only that, but she was shocked to see how small he looked when she opened the door. Not that he was short, but that he was only a little boy of eleven, with his little shorts and his white face and blond hair, like a baby, despite his frown, despite the sneer inherited from Paulina. The entire time in the church, Paulina had been imagining him as a man and as a godless man, and herself as the guilty party. Although she couldn't quite fathom of what offence she was guilty.

A quick glance was enough to tell her that he'd skipped his shower. He hadn't washed his face and he was already dressed. Yes, he did need a lot of looking after and not simply when it came to material things.

Miguel was in a serious mood. His eyes looked almost black. The boy was upset about something. His refusal to go to Mass with his mother was not a coincidence. He ate his breakfast in silence. They could hear birds singing outside the window; the neighbours had put their cages out in the sun. Paulina wanted to make things better between them, and asked her son about his exams. Miguel rewarded her with a trembling smile. The termly exams were coming up at the end of March.

"How do you think you'll get on?"

"I think I'll do well, mother. I'm top in maths, and that's the one everyone finds the hardest. I'm also good at natural sciences; I want to be a vet."

Paulina was smiling, looking at her child's hands. She loved those little hands, square like Eulogio's, with their bitten nails, and the white skin, a little ragged around the nails where he'd picked at it.

She leaned over the balcony to watch him come out onto the street. Again, she was touched. She liked to see his funny little figure, his blond head… Paulina had never been overly affectionate with Miguel. She'd been scared she might spoil him. But she enjoyed doing things with Miguel, as if they were friends rather than mother and son. They'd always got along well, though they could be separated and not miss each other too much. But now, Paulina had the sense that her work was not done. That God had given her this child for something more than simply for her to be kind to him. After a morning of feeling cross with herself, she observed the boy keenly at lunchtime.

Miguel was very cheerful and there was no trace now of the strange expression he had worn early that morning. He chatted away like a parrot and kissed his mother goodbye, in the same affectionate way he always did. Paulina wondered if the rebellion she had seen in Miguel was simply a result of her own fears. But it was a kind of dull pain, a kind of infection, like when pus begins to make your skin feel sore, even before it's visible.

In the afternoon, when her classes finished, she took a long route home, filled with the same uneasy feeling, the sense that something was happening in her child's soul, that only she could relieve.

She walked through the Retiro park, full of birds and children, full of the first buds of spring. She remembered when Miguel was very little and how on Sundays, she would bring him here as a special day out. Thinking, thinking, she rewound back to the first moment of intimacy with her son, there, in the prison cell her fellow prisoners called "the birthing pen" where the child had been born eleven years earlier.

The recollection was so intense that she forgot the park surrounding her and could almost sense again the tang of disinfectant, the hot smell of blood from her own body and the unique stench of the blanket covering her, a blanket steeped in the sweat of so many other women prisoners.

She remembered vividly the dripping of the tap; the cell had a small basin with a tap, and for that reason had been fitted out as the birthing room. She remembered, too, that as the dawn broke a dirty, ash-coloured light was trickling in through a small skylight, and that in the next bed a woman, an alcoholic, who three days earlier had given birth to dead twins, was sleeping… She remembered all of this and how her body had seemed broken yet at peace after the birth, when they left her alone with the baby beside her. She had stifled a groan as she raised herself up slowly, propped up on one elbow, to see her child's little face, that first time. Miguel had moved his head like a tiny, blind puppy, searching anxiously. Then, happy to be alone—hearing the slow breathing that told her the other prisoner was asleep—she had pressed her breast, still empty of milk, into the baby's tiny mouth and felt him suck vigorously. With him attached there, she had lain back down cradling him in the crook of her arm, and had felt a pure, instinctive happiness, a physical happiness, a joy that lifted her out of all her worries, her insecurity, her misery back then, in that warm intimacy with her little boy.

It had been beautiful. A beautiful, deep, and pure feeling. She couldn't compare it to anything, because it was unlike anything else. It had burst out of the very depths of her humanity, and she was sure, as she looked back on it, that it was part of the flow of beauty and harmony that brings men closer to God.

By the time she arrived home she was desperate to be with her child, to feel his love, and to devote herself entirely to him.

The boy was in the dining room, with the lamp on and his books open on the table. Paulina observed him from the hallway, and he seemed tired and preoccupied, but he straightened up when he saw her come in, as if he were ready to work hard.

Paulina left her students' notebooks on the table and distractedly cupped her hands around one of the bulbs in the lamp. Miguel watched the shadows of her hands, silhouetted on the wall. Then Paulina placed the alarm clock on one of the sideboards. She did this every day, so he could see when it was time for dinner. It was the only clock in the house. The boy continued to watch her.

Without thinking, she sat down in "Eulogio's armchair" next to the radio and looked at her son: the boy looked at her. She gestured to her lap… The boy ran to her, sat on her lap and threw his arms around her neck. Paulina felt the rapid beating of her child's heart.

They had not been close like this since Eulogio had come back from America. She whispered into his ear.

"I'm cross with you, Miguel… You left me on my own this morning. You didn't want to take communion. Why not?"

The boy, without moving, seemed to shrink. Then he spoke…
His mother had taught him to tell the truth.

"I don't want to spend all day in church, like you do… You're
mean now." Paulina felt a bitter shock. She prised the little
boy's face away from her shoulder to look at him. Miguel was
red-faced, his eyes moist, about to burst into tears.

"Tell me son, how am I mean now?"

"It's true. Before, you used to love Papá, you lived with him,
like all the other mothers. Ricardín's mother doesn't go to Mass,
not even on Sundays, and she spoils him, and she and his father,
they love each other, and… at Christmas in the castle Grandma
said you wanted to become one of those nuns that no one sees
ever again and… and… that neither my father nor I had ever
mattered to you, and…"

Eventually, Miguel cried. Paulina felt devastated at his sob-
bing. She had known that this moment would come. She had
read the story of a female saint who had even clambered over
the body of her twelve-year-old son, lain across the door of
her room, to go and join the convent. When she read it, she'd
thought that she, too, would have to go through something like
it. It didn't seem much to leave a son in order to dedicate an
entire life to God, given that she'd once imagined abandoning
this same son to pursue the love of a man. And yet it was a
mistake, down to her stupid pride, to have thought it and in
the meantime, she'd neglected the real and very personal task
that God had placed in her hands when he gave her the child.
She began to rock him, as if he were a tiny baby. They remained
like that for a short while, almost as unified then as the day
she'd given birth to him. The house was like a cocoon protecting
them. The furniture was no longer hostile, after witnessing this

outpouring of affection; even the alarm clock, beating softly, instilled a kindness and goodness into everything.

"No, little one; no, little one. I'll never join a convent, not while you still need me."

Miguel fell asleep that night with one of Paulina's hands clasped in his, like he used to fall asleep after daytrips, worn out, content.

Paulina watched him sleep for a while, and it felt as though she had narrowly held on to him, that she had been on the point of losing him through a misunderstanding, in her eagerness to be with God. And again, she asked God to keep her spirit alight with the truth.

Sitting in the boy's room, she could see the March moonlight spilling over Miguel's desk, illuminating the shelves with his little boxes of insects… And beside them, empty cartridges from Eulogio's hunting rifle. These were the boy's special treasure. Paulina had seen him playing with them, lost in his own world. He would place them on a map spread out on the floor, and they became soldiers. At other times, he turned them into bridges, houses. Paulina remembered her favourite doll when she was a child was a stone from the riverbed, wrapped in a chamois cloth duster. Children prefer toys where they create the fantasy themselves.

If those past few days felt dry, now her emotions were like a rain shower, like a victory. She was sure that if she accepted this pure and natural affection, he alone would free her from selfishness, he alone would fulfil her.

She was determined to dedicate herself entirely to Miguel. He must grow up with her by his side, and know God from her lips and from her deeds.

*"When he's older, Miguel will understand that Eulogio and I didn't want to marry without love, that we didn't want a loveless sham of a marriage."* Once Miguel was grown up and could understand, perhaps that would be the time to think about a life of solitude and contemplation.

Paulina tossed and turned in her own bed, wondering why she couldn't sleep. There was something in her own reasoning that was doing her harm, that didn't fit, like a painful stone lodged in her flesh. There was something false in all of this, but she couldn't figure out what it was. For a long time, she lay with her eyes open, watching reflections of lights and shadows from the cars on a nearby street flit across her bedroom ceiling.

# XV

A group of shaven-headed little boys were milling around underneath the roof canopy of the Estación del Norte, having emerged from the depths of the Metro. They were accompanied by two young ladies and some rather down-at-heel women, who looked slightly out of place among the swarms of travellers and workers, not because they were poor, but because they had a strange wild look about them.

One of the young ladies, the shorter of the two, was getting very agitated.

"Let's see… The register… One, two, three… twenty. We've got twenty, right? Jacinto and Lola should be here by now. You, get going… You're going to be late. Get going, for goodness' sake."

"The office doesn't open for another half an hour…"

It was nine o'clock in the morning and it was already hot. A heat that was sticking Señorita Rosita López's short, blond, fine-as-silk hair to her forehead. Both she and her companion were enveloped in thick overcoats, with long sleeves, buttoned up collars and thick stockings. Marina Pérez, the other young woman, wearing a skirt and smart blouse, looked as if she'd stepped out of a postcard from an elegant bygone era. Rosita had on a striped gingham suit, and white canvas shoes, because she was on summer holidays. She was slim, and if you didn't inspect her features too closely, very nice-looking. Neither of the two looked much over twenty. Amid the din of the taxis constantly pulling up outside, the porters running around with luggage, people coming and going, and the children, each carrying their little bundle of belongings, running, fighting, trading insults and playing with one another, plus the group of women all talking at once, the two friends felt a little shell-shocked.

"Oh my goodness, they told me they'd be arriving by taxi. Lola was going to pick up Don Jacinto, who promised to help get all this lot sorted. Don Jacinto had the twenty bags of children's snacks at his house, the ones donated by the Charity Secretariat. What if they're late? By the time we hand all those out, and the tickets… But Marina, you must go!"

"There they are," shouted Marina.

Two taxis had drawn up. Marina rushed over to one of them, and Rosita—excitedly—to the other; but she was taken aback to see step out, not her friend Lola Díaz, but a slim, very elegant, young-looking lady, who Rosita thought she'd seen somewhere before… And instead of Father Jacinto's large frame, grey hair and cassock, an older lady, dressed in a smart navy and grey suit with a simple grey turban covering her hair. The lady was rather intimidating, and, unlike the young black-haired woman who had smiled vaguely at Rosita, she greeted the young woman with a cold, hard stare. Behind the ladies, a little blond boy with long legs jumped out.

Rosita sighed… A moment later she felt a tap on her shoulder and saw her friend Lola, tall and cheerful, with her sparkling blue eyes and her always discreetly painted lips, and her beige-coloured jacket. Her energy and cheerfulness were infectious.

"Chop-chop! Don't just stand there! We're handing out the bags to the children. We'll have to watch the mothers don't take half of it, mind… I saw one of them put a banana in her pocket."

Marina hugged them.

"Goodbye, goodbye."

"See you there in two weeks," Lola reminded them.

The porters were trying to move the friends to one side.

"Mind out!"

While the young women lined them up in pairs the boys were singing something they'd often sing when they won at football.

"Let's go," Rosita said as she took her place at the head of the line and Lola brought up the rear. In this formation, they set off leading the children down the steps towards the platforms at Príncipe Pío Station. Rosita turned around in a panic to shout to her friend:

"What about the women? They all wanted to come to say goodbye to us!"

"Father Jacinto is getting them platform tickets."

The crocodile of shaven-headed boys broke apart, wriggled about and lengthened, until the once neat line of pairs was in complete disarray.

"Frightful! I've never seen so many frightful children… and those grey smocks are simply ghastly."

Mariana said this, her gaze sweeping over the group, as she, Paulina and Miguel descended in the lift along with several other passengers. They had a good view of the stairs through the glass panels.

"Frightful," she repeated as the lift came to a halt. "Those children are not normal. Of course! It must be a school for abnormal children. The teachers look abnormal as well…"

"No, Mariana… Not at all, I'd say one of them looks very elegant. And the little blond one at the front is pretty."

"She looks like a horrible dwarf and she's dressed up like a mattress."

Paulina didn't insist. Mariana was in a bad mood and was not inclined to agree with Paulina on anything. Paulina didn't blame her. Mariana's pride had been wounded; she could not understand that Paulina, who in the end hadn't become a Carmelite nun, didn't want to get back together with her son Eulogio and had accepted, not only uncomplainingly but enthusiastically, the idea that Mariana was free to find Eulogio a more suitable fiancée. Mariana was offended, disparaging, and cold. She had been like that for the entire length of her visit to Madrid—ten days—lodging, fortunately, in a hotel. Any little thing would cause her to explode, for example when Paulina told her that she'd been promised a cheap flat that would be ready in October, and she would like the furniture from engineer Goya's house sent up. Mariana had replied that, obviously, she would be delighted to get rid of the awful furniture, currently stored in the attic of the Nives mansion, but that it wasn't worth Paulina paying for a removal van.

"If I were you, I'd sell it for firewood. Your family lived like gypsies in that house. Your parents had appalling taste… and to be honest I'd say their manners were no better."

Paulina knew that the furniture was well-made from decent wood, and that she could polish it up. But she put up with the stream of insults, as well as a string of acerbic remarks about the war-induced madness that had led to men saddling themselves with women who were beneath them in class, wealth, everything.

"Luckily, in your son's case, everything is fine, given that he's free."

It was because of this comment that Mariana hadn't spoken any more than strictly necessary for the past three days. Only when she caught sight of the missal, one morning when she'd gone to pick up Miguelito, did she complain about people putting on a pretence of religion and writing lies to deceive decent people. A reference to Paulina's letters.

Fortunately, she was about to leave. She was taking Miguel to spend the holidays in the village. Paulina sighed as she showed her platform ticket to the inspector. She turned her head for a second while she did so, because of a racket that was drowning out the usual noise in the station. Coming down the stairs was a motley group of women who looked more like a band of revolutionary fire-raisers than would-be travellers. They had clearly washed, and even ironed their clothes for the occasion; but most of them had a wild, dishevelled air. One huge woman was walking barefoot... The curious thing was that the group were all gathered around a very short, plump, grey-haired priest. Paulina smiled as she recognised the priest. Things began to fall into place in Paulina's mind. She had to quicken her step to reach Mariana and Miguelito, who were ahead of her, at the bottom of the steps, following the porter who was carrying their luggage.

Father Jacinto's ears were ringing with the women's warnings and advice.

"Listen, I told that Señorita Rosa straight, my Tiburcio is not so sick they should've brought his brother and left him behind…"

"Excuse me, if they're getting them vaccinated, I'm not letting my Pepe go…" "Excuse me!"

The priest allowed the group of women to pass in front of him, as he held out a fistful of platform tickets and waved them in the air above the gaggle of women's heads, so that the inspector could see them.

"I don't envy you, Father. Where are you taking this lot…Jail?"

One of the women, the tallest one, with the bare feet and bushy eyebrows that met in the middle, placed her hands on her hips at the man's remark. Father Jacinto winked and put his finger to his lips. Unexpectedly, the woman calmed down… Perhaps because the others were running down the last flight of stairs separating them from the platform, eager to catch up with the children. The little boys were already disappearing into a third-class carriage…

It was a hot day. The summer of 1950 was dreadfully hot. There had been no rain in the central region of Spain since the spring, and in June water and lighting restrictions had been put in place. There was a horrible dryness and a dirty germ-filled dust in the air, which seemed to get into one's lungs. Apparently, there were several cases of typhus. The temperatures were creeping up every day.

The vast station canopy was boiling as if the high ceiling boards were red with heat. The soft, dappled light, however, gave some relief. The trains, ready to depart, the tracks being cleared to let other trains in, the smoke from the locomotives, the smell of grease, coal, even of leather suitcases; all this Father Jacinto liked. The women were all shrieking, tightly packed together beside the carriage, their children's faces peering out of every window.

"What a day!" thought Don Jacinto, wiping the sweat from his face. His complexion was grey and sickly. For him, his obesity was terribly embarrassing. Many people insisted on believing his life was easy and made jokes at his expense.

It was even difficult to convince his neighbours in the poor area where he lived, that their priest was as poor as all of them put together… And this, he felt, was something he needed them to understand!

"You're very fat," they would tell him.

Now, Don Jacinto was smiling at the youngsters, the young women who were escorting them, the women; he blessed them all.

One of the lads, ugly as sin, with a wonky eye and a lumpy face managed to get his hands out of the train window. In his dark hands, he was holding a catapult and a small, hard piece of bread. His tongue was hanging out of one side of his mouth. He carefully took aim and fired the little piece of bread straight at one of Don Jacinto's eyes.

At that moment the train moved off. The shrieking increased in volume; some of the women were running along the platform screaming out words of love to their little ones as they went.

Don Jacinto, his hands over his eyes, felt the tears in his eyes and painful purple and blue circles forming, expanding and then disappearing behind his eyelids.

"Don Jacinto…"

"Father…"

"Excuse me, Father…"

"Father, excuse me…"

He opened his good eye. Then, slowly, the other one. He began to hand out the platform tickets the women needed to exit the station.

"God be with you, ladies, God be with you. And don't worry about the boys. Remember last year, the little girls came back safe and sound."

"Right!" retorted one of the women. "Mind you, some mothers would be happy if their kids never came back—it takes all sorts—but one mother never got the choice, because of those do-gooders…"

"Do you remember Micaela's little girl, woman…" she turned to her friend. "What use was the summer camp to her? She got run over by the sawmill truck in November."

"What if the same thing happens to my Paco… because I let him go?"

Don Jacinto was anxious to escape the throng. He had to meet a relative from the ten o'clock train. This was the reason he'd decided to accompany the group to the station.

"Go with God, ladies, go with God… I must stay here."

It wasn't that easy to escape. One of the women wanted to know if they would receive some nice gifts from the young ladies at Christmas.

"Because, after all, we're leaving them our boys!"

"For Christmas? Ladies, it's only the twentieth of June… But I'm sure the poor young ladies will arrange something…"

"Poor… I wouldn't mind being as poor as they are!"

Just then the priest noticed, behind the women, a tall lady with large black eyes, who looked vaguely familiar. And she was definitely smiling at him. She looked incredibly neat, refined and self-assured next to the other women.

"May I?" she asked the most fearsome of the women, who let her through, looking her up and down.

"Father. I've been waiting some time to talk to you. Don't you remember me? I'm Paulina Goya. You're not busy, are you?"

"No, no not at all Señora; in fact, I need to stay here in the station for a while and these ladies are leaving now…"

The women remained there chatting in groups for another few seconds, while the priest and Paulina began to walk beside each other towards the far end of the platform, away from the exit. The priest was much shorter than the lady; in the light filtering through the canopy his cassock looked green.

"Father Pedro González introduced us; I came to your house with two ladies who were delivering some medicines or other for you to distribute. It was some time ago, almost a year. Perhaps you might remember the surname Nives?"

Father Jacinto's wrinkled face completely relaxed.

"Nives? Yes! That rings a bell! But in any case, Señora… Please feel free to talk to me about whatever you like."

They had walked nearly to the end of the roofed part of the station, towards a yard full of rails and locomotives gleaming in the sun. The engines, the ones being tested, puffed out long tendrils of smoke, which turned iridescent, forming a ghostly forest before disintegrating into the grey-blue of the sky. Paulina and the priest paused at the very edge of a pool of light that, at their feet, seemed to threaten them with its waves of molten metal.

"Father," began Paulina, "I am a completely free woman. I have almost no one in the world except for my eleven-year-old son, who is now on holiday with my… with his grandmother."

Father Jacinto gave Paulina a sideways look, wondering where she was going with this opening sentence. Nearly everybody he met wanted to talk about their misfortunes.

"Yes, it can be miserable, yes, the loneliness…"

Paulina interrupted him impatiently:

"I think, quite the opposite, that it's a gift from God."

She paused and then said, almost to herself:

"I would have liked to join a convent, as a cloistered nun, do something meaningful… You know? I'm a true believer in the power of prayer. I think in today's world, where the values of Christianity are so often faked, the work of the contemplative orders is vitally important for the Church"

"True… True…"

The priest looked at Paulina's pretty, smart dress, her slim, bare arms. There was something unusual about her, that differed from the appearance of other young women who had talked to him about similar things in the past.

"But I have a child, you see? And I must dedicate myself to him. I don't regret that, it's marvellous, the joy of having him is a gift from God. And, yet, I can't go on like this, as I am, self-indulgently praying, living my comfortable life. Every day the same thought occurs to me. We Christians should be heroes… Don't you think?"

"It's true… Yes…"

Father Jacinto, unconsciously, had turned slightly to look at the great central clock. In his pocket the newspaper he'd scarcely had the time to flick through this morning crackled.

"Are you in a hurry, Father?"

"Not in the slightest… I was told the train I was waiting for would come in on this platform…"

"Then could you possibly listen to me for a few minutes? I know that you don't lead an ordinary life, that you live among the poor, and that you're even poorer than they are, that even though you're attached to a parish, you go out of your way to help the most needy, and you sometimes help in quite an eccentric way."

"I don't know…"

"And those girls too. The ones who came with those abnormal children… I've heard about them and I liked the sound of what they were doing. Today, when I saw them, I thought I could join them. Of course, not as a member of any of those organisations that have strange rules about how to dress and things like that…"

The priest laughed.

"Slow down a little, Señora. Those children aren't abnormal… And what do you mean about clothes? Didn't you say you were going to become a nun? How would you have managed in one of the orders where you do indeed have to wear strange clothes and several kilos of wool in the summer?"

Paulina had thought about this.

"It's different. There you leave everything behind. The normal rules don't apply, there is no contact with the world. But if I live among people and I must teach my son the notion of good and evil, and if I start by telling him that evil exists where I don't actually believe it does… How will I convince him of the things that really matter? But really, we're going off topic. You seem tired…"

"Look… Shall we go for a little walk and see if we can find a bench? Yes, I am quite tired, as it happens. But if we don't find one it doesn't matter, Señora Nives," he frowned. "Or should I say Widow Nives?"

The priest was struggling to remember, there was something about her surname. His expression was utterly perplexed. Paulina blushed. She said coldly, "Nives is my son's surname. I'm single."

Father Jacinto took out his handkerchief and wiped his brow. His ears turned red.

"Forgive me, my goodness. You'll think I'm an old busybody…"

"So, Father… Tell me exactly what those young women do, the ones that came with the group of children. I was told some time ago, but I've forgotten. I didn't pay enough attention back then… Today, when I saw all of you, I felt perhaps this was my calling."

"They're from Acción Católica. They don't mind wearing stockings. I think they don't see that as important. But they've set up their own charity initiative, that's what you'll have heard about. There are people who can't be reached by the parish or the State, people whose lives don't exist according to any civil records, who don't register the births of their children, and who wouldn't go near a priest. The young women go among these people, sort out so many things for them, give them aid… in whatever way they can… Last year they took twenty little girls to a farm belonging to Lola's family. This year they're taking twenty little boys. They don't have any money and it's miraculous how they manage it; even though Lola's family is rich, she doesn't have access to the money, as you'll understand. The others are poor, they work. So, you see… Everything is sustained by their faith."

"I understand… But do you believe that all this effort… is it worth it… does it solve anything?"

"Socially? A drop in the ocean! No, it's not that. They don't do it believing that… They're not sociologists, they're concerned only with giving what they can, their time, their self-sacrifice."

"They must love them."

"Oh… Well… I think not… They work in a very difficult environment. With people who are uncivilised, resentful… They think that anyone who gives them anything wants something from them, and even suspect the young women of ulterior motives. You can't ever convince them otherwise. But the young ladies aren't looking for gratitude, that's the best thing about them; they don't demand to see the fruit of their labours either. If that was what they did it for, they'd be making a foolish mistake turning their lives upside down. All they want, if anything, is for even one of these people to feel the presence of Christ through their work… Well, I believe that's how they must feel, as they don't appear to get discouraged, and because they have faith, everything works for them… Yes, they have a lot of faith. They are three of the best young women I've ever known, and I have known many good people… which compensates for the many bad people there are…"

Paulina thought for a while. She could see herself being as heroic as these young women, resisting all their failures through their love of Christ. She would be able to resist anything, if she could have blessed solitude, the love of her son, the hours of prayer. Yes; this chance meeting, today, when she'd felt so alone, meant something perhaps…

Father Jacinto noticed her silence and told her that there were ministries which were more rewarding, that there was huge scope for any good-willed person. He began to explain one of his many tasks.

"As a matter of fact, when your relative, the Countess… Didn't you tell me that Doña Blanca was a relative of yours, or did I dream that? Ah, of course! The surname Nives… Yes, yes, now I know why it sounded familiar. And by the way, would you have Doña Blanca's address in Switzerland?"

Paulina laughed because she found Don Jacinto amusing. She knew he was a good man. Goodness was such a rare quality, Paulina thought, that his unkempt appearance and absent-mindedness were of no importance.

It was comical watching him squint his eyes, trying to seize an idea at the edge of the conversation and then, suddenly, unexpectedly ask for Blanca's address in Switzerland.

"Yes, Father; I know her address. You know she's with her daughter who's unwell…"

"Unwell? No! The daughter has died! That's why I wanted the address… to send condolences… I happened to see it in the newspaper this morning… Look."

The priest put his hand in his pocket and took out a very crumpled newspaper. He began to unfold it. He turned his gaze back to Paulina and saw that she'd sat down on the edge of one of the luggage trolleys that stood empty, waiting to be used… Paulina's face was white, stunned. The priest didn't notice.

"See?" he was pointing to an obituary. "It's true… She died the day before yesterday, in Switzerland. Her widower… Nives… That's why I said earlier that Nives and widow or widower rang a bell! Ah, forgive me… look, she was so young… poor…"

Don Jacinto stopped looking at the paper and saw something amiss in Paulina's face.

"Señora… Perhaps I shouldn't have told you the news like that, so abruptly… I didn't know."

Paulina wasn't listening to him.

"My mother-in-law didn't know!" she said as if to herself.

"Your mother-in-law?"

Paulina blinked.

"No… My son's grandmother… What does it matter now? It's all nonsense…"

Her voice sounded tired.

Don Jacinto was a little surprised. Then he felt uncomfortable, saw that the woman didn't feel like continuing their earlier conversation… The hubbub around them grew louder, the platform was filling with people, bells were ringing… A porter said, "Excuse me," to Paulina, and she found herself standing a little shakily, as the trolley she'd been leaning against was driven away by the man, tooting a horn.

"My train's coming in… Señora… Hmm… I'm so sorry to have to leave you like this… You seem very upset."

The train was arriving. They could hear its powerful, slow breath tempering its pace. Don Jacinto was watching the engine's slow approach from the far end of the platform. He watched as if hypnotised. He almost couldn't tear his eyes away even as Paulina spoke to him.

"I'll come to your house in the next few days, Father, if you'll allow me… and we can talk some more… I need so badly to find my path!"

"Yes, my dear, yes… Come, come… We'll talk soon."

They shook hands. Don Jacinto carried on looking excitedly

towards the train; the first windows were coming into view…
Afterwards, he thought he'd been rather rude to Paulina and
turned around dismayed… She wasn't there. She had walked
away and disappeared into the crowd in an instant…

Don Jacinto thought vaguely that Paulina seemed a rather
impetuous lady and that she wouldn't ever come to his house to
arrange a meeting with the young ladies. "She won't be back," he
said to himself, certain, before waving his hand because at last
he had spotted his cousin Ignacio in one of the train windows.

Paulina had spoken more sincerely than he gave her credit
for when she explained her wishes to him. But as it turned out
Don Jacinto's hunch was right… She never did go to his house
to talk about that topic, nor about any other.

Paulina, in the taxi that took her from one end of the city
to the other, felt slightly unwell. Inside the vehicle, the hot air
reeked of old leather, paint, and dry rubber. The heat was suffocating; she remained slumped on the seat and quiet for a while
with her eyes closed. The taxi had a radio and it was turned on,
but too quietly. That made her feel worse.

The atmosphere in the station, with its greyish air and its
smell of soot and the dusty rays of sunlight that seemed to
break everything apart as they stole through the roof. Those
horrid little boys with their crew cuts, the young women who
were escorting them, who had suddenly inspired her longing
for heroism… The slightly absurd conversation with the old
priest, and at the end the unexpected news of Rita's death which
had struck her like a stone thrown from another period in her
life… Paulina was reliving all this, all of it was making her
head spin, making her temples throb painfully as if they were
about to explode.

Despite her cool attire, she felt dirty and shabby. She knew that when she arrived home she would find the taps dry; the water would be turned off—because of the restrictions—at that time of day, but she had a full bath, ready to step into. She was longing to do so.

There had been a time when a painful hatred had made her wish for the death of a young person, a truly beautiful woman called Rita. She was very different now to that selfish, blind creature who had hoped for Rita's death. Different, yes, but still she felt she deserved the intense pain, the sharp pang of remorse she was experiencing. She felt a sudden need to show solidarity in some way after Rita's death, and she spoke to the taxi driver because she wanted to send a few telegrams.

The simple act of writing a few words of condolence for Rita calmed her down, made her less tense, and even gave her some respite from her memories of the dead woman, dispelling them in her imagination.

The young women who had taken the twenty small boys on summer camp came back into her mind. Again, she felt the urge that had drawn her to them; a desire to repair things, like her ill-will towards Rita, and also the hope that she might, at last, embark upon a concrete mission that would accommodate her desire for religious perfection, for love.

"Anyone who thinks prayers are simple murmurings to numb one's mind, and quieten life down is so wrong! I feel harried every day by a force greater than my will, I feel spurred on, like a horse, to gallop, to jump, to be heroic… But I whirl around unable to find the task I must throw myself into."

Her eyes wide open, Paulina watched the streets rushing by, their colours bleached by the burning sun, and she saw other things too, not filing past the windows of the cab, but inside her, and inside her they were beating fast.

She saw her comfortable, pleasant life, the love of her son, which she felt intensely, more than ever, and which seemed to fulfil all her emotional needs. Boredom had been driven away for ever, since she had thrown herself at God's feet. And, yet, that tremendous power, that she sensed anew each day as she took communion, worried her, because, by contrast, she became aware of her half-heartedness, her cowardice, her indecisiveness, and her rootlessness.

Eventually it would always propel her to ask God to allow her to see to the core of her duty, to the core of what He wished her to do...

The cab turned into her tiny street, raising a cloud of dust as it came to a stop. The shade in the entrance was warm and unpleasant. The lift, without electricity, wasn't going anywhere. She had climbed the first few steps up to her flat when the concierge emerged from her den and held out a telegram. The long hairs that graced the mole on her chin quivered as she spoke. She pointed to the slip of paper.

"It's from abroad..."

"I know, I know..."

Paulina put the telegram in her handbag, without opening it. She assumed that someone was informing her of Rita's death... Blanca or Antonio, possibly... Yes, possibly Antonio.

She was shocked when she realised that until that moment she hadn't connected Rita's death to Antonio. The torment of having to banish him from her mind, a few months before, had been so great that possibly because of this, it was hard to think about any of it, as if she expected to feel pain, and her entire consciousness was tensing, preparing to defend itself. "Like animals trained with a whip," she thought to herself, "that do only what their master allows."

She couldn't imagine Antonio either upset or indifferent at Rita's death. It was as if he'd never had anything to do with the young woman who had died, as if the couple had never existed and the problems that had led to Paulina's separation from him were quite distinct.

She frowned. And pursed her lips. She didn't want to think about it now either.

Paulina pushed the key firmly into the door of her flat and this one action seemed to drain her energy. She recalled, horrified, that she was expected at Concha and Rafael's house that evening. Her presence was required for a dinner they were giving before leaving for the summer.

"Nobody's staying in Madrid this year and all the ladies are away. We have two male guests attending, high-ranking, very important, so it won't work if I'm the only woman… Paulina, you've lost none of your charm as far as the gentlemen are concerned. I know the evening will be a success if you come."

Concha flattered all her friends in the same way, but Paulina couldn't say no. Concha and Rafael had used their connections to secure the small apartment she was to move to in October.

"I'll soak myself like salt cod. Then I'll try to sleep all day, without eating anything. Perhaps then I'll be presentable this evening." The flat was filled with hot, heavy air, which she inhaled forlornly.

Paulina needed to telephone the woman who did the ironing. She decided to do it right away. Her last task for the morning! When she put her bag down on the dining room table, she remembered to open the telegram she'd placed in there. It was from Antonio.

"Rita died yesterday. Very distressed. I beg you write to my Barcelona address. Will pass through in three days. Anxiously awaiting letter. You decide our future."

She read it twice, in a daydream, without understanding its content. It had been a while since she'd got used to the idea that forgetting Antonio was necessary, non-negotiable. For a few moments, her face took on a stunned, almost rigid expression. Afterwards she slowly inhaled some of the warm air in the flat, as if, after all, she had missed it. Her movements became automatic. With the telegram in one hand, she looked for the ironing woman's number and spoke to her, making sure that she would have the dress she needed for the dinner in her flat by six o'clock.

A short while later, her skin, fresh and damp from the bath, gave her a profound sense of relief. She stretched out fully on her mattress in the darkness of the closed-up house.

Then, gradually, Antonio ceased to be a ghost and became once again a real person, a person whom she loved, whom she sensed beside her, sharing with her his love and his message, which seemed to soften her feelings by its presence, reminding her slowly and tenderly what he had meant, what he still meant in her life.

Later, Paulina realised that the hours after she arrived home that day and the ones she spent in the evening with Concha and her friends were edging her closer to her destiny. She didn't know it then, she simply let herself be carried along by a tide of sensations and a spiritual struggle that threatened to keep her from going anywhere.

She arrived at Concha's house with a bad headache, having written a long letter to Antonio, an incoherent letter which she left on her son's desk to post the following day, but which she forgot about. Only after much time had passed would she come across it unexpectedly. In the letter, she declared to Antonio her love for him, her regrets, and the impossibility of accepting a life with him, given that she had decided to dedicate hers to God alone.

But when she arrived at her friends' house, pale, with dark circles under her sparkling eyes, she was not so sure that this was what she wanted.

Concha appeared worried. Paulina reflected as she looked at her well-dressed friend with her warm manner and her kind expression, that Concha was nicer than she had thought. That she was avoiding her for no reason, and that she'd been unfair.

"It's nothing. A headache I can put up with perfectly well," she said.

"Have you tried aspirin?"

Paulina's surprised expression made Concha laugh.

"For goodness' sake! Come with me… Had you forgotten there is such a thing as aspirin?"

Paulina had forgotten, the same as she'd forgotten about many helpful things, basic things, during her time on her own. She felt relieved to find something so simple… There were aspirins in the world and friendly people. She remembered the favour that Concha and Rafael had done her, and she thanked them again. Looking around her friends' beautiful house that night, she wished she could have a nice place of her own.

"Don't mention it. We're only sorry that it didn't occur to you to come and see us to ask. You do everything by telephone. If we hadn't begged you, you wouldn't have even come tonight."

Paulina realised with amazement that her friends appreciated her. She didn't know why she found it so hard to believe that people might be fond of her. When she thought about it, she'd only once been let down by someone she loved. And it wasn't clear-cut; after all, Eulogio didn't want to separate from her.

"How lovely you've made it, what a lovely evening."

She said it with so much sincerity that her friend thanked her.

"You're like Sleeping Beauty when she wakes up," Concha laughed. "I've heard you've been leading a very strange life. I know some of your husband's relatives. They've told me about your fit of saintliness."

Paulina blushed.

"It's not saintliness."

Suddenly, those shaven-headed kids, the women escorting them, all of it seemed like a bizarre nightmare. A few hours before, she'd wanted to dedicate herself to helping people like them, for the love of Christ, but she wasn't born for that life. She was sure of that now.

Concha's dinner party was larger than Paulina had been expecting, and it struck her once again that they really wanted her there, they actually wanted her presence without needing her for anything else.

Concha had prepared a dinner for twelve people; the men were in the majority, but as well as Concha and Paulina there was a stunningly beautiful South American lady. Paulina let herself be carried away by the affable conversation, as well as the amazement that it was so simple to relieve a headache by something as convenient and as old as aspirin. "Maybe everything I think of," she thought, "has a simple remedy, as simple as the one for a headache. Why invent a strange saintliness? My desire is for Antonio. When I found out he hadn't forgotten me, everything looked so different, I felt such peace inside... He's a free man now. I'm a free woman. There's no problem whatsoever."

She caught herself laughing. She thought about how long it had been since she laughed and how good it felt to laugh. The light-hearted atmosphere, the sweet, passionate songs the South American lady sang after the dinner, everything was inducing a state of euphoria and tenderness in her.

"I'm alone so much," she explained to Concha, "that I'd forgotten the pleasure of being among educated people, with culture, with flair... I'm very grateful to you. Just this morning I thought I'd been called for greater things, you know? This gathering of yours has made me see myself from a more balanced, calm perspective."

She was in front of a dressing table in a room filled with wardrobes, it smelled of good wood, of Concha's perfume, and of the lipstick she was reapplying.

"Do you think?"

Concha was laughing, her eyes sparkling, because Paulina as she said this, didn't appear very calm at all. She'd drunk quite a lot.

"Yes, I now believe in fairy tales. This morning I thought that human happiness was incompatible with my life. Today I've seen that goodness and happiness can often go together... How pretty that lady is! And how kind. She tried to give me a chance to shine, she got me to sit beside her and tell her my favourite songs. Apparently, she's a millionairess and her husband adores her.

That young man with the freckles also seems very fond of her."

They were in Concha's dressing room. The guests had left. Concha and Rafael had suggested a drive around the sleeping city before taking her home. Concha insisted Paulina borrow a cardigan. She said it would probably be a little chilly. It was after three in the morning. Now Concha put her hands on Paulina's shoulders and shook her head smiling.

"Paulina… Many women don't like you because men like you a lot… But I do. I've always known you're very naïve. The lady you're talking about, isn't a very nice person… And she certainly isn't happy. Anyway… Let's go, I'll tell you all about it another time… But I'm glad you had fun. You always seem to seek out such utterly uncomfortable and uncivilised ways to live your life. And someone always has to yank you out of it. But I don't know, I've a feeling that one day you'll get yourself so entrenched in something, no one will get you out."

Paulina thought about all this during the drive. It was a marvellous night. They drove to the end of the Paseo de la Castellana which opened out to them, revealing its illuminated trees, perfectly still, with a magical serenity and charm.

"Sleep well, my dear. I've enjoyed helping you recover. We've been plotting for a while to tempt you back again. When we come back from the beach, we'll call you… So, you won't play hard to get now, will you?"

"No, I can assure you, you'll see me soon."

"Don't think you've got me fooled," said Concha. "Don't you believe it."

Paulina thought she would see Concha soon, with the same sincerity that she'd thought she would visit the priest she met at the station… But she didn't do either of these things.

The morning after the night at her friends' house Paulina was exhausted and got up late. She didn't go to Mass.

She already knew that she was going to tell Antonio to come and pick her up, but she was struggling with a feeling that it wasn't right. In the afternoon, she went to church for a short while. It was so terribly hot that she came out feeling suffocated by the smell of wax and incense, even by the jacket she'd put on expressly for the visit. She went for a long walk and, gradually, in the dusty twilight of the city a sense of calm and wellness came over her. People didn't necessarily need to be miserable to be profound and good.

Rita was in a place where she would be able to know and—Paulina took great comfort from imagining everything as she wished it—understand Antonio's love for her. Rita already knew that out of thousands and thousands of women, only Paulina knew how to love Antonio and would be able to free him from his frivolous nature. Because if they were to be truly deserving of the incredible good fortune of being together, they would have to start something beautiful and good together. Antonio would finally grow out of his boyish superficiality and his obsession with physical pleasure. With her he would become a man.

She allowed herself to imagine this fairy tale for a while. Her son Miguel would be with them for most of the year... She would be able to give Miguel whatever he wanted. Eulogio, over in Villa de Robre and in Las Duras, would certainly be happy too. It was a happiness that hurt no one. She would be with Antonio legitimately. Her human joy would be blessed... She had already suffered enough.

When Paulina examined her own thoughts, she concluded that they were foolish; things never work out like that. It was when she realised too that the beauty and value of human relationships lie precisely in their difficulties, that she finally admitted defeat. She knew that a marriage requires self-sacrifice, a bending to the other's will, which is only possible with a very great love. She had achieved this happiness during the war, when Eulogio's jealousy and caution had isolated her; and she couldn't hold on to it when that love had ceased to exist. Then, instead of happiness, there had been misery, meanness, hardness, total incomprehension.

But now she felt that her love for Antonio was still alive. She knew also that this love could make the man she loved more complete, a better person and that this love of hers would never be taken by surprise, because it wasn't the blind love of youth. She recognised the flaws, the weaknesses and the shallowness of the man she loved and accepted them generously, as she would accept the sheer joy of desiring and loving him, with God's blessing at last.

Her decision made, she fell asleep, worn out. She slept so deeply that she awoke with her imagination wiped clean and her body strong and willing.

It was so early that stars lingered in the summer sky. Her soul turned naturally towards God, and she felt as if she had emerged with supreme ease from a sea of anxiousness and doubt.

She had asked God to light her path with the truth. Why not accept this truth of human happiness that the Lord was offering her after all her suffering? To reject it through pride, now that it was falling straight into her hands, would be so false and perhaps as harmful as taking it by force when it was forbidden.

She went out early. Her footsteps had never sounded so light to her as they did now, in the fresh, pure silence of the dawn.

Paulina was going to church. Every day she took communion, and she was anxious to do so today, as she'd missed it the day before. She felt as if it had been entire years that she had been deprived of this great consolation, this great mystery of love and strength.

How had she thought that her love for Antonio would weaken the strength of her relationship with God, who nourished her life? It had all started the day she had found out about Rita's death and had made perfection plans which were not God's will.

It was foolish to have done so even for a moment. Before writing to Antonio she wanted to offer up to the Lord her decision to hold on to this human love, whose pains she knew, whose joy ran through her. God would bless her. God would help her, as she had fought so hard for his Love, and against this other love for a man, which now He offered her anew, purified.

For hours, the world had been submerged in a pale blue, milky light. Paulina could see out there, towards the east, at the end of the streets, a blood red sky streaked with dark clouds. She paused for a moment to look at them. It occurred to her that the clouds were like mysterious black fingers, outstretched, motionless, in an incomprehensible warning… She shuddered.

The church showed off its bell tower, dark against the sky. A faint, indecipherable emotion made Paulina stop in front of the entrance. She sensed that something surprising was waiting for her there. She pulled herself together, annoyed and surprised at her own nerves, and went in.

She always arrived a while before the first Mass started. She was used to a discreet and cold half-light and blinked a little when she saw one of the small side altars brightly lit and covered in flowers. She approached and then smiled. Here was the surprise, then. But it wasn't anything bad, it was touching. Nothing worrying, but something that for her held a special charm; on that decorated altar, a wedding was being celebrated. She felt her eyes well up with tears, unexpectedly, and stepped closer very respectfully... An old couple, both white-haired, were getting married. The children were the witnesses. The man seemed more emotional than the woman, who was stout and serious. They looked like country folk. They were probably marrying at that time of day to avoid people commenting on their age.

Paulina approached the group and knelt close to them, listening to the vows that the couple made to each other, and afterwards she began to listen with them to the wedding Mass.

Slowly, profoundly, the words of the Mass for the newly-weds caressed her soul with their beauty, and at the same time, revealed something deep and real to her that she hadn't thought about very much until that moment.

She felt she understood, more than ever, the greatness of Catholic marriage, that it is not simply a contract, but a sacrament. An indissoluble union of two people who wish to unite their lives until death, supporting each other spiritually, materially, and bodily. A union before God. A union that is binding only in relation to God, not simply a selfish desire for love or convenience. It goes beyond love, beyond convenience and attraction. Even when love ceases, the sacrament is not broken and whoever receives it, receives also sufficient grace to carry on to the end. And it has God's blessing, because it is a path where men's every act of self-denial and every perfection and every depth can reveal itself. Precisely because it is a huge commitment which excludes selfishness.

Paulina understood. She was imbued with this deep wisdom. She understood what perfection and what truth can be achieved by simply living the Christian married life to the full. If she ever married Antonio, she could not be separated from him by a falling out of love or by misfortune. She would be engaged in a far greater task than the satisfaction of a simple instinct.

She looked at the old couple. The woman remained serious and calm, her dark hands holding her rosary beads. The man was wiping his runny nose with a handkerchief. What was their story? What had brought them to this significant moment of giving each other this sacrament? Because they had indeed granted it to each other. It was moving to think about it. One to the other, two human beings, who are free and who wish to be united for life, grant each other the wedding sacrament. The priest is simply an authorised witness who blesses them. Paulina went over the catechism lesson in her head, distractedly, and smiled gently because there was something she found very touching in that old couple's wedding ceremony.

The Mass was finished. The smile disappeared from Paulina's lips. She felt a little as if her knees were turning to lead and she wouldn't be able to stand for the Last Gospel.

"Every one to whom much is given, of him will much be required"... She didn't know who had said this, she thought it might be Saint Peter... She had asked for the great gift of truth.

Paulina's face took on a concentrated expression that made her look almost ugly. Outside, dawn was breaking, and as the stained-glass windows began to glow pink, it felt to Paulina as though the understanding that she had so often asked for was flooding into her soul in a soft wave of light… The small altar was illuminated by the flames of several candles. The flowers that adorned it gave off a warm scent. Paulina thought she could smell newly cut grass. She remembered Eulogio's serious blue eyes looking into hers: "For ever, Paulina… For richer, for poorer, for better, for worse,…" She, too, had given herself to him. Not in a love affair, but for life.

Forever. It didn't matter that she no longer felt those selfish impulses towards Eulogio. It didn't matter that she was more terrified of living with him in the countryside than locking herself away in a convent for her whole life. It didn't matter that it would be far more difficult to dedicate herself to God amid pregnancies and obscure country housewife chores, than somewhere where time was mapped out, for prayers and for silence. It didn't matter that she'd imagined an earthly happiness with another man. Nothing mattered. God would give her the grace she needed to follow her path, because she was Eulogio's wife, and this is what had been shown to her constantly, throughout her life, but she, blinded by her own imagination, had been unable to see the simple truth: she was Eulogio's wife, since the two of them, being free, had given themselves to each other, openly and honestly, for their whole lives.

Her blindness had been her selfishness, both when she thought of her happiness with Antonio and when she dreamed of the great penitential heights of the convent. Everything was simpler and for her more deeply mortifying than she had supposed. She had not been called to a life of solitude among the contemplative nuns in a convent, nor had she been denied a great initial sacrifice in the call to Christ that all the baptised hear, each according to their circumstances. Her path to perfection must have been marked by the stripping bare of those whom God wishes to fill with light, but outwardly it was the simplest and the most anodyne path: the total realisation, body and soul, of her abandoned marriage to Eulogio.

# XVI

The telegram from Eulogio announcing his arrival didn't reach her until the end of September. He hadn't written to her the entire summer, and Paulina was beginning to wonder if he'd decided not to come after all. She had considered this last possibility with a deep sense of calm. In fact, when she did receive the telegram that afternoon she began to feel very anxious.

Paulina had written faithfully to Eulogio, after being absolutely convinced of her duty, as she saw it in the light of Christ. As she, the new woman she was becoming through her love of Christ, saw it.

There had been no answer from Eulogio for two months, and eventually his very thoughtful, sensible letter arrived, apologising for the late reply, but telling her that her letter had arrived at Las Duras—where he was—very delayed, and that he too had wanted to take some time to resolve the matter of the two of them; given that he had become accustomed to the idea of living alone; and neither could he be sure that Paulina wouldn't change her mind again, although he did believe she was sincere.

In the end—he said—he'd decided to accept the marriage, thinking of Miguel, and provided that Paulina could adapt to the kind of life he would ask of her in the solitude of the countryside. Paulina should think hard, think about whether she was prepared to put up with winters in Las Duras, where she would certainly have to forego the company of any ladies of her class and level of education. If she was prepared to learn all the skills a country lady needs to manage her land and her servants, if she was prepared ultimately to support him entirely in the new life he had embarked upon. He added that he understood it would be in no way easy. Paulina should know, on the other hand, that if she said no he would not hold it against her, not at all…

The letter from Eulogio had arrived after those terribly lonely months when, having given up Antonio for good, Paulina entered a period in her life that for her was truly penitential and purifying. Not only because of the heat, the solitude and the dry air that she was living through at that time, but because once the initial struggles had passed, Paulina no longer felt God's presence in her prayers in the same way, and she realised that this was the beginning of the phase that theologians call the spiritual desert. A path paved with nothing but pure faith, with no more strength than that needed to live, to dream and to think…

Antonio hadn't written either, and this, by contrast, felt like a relief. She even came to suspect that her refusal might have relieved him of a burden. The Nives, all of them, were capable of compromising their entire lives through stubbornness, purely to get their own way. But the thought of Antonio falling out of love with her was something that caused her unnecessary pain, so she learned to keep pushing it aside.

One day, after receiving Eulogio's letter towards the end of August, Paulina paid a visit to Amalia to tell her that she was going back to her husband and her village.

The woman was a wreck. She was desperately putting a brave face on it, which came across as farcical and absurd. She lived holed up in the darkest reaches of her house, no longer going out at all. She had given up trading in dresses and was focussing solely on the boarding house. "I'm not up to all that, Paulina. Look at my legs."

Her legs were swollen. Her face, too, looked puffy. In a mere few months, Amalia had grown fat and old. Her house was full of female tenants, members of the social class that she called the "substitutes." She spent all her time playing cards. It was an obsession… Every evening she had her circle of players in the dining room. The son was never mentioned. Paulina had been told that she drank a lot and one day Amalia herself showed her a bottle of anís, assuring her that this was the only true consolation she knew. This had been some time ago, on one occasion when Paulina had tried to convert her.

"Go for it Paulina! You mean you're finally going to the village? I thought your husband would never forgive that little affair… Or, did he never find out? Don't blush, we all know your secret. You're very lucky, sweetheart, to have such a good, and more's the point, rich, husband. I always said you landed on your feet. You pious women are always lucky. You didn't use to be pious. And you weren't lucky either, poor dear… but your time has come."

"And you're not going to marry, Amalia?"

"What for, my dear? Rosendo, my man, already lives here. When one has been what one has been, and looks how one

looks! I tell you, Paulina, you have a lot of luck. Believe me…
But we can't all have your luck…"

That was Amalia's verdict on her decision.

In Eulogio's letter, a postscript explained to Paulina that he
was thinking of coming to Madrid in September or October.
If by then she hadn't changed her mind, they would marry in
secret to avoid rumours that could be damaging for Miguel,
and they would return to Villa de Robre together.

Paulina had been waiting day after day, almost in anguish,
for the telegram that had just arrived.

Though it was now the end of September, it was a hot day.
The eternal backdrop of the illuminated, open windows of the
city filled the night. Paulina leant on the balcony, as she often
did, watching the spectacle. "Soon I'll leave all this behind," she
thought. She had grown used to the flat, the neighbourhood,
the ugly furniture. It's possible to grow fond of the things that
surround us, witnessing our suffering and our joy.

She took a mattress, pillows and blankets out onto the balcony. She had decided to spend that last night of solitude in the
same way she had on other nights the previous summer. She
wasn't feeling sleepy. Sometimes she dozed and then woke again.
When she did she loved opening her eyes to that marvellous
starry sky. Sometimes, a shooting star would fall leaving a trail
of light that gave her vertigo.

Paulina couldn't help thinking about Antonio that night.
What her life would have been like if she'd closed her eyes and
ears to the truth that God had imparted to her so vividly, and
accepted him.

She imagined the adventure that could have been hers, the
marriage with a man eight years younger, who with one kiss

could have made her fall in love with him all over again. The Church, without any proof of the vows she and Eulogio had made to each other, would have blessed the marriage. And then Miguel could not have been ashamed of his mother, and might even have been happy when, as an adult, he learned of his vast material wealth. She, Paulina—she didn't hide it from herself—would for a time have experienced an intense joy, though her conscience would have told her that she was betraying God, and that it could not be. Afterwards, her conscience would start to weaken; it would quieten down too. She would experience only human pain and enjoyment. In everyone's eyes she would be respectable. In the best case, if there were no betrayal, or jealousy, or desperation or one putting pressure on the other, which tends to happen eventually in great love affairs, if none of this were to happen, she would feel constantly happy in the human way. And she might even gain a reputation as a saintly, charitable lady, given that she would be able to carry out ostentatious acts of charity with all her money. But her spirit would die if it were not sustained by the truth. And in the end, everything would go. And before God, and in the depths of her being, her life, if she took that path, would be empty and a lie and nothing.

She tossed and turned a little. The starlight was in her eyes. She couldn't sleep.

She would suffer somewhat when she returned to Eulogio, but the sacramental grace would always help her, and in every vacuum, every self-sacrifice, God would fill her. Eulogio's and her life would, after all, be fulfilled by something more than their own selfishness.

It was a long night, during which her soul was deeply immersed in a serene pain. In a pain that in no way blurred her sharp perception of things. It was a very pale dawn. Paulina, however, felt as though her heart had been set free.

At midday Eulogio arrived. When Paulina opened the door to him she thought he looked stockier, more countrified than the year before. His face was very weather-beaten.

They looked at each other for a few moments with awkward, embarrassed smiles. Paulina knew that Eulogio was noticing the grey hairs that had appeared over recent months.

"We're both getting older," Eulogio said eventually.

And in that moment, when she saw his smile, Paulina felt sure that her life with this man could be deeply satisfying.

At dusk, they went "for a stroll," as Eulogio liked to stay. He explained to Paulina that since he'd grown used to living in the open air in the countryside, he couldn't bear being confined within four walls. He found these crate-like city flats suffocating.

They arrived at the Retiro, the air ringing with the last shrieks of children and birds. Some of the trees already had a reddish tinge to their leaves. Autumn was coming, and its presence seemed to hover over everything, cleansing the air and imbuing it with poetry.

Eulogio spoke slowly and deliberately about his work and other things connected to the countryside. Now and again he would come out with a swear word.

"I'm glad to hear you're giving up smoking. In Villa de Robre it doesn't matter, but out there in Las Duras, people would think it odd and… My work is more and more based there, in those forests. You're afraid of them, aren't you?"

Paulina was gazing at a small, young tree, with leaves that were entirely yellow, like gold coins. It stood among other intensely green or reddish trees.

She imagined life in Las Duras. The leaves raining down from the old oaks, in autumn, must be very beautiful. Now she knew for certain that she would appreciate the beauty of those great trees and that the solitude would suit her, because when a person has God, solitude is not a burden, but a great wonder, a gift from heaven.

She said that not only was she not afraid, she was looking forward to it.

Eulogio held her, his arm around her back, and his strong hand rested on her shoulder. It was how they had used to walk together sometimes, during their short courtship in Villa de Robre. They walked like this now, along the footpaths in the Retiro, through the first fallen leaves, dried by the summer heat.

Paulina noticed a great confidence growing in her. And a profound peace. The peace at having begun, at last, walking her path "in spirit and in truth." That peace of Christ "that surpasses all meaning," and that enveloped her entirely, as they turned back towards the house.

9 780813 239804